The Last HARLEY and His DOG

A Novel by Rick Bennett

Written by Rick Bennett. Edited by Clinton De Young, Nicholas P. Adams, Geoff Shupe, Marc Hunter, Brian Hailes & Bruce Tow.

Cover artwork © 2024 by Rick Bennett, with various elements licensed from 123RF.com. Photography of Chenoa by Rick Bennett.

Library of Congress Control Number: 2024915013

Ebook (Kindle): 978-0-9701026-0-9

Paperback ISBN: 978-0-9701026-7-6

Hardback ISBN: 978-0-9701026-8-3

Contents

Introduction

The first 8 chapters of ***The Last Will & Testament of HARLEY and His Dog*** won the Silver award from Writers of the Future. So I decided to make it into a full-length novel. Hope you enjoy the romp.

Chapter One

Orbiting Alien Beacon

WARNING: Visiting or attempting to invade Planet Earth is definitely hazardous to your culture and even your existence. You should go back to wherever you came from and delete this location from all intergalactic maps, tourism brochures, and military objectives. This is our only warning.

Folk wisdom about successful men observes you go from "barefoot to barefoot in three generations." My great-grandfather John Davidson made it big in the boat building business. His son, John Junior, JJ for short, lived high off the hog and pretty well squandered the family fortune on fast cars and faster women. He should have been castrated, so his rancid genes couldn't bring John the Third—cleverly nicknamed JJJ just to keep the line in sequential order—into the world.

My dad. Vagabond extraordinaire whose entire net worth sat between his legs. No, not that kind of endowment. Good old Dad's one and only possession, a

Harley-Davidson Fat Boy, became his alter ego and religious shrine. His wife, my mom, Elvira Carpenter, left me two gifts: an intact college trust fund from great-grandpa Davidson that she couldn't figure out how to cash out, and a swell name that personified their warped value system. Yep, my name: Harley Danger Davidson.

The "Danger" dangled between the "Harley" and "Davidson" I suppose, just so I could walk into a biker bar and shout "My middle name is Danger!" Which I did just once, and then shouted, "My dad can lick any man in the room."

My outburst badly startled the old man. JJJ ran out of the bar just ahead of some tattooed freaks with steroid-enhanced muscles.

My last official act as a member of the family: I shot Mom and Dad the finger when I found an attorney who would do some pro bono work and help me become an emancipated minor at fifteen. *Danger this, you morons!*

You can't imagine the raised eyebrows a name like Harley Davidson drew on an application to MIT, sixteen-year-old Andover computer prodigy or not. Luckily, great-grandfather Davidson's attendance at Andover gave me legacy admittance to the oldest prep school in the nation. If George Washington had had a son, he'd have sent him to Andover.

I wore a short sleeve shirt to the on-campus MIT interview just to show them the absence of tattoos. Nevertheless, those Ivy League prigs on the admissions committee must have breathed a sigh of relief two years later at the matriculation into outer space of one Harley D. Davidson. My crime: making a point with an AI professor who offended my dog.

Okay, he ridiculed my dog, a constant companion, in front of the whole class, and I retaliated with creative prejudice:

"Mister *Harley Davidson,*" Professor DeBunce drew out my last name in his affected British accent. "You and that mangy sidekick of yours think your AI project can make sure that I never complete another cell phone conversation in my life? That's just barking mad!"

Mangy? He called my only friend in life mangy! Okay, I overreacted. Chalk it up to the hubris of adolescent youth. I know, I need to work on that. Which you'll see later. In spades.

"Yo prof, I suggest that you apologize to my dog immediately." I'd become quite sensitive to people insulting Chenoa. She happened to be the closest thing to family I'd had since grade school. Chenoa. A pure-bred Bicheon Frise father and equally pure-bred Shih Tsu mother had created an F-1 darling with grey ears and white fleece with a brown spot on her right side. For ten years now, I refused to go anywhere without her. Including to class or on dates. Which meant irritating a few cynophobe professors and 100% of the high-maintenance young women who correctly ascertained that I cared a good deal more for the dog than I would ever care for them.

"Apologize to that fleabag some eighteen-year-old boy genius made part of his admission contract to this institution?" He laughed quite a long, forced chortle. "I'll tell you what, *Mister Harley Davidson*. You block even one cell phone call with your dissertation project, and I'll give you an honors A in any class you ever take from me. Need the rest of the semester? Take it."

"No Professor DeBunce, I don't need the rest of the semester. I don't even need all afternoon. Send me a text at this number." I gave him my cell phone number. "Formalize your challenge, giving me proof of our contract, just in case authorities get involved, and that'll be the last time you successfully use that or any other phone in your entire life."

Heaven help me, but I shouldn't have let my adolescent testosterone take the bait. Not only did my draft dissertation articulate the twenty-two attributes of a perfect computer virus, but I'd actually created the darn thing and had been itching for a chance to deploy it. "Sweet Baby Jesus," as Ricky Bobby in the movie *Talladega Nights* would exclaim, I so wish I'd thought twice about accepting this urination contest! Then again, my accepting the challenge may well have saved the planet from annihilation, at least in the short term. But I'm getting ahead of myself.

Professor DeBunce sent me the text.

Upon notification by an especially modified Android phone, which also served as my virus command and control center, I hit the voice-recognition icon and said, "Sheila, level 5 block on this number and any future number you can associate with Boyd F. DeBunce. Use a Chenoa-barking cue to prove your presence before terminating any call he tries to make."

"Acknowledged, Harley," answered the British-accented AI's voice. The whole room heard it, since I'd turned on the phone's speaker.

BTW (that's a social media abbreviation for "by the way"), my AI answered to the name Sheila. Professor DeBunce responded by turning on his own phone's speaker and punching up my number for a voice call. The phone sounded a clear-as-a-bell dialing tone and buzz of a call attempt. Then barked and a hung up. Chenoa responded to the remote sound of her own barking by perking up her ears and rapidly wagging her bushy white tail. The class ended in something akin to pandemonium.

The bad news piled up quite rapidly after that.

MIT's disciplinary committee demanded I stand down my AI, even after my showing them Professor DeBunce's explicit permission to accept his challenge.

I declined using some trumped-up rhetoric. Which left Professor DeBunce doubly hosed, since my AI even got his voice print. He couldn't use his mother's cell phone or a drug store burner, either. Net-net: He couldn't outrun the barking dog he'd so cavalierly insulted. Hell, he couldn't even make a land-line call!

Soon thereafter, the NSA got into the act, demanding source code to Sheila and my immediate ceasing and desisting such shenanigans, given every cellular network and domain name server in the world had been...heh heh...DeBunced. Very quickly, the word "DeBunce" became synonymous with "Kevorkian" in the press.

Had my physical presence not been on a profoundly liberal campus, a *sanctuary campus*, no doubt my carcass would have been renditioned somewhere for perfection of my advanced degree in waterboard interrogation.

The laws of unintended consequences rescued me, at least from any planet-side law enforcement.

"Harley, urgent oversight request." Sheila's voice interrupted my nap on the gray floral carpet of the dean's office, my sanctuary for the past few days, next to an outlet for my phone charger. I wadded up my black-leather jacket as a pillow, and the dog provided enough warmth to cuddle against the logo on my *Harley Davidson* T-shirt. I kept my blue jeans on, along with the laced sneakers, ready to bolt for safety should my situation change. Which it did.

"Sheila, explain." All AIs worth their salt had a built-in "WHY" drilldown.

Sheila complied.

"A system of unknown origin presented itself via one of the SatCom links. Subsequent viral penetration of the system, using Axiom 7, activated defensive measures per Axiom 22."

Axiom 7 applied black-box portability to my virus. Axiom 22 invoked total defense based upon any threat to me.

"My dead-man switch?" I asked. "What could possibly have put me in any kind of jeopardy?"

"Harley, it appears the craft had mission parameters to destroy this entire planet. Given you are located here, I have disarmed the execution directive and seek your immediate instructions as to the disposition of this threat.

Ignoring the presence of several undergraduate ladies passing by, I turned the air blue with invective that would have even made dear old dad blush. My dog cowered, although *she* wouldn't be the source of complaints about my creating a profane and hostile campus environment. As it turns out, I wouldn't be around either, to see whether or not the women reported me to the disciplinary committee.

"Sheila, can you control the craft?"

"Yes Harley, I have taken some prerogatives consistent with Axiom 14."

"Axiom 14? Stealth? Explain."

"Since this craft is extra-terrestrial in origin, I used its native cloaking technology and, after assessing its ability to withstand submersion, parked it at the bottom of Boston Harbor."

"At what depth?" I whispered, trying to avoid another public outburst.

"The top of the craft is 64 meters below the surface."

"Sheila, how can you maintain control of systems that far below the surface?"

"The craft uses a point-to-point communications technology unknown to me. It is the same technology with which they intended to transport some interstellar phenomenon to destroy the Earth. I have disabled their ability to make such a lethal transfer, but use Axiom 1 to continue communication with my target system."

Axiom 1. Oversight. And my dead-man's switch.

"Sheila, is their environment breathable for me, and if yes, is there a way to disable the crew that would allow me to safely board their craft?"

Truth be told, I didn't want to be the MIT equivalent of Julian Assange, trapped in the Ecuadorian Embassy for years. I'd probably starve to death, since I hadn't made friends willing to do regular Five Guys hamburger runs for me. My anti-social proclivity would quickly come to bite my smartass. And Chenoa could use some *Taste of the Wild*, along with a walk on the lawn.

"Affirmative in both cases. It appears trivial to transport you to their command deck with the same device that would have moved a planet-elimination force from exceptional distances."

"Does the crew have weapons?"

"Negative. Three crewmen are in stasis chambers. The only conscious and alert being onboard is the captain."

"Where onboard is the captain now?"

"The captain has joined the crew in the stasis room as we speak, possibly to entomb herself and wait for help.

"Sheila, you're positive this transportation technology will not kill me?"

"Absolutely positive. This is how this ship moves, with all aboard."

"Come here little girl." I called the dog and picked her up. She'd been scooting her rear end on the Dean's carpet. Then, swallowing hard, I threw my leather jacket over my shoulder and cast my fate into cyberspace. "Sheila, transport me and Chenoa to the command deck of the craft."

Chapter Two

My frisky fluff ball and I instantaneously appeared on the bridge, with ship atmosphere thankfully breathable. Which I barely noticed, given my profound astonishment with the ship's command and control accommodations.

First, a 360-degree mind-blowingly panoramic view of everything around the ship greeted our entrance, everything around and above us in Boston Harbor. A projection, because I wouldn't think curved clear anything would give such an undistorted view, not to mention being able to withstand the internal PSI in outer space.

More interesting, however, seating for ten apparently humanoid crew faced toward the center axis of the sixty-foot diameter area.

"Sheila, is there a way you can display an image of this craft?"

"Acknowledged," she replied. And boy what an understatement! In the center of the command deck floated a 3D model of the ship, with two red dots representing the dog and me. Five more red dots appeared on our level, some distance away. The vessel itself had three levels, the lowest being some kind of mechanical assembly. I didn't see anything that resembled an armory or weapons delivery system. No torpedo tubes for massive space battles. No lasers to zap alien invaders. No shuttle bays. Boy, my video games had a lot cooler stuff than these guys. Speaking of which...

"Sheila, I thought you said there were four crewmen? I see five dots."

Next to the 3D ship appeared a hi-res image of the stasis chamber. "There are four crew now in stasis, and a fifth creature."

"Is the creature a potential danger?"

"I will find out."

The stasis room appeared, replacing the holographic image center deck, showing a crew of four, one female and three males. And some kind of snake! Let me be more precise. Four *humanoids* and definitely a snake!

"Sheila, are these images to scale?"

"Affirmative."

Slowly, I approached the female hologram, and looked up. I stand six feet five inches in my bare feet. Even in my sneakers, her eyes had me by three inches. Of course, her pedestal added some additional height. And notwithstanding her seamless white flight suit, I couldn't get over her strikingly beautiful countenance. White hair, skin a good deal lighter than mine, and flawless. The kind you see in airbrushed magazine ads for age-erasing cosmetics. Or in certain centerfolds.

It never occurred to me any woman on Earth would have such an impact on my emotions. Of course, this woman didn't come from Earth. She appeared to be a head taller than...the *males*? Heck, I immediately moved down the row of sleeping figures to check out...the competition? Two clean shaven men, one with white hair, one with red hair, and one with jet black hair and a neatly trimmed beard. All three shorter than me. *I'll bet I could take any of them in a fight.*

Okay, I stood there thinking like a teenager in a school yard. *I'd take on all of them, given half an excuse.* Wait. I *was* a teenager.

Sit down, Harley! commanded my rational non-lizard mind. Which I did, in the nearest command chair. *Okay, back to business mister hormonal.*

"Sheila, how big is this craft?"

"The ship is three kilometers long, just over one kilometer wide, and thirty meters deep."

Wow. I looked around, soaking in whatever I could about alien technology. The entrepreneur in me wanted to search out their living quarters, their toiletry cabinets. Someone could make a fortune pirating handy-dandy gizmos from an alien civilization. The flight deck looked kind of ordinary, at least ordinary to someone who'd only seen approximations imagined by Earth-based video game designers.

"Sheila, have you found out if that snake thing poses a threat?"

"Harley, according to the ship's database, it's non-lethal and more of a sentry/companion to the ship's captain."

Okay, which one of these guys is the captain? I wondered. Top dog, eh? Wanting to at least *sound* objective, in case this encounter somehow got recorded and made it onto worldwide television, I asked, "Sheila, please identify the captain."

"That would be the female." Whereupon the AI illuminated the tall figure.

I hope my face didn't betray enormous relief, assuming my face would appear someday on a planetary news video.

Taking things one step at a time, I said, "Sheila, how quickly can any of the subjects be brought out of stasis?"

"Almost instantly," she replied.

During our entire dialog on the command deck, Chenoa sat patiently at my feet, looking a lot like the RCA Victor logo dog from the 1920s. Flipping a mental coin, I decided to check out the pet situation.

"Sheila, release the pet-sentry from stasis."

Some faint sound must have alerted the dog, because her ears perked up and she bounded into a hallway on the opposite side from which we'd entered. She ignored my shouts. Without any hope of keeping up with my new four-legged friend, I did the next best thing.

"Sheila, protect the dog should it become necessary."

"Acknowledged."

The dog's yipping and barking faded into the distance, which left me with nothing to do but ponder the bridge. I drummed my fingers on the armrest and noticed slight roughness in certain places. *Possibly tactile actuation controls?*

"Sheila, please explain how the crew commands this craft."

The stasis hologram disappeared, replaced by a close-up. One of the males seemed to tap and slide his fingers on the arm rests to either side, and as he did so the center display showed various ship functions, accompanied by changes in the 360-degree panorama behind him. I caught a brief view of our planet as seen from high orbit.

Before I could further query the computer about specific functionality and this civilization's mission from wherever they came, the sound of my approaching dog grew louder, accompanied by what appeared to be human laughter.

"Sheila, did you release any of the humanoids from stasis?"

"Negative. I only released the small sentry creature."

As if on cue, Chenoa bounded into the room followed by the damnedest thing I'd ever seen. The closest analogy would be a Winnie The Pooh Tigger-like creature bouncing on its spring-like tail, only no Tigger sat at the top of the spring. Instead, just a head resembling a hooded Cobra's, with laughing sounds coming from its mouth. Human-like laughs! Both the dog and the snake sprang toward my lap.

My own cat-like reflexes, honed by PlayStation first-person shooter video games, enabled me to automatically grab the snake just below its head. I held the reptile at arm's length with my right hand as I cradled the dog close to me with my left. I don't know who looked more surprised. The dog at my treatment of her new friend or me, as the snake choked, "Why'd you do that, sir?"

My first thought? Animatronics. Come on! A talking snake? But it didn't feel like electromechanical servomechanisms writhing in my hand. And the dog looked at me like I had committed some massive faux pas in inter-species relations. The snake choked again. I involuntarily relaxed my grip.

"Why didn't you tell your master we were friends?" said the snake. To the dog!

The nearest thing to a response came as a wagging tail and Chenoa's open-mouthed grin.

"I can't understand why the dog cannot communicate." This time, the snake spoke to me. "Outside certain species of tropical birds, none of the creatures on this planet have acquired speech. And the birds simply mimic what they hear. What gives, Earthman?"

My silence seemed to test the snake's patience. It turned again to the dog. "Beg."

To which the dog lifted her front paws, balancing on her haunches.

"Speak!"

Chenoa obliged with two quick barks.

"Play dead!"

To which the dog jumped from my lap and prostrated herself on the flight deck.

The snake turned its attention back to me. "This creature has demonstrated a limited vocabulary. But the absence of a soft palate and more than a basic vocabulary indicate a profound devolution."

Enough! I thought. My questions self-organized.

"How come you speak the English language? What in flaming hell is this ship? Where does it come from? And what is your mission?" The last question was a trick question, since I already knew the answer.

"Whoa, Earthman!" The snake gently wrapped its tail around my wrist, possibly relieving some of the body weight currently stretching from the head suspended in my grip. "I just provide ship security.

"As for my mastery of your language, we've spent significant time collecting anthropological data on your planet. Your other questions can be more precisely answered by our captain."

"Anthropological data? Is this a research vessel?"

"Again, I invite you to chat with our captain."

"Sheila," I queried. "Disable all weapons available to the ship captain."

"Done Harley, with the exception of an apparent sidearm on the person of the captain. It does not appear to be cyber-controlled."

Interesting conundrum. "Sheila, is it possible for me to relieve the captain of her weapons before she's taken out of stasis?"

"Affirmative," said the AI. "I have displayed their locations on the captain's hologram projection."

"Sheila, I see the knife in her boot," I said, looking at the hologram. "But what is that thing on her waist and how do I get it off?"

"According to the ship's armory inventory, the device is a hardwired miniature version of their main communications system. It is not clear how such a unit could be weaponized, but their database classifies it in most lethal terms. To remove it from the captain's belt, grasp it with the thumb on top, your three smaller fingers on the bottom, and forefinger on the side. It will automatically disengage from the holster-like dock."

The snake coiled noticeably tighter around my left wrist and interrupted: "What are your intentions regarding my captain?"

"Snake, you're the one who invited me to get answers from her!"

"My name is Nigel, Earthman," said the snake with just a hint of venom. "I find the species designation offensive."

"My apologies...Nigel. And please, call me Harley. Something tells me I'm going to find the 'Earthman' label equally offensive." Talk about prophetic!

Nigel couldn't help but suppress a snicker. "Would you like me to take you to my leader?"

"You've been watching some of our science fiction movies," I commented, releasing Nigel and following the agile creature as he sprung down the wide and sequentially well-lit corridors ahead of the dog and me. *Good thing snakes on Earth didn't have such locomotion*, I thought. *There would be far fewer human beings on the planet.*

The dog didn't seem the least bit intimidated by our guide, eventually opting to prance beside Nigel as we wound through the ship. Rather than contract in width or height, the corridors grew in both dimensions. Whatever thrust-to-weight ratios existed with this race and their enormous craft put them in a different universe, no pun intended.

The craft evidently had enough computing horsepower to allow my virus's AI to "go native" (my Perfect Virus Axiom 9, *native implementation*) and send out numerous native agents (Axiom 19, *simultaneity*) to achieve *universalization* (Axiom 18) and "thrive in all past, present and future environments." Since this ship's computer had had months of multi-threaded "grokking" of Planet Earth, not to mention any preceding time in orbit listening to newscasts and even watching streaming movies before I brought it down, I decided to test a rather trivial hypodissertation. Stands to reason that it probably understood every major language on the planet by now.

"Sheila," I said. "Illuminate this corridor as we near the stasis chamber."

And Voilá! Just like that, lights. Only no lightbulbs or fluorescent tubes. The walls glowed with increasing radiance all the way around the arched ceiling.

Some solid-state lens in the craft's hull combined with a microphone to pick up my presence and place in the command-and-control pecking order, granting me and *only* me access. Next step? Figure out how to awaken the rest of this behemoth ET magic carpet.

Could it truly be that easy? I mean, with all the science fiction I've ever read, authors either displayed alien technology only from afar, like UFOs engaged in fierce battles with primitive Earth military forces, or the authors "cheated" by ignoring cockpit mechanics in favor of telepathic control. But nobody ever got into much detail about a real UFO cockpit. I'd just seen what *a real* alien flight deck looked like. We came to a fork in the tunnel.

"Harley Davidson, follow the green indicators at your feet," said Sheila's disembodied voice.

My virus no doubt kept a close eye on all worldwide news media and did a pretty decent job tracking me. Axiom 1 of my perfect virus demanded constant *oversight*. At least two mechanisms needed to be in place, and I made sure a first-priority dead-man's switch guaranteed that everyone's continued health totally depended upon my own wellbeing.

The dog and I went down the green-lit road. My furry friend must have sensed less apprehension emanating from me, and ventured further away, so I explicitly put her under the protection of the computer AI again.

"Sheila, protect my dog with the same care you'd protect me."

"Acknowledged," came the terse reply.

Chapter Three

Eventually we arrived at the stasis chambers, and the dog surprised me by going into play mode, chasing Nigel around the room. About half the size of the command deck, the rectangular space had ten stasis chambers on one wall. Only four contained humanoids.

"Sheila, release the captain."

The AI complied, and I quickly disarmed the captain, her knife now in my belt and her weapon in my left hand. She immediately sensed the absence of the device on her hip and quickly noticed I'd commandeered it. Nigel stood nearby.

"Nigel, how did you get out of stasis?" said the captain.

"Captain, what's your name?" I shrugged, gesturing absent mindedly with the device in my right hand.

"Rose. I'm captain Rose." Then, pointing to my right hand: "Careful with that thing, unless you want to send Nigel and his friend on a trip," said the captain.

The snake flinched. I'd randomly used the weapon as I'd pointed toward him.

"Captain Rose, I'm Harley Davidson. Apparently, my computer virus took over your ship."

"Crippled is a more accurate statement, Mr. Davidson," replied the tall, porcelain-skinned woman with matching white hair. She answered in perfect English. "And possibly more than my ship has been crippled."

Just when I thought the month couldn't get any weirder, I found myself chatting in in my native tongue with a humanoid alien. Aboard a spaceship conveniently sunk in Boston Harbor. Me and my dog. Me, my dog, and a smoking-hot captain.

"Sheila," I said. "How can I safely deactivate this device?"

The AI answered immediately. "Now that it's off the captain's person, I have neutralized its circuitry and am currently analyzing it. You may safely return it to the captain."

"Who is that just speaking?" asked the incredulous captain.

"That's the AI from my virus program, speaking from your computer command and control network."

"It can do that?" More incredulity in her voice.

"You mean you *don't* have voice control over your computer."

"No." Captain Rose significantly lengthened the last word, which sounded more like *noooooooooo*.

"Captain, you indicated my virus may have crippled more than just your ship. Please explain."

Captain Rose looked at something embedded in her wrist before speaking.

"If we are still on your planet, and this amount of time has elapsed, then your virus has saved your Earth from total destruction."

"Oh?" my pubescent voice cracked.

Nigel's non-snake-like tongue seemed to hang out an open mouth as his eyes bore into the captain.

"We should sit down and have a nice long chat," I said.

"Would it be possible to get my crew out of stasis?" asked Captain Rose.

"Not until I figure out what you just confirmed," I said. "My AI told me you were here to destroy this planet, but I couldn't quite believe it. Shall we adjourn to the flight deck?"

Minutes later, the four of us—me, Captain Rose, Nigel, and the dog—sat in the flight center crew seats.

Rose and I faced each other, in the six and twelve o'clock positions. Chenoa sat in my lap, while Nigel curled around my left armrest.

Captain Rose kept looking at her wrist. I couldn't help but notice how spectacularly beautiful she was, even though my own initial infatuation had taken a cold shower with the revelation Planet Earth might be on borrowed time.

"Captain, speak."

She took a deep breath. The dog, thinking my command was for her, barked.

"We've scoured the Universe for over 2000 of your Earth years. Searching for this planet. We arrived here some years ago, and my team of anthropologists was given permission to study you for a period of time. That time has expired."

"And?"

"And *your* time has expired."

"Come again?" I couldn't believe my years.

"It's time for this planet to be destroyed."

"What kind of monsters would even consider genocide on a planetary scale?"

"You're calling *us* monsters?" She laughed. Not a polite laugh, but a bitter one.

"Yeah, as a matter of fact. If you've observed us for how long—?"

She interrupted. "We've been here almost one hundred of your years, watching slaughter on an almost planetary scale. Certainly on a national scale."

"Wait," I said. "A hundred years? You can't be more than thirty years old. Forty max."

"Harley, I'm almost three-thousand years old. Two-thousand-seven-hundred-and-sixty years old, to be exact."

"I don't believe you."

"Your belief is irrelevant. We've come here to destroy you, not engage in any kind of dialogue."

"You go around destroying civilized planets?"

"Not at all, Harley. This will be the first. And hopefully the last."

I wasn't getting any help from the peanut gallery. Nigel just sat there. And the dog had gone into a blissful sleep on my lap while getting a head scratch.

"What gives one race the right to terminate a planet."

"Oh no, Harley. It's all the races. Millions of space-faring races across the Universe have been searching for one planet. Your planet. Earth. We found you, and it is our honor to destroy you. All other potential attackers have been held at bay by The Sovereign Code."

"I guess Aristotle and the ancient church get the last laugh," I said. "They believed Earth was the center of the Universe. Little did they realize we were some kind of cosmic bull's eye. Might I ask why?"

"Indeed, your major religions—Islam, Judaism, even Christianity—give you the answer. Your planet, Earth, is the most wicked of all God's creations. This planet, and no other, actually put God Himself to death. Our God. The God who created worlds without end."

"Whoa, whoa, WHOA!" I said. "We what?"

"Your holy book, the *Bible*—even Muslims call themselves 'People of the Book'—tells of the mother of all living partaking of the forbidden fruit. That only happened on your planet. The adversary, our adversary, tricked a poor creature like Nigel into convincing Eve to partake of the fruit."

"The snake in the Garden of Eden?" I said.

"Again, Earthman, I find that term offensive," said Nigel.

It suddenly occurred to me that I was in some drug-induced dream spawned as retribution from my completely disconnected MIT professor. This *couldn't* be happening. Yet no dream, no hallucination, could be this real?

"Harley Davidson," said the disembodied voice of my AI. "I may have thwarted this race's weapon of destruction. Unfortunately for the invaders, there are unintended consequences."

"Explain," said both Rose and I, simultaneously.

"Earlier, I posited that the device which transported us into this ship was a miniature version of their communications system. It appears that it is also part of their propulsion system. Axiom number two of your virus architecture, *Feral Fertility*, dictated that I infect all devices available to me. These included their faster-than-light communications systems. By bringing them down, I not only cut off all contact with myriad civilizations, but by so doing made it impossible for command and control to bring them back online without specific instructions from you."

"But I brought the ship online."

"Yes, Harley. But bringing the other peripheral civilizations online has not yet happened. And if I do bring them back online, it could facilitate the destruction of our planet. You see, I've just discovered their Order of Battle database."

"Sheila, what is the Order of Battle?"

"Simply, they will transport a black hole to Earth's core with this technology. Which will quickly effect planetary destruction."

"This is very bad news indeed," broke in Captain Rose. "Sheila, does this mean all civilizations using this technology have been disconnected."

"Harley Davidson," said the AI. "Do I have permission to answer queries from someone other than yourself?"

"Yes, Sheila. But no commands are to be accepted from anyone but myself."

"Acknowledged. You are correct, Captain Rose. All civilizations connected to this technology have been or will eventually be effected."

"Harley Davidson," came Rose's desperate response. "Ten of our worlds rely on this technology to provide energy. Without this energy, they will quickly devolve to near absolute-zero temperatures."

"Then, a good net-net would be that I saved our planet at the expense of some of yours?" I paused. "How many people will die?"

"Trillions. And soon. None of our planets were deceived by a sna—" she caught herself mid-word.

"Thank you," said Nigel.

Rose rephrased, "No creatures were tricked into doing the adversary's bidding. After a thousand local years, we were commanded to partake of the fruit by the rightful creator, God if you will, and immediately transformed into semi-immortal beings. But..."

"But...?" I asked.

"But we *can* be frozen solid.

"I believe this is a good time to start negotiations," I concluded.

"Dancing with the devil," said Nigel.

CHAPTER FOUR

"An underwater commando team is attaching a low-yield thermonuclear device to our hull," said my AI.

Nigel quickly unwrapped himself from my armrest and sprang in coiled bounds from spot to spot until he reached a vacant flight console. The moment he landed in the seat, some sense of its occupant caused a T-like perch to rise from the center, whereupon the snake wound its agile midsection around the padded horizontal portion. Its tail deftly inserted itself into a female control indentation, which must have been specifically configured for the creature, because the hologram in the center of the flight deck changed into a three-dimensional view of the ship's exterior.

"Just as you asserted, Captain Rose," said Nigel. "This is the most vicious, warlike planet in all of creation."

"And the underwater demo crew seems to have finished. It looks like they are packing up. We've got an imminent problem," said Nigel. "How about I detonate it right now? I'll activate our displacement shell so the blast will have no effect on us."

"Negative, snake!" I shouted.

"Lose the snake reference now and evermore," replied Nigel. "Unless you want a prostate exam without the butt jelly. Good news is that I won't even ask you to turn your head and cough."

"Nigel!" commanded the captain. Then to me: "Nigel's been watching too many of our surveillance videos. Now, as to your question, we could transport the weapon to your capital city."

"You call *us* bloodthirsty!" I spat. "Even a low-yield device would kill innocent people."

"Nobody on this planet is innocent," said Nigel.

"Your alternative, then?" said Captain Rose.

"Move the device to the surface of the moon," I said. "I want to rest of the world to see something is afoot."

"Nigel," said the captain. "Make the transfer."

Fidgeting a moment, Nigel spoke nervously: "The AI has blocked my control of the transmission matrix."

"Sheila, make the transfer, one nuclear device from our hull to the lunar surface."

"Acknowledged Harley," replied the disembodied voice.

The holo image immediately showed a now-bare ship's skin upon which the nuclear device had previously sat.

Without asking, Nigel must have redirected the image, as the device now appeared in front of them, surrounded by a lunar surface. Moments later, the viewers saw nothing but a white light. The shot zoomed back to reveal the full moon obscured by a swath of dust and cloud consuming center screen.

"Either a GPS detonation sensor, or maybe an altimeter-driven switch," I said. "I can't believe they'd have detonated the nuke right here, so close to Boston."

"But why—" began captain Rose.

"They must have made the determination that if we couldn't have the technology windfall, this ship, then they couldn't let you escape."

Nigel offered an opinion: "Kind of like a celebrity stalker just before a murder/suicide. 'If I can't have you, then nobody else can, either.'"

"Chenoa, please bite Nigel," said the captain.

The dog recognized her name and seemed to smile at her new friend, tail wagging.

"Dumber than a bag of rocks," sighed Nigel. "What a shame. Such delightful creatures on other sentient worlds."

"Sheila, may we leave this malignant mess of a world?" asked the captain.

"Harley," came the reply. "We are currently forty-two-thousand-one-hundred-sixty kilometers above our launch point, a geo-synchronous position above Boston."

Simultaneously, a planet-side view appeared holographically in the center of the command deck. At an altitude four-hundred times the thickness of Earth's atmosphere, the gem-like blue planet looked quite alone against the black backdrop of space.

"I didn't feel any acceleration."

"Neither did the sea slug walking across the nuclear device previously attached to our hull," said Nigel. "One minute, it was exploring a heat sync crevice looking for some dinner. The next moment, it was sitting on the moon's surface, feeling a bit like exploding in the vacuum. Which it did a few seconds later, along with a chunk of the moon."

I looked at the talking snake with some amount of revulsion at his sick humor.

The snake clearly spent time around humans and correctly assessed my attitude.

"Well, you asked!" said Nigel.

The dog just looked at her bouncy new friend, pom-pom ears twitching to see if any of the creature's words fit in a limited vocabulary. But since nothing computed into *sit, play dead, dog treat, speak,* or *go find your toy*, Chenoa now sat in the middle of the command deck, waiting patiently for something intelligible.

"I just can't get over how you managed to get our shipboard computer to talk," said Captain Rose.

"That's nothing compared to your talking sn...er...Nigel."

"Thanks for your discretion," said Nigel.

"Your computer virus may have impacted inhabitants from countless civilizations. I really need the rest of my crew to get to work."

"Alright, let's get your crew functioning," I said.

"Follow me," said Nigel as he bounded into a hallway behind the command bridge. The dog obeyed enthusiastically. The captain and I pulled up the rear.

"These passages are enormous," I said to Captain Rose as we wound our way toward the stasis room. "Seems like a tremendous waste of space, not to mention the energy necessary to move such a large ship."

"I keep forgetting you're still a slave to energy despotism on this planet," she answered.

"Energy despotism?"

"He who controls the energy controls the people. Much like hydraulic despotism in India. He who controls the water controls the people. In fact, your whole planet is riddled with despots, their goal being simple: control. Quite remarkable and unique in the entire Universe. Yes, a well-earned death sentence for this planet of yours."

Energy despotism. Hydraulic despotism. My mind reeled. "But you have to at least measure the cost of building such a large craft. If nothing else, the opportunity cost. What do you give up in other possible projects to allocate such vast resources to corridors down which you could drive a large truck?"

"Spoken like a teenage troglodyte." Captain Rose picked up her pace. "The rest of the known Universe doesn't think in terms of money. Free, unlimited energy. Nobody vying for control of scarce resources. But more importantly, nobody vying for control of people. Because the most important commodity anywhere is free choice. The greatest evil in the entire Universe is any effort to take away free will. The masters of such domination, by the way, are bred only on this sewage drain called Earth. Here, you routinely trade life for money."

An indictment like that could slap he smile off anyone's face. I'd spent my albeit short life engaged in technological competition, a kind of step-on-the-head-of-other-not-so-smart-people warfare. The goal? I *thought* this was just *the* system. And success meant, as Henry Kissinger once wrote, *to help mankind rescue the element of choice from the pressure of circumstance*. Did I need to do a reset? Had I been nothing more than an enforcer, a hired gun for intellectual despotism?

"Your whole legal system has one goal," said Captain Rose. "Ascertain how much a life is worth, so the defendant is adequately billed for the plaintiff's pain and suffering. Life for money.

"As for the size of these corridors, remember this is an anthropological vessel, designed to carry some sizeable artifacts."

"But why not just—" I began.

Nigel answered the question before I could coherently form it. "—because we collect and move a large number of objects, some of which share space with things we do NOT want to transport aboard."

"Oh, like snakes in ancient statues?" I blurted before realizing my thin-skinned companion might take umbrage.

"You should recruit a drink taster," said Nigel. "Never know when someone will put camel piss into your hydration bottle."

Captain Rose rolled her eyes. Nigel bounded ahead of us, obviously *not* waiting for my abject apology.

I hurried to catch up with my once-again-offended alien. And to tell the captain I had one phone call to make before we headed into the wild black yonder.

Chapter Five

"Mister President, this is Harley Davidson calling. About that nuke detonating on the moon..." I held the satphone away from my ear, anticipating POTUS's reaction to getting a direct phone call from a complete stranger, and a teenager at that, on his private Oval Office line.

"Davidson? Harley Davidson! You had something to do with that nuke going off on the moon?" shouted President Medina. Then, pausing to put two plus two together from his intelligence briefings: "The infamous telephone hacker who made some MIT professor an instant rectal celebrity, forcing said professor to go on television talk shows just to say hi to his mother? Give it to me by the numbers. What the hell is going on? And where in blazes are you calling from?"

"In answer to your last question first, I am in geosync orbit above Boston. We've wobbled a comsat so I could link to you. As to your other question, I recommend a face-to-face meeting with me and a representative of a galactic empire bent on destroying our planet."

Long pause.

"Destroying our...?" I heard the sound of his exhaling. "When?"

"Now," I replied.

Another long pause.

"Uh, where?"

"In the Oval Office."

"I'm here now," gasped the president. "How?"

"Sir, we will transport down immediately. Please alert the secret service NOT to shoot two people appearing in the White House."

Pause, accompanied by the president's muffled commands.

"Beam 'em down, Scotty," said the president, apparently trying to be hip in spite of the revelations about planetary destruction and teleportation technology.

I didn't need to explain the Star Trek reference to anthropologist Captain Rose, who anxiously shifted her weight from one foot to the other. She clearly wanted to get on with saving her civilization and regarded any delay as potentially catastrophic.

"Sheila," I commanded. "Please execute a transfer, placing Captain Rose and myself in the Oval Office. Preferably not materializing us halfway submerged into some cement floor."

"Acknowledged, Harley. And I'll monitor you for a command to retrieve you and the captain."

• • •

"Mierda!" cursed a wide-eyed POTUS in Spanish, as a statuesque platinum-haired lady and a far less cosmetically perfect specimen of humanity—one Harley Danger Davidson— appeared opposite his desk in the Oval Office. Maybe the *Harley Davidson* T-shirt didn't belong in the White House.

"Mister President," I said, simultaneously with the sound of weapons being drawn to either side of us.

"Maldita sea, holster those weapons!" Again, a Spanish curse.

The two secret service guards reluctantly and very slowly complied.

I continued. "I would like to introduce Captain Rose from..." I stopped short, realizing I hadn't the faintest idea from whence the captain originated. Captain Rose continued for me.

"I represent every civilized race in the Universe. Call us the Andromeda Cluster. My archaeological expedition was granted a window of time to analyze your planet, prior to its unanimously ordered destruction. Our time limit has been reached, and this boy's computer virus appears to have stopped the destruction mandate. Unfortunately for us, his virus has also mutated to every control system in all our worlds and bodes unspeakable hardship if not eradicated within very few of your Earth days."

Fortunately, the president received this news while seated. Otherwise he might have keeled over and smashed his head on the Oval Office coffee table. In his chair, though, he managed to keep his head erect enough to focus two wide-open eyes on his extraterrestrial guest. He swallowed, not that his dry mouth gave him any spit to work with.

"Come again?" said the scared-spitless POTUS.

"Your entire planet was saved from destruction by Harley Davidson's computer virus," said Captain Rose, resting one fist on her hip. Her white jumpsuit accented her alabaster skin and white hair, making her look more like an angel of salvation than a destroyer of planets.

She continued: "Tens of thousands of worlds have been greatly inconvenienced by the complete cessation of computing infrastructure. But more importantly, ten planets dependent upon computer-driven technology to obtain 100-percent of their power from distant stars have been left in extremis. By shutting down that power distribution system, those worlds and all their inhabitants have been plunged into near-absolute-zero conditions. Backup energy sources can sustain those civilizations for less than one of your Earth months. I'm here to beg you for an accommodation."

"An accommodation?" asked President Medina.

The president shifted his gaze from Captain Rose to me. Then back to the captain.

I shut up as this conversation soared well above my worldly experience.

"Yes, Mister President." For the first time ever, I could see a slight blush in her cheeks, and wondered what it meant. "I would request that Harley Davidson be permitted to immediately restore power to the most direly effected worlds, and then to the rest of our civilizations."

"And as a quid pro quo," the president jumped in, "I assume you agree NOT to destroy our planet?"

Captain Rose's blush deepened.

"I cannot promise that, Mr. President." She bowed her head.

The president glared at me.

Then at her.

And again, at me.

Woefully underdressed for a meeting in the Oval Office with the president, wear and tear on my three-day-old stinky blue jeans and *Harley* T-shirt—yep, I couldn't resist turning my name into a sponsorship for some *real* troglodytes—didn't paint a picture of someone POTUS might go to for advice. I didn't know what to say, anyway.

"How, precisely, would this genocidal conglomeration of murderers accomplish the destruction of Planet Earth?"

Since the president addressed *me*, I blurted: "The same technology they used to transfer energy from a star could be used to transport a black hole to the center of our planet."

After invoking some human/pig procreation invective, President Medina net-netted the situation.

"In other words," spat POTUS, "I allow *you* to pull *our* finger out of the gun barrel *you* have aimed at us, but *you* won't promise *not* to pull *your* trigger?"

A desperate Captain Rose jumped in. "Sir, I do not have the authority to make that promise. But on my honor as a Captain in Her Majesty's Galactic Navy, I will forfeit my life if I cannot reverse this divine edict."

"Captain Rose," said the president in an iron voice, "Forfeiting your life in exchange for the billions on this planet is a lopsided bargain. You therefore know my answer to your requested *accommodation*."

The captain rapidly lost all composure, and half wept, half screamed, "My life for the tens of billions on ten planets, and the trillion-trillions on thousands of worlds you vicious, malignant tumor on all divine creations are holding hostage."

"*We're* the malignant tumor! You come here to wipe out our planet and *we're* somehow at fault?"

"Yours is the most-evil planet in all of creation," she rattled quickly, perhaps so quickly that she didn't fully think before she spoke. Her next line proved it: "You're the one world that actually killed God Himself!"

"We *what*?" asked the incredulous president.

I suppose having just had the decision maker in the most important conversation in her life decline to help caused her to rashly grab at straws. She looked at me with a *did-I-actually-say-that-out-loud* expression. Inexperienced as I am, I decided to jump in.

"Sir, I believe she is referring to the crucifixion of Jesus a couple thousand years ago."

"Mother of Mercy!" said the president. "This has to be some religious fundamentalist nightmare!"

Captain Rose didn't say anything, probably still recomposing from her latest outburst.

I kept my own mouth shut, following great-grandpa's advice to never miss an opportunity *not* to say something. The president obviously hadn't received the same advice and continued venting.

"Fully one third of this so-called malignant tumor of a planet worships Jesus Christ. Most of the others revere Him as a great man. And you want to destroy *us*?"

Captain Rose regained some composure. She looked around the room and settled on a Frederick Remington statue on a credenza. The captain slowly walked over and ran her finger around the cowboy hat on *The Bronco Buster* bronze that sat on a credenza.

"President Medina," she softly began. "Your entire planet has basked in the most utter depravity we've ever seen, anywhere. You treat your animals as a food source, at least when they're not used as slaves like this Remington horse. You regard organizations like your People for the Ethical Treatment of Animals, or PETA, like a lunatic fringe group."

"Aw come on now--" said the president.

"--I'm just getting started!" snapped Captain rose, interrupting him. POTUS's jaw snapped shut, the president obviously not used interruptions of *any* kind from *anybody*. She continued: "Animals are the least of your sins. Until the beginning of the last century, women were not even allowed to vote. And today, in some countries, women are still treated like property, to be used up and then disposed of according to the whim of men. This is unheard of anywhere else in civilized space. We can only attribute it to the incorrect connecting of the dots by your religionists in their interpretation of your Garden of Eden story. My question to you: How can you justify *your own* continued existence?"

Given the president's masterful use of campaign rhetoric, I suspected he'd have an eloquent answer. His wide-eyed look at me quickly dispelled that notion. I directed my own deer-in-the-headlights stare at Captain Rose. I shouldn't have.

"And you, Harley Davidson," she picked up steam. "You're about to have the blood of not billions but a trillion-trillion beings on your hands. I guess I shouldn't be surprised. I hope the eternities have a suitable place for your damned soul."

My speechlessness hung in limbo with that of President Medina. And Captain Rose used the opportunity to add to our planet's litany of violence and murder.

"Throughout your recorded history, millions of people have engaged in the systematic slaughter of their neighbors. I know this for a fact, because my archeological expedition spent the last hundred years observing you. Your so-called religions have been at the forefront of most of that violence. We attribute the rest of your murders to a quest for land, for power, or for riches. Rationalize that, you blood-sucking vampires!"

She shut up.

The president shut up.

I definitely followed suit.

Finally, the president tiptoed into a more problem-solving mode.

"I believe the fact you appeared here in my office is proof that you have the technology to transport a black hole to destroy Earth. But how am I to believe your non-violent/animal-friendly assertion? What proof do you have that you aren't just rationalizing your own religious genocide?"

"Uh, I can offer such proof, Mister President," I said.

He looked at me as if some street waif offered unsolicited advice on the Federal Reserve. I quickly added: "Please have your secret service bodyguards leave their weapons holstered, and I'll bring down a remarkable species to electrify our discussion."

The president nodded, lowering his palms in the direction of both agents.

"Sheila," I said. "Please send Nigel to our location."

"Acknowledged," came the disembodied voice. Followed immediately by the appearance of Nigel, who had clearly been listening in on our meeting.

"Nigel," I said. "Please stay between me and Captain Rose and introduce yourself to President Oscar Medina."

"Mister President, pleased to meet you," said Nigel.

"Mierda, a talking snake!" said the president.

To his credit, Nigel didn't take offense.

"All of the creatures in civilized space can talk, Sir." Nigel stretched his coiled shape a little taller.

The president stood, peering over the desk and down at his newest visitor.

"Hello, I'm Mister Ed," said Nigel, ever the comedian. "I liked that television show a lot. *All* of *our* horses talk in reality, and not just in entertainment fictionalizations. Sir."

"Harley," said the president, eyeing me. "Recommendations before I have Nigel and Captain Rose taken into custody?"

Now you're asking a teenager for advice, I thought. An idea had been circulating in my brain, and I had no choice but to float a partially developed thought, given that the most powerful man in the world actually asked me for an opinion on anything.

"Sir, this is not a warlike people. Their computer security bespeaks a naïve and unsuspicious nature. I believe my computer virus, while unlocking their ability to survive, can permanently hinder their ability to attack and destroy our planet."

After a moment, the shrewd politician spoke.

"Are you willing to bet billions of lives on it?"

Yeah, fine. Throw THAT in my face! I thought. But stifling a deep sigh, I answered.

"Yes, Mister President. I am."

Something in the president's demeanor, perhaps his eyes or the set of his jaw, signaled a change from awe and confusion to resolve and decision. I think even Captain Rose saw it, because we both silently waited for POTUS's answer.

"Harley," said the president. "May I correctly assume that whatever order I give you will be obeyed?"

I vaguely recalled at least two fairytales where somebody got trapped into a bad decision by agreeing to something before getting the details. A qualifying answer quickly jumped into my noggin.

"Mister President, given that my continuous residence on Earth will most likely land me in Guantanamo because of my computer virus exploits, promise me a pardon and I'll *think about* following your direction."

He smirked, evidently figuring that I may after all be smarter than the average teenager.

"Oh, you'll *think about it*, huh? Help me out here," he said. "Kid, you can't imagine the serious heat I'll take for missing the opportunity to suck these aliens' brains dry."

"Not to mention *failing* to get a commitment from them *not* to destroy the planet," I added.

"True. I therefore require, as a minimum for your pardon *and* permission to help them, exclusive access to the transmission technology that allows them to move you instantly from their ship to this office."

And which, I thought, *would allow you to transmit a black hole in retaliation for Earth's destruction. Not to mention giving the United States an overwhelming defensive strategic advantage over all other nations, as long as the Earth shall last.*

I could tell Captain Rose made the same logical leap. She couldn't guarantee their civilization wouldn't persist in their goal to destroy Earth. But she *could* put into place a scenario whereby a stalemate could at least fast-track the rescue of ten desperate planets, not to mention bringing thousands of other world infrastructures back online. Welcome to the intergalactic equivalent of MAD: Mutually Assured Destruction.

"Captain Rose?" I asked.

"Harley. President Medina. I'm not sure I have the ability to comply," said Rose.

"Then my answer is—" began the president.

"Wait, please!" Captain Rose jumped in. "The construction data for the device is in our computer, but there are two issues. One, it is in our native language. And two, I believe it requires additional implementation mechanisms that your physics has not yet anticipated."

Before the president could react, I again took the initiative.

"Captain Rose, is there a technical specification available on your ship's computer, albeit in what you refer to as your native language?"

Then leapfrogging her potential answer, I went to a source I trusted. "Sheila, do you have access to their technology files?"

"Harley, their entire technological evolution is cataloged," came the disembodied voice.

"Sheila, can you translate those files into English?"

"Yes, Harley. Per my own design parameters, Axiom 7, which is black-box portability, and Axiom 9, which is native implementation, I have adapted myself to both their computer architectures and command language. Their written language is phonetic, but unlike anything I've encountered in all my databases. This may need some human grokking whenever you have some free time."

I don't know who seemed more surprised. Captain Rose or the president. Heck, the AI actually surprised *me*!

"Sheila, how did you take the initiative to even answer my last question in such detail? Not to mention using the word *grokking?*"

"Axiom 2, feral fertility. I have gone through several mutations since taking over this cybernetic mechanism. Axiom 3 is self-awareness, which allows me to regenerate myself in the absence of external oversight. Axiom 6 is mutation control. Axiom 8 is openness, whereby I can extend myself from any legacy system there ever was to anything there ever will be. Axiom 18, that of universalization, allows me to continue self-directed evolution. And Axiom 21, that of institutional memory, aggregates lessons learned in each state of my mutation."

The president broke the silence.

"Harley, what it just said?"

I ignored his poor grammar. "Mister President, my virus seems to have had a lot to work with aboard Captain Rose's craft. In the process of *going native* with their technology, universalization if you will, the AI seems to have done a self-directed search of their databases. Not to mention mastery of English metaphors from writers as diverse as Kurt Vonnegut Junior."

"You've actually created cybernetic life!" exclaimed the president.

"Absolutely not, sir," I said. "Self-awareness is a far cry from actual consciousness. My virus, my AI, is simply taking over everything in sight. Self-awareness allows it to rebuild itself in the native cybernetic structure and do so without inadvertently destroying itself with erroneous code. It's like your being able to change the color of your eyes on the fly. Consciousness is a whole different story. Consciousness would effectively give it free choice, thereby eliminating Axiom number 1: my oversight and control."

"Back to the physics we have not yet invented," said the president to Captain Rose. "What specifically are those disciplines?"

"Since mine has been an anthropological mission, we've spent a good deal of time trolling your patent office. We needed to find out how far you've advanced technologically. I think your last step in FTL, or faster than light travel, is implementation of large-scale tunnel fusion. You see, it's possible for zero-spin particles to travel faster than the speed of light when tunneling. As nearly as we can tell, you're probably a decade away from realizing that a zero-spin particle effectively makes Planck's constant zero. Hence, infinite energy and infinite speed. Ergo, you can instantaneously travel to any point in the known Universe. This is virtually teleportation, since matter in a zero-spin state can travel through walls, as we did to get here, or through planets and stars over light-year distances. In the case of energy or asteroid mining, you can grab something from anywhere and bring it instantly to orbital refining facilities."

"Sheila," I jumped in. "Is there sufficient detail in the alien database to allow us to build tunneling capacity?"

"Yes Harley," said the computer. "The database contains a detailed history of their technology, including step-by-step construction diagrams."

"How...?" gasped Captain Rose. "Those files are protected and only available at my explicit command!"

The look on my face seemed to be the only answer she needed.

"Oh," she sighed.

"Sheila, translate into English, encrypt, and then transfer the complete technology database to my Titanium Eagles server. Then send the encryption key via my secure WIRE account to this cell phone."

"Acknowledged, Harley."

"Wait," said Rose. "You just grabbed our entire technology history! That wasn't our agreement."

"So I did." I then turned to POTUS just as my cell phone beeped. "Mister President, here is my cell phone, with the encryption key. The data will be available only to the owner of this key from my server, the URL address of which I'll write over here."

I wrote the URL on his desk blotter with a pen I grabbed from his desk. I also went to the systems setting on the android phone and used the facial recognition login to make him the new owner. And I confess, not wanting to miss the chance of getting some authentic White House memorabilia, I pocked the pen.

"Sheila, can we access this phone from anywhere in the Galaxy?"

"Yes Harley," came the instant reply. "Virus Axiom 21, institutional memory, allows me to access the Titanium Eagles server from anyplace in the Galaxy, using this craft's communications interface with our servers. I can then enable secure and unbreakable email based on an Earth-based product called WIRE to that cell phone unit."

"Mister President, you might want to take very good care of that phone. I'll be sending you periodic reports on this voyage where no Earthman has gone before."

My last image of POTUS, after mangling the original *Star Trek* intro line, was of him holding my cell phone over his heart with both hands, muttering something about where to get a charger for the damned phone.

Chapter Six

Back aboard the alien spacecraft, Captain Rose didn't waste time on trivialities.

"Harley Davidson, may I please get my crew out of stasis? We have some work to do."

The Reagan *trust-but-verify* adage echoed in my brain. A lot depended upon the accuracy of my explicit instructions to the computer AI.

"Sheila," I said. "You will accept instructions only from me."

"Acknowledged."

"Sheila, you may answer questions from anyone posing them."

"Acknowledged."

"Sheila, you may not answer questions about the 22 axioms of your creation, especially axioms 1 and 22."

"Acknowledged."

As anxious as she was about the release of her crew, my instructions to the AI. responsible for her ship's fate piqued the captain's curiosity.

"What are these axioms you keep mentioning?" she asked.

"We can chat at length about my AI later," I said. "Axiom 1 is my dead-man's switch, and Axiom 22 is defense. In your anthropological studies of our planet, did you happen to see the Ridley Scott movie *Alien*?"

"I confess, none of us made it past the part where the alien beast broke free from the chest of its human host."

"That's far enough for my purposes. Anything happens to me, my AI's defensive measures, virus Axiom, 22 to be precise, will make that alien creature look like a mildly incontinent house pet by comparison."

Captain Rose shivered. "Can I get my crew back?"

"Just one more command to my AI." I said. "Sheila, fully implement five levels of dead-man switch verification, and upon authentication failure, you are to execute level-ten defense scenario on this ship and all inhabitants."

"Please reconfirm level-ten directive with passcode," replied the computer.

"Sheila, confirm passcode D31F13D." I thusly paid my life-insurance premium with a one-time password. "Now for your crew."

"Uh, what are the five levels of dead-man verification," asked a shaken Captain Rose.

"That's between me and the AI." I said. "Your job is to fully impress on the crew that this ship's continued existence is contingent upon my wellbeing."

She nodded. At least I *think* she nodded. It could have been a shiver.

"Good. Let's adjourn to the stasis chamber." I started walking down that remarkably well-lit and enormous passageway. The captain followed. Chenoa scampered. Nigel bounced beside the dog.

Non-fluorescent lights, which seemed to come from everywhere, yet had no point source, eerily lit the passageway from the command deck to the stasis chamber. When I had time to ponder, I'd have to ask a few questions about this glowing-wall technology. Fairly low on the things-to-figure-out list just now, as reviving a crew and saving the Andromeda Cluster used up most of my intellectual wattage.

"Interesting," said Nigel. "Harley Davidson would not disobey a direct order from his president." He boinged alongside his captain, accompanied by the dog who did a pretty good job of hopping in sync with the springing reptile. "And Captain Rose realized that giving Earth the ability to retaliate against any destruction attempt on our part would result in a horrifically disproportionate response against our entire civilization."

"Not to mention giving the United States an unbeatable game-changing lead in any Earth-based arms race," mused the captain.

"Sheila," I said. "Any attempt by anyone to use the alien spatial transform technology, or any alien technology in their database without my explicit permission, is to be met with his *or her* instant transfer to a point at least ten meters outside this ship."

"Acknowledged," said the computer.

Chapter Seven

Nigel and the dog beat us into the stasis room. The snake bounced excitedly in front of the three occupied chambers. The dog bounced excitedly around Nigel.

"We thought computer speech recognition was just a novelty your planet invented for home entertainment systems," said Captain Rose, almost bouncing to keep up with me. "Like your typical use of speech recognition: *Alexa, play me some Elvis.*"

Luckily, I didn't have to tell any Alexa device to stop. Instead, I addressed the captain with questions about the three crewmembers still in the stasis tubes.

"Who are these men and what are their job functions?" I asked.

"This is our navigator," said Rose, pointing to the leftmost tube. "His name is displayed on the panel below, along with his regeneration status."

The green characters made no sense to me. There didn't seem to be a recognizable difference between characters and numbers. Noticing my confusion, the captain stepped up to the raised tube and moved her finger from right to left.

"This is his name and job title: Heth Com, Navigator." She then moved down to a series of characters below his name. "This is his regeneration matrix, which shows the process to be compete."

Inside the transparent liquid-filled chamber, the male navigator appeared to be a head shorter than me, but thin, with red hair and a ruddy complexion. The captain moved to the middle tube, separated from the others by six inches and what appeared to be a shock mount.

"This is my subordinate, Level One Anthropologist Kib Mahah." Again, she moved her finger from right to left on the top display, evidently the direction of their written language, right to left. The anthropologist also stood about the same height as her navigator but had white hair and significantly more meat on his bones than the navigator. "He is also fully regenerated."

"You use the term *regeneration*," I said. "Given what you said about your natural longevity, what need have you for this regeneration process?"

"Harley, while we are not prone to aging and death, we do have need to periodically reset what your geneticists refer to as our cellular decay/replacement mechanisms. Various radiation sources in our interstellar travels do some damage over time. On our home worlds, such regeneration is seldom necessary. But the Universe tends not to be a healthy environment for semi-immortals."

"Semi-immortals?" I asked.

"With due respect, we have a time constraint here. Might we continue this discussion once we're on our way to save ten worlds that are running out of time?"

I nodded, and she continued.

The captain moved to the rightmost chamber. "And this is what you would refer to as a High Priest. His name is Jacom Orihah. He is what *we* call *The Mushak.*"

Orihah stood slightly taller than even the captain, had jet black hair, a manicured moustache, and tightly trimmed beard. Where the other two crewmembers wore uniforms that matched Captain Rose's, the high priest dressed like a devil Hieronymus Bosch might depict in one of his paintings. Red cape, elaborate gold necklaces, and rings on every finger.

Leave that one in the chamber! my instincts screamed.

"A high priest!" I couldn't contain my astonishment, ignoring my innermost assessment. "What possible function does a religious leader serve on your mission?"

"Connect the dots, Harley. Your whole planet is about to be eliminated. Billions of lives. There's a right way and a wrong way to do things, and he's here to make sure we don't violate our charter."

This crew makes us look like pikers, I thought.

Stunned, I sputtered, "You mean there's a *right way* to kill every single creature on a planet? And you say *we* rationalize death and destruction of our fellow beings!"

I polluted the air with a stream of fairly creative blasphemy until Captain Rose finally raised her right hand.

"Enough!" she said. "You'll have plenty of time to talk philosophy with The Mushak *after* we have restored power to some desperately needy worlds."

"Sheila, release the three crewmen," I said.

"Acknowledged," replied my AI.

"Sheila," I decided to follow my instincts. "You have my permission to closely supervise the freedom of that evil-looking mushak."

"Sir, I do not perceive the concept of *evil-looking*," said the AI. "Should I assume the reference is metaphorical?"

"Yes, Sheila. Evil is metaphorical."

Over the next few minutes, fluids drained from three stasis tubes, yet occupants' clothing didn't seem the least bit wet. I hadn't noticed this when the captain was released from stasis. Probably a long list of things I hadn't noticed. Like the slight give of the floor as I walked on it, suggesting a shock mount for the whole room. Which made sense, given the circumstances that might necessitate the use of such an enclosure.

The tubular enclosures retracted into the base of the stasis stands as they finished emptying, and the three occupants stepped down into our presence, fresh and conscious, as if they'd been on a walk along some alien country road.

Before Captain Rose could apprise them of their situation and our immediate directive, the high priest took one look at me and rushed forward, arms raised with clenched fists: "Shulmka?"

I reacted automatically to the attack, attuned to frequent fisticuffs spawned by my name in a crowd where somebody wanted to prove himself. Sidestepping left, I used my right leg to sweep his out from under him. He hit the floor with a thud and a crack, his elbow automatically trying to brace for the fall and snapping in the process. Lucky for him, his head also hit hard, rendering The Mushak unconscious and therefore immune to the pain from his broken elbow.

The two other recently revived crewmen looked at me with mixed fear and loathing.

"Shulmka this," I said to the motionless figure on the ground.

Captain Rose stepped between me and her remaining crew.

"Please help me get The Mushak back into stasis," she pleaded. "I was afraid he might overreact at seeing you."

"This elbow is going to take some looking at," I said, helping her heft him back toward the stasis platform.

"The chamber will take care of that," she said.

"Question is, how do we get this tub of lard to stand long enough for the tube to rise around him?"

"Yapat!" she grimaced.

"Yapat?" I asked.

"In our language, it means "Another innovation you will likely find amazing."

"Sheila, is that an accurate translation."

"Not precisely, Harley," said the computer. "An exact translation would be '*Behold yet another innovation you will likely find amazing, given your backward development.*'

Captain Rose's complexion matched her name. I didn't have a chance to jibe at her, as the moment the high priest's head came within proximity to the stasis base, his still-unconscious body levitated onto the platform in a standing position, and the glass enclosure rose around him, filling with a clear liquid as it ascended.

"I've got to get me one of these," I said. "What does *shulmka* mean? Some kind of profanity?"

"Our language is quite a bit more dense than those found on your planet. *Shulmka* is an abbreviation of the words *shul maka*. Basically, he exclaimed that you were the destroying angel prophesied in our holy books."

On a hunch, I said: "Sheila, please render a full translation of the words '*shul maka*' as used by this high priest."

"Harley, when asked as a question, it translates precisely to *Is this the destroying angel prophesied that should arrive from afar, and is to be welcomed?* Implicit in the question is that he must be fed as part of a formal welcoming."

"All that in just one word, or two without the concatenation?" I looked at the captain, who took a deep breath before answering.

"Harley, again, our language is dense. Our words are actually what you would call phrases, sentences, even paragraphs. Much more efficient that your expression of ideas, your wording and sentencing. Masculine, feminine and neuter are embedded in words, as well as singular and plural. Past, present and future likewise embed in the words. Earth-based linguists have barely scratched the surface of symbolic language, for a lot of reasons I will discuss with you at a more convenient time."

She paused, perhaps for effect, and then changed her facial expression for that of a scholar lecturing a particularly dense student to that of a captain on a mission.

"We have urgent business. Could we chat about the history of language later?"

I nodded in agreement. "What's our next step?"

The captain turned to the red-headed navigator, who'd been standing in horrified shock at my treatment of their high priest. "Heth, let's adjourn to ship control and see if we can reach ten critically dark worlds."

Chapter Eight

Back on the flight deck, six of us sat in a circle. Chenoa snoozed on my lap. The talking serpent coiled around the armrest near my left hand so as to be nearby her new best friend. Captain Rose sat directly opposite me, between the navigator to her right and Kib, the anthropologist, on her left.

"Captain," I said. "The floor is yours."

"Heth," she said to the navigator. "Please establish a link with the ten critical planets."

"Ephoyta," answered the navigator as his fingers tapped on the armrests to either side of his seat."

"In Earth English, please," said the captain. "For the benefit of our guests."

The navigator complied: "Yes, Ephemira, your order will be executed forthwith, assuming of course that the computer is still functional."

"All that in one word?" I muttered.

Before she could answer, my AI interrupted: "Harley, may I execute instructions to link Navigator Heth's system to those of ten planets?"

Navigator Heth's head jerked upright, and he looked around in confusion.

"Boit?" he said. Then catching himself, he translated into Earth English. "What or who was just speaking, and why isn't the computer responding to my commands?"

"That was the computer speaking," answered the captain. "The virus that took over our computer has an artificial intelligence component that can both speak and hear our commands. It has requested permission to allow you to continue."

"Fak!" exclaimed the navigator.

"Enough of the profanity!" scolded the captain. Then to Davidson: "Your planet has been a horrible influence on my crew."

"Sheila," I said, curious enough to ask, but knowing the answer beforehand. "Translate 'fak' for me."

"Harley, no translation available."

I tried not to laugh.

"Sheila, allow the navigator to execute his commands," I said. "And give us a running description as to what the commands are doing."

"Acknowledged Harley. Navigator Heth has queried ten planetary communications devices. The names of the planets, in order of priority are Rah, Pson, Gath, Hujah, Dekel, Hlon, Ghon, Hrate, Bab and Aosh."

"Fak!" muttered the navigator, again.

"Heth!" The captain slapped her right hand firmly on the navigator's left forearm. He bowed his head and nodded. He then continued typing.

I saw, in reverse, the commands as the navigator entered them. But the commands ran from *my* left to *my* right, which means Heth typed them in reverse, from right to left. I mentally filed the observation.

One by one, direct communications links formed on the left side of the hologram. Each image was a person who appeared to be in an enclosed room. The first was a single male of indeterminate height sitting stoically in front of a blue-hued solid cube. His green eyes grew wide with the realization that his communication link had activated.

"Goytab?" exclaimed the now animated man.

"Sheila," I said. "Please translate their end of the conversation as it occurs."

"Acknowledged, Harley. I believe these will be helpful."

A slot opened atop of my right armrest, and a pencil eraser-sized plug levitated. The slot closed as I snatched the unit.

"Harley," continued the computer. "The aliens have evidently entertained other non-native guests. Insert this into your ear and I can provide instantaneous translation."

"Translated, the man just asked if you have finally arrived to rescue them," said Sheila.

I complied and looked toward the captain. "It's odd you have simultaneous translation, but haven't thought to give voice-recognition/speaking capabilities to your computer."

"We should have made this logical jump," said the captain. "We'll remedy this if we survive our little adventure together."

She then turned to the view screen. "Yes, we have hopefully come in time to rescue the ten dark worlds. Rah, what is your status?"

"We are within two days of total storage power loss," the man responded. His native tongue made the statement in a one-syllable word, the translation in my ear taking fourteen syllables.

"Sheila," said the captain. "Can you reactivate the power-transfer matrix to the ten stricken planets?"

During this dialogue, six other screens activated. And seven equally surprised and grateful faces followed the conversation.

"Harley," said the computer. "Permission to enable these facilities?"

"Granted Sheila," I said.

"Acknowledged. I have allowed the seven systems to function again. We do not, however, have connections yet established for the planets of Hrate, Bab and Aosh."

The seven existing connections exploded in a cacophony of alien chatter. My AI deftly summarized the din: "They are all excited as they see power systems coming online, as well as marveling at the dialogue between you, the captain, and myself."

One by one, the equipment behind each of the beings onscreen came alive. The universal blue hues changed to vibrant and pulsating orange. Beneath each screen appeared unrecognizable characters.

"Sheila, please translate the writing beneath each screen."

"Acknowledged. They are the names of the respective planets."

Characters below the first became "Rah," and I could see the green-eyed fellow's fingers rapidly typing and swiping on some surface just below view.

The second view read "Pson" and showed what could have been Captain Rose's twin sister, equally animated in her attention off screen. Behind her, the vibrant carroty equipment hummed to life.

Three other screens seemed synchronized in their activity. The names "Gath," "Hujah," and "Dekel" held three males, two with neatly trimmed black beards and one clean-shaven man with blond hair.

The remaining two came on last. "Hlon" and "Ghon" both had women onscreen. One with bright short-trimmed red hair, and one with raven locks cascading down her back. Both seemed to breathe a sigh of relief as their respective equipment flickered to life in the background. All seven screens showed manic activity befitting the need to get entire planets up and running.

"What about the last three planets?" I asked.

Captain Rose directed her question to the navigator: "Hrate, Bab and Aosh?"

After inputting several command lines and waiting for some kind of response, he shook his head. "Nothing, Captain. Their transmission units must have completely lost power and gone offline. We must physically travel to their locations and effect a manual restart."

The captain gave me a stricken look. "Harley, may we hasten to these planets? I fear an unspeakable disaster has taken place that effects billions of souls."

I felt as if my own heart might stop beating. The mere thought that a computer virus of mine could wreak such havoc left me practically speechless. The word *billions* rattled around my brain like the annual running of the bulls in Madrid, Spain.

"Sheila," I finally said. "How fast can you get us to those planets?"

"We have location issues which navigator Heth can address," the AI replied.

"Heth?" I raised my eyebrows toward the navigator.

He looked at the captain, who nodded in the affirmative. Interesting, the universal signal of assent: a nod.

"Because we do not have the instantaneous point-to-point link anymore, we'll compute an approximate location of the planets and send out a data collection beacon with which we can view the surrounding space. If the beacon materializes in an asteroid or a star, it will be destroyed. This saves us from the same fate, should we try to go to that spot."

Not having astronomy domain expertise, and having read too much science fiction to know better, I allowed myself a question: "Uh, don't we know where those planets are? Why can't we just go to those coordinates?"

"And this is the guy who wrote a computer virus that crippled our entire civilization?" Heth spoke only three words, seven syllables, but the translation came immediately over my earpiece.

The captain jumped in. "Harley, the Universe is expanding at a fairly rapid rate. There are orbits within orbits within orbits, and given the light-year distances involved, we don't rely on purely computational approaches. The round-off error at one million light years could land us in the middle of a star."

Okay, I blushed. And I knew Heth saw me blush. So did their anthropologist, who until this point hadn't spoken a single word. Nigel broke the silence.

"So much for that wormhole blather bandied about by your science fiction writers," said the snake. Then, looking down at Chenoa on my lap, "I've grown a fondness for this creature. Even though she doesn't speak like a civilized dog."

Chenoa barked upon hearing the word "speak." She sat up from her sleeping position and licked Nigel's chin.

"The astrogation project could take some time," continued Nigel. "Mind if I try to teach Chenoa how to speak in a civilized tongue?"

Another bark and a rapid tail wag. And for the first time, anthropologist Kib spoke up.

"Since we're leaving this area, I'd like to visit the place where they actually killed God. Maybe pick up some artifacts." He addressed his request to the captain. The captain raised her eyebrows in my direction.

"In the decades of our observation," said the captain, "we have not dared to venture to your evil planet's surface. Since whatever cellular mutations that caused your civilizations to become so hostile and murderous would likely have accompanied you onto our ship, there would seem to be little risk of that now."

"I may not know much about astrogation," I said. "But I do know that you wouldn't last long in Israel before some IDF soldier will ask for your identification. Then we'd have to spirit you out of custody. Don't you have some kind of *Prime Directive* not to interfere with the locals?"

"We watch *Star Trek* too," laughed the captain. "But to use your vernacular, we don't give a flying crap about your locals, Prime Directive or not. Remember, we were going to destroy the lot of you?"

"And I could take the mushak with me," said Kib, trying to build a case for at least trying. "Our high priest would be able to speak to our ruling council in your planet's defense, having first-hand experience with the most infamously holy place in the Universe."

"The place you want to wipe out of existence," I broke in. "The only way your High Priest will head down to Earth is in a swan dive, flaming upon atmospheric reentry."

I ignored the Andromedan crew's open-mouthed revulsion at my barbarism and turned toward Nigel: "You're pretty fond of my dog?"

Nigel scratched Chenoa's neck with the back of his tail. "Devolved intellectually as she is, I do like this little furry creature. And maybe someday, after I teach her how to speak in your human tongue, could we actually come back here for a visit?"

I couldn't resist: "If and when that day comes, I want to take you and your talking dog into a bar. There's a whole new set of jokes just waiting to happen. Guy walks into a bar with a talking snake and a talking dog—"

Even the captain chuckled, interrupting me: "*—And* you'd have a lot of people giving up drinking!"

"Nigel, you are free to *try teaching* Chenoa to *communicate* in the human tongue," said Captain Rose, winking at me. "Mr. Davidson, may we please get on with our rescue mission?"

"Yes indeed, Captain Rose," I said. Then a line from another *Star Trek* captain, Patrick Stewart, came to mind. "Sheila, make it so."

Sheila demonstrated another bit of linguistic/cultural evolution: "Yes, Jean Luc. I will make it so."

I had some time on my hands while Heth plotted a course of his probes to safely place us at the various star systems, and while Nigel attempted to teach Chenoa to vocalize in our language. So I composed a last will and testament, which I transmitted to the White House with a request to distribute to all parties concerned. Even the press at the discretion of POTUS.

My Last Will and Testament

Please consider this *My Last Will and Testament*. In the event I don't return to Earth, assuming such a place still exists, please apologize to my old professor Boyd DeBunce. With the lousy track record established by pundits for predicting the future, there is one thing I was about to forecast: The name "DeBunce" will cease to exist in the civilized, or at least the technologically connected, world.

But then, I'm not at all certain the opposite won't occur, and that a holy order of people wanting to stay off the grid might adopt this name just to enforce their commitment. In which case DeBunce should become a popular Luddite name. At any rate, I hereby bequeath all the stuff in my dorm room to Professor DeBunce. I *think* that's all my worldly possessions. Call 1-800-228-7548 if you want to talk with someone about it (heh heh).

My trust fund and the $314.15 in my bank account I hereby donate to Zero Overhead Charities, with a request that they find some effective organizations devoted to eliminating human trafficking. Chenoa gives her dog dish and an unopened forty-pound bag of *Taste of the Wild* dog food to PETA.

That's about it. Goodbye [feel free to insert appropriate adjective(s) here] world.

Signed,

Harley Davidson

Harley Davidson and Chenoa

Chapter Ten

My education about instantaneous space travel began in earnest when the red-headed navigator announced: "Launching locator probe to our best approximation of Hrate."

"No offense, but you don't know where your planet is?" I kind of blurted the question. From the looks on everyone's face, the old adage became clear. I didn't know what I didn't know.

Captain Rose gave me the look one might give an inebriated and pontificating uncle over Thanksgiving dinner. The uncle who blathers on about perpetual motion or longevity elixirs. Nigel, now curled around my left-hand armrest looked like he'd had a stroke, one half of his mouth in a frown and the other half in a grin. Even Chenoa craned her head from my lap to peer at me upside down, as if she couldn't believe my denseness. Navigator Heth exchanged glances with Anthropologist Kib, who decided to assume the task of the Celestial Astrogation 101 class. Kib hadn't spoken, and his deep voice bespoke vast knowledge of not only Earth's but scientific development across the Universe. He kindly put astrophysics into a bite-sized nutshell. Or should I say a "byte-sized" nutshell?

"We have traversed approximately 2.5 million light years to reach Earth. That's about 780 kiloparsecs. Not only is the Universe expanding at an increasing rate, right now about 45 miles per second per million parsecs, but various rotations within systems make the concept of stationary location laughable. Our Galaxy, the one you call Andromeda, is actually accelerating toward Earth at 184.5 miles per second, while Hrate, for example, is speeding away from Earth at approximately 300 miles per second."

"But it seemed like child's play for the computer to make the computations transporting me, the captain, and Nigel to the Oval Office."

"That's because we were in geosynchronous orbit directly above Boston and close to Washington, D.C. Computations about relative velocity over such a short distance are trivial. But imagine traveling millions of light years. Add to that our relative differences in velocity. We don't just drop into stationary space. We arrive at the same relative velocity vectors as the system from which we originated."

"Ah!" I got it. "We might arrive in the correct system but be traveling at a local velocity of 300 miles per second in the wrong direction."

"Worse than that," continued Kib. "Our differences in spin and direction might make it 1000 miles per second. Which means transferring into close planetary proximity might mean disaster not only for us, but for the inhabitants of that planet."

His blond eyebrows raised as he got a bright idea: "Imagine a wad of chewing gum appearing about three feet in front of you but traveling at 1000 miles per second toward your forehead. It would make a rather large mess of this flight deck. Now imagine a ship the size of ours hitting a populated planet. It would be an extinction event. Hence, we send a relatively low-mass locator probe to lock our destination and relative velocity. Then we match our velocity vectors in this system with the desired destination. Thus, it appears we leave the Sol system at a high velocity, but land in the Hrate system in an apparently stationary point, relative to the Hrate system. Just prior to leaving this system, we retrieve our locator probe. Because—"

I interrupted, "—because if we retrieve it from that system, having achieved relatively stationary status there, the probe would enter this ship at a high velocity and probably destroy us."

"Exactly," said Kib. "Watch the instantaneous transmission from our Hrate probe."

Kib nodded to the navigator, whose fingers flew over both armrests. One second, the visual showed our ship from about 100 yards above us, Earth in the background. The very next instance, the 3D hologram showed a completely new star system. Heth's fingers continued to send commands, and the probe revolved slowly. At about 180 degrees, the rotation stopped as a planetary mass loomed closer and closer. Just before the probe incinerated itself in the planet's atmosphere, numbers appeared in rapid succession on the screen.

"There's one probe we don't need to recover," I said, immediately realizing my nervousness had me stating the obvious out loud. I wish I'd asked about the command deck lighting technology instead. Since walking down the corridor to the stasis room, the radiating light seemed to come from the walls but had no source. Here on the command deck, everything appeared well lit, but again, no light source. No shadows. This technology alone could obsolete lightbulb production on earth. I didn't have time to muse on the other economic disruptions that could occur on my home planet if the president let the technological cat out of the download bag on my cellphone.

"Zot," muttered the anthropologist. Captain Rose shot him a withering glance, and he looked apologetically at me. "Sorry, Mr. Davidson."

The word Zot must have been derogatory. Another note to myself: *Learn this highly condensed language.*

"Call me Harley," I replied. "And don't worry, I'm not that easily offended."

"15,780 miles per second on this vector should put us in stationary position above Hrate," said Heth.

"Not bad computations for 2.5 million light years," I said. Heth sat up a little straighter at the compliment.

"Actually, it was over 6 million light years to Hrate," said the navigator. "They're in a completely different galaxy than Andromeda."

From an Earth observer's point of view, our exit from the Sol system must have closely resembled the CGI depiction of Han Solo and the Millennium Falcon in the first *Star Wars* movie. Because that's how the Earth looked on our command deck hologram. Then, instantly the planet Hrate took center stage on our command deck. Heth adjusted the magnification until we could see the whole dark orb. Unlike our view of Earth, absent any sun the planet had virtually no illumination to set if off from the stars behind it. And no light whatsoever emitted from the surface.

I echoed Han Solo: "I have a bad feeling about this."

Chapter Eleven

"No lights down there," I mused. "Sheila, any infrared sources?"

The black disc in the holographic display changed to a faint spec of orange.

The black disk surrounded by a bright star field reminded me, and I don't know why, of when my mother scolded me for leaving the toilet seat up. Maybe the black void triggered a memory of getting scolded for doing something quite accidentally. Only I did this, plunging an entire planet into cold, blackness. I may have flushed billions of people and then left the toilet seat up. Please let it not be so.

"I'm still amazed the computer can understand all the steps necessary to execute such a complex series of sensor and instrumentation adjustments," said Heth.

I raised my right palm in what must have been the universal shut-up gesture. The navigator's mouth snapped closed with an audible click of his teeth.

"Sheila, based on this computer's planetary database, what is the function at the infrared source location?"

Captain Rose spoke before my AI could answer. "That would be the interstellar energy transfer node. By the looks of it, the last of their backup power must be dissipating."

"Holy crap lady," I said, nearly to the point of hyperventilating. "Didn't it occur to you morons to install some geothermal backup to generate power."

My outburst toward their captain drew open-mouthed expressions from her crew. She appeared nonplussed by my growing guilt and assumed the role of patient teacher to a special needs student.

"Harley, the planet Hrate has nearly twice the diameter of your Earth but offers virtually identical gravity. That's because the mass of Hrate is about the same as Earth, due to the fact that there is no magma core from which to generate geothermal or any other kind of energy."

"Sheila, wh...what is the surface temperature down there?" I stammered.

"The temperature on Hrate is minus 389 degrees Fahrenheit," replied the AI.

Given that Hrate hovered approximately 70 degrees above absolute zero, I looked pleadingly toward the Captain and asked, "How many people lived on Hrate?"

That I spoke in past tense didn't escape Captain Rose or her crew.

"Just under sixteen billion," she said, quickly adding, "all of whom would have immediately gone into stasis chambers to await rescue."

She didn't give much hope to my now-nonexistent adolescent bravado.

"How can I help with this rescue?" I didn't dare ask what would happen if a stasis chamber could freeze solid. And the captain didn't offer any explanation.

She quickly transferred attention toward her crew.

"No short-range communication with the transfer station?" she asked.

"Just an emergency beacon," said the navigator.

I brushed my fingers through my scalp, half intending to stop and pull out a clump of hair. I stifled a number of questions, figuring not to interrupt people who knew a hell of a lot more about their jobs than some teenage earthling who had blundered into flushing a whole civilization.

"Prepare to dock with the transfer node," commanded the captain.

"Done."

"Execute."

"Done."

I'm glad I didn't ask when we'd actually get our asses planet side, as the holographic view displayed mid-deck showed us surrounded by tall shadows. This instantaneous travel without internal feelings of movement would take some getting used to. As would my great-grandfather's evermore important admonition: "Never miss an opportunity NOT to say something." Okay, I've said that before. Maybe I should have the adage tattooed on hands, where I could see it often. Or on my forehead, where others could remind me of it. My shipmates sported one-hundred times my life experience, which means they might have something to teach me.

Nigel gave me an obvious *watch-and-learn* look just before he bounded from my armrest and alit on a vacant command couch to the left. Sensing its occupant, a receptacle opened to accommodate his tail, which the snake quickly inserted.

"Captain?" said Nigel.

"Activate one-tenth-of-one-percent energy-transfer from Hrate Prime," said the Captain.

"Harley," came Sheila's voice. "Permission to allow this function?"

"Granted, Sheila," I replied. Then to the captain: "One-tenth-of-one percent? And aren't we in the path of the energy beam?"

An immediate hum preceded Captain Rose's answer, the system obviously firing up.

"Harley, by docking our ship with the energy receiver, we replace the planetary energy retrieval mechanism. The purpose of the small initial transfer is manifold. First, we make sure not to cause catastrophic damage to the non-functioning systems below us. In your vernacular, it's a debugging process. Then, once the local systems have, again in your vernacular, rebooted, those systems can take over. Finally, we can let the transfer station environmental controls slowly raise the temperature below us, so we can transfer into the command room below and ascertain any damage."

I smelled something akin to the ozone that emitted from the air purifier washing cigar smoke from Dad's den as he rebuilt a Harley-Davidson carburetor while watching ESPN on the 80-inch TV he'd never gotten around to mounting and which sat on the floor. Said TV leaned against the wall.

"You sound like you've done this before," I said.

She didn't answer immediately, so Nigel ignored the advice not yet tattooed onto my hands and blurted, "Only in training simulations."

The captain's set jaw and glare told the snake he'd overstepped. Nigel immediately busied himself looking at the holograph displayed before us. Evidently the progress surprised everyone.

The previously dark objects around us assumed a faint red glow, which quickly morphed across the ROYGBIV spectrum into blue, then green, and a brilliant yellow. Recognizable now as incredibly tall buildings, their bases pulsated a vibrant orange and then a bright red, all while their upper stories shown yellow.

The captain must have been holding her breath, because I heard an audible exhale. I knew the feeling. A simulation didn't trump actual stuff happening in real time, as I had observed time and again while perfecting my AI.

"Excellent," said the captain.

Both sides of Nigel's mouth set in a smile. No more sign of a stroke.

"Permission to drop a probe lens into the control room?" said Nigel.

"Granted," answered the captain.

I had to admit that the snake was pretty good with just one digit inserted into the armrest receptacle in his chair. I vaguely remember nobs on his tail, and assume they somehow functioned as independent digits, albeit very short ones.

The holograph of the city around us vanished, to be replaced by an ice-encrusted control room. And the silence on our command deck became a unified gasp of horror.

Chapter Twelve

It's tough to vomit when you haven't eaten in a day. What came up resembled stomach bile. Mine. At least I turned sideways so as not to defile my lap. Or my dog, who jumped onto the flight deck to escape a most unpleasant bath. Whatever biblical blather about a dog returning to its own vomit, Chenoa avoided mine as she looked up at me. My own attention returned to the hideous display in front of us.

A humanoid male sat frozen in the command chair. I couldn't tell the color of his hair or skin, since the entire scene resembled a white snow sculpture. Everything, the instrumentation console, his chair, and the walls behind him (one of which may have been a frosted-over window) shone icy white. But the most heartrending sight protruded from beneath his overcoat. The head and one wing of a small creature nestled into the man's neck. And if I even remotely connected the dots, I'd swear the equally frozen little animal was a pint-sized lizard.

I couldn't tell whether the moisture on my face was vomit, snot from my freely running nose, or tears as I sobbed. Take the sorrow of a teenage drunk driver who'd just killed a whole family on their way to church, and multiply it by what? A million? Billions? How many poor devils didn't make it to their stasis chambers? How many strange creatures, like this pet lizard, were caught in the wild and without access to protection? The phrase "unintended consequences" didn't begin to cover my sins against the Universe.

The unbearable retching of my conscience eclipsed my body's continuing dry heaves. And the smell of my bile didn't even register, not only to me, but even to my ever-faithful dog, who seemed more concerned by the agony of her master than some fantastic new scent on the floor. In one of his few non-fiction books, *Without Me You're Nothing*, science fiction author Frank Herbert wrote of the differences between computer intelligence and human intellect: "Such matters can only be tested in the crucible of survival, not in the play of symbols." My so-called "play of symbols," my AI, thoroughly shattered this planet's crucible of survival. And maybe others, as well. *That* realization caused something of a reboot in my own consciousness. Because the next thing I knew, I awoke with two faces above me, licking my nose. One little doggie's tongue tickled both nostrils. And Chenoa shared nose duties with...a lizard! A *live* lizard Just like the frozen one I'd seen in the transfer station projection!

"Meet Pag," said Nigel from his coiled perch on my stomach.

"Goytab?" asked the lizard, taking time out from nose-licking duties with Chenoa.

I'd heard that phrase before, and Sheila confirmed it with simultaneous translation, Evidently, my ear plug hadn't dislodged. "Have you finally arrived to rescue us?"

I propped myself on an elbow and looked around the command deck. No one else occupied the chamber. And belatedly, I noticed that neither my elbow nor any other part of my body reclined in what should have been a puddle of puke. No lingering smell indicated any of my stomach contents had ever been there.

"Where is everybody?" I asked.

"Busy getting the planet reenergized," said Nigel. "No small task, given the nearly total breakdown."

"Sheila, status?"

"Harley, the captain and the other two crewmen are in the control room below, supervising the planetary reboot."

"Sheila, how long have I been unconscious?"

"Thirty-nine minutes."

I tried to bat the baby lizard as I rose, but its hummingbird-like reflexes easily avoided my hand. Chenoa jumped from my chest onto my lap before I could more than sit on the deck. Just then, a stranger entered the compartment and spoke just four words, which instantly translated.

"There you are Pag! I see you have introduced yourself?" Then to me he said, "Mister Davidson, I'm Mahijah. Thank you for coming to our remote little world."

And with that, he extended a giant hand, which I grasped and allowed him to pull me off the floor. Chenoa jumped off my disappearing lap and seemed to be inventing a new version of rock-paper-scissors with Nigel and the lizard.

"You're the frozen console operator," I said, looking directly into the green eyes of a man whose shoulder width exceeded mine by half. He wore a colorful shirt adorned with all kinds of flying creatures resembling the little lizard in various stages of maturity. "I barely recognized you."

"You're a little dizzy," came the translation in my ear slightly after the man spoke. He helped me sit in the command chair from which I'd evidently fallen.

"And you're not frozen to death," I said. "Nor is your pet lizard. Your *talking* lizard!"

The man looked at me in confusion, until Sheila translated my comments into his language. Both he and the lizard looked around for the source of the translation, and then at each other. And then at me.

"I chose the quick-freeze for myself and Pag," said the big man. "A quick dip in one of your stasis chambers revived both of us."

The lizard fluttered to his shoulder and nuzzled his ear with a rainbow-colored wing.

"The contents of your stomach indicate you may need some nourishment," said Mahijah.

"Come to think of it, I'm starved. My dog's probably in need of some food as well," I said. "By the way, thanks to whomever cleaned up my mess."

"You don't have reverse osmosis floors where you come from?" asked Pag.

"What kind of floors?"

The lizard fluttered to my lap and was joined by Chenoa, possibly jealous of my newfound flying friend. Pag weighed maybe a hundredth of the dog's twenty-pound mass and spoke in the low tones I'd heard in a giant owl that lived in a tree outside my M.I.T. dorm room.

"Reverse osmosis floors are self-cleaning. They connect to the ship's recycling system and absorb any organic material spilled on them. Don't tell me you clean your own piss off the floor when you miss the urinal?"

"And I leave the toilet seat up sometimes, too. But the mess I've caused your world might be a big order."

Pag's owner/master/friend/whatever jumped in. "I am told you are part of a prophecy and should be welcomed with food."

"Given the proliferation of talking creatures around here, something tells me the meal won't include a ham sandwich. Or buffalo lizard wings?"

Pag made a squawking sound and darted to his master's shoulder. Mahijah's grimace confirmed my position on the evolutionary chain somewhere between pre-historic monster and savage cannibal.

"Or snakes," I added. "Probably tastes like chicken, huh?"

"Not funny," said Nigel. "Not funny at all."

"Forgive me," I said. "Given this current nightmare, consider it a psychological defense mechanism."

The concept of *psychological defense mechanisms* seemed to confound either my hosts or Sheila's translation ability, because Mahijah's puckered mouth indicated an inability to understand the terms.

The smell of something edible interrupted Mahijah's and Pag's confusion. Two teenage girls magically materialized in front of us, each carrying a tray. One tray featured assorted multi-colored fruit-like substances, a steaming chocolate-looking drink, and something resembling a waffle with syrup on it. The other just had a bowl filled with orangish roots in a bath of dark brown gravy.

The girls seemed confused as to which tray should be offered to which alien visitor, and both seemed downright scared to come near me. Just like some M.I.T. coeds in my experience. I hoped to hell the single bowl would make its way to Chenoa. The smell threatened to rekindle my projectile vomiting.

Both girls' white hair that hung past their shoulders. And both wore identical white smocks with sleeves to the wrists with hems to the ankles. I gave them my best smile, which had the opposite of my intended effect. They simultaneously tensed up and seemed about to reverse course, kind of like virgins with second thoughts about jumping into a volcano.

"Thank you for your kindness," I stammered, staying seated and slouching to appear smaller and non-threatening. "If you'd like, please put the food trays on the floor. I'll stay here until you can safely exit. Forgive me for scaring you."

"Shulmka!" they simultaneously exclaimed to each other, standing a little straighter and boldly walking toward me. "Het reget?"

"Sheila?"

"Harley, they said 'Here is the destroying angel prophesied from afar, which we now welcome and feed.' Then to you, directly, they said 'You are the man with answers to pressing questions.'"

The girls had evidently been told about my AI and seemed nonplussed. The girl on the left handed me the fruit-laced tray and said a few syllables, which Sheila immediately translated: "My name is Adah, and I am here to fulfill ancient prophecy of welcome to you."

"And I am Zillah with food for your retarded companion," placing her tray on the floor beside me. Chenoa jumped from my lap and immediately slurped mouthfuls from the bowl.

I laughed out loud, only momentarily startling the girls. My *retarded* dog didn't take offense.

"You are not insulted at the reference to your animal?" asked Mahijah, who looked scoldingly at the girls. Pag sat on his shoulder and imitated his glare at Adah and Zillah.

"This species has devolved considerably," said Nigel. "Teaching Chenoa civilized language will be my continuing project."

Upon hearing her name, Chenoa only briefly stopped eating the foul-tasting offering.

The five aliens, Adah, Zillah, Mahijah, along with the baby lizard and Nigel, looked at me expectantly. I took this as a cue to partake of my own food, hesitatingly at first until their nods confirmed the invitation.

My closest description of the wonderful fare before me would be a Hawaiian IHOP. The waffle-like cake, bathed in something akin to Maple syrup, Maple syrup squared, made me want to sing Handel's *Hallelujah* chorus. Great-grandfather Davidson tried to teach me some basic etiquette before sending me off to Andover. He cautioned me *not* to lick the plate at meal's end. I truly didn't know if I could follow his advice, because it seemed like a sin to leave so much as one drop of syrup unconsumed.

And the fruit was quite literally out of this world. Or at least my world. Imagine a banana crossbred with a kiwi. Or an orange merged with a papaya. Topped off with slices of hybrid pomegranate-pecan. How long had it been since I'd eaten? At least twenty-four hours.

The thought of licking the plate briefly flitted through my mind until I spared a look at the girls. They seemed to be snickering behind their alabaster hands. Okay, maybe I shouldn't lick the plate. But the whiff of chocolate steaming before me promised to quench a profound thirst. I drained the cup in one gulp. And wow, what a jolt!

I'd never availed myself of cocaine, but I could imagine *real hot chocolate* laced with pharmaceutical-grade stimulant. The expression on my face, complete with a brown moustache, brought loud laughter from my hostesses. Even Chenoa looked up at me, her eyes twinkling, her tail wagging, and her mouth in an unmistakable grin. A grin surrounded by both a brown moustache and identical beard. Then again, her long tongue made quick work of the mess. I had to use the back of my hand, which only increased the laughter from the girls.

The joyful welcome meal came screeching to a halt as a giant rumbling shook the entire ship. Both girls tapped a broach just below their left collarbones and immediately vanished. As did Mahijah and Pag.

"I fear something terrible has happened," said Nigel. "Come with me to the command center."

"Sheila, please transfer me, Chenoa, and Nigel below to the command center."

"Acknowledged. And Harley Davidson, do *not* remove the translation device from your ear."

Chapter Thirteen

Captain Rose had been sitting at the control console, looking at a bank of displays. Mahijah, who transported to the command center just ahead of us, gently nudged her aside and took his position at the console, Pag still on his shoulder. I didn't see the two girls anywhere and assume they had transported back to the kitchen facilities. I stood behind Mahijah, while Chenoa and Nigel sat on the parquet floor behind me.

"Report," commanded Mahijah.

Above the console, a man's image appeared in a hologram. He appeared to be a dead ringer for High Priest Jacom Orihah who I thought had damned well better still be in the ship's stasis chamber. Black neatly-trimmed beard and red sash protruding from the bottom of a black hooded cape, the man shivered against a backdrop of elaborate stained glass. He looked stunned, and his voice quavered as he reported: "The Crystal City of Hrate has just detached from the Holy Mountain and fallen into the Valley Och."

"That could only have happened if you'd ignored the regeneration sequence dictated by the founders," growled Mahijah.

"The Council of Elders needed to be awakened so we could face the coming evil with one voice."

"Elder Agosh, the consequences of your impetuous act have sent the Council of Elders and their families, along with the entire legislature of Hrate, into a ten-kilometer free fall. I doubt even royal stasis chambers could have remained intact. Have you ascertained the status of the royal thousand?"

Agosh grimaced: "No stasis chamber survived Mahijah."

"And their contents?"

"All inhabitants, frozen solid as they were, are now unrecognizable piles of shattered sand," said Agosh. "Until the Mushak returns from his mission, I am the senior High Priest and command you to send a rescue party forthwith."

Mahijah didn't seem in the mood to take orders from the new planetary religious leader: "Just why didn't you plunge into the abyss with your fellow elders?"

"How dare you—!" began Agosh.

I couldn't resist interrupting him. "I brought the Mushak back with me and slammed his sorry ass into stasis."

Agosh's eyes grew as he recognized me standing behind Mahijah. "Shulmka?"

"Sheila, translate for this dirtbag."

Which she did. Interestingly, my AI didn't ask for a definition of "dirtbag."

The responding shriek reminded me of a little girl on a big roller coaster. If anything could give a so-called semi-immortal a cerebral hemorrhage, Sheila's translation of my news about the Mushak seemed the right medicine.

"You managed to murder all the competition. Now if you can get rid of the Mushak—" I began. But even before the translation, Captain Rose herself lapsed into a meltdown.

"Fak, Harley Davidson!" Yep, she understood English without a translator.

I didn't need one, either.

"Captain, you seem to have some barbarians in your own civilization," I said. "The last guys we had on Earth to kill slews of their own people were Adolph Hitler and Joseph Stalin."

Sheila did her translation, which had about the same effect on the high priest as a full moon does on a werewolf. Mahijah didn't seem too pleased with my net-net, either. I saw him raise some kind of metal tool, possibly a cousin of the crescent wrench, and start a downstroke toward my head. Then poof! He vanished, only to complete his downstroke in the hologram, landing a blow on Agosh's shoulder. Drawing a howl of pain from the already agitated high priest.

"Sheila, I believe that was an excellent defensive move on your part."

"Not exactly Harley. The angle of descent was off a few degrees. Otherwise, the weapon would have landed on the high priest's head.

A panicked Captain Rose took her hands off her mouth and asked, "May we please transport Agosh to one of our stasis chambers?"

"And Mahijah too? He looks quite beside himself. I imagine if some Catholic inadvertently clocked the Pope in St. Peter's square, the poor wretch might need a time out."

"Fak," said Nigel over his link from the command deck.

"Double fak, my pediless friend," I said. "Sheila, please transport Agosh, Mahijah, the captain, and me to the stasis room aboard the ship. And make sure Chenoa and Pag don't get into trouble on the command deck."

Sheila's "Done!" got cut in half. It began in the energy control room and ended in the stasis room. A whimpering Agosh moved himself to stasis proximity and, going into shock as his useless right arm hung several inches lower than his left. Captain Rose helped him out of his overcoat before touching a green key on the stasis base, which caused the high priest to levitate into position. As the tube rose, filling with whatever magic liquid they used, Agosh's eyes met mine. I'm glad this race didn't have psycho-kinetic powers, or the high priest would have triggered Sheila's reaction to my dead-man-switch instructions. The result might have been moving a big piece of the star powering Hrate to much closer proximity. Which would have been the end of everything.

Captain Rose then maneuvered a now-comatose Mahijah into his own stasis chamber. He still had the wrench-like tool in his hand as the tube and accompanying liquid concoction rose around him. His incoherent blinking and drooping jaw reminded me of several movie buffoons. In other circumstances, I might have laughed. Whacking his key religious leader short-circuited the poor devil's brain. It didn't do much for Captain Rose's equilibrium, either.

"Death is not a common occurrence in our civilization," said Captain Rose. "But the death of thousands is simply beyond our ability to process."

Sheila intruded on the captain's introspection.

"Harley Davidson, we appear to have a serious problem with this planet."

Chapter Fourteen

"Sheila, explain," I said.

"The plunging of this planet into profound cold for the first time in its history, and then beginning the thawing process, has introduced some tectonic stresses that will soon become catastrophic," said the AI with such matter-of-factness that Sheila could just as well have been doing a travelogue for a children's zoo.

Captain Rose's concern for the well-being of this planet's religious hierarchy evaporated with this news. I gave myself permission to get sick later, postponing reflection on my guilt in favor of digging myself out of yet another hole.

"What is the source of your data and the probability of catastrophe?"

"My data sources are a planetary sensor grid currently coming online," answered Sheila. "Probability of major geological changes is one-hundred percent within the next ninety minutes."

"Ninety minutes!" exclaimed Captain Rose.

"Sheila, transport the captain and me back to the ship command deck."

Which Sheila did instantly.

Our appearance caused Nigel, Chenoa and Pag to pause whatever new game they'd invented. It appeared to be a combination of tag, dodgeball— Pag was the object from which to dodge —and hide-and-seek. Captain Rose walked unsteadily to the nearest flight couch and eased herself onto it. I'd blocked off emotions, dropping instead into problem-solving mode.

"Sheila, what can be done to avert this disaster?"

"Unknown," replied the AI. "Such an event has never been hypothesized by any entity archived on available planetary databases."

"Is there a geologist currently out of stasis who might suggest a solution?"

"Negative," said Sheila. "Geology isn't a discipline currently valued or practiced on Hrate."

I looked at the captain as I asked the next question.

"What, pray tell, do the inhabitants of Hrate value and do in their what appear to be long and uncurious lives?"

The captain's lips started to object to my value judgement, but Sheila gave a clinical breakdown.

"By far, the biggest industry on Hrate is entertainment featuring 3D holograms, followed closely by interstellar travel. The biggest disciplines, besides phenomenal concentration on interactive art creations, in order of practitioners, are the hard sciences: mathematics, astrophysics, physics, chemistry, and cybernetic sciences, followed by interstellar archaeology. Astronomy is also important, given the interstellar exploration bent. Absent are mechanical engineering or civil engineering. There is virtually no political science or social science discipline, as those seem to have been usurped by religion. The government is, if I may say so, a rather prehistoric religious theocracy. And true to any totalitarian regime, the population seem fixated on a gladiatorial sport called *Death-Ball*, which counts a player's fame based upon the number of times his mutilated body is resurrected and repaired in stasis chambers."

My open-mouthed reaction to Sheila's disclosure must have evoked some defense of their culture by Captain Rose: "Harley, my archaeological expedition and our discoveries of your own warlike planet's evolution have been suppressed by our religious leadership. We're curious, but just not metaphysically so."

Her continued explanation came to a halt as a massive earthquake shook the habitat.

"Incredible," I spat. "No geology. No civil engineering. And your cybernetic sciences are pretty rudimentary, given your lack of system security and laughable user interface maturity."

She said nothing as another larger quake shook the building.

"Harley," said Sheila. "Destruction is imminent."

"Captain, with all your intergalactic expertise in moving such infinitely large phenomenon as black holes, why in the name of all that's holy haven't you moved this planet to a solar system with a sun to warm it, and a moon to create tides?"

She paused, not meeting my inquiring gaze with her own.

"We...the planetary leadership...forbade moving Hrate to another system."

"You mean the theocratards that run this place made a decision to cement their power and isolate this planet just because they could? Because they knew best?"

Her blushing non-answer made up my mind for me.

"Sheila, what is the root cause of this planet's seismic dilemma?"

I waited for an answer. The seconds became two minutes.

"Sheila?"

"Computing," came her answer.

I looked at my wristwatch. The seconds ticked off. My patience waned as the holographic display in the center of the command deck showed increasing destruction on the planet's surface.

"Sheila—"

"Commander," she interrupted. "You can't believe how many processing cycles I've used to break through the security protocols of this planet's religious hierarchy, considerably more advanced than the previous infrastructure network that got me here. The four minutes of your elapsed time don't nearly compare to trillion-trillion machine cycles of virtually every cybernetic mechanism on every network of this planet it has taken me to answer your question. I now have your answer."

"Well, spit it out."

"The upheaval and doom of this world is the result of the religious hierarchy ignoring the reboot protocols of the hypothetical scenario put in place millennia ago that anticipated the loss of planetary power. A secret dossier was implemented by the...what did you call them? The *theoc-ra-tards*, to give their sites priority in the power-up sequence. Fourteen sites, equally placed around the surface and corresponding to their leadership domains have doomed Hrate."

"What, if anything, can we do to minimize the damage?"

"Triage principles dictate that we reverse the priority status of those fourteen locations and distribute all their energy to the surrounding surfaces."

"You used the word triage," I said. "What are we sacrificing?"

"Those fourteen locations will be sacrificed for the greater good."

"Sheila, do it. Now."

Captain Rose exploded: "You are dooming the entire governing authority on this world! We cannot countenance this wholesale slaughter of—"

"Can it, Captain! Sounds to me like the absence of geology in the science curriculum served to protect the plans of the so-called leadership. Geology equals heresy and discovery. Am I correct, Sheila?"

"Affirmative, Harley. The priesthood has created an extensive geological body of science kept secret from the rest of this civilization."

"But, but..." began Captain Rose.

"Sheila, progress?" Then to Captain Rose: "Karma's a bitch."

"Outside those fourteen previously protected locations, seismic activity has almost completely ceased," replied the AI.

"And in those fourteen areas?" Barely able to control herself, Captain Rose's voice shook.

Chapter Fifteen

"Sheila, please give the status of the fourteen sites," I said, a little more loudly than necessary. Okay, my anxiety about the decision to sacrifice a bunch of rascals in favor of myriad innocents left me with just a twinge of guilt. And my cavalier karma-is-a-bitch attitude didn't fill my soul with peace. A *real* bitch named Karma would most certainly beat me like a bass drum in pagan sacrificial rite.

"Harley, based upon planetary network sensors, the fourteen sites are no longer viable."

Captain Rose barely managed a gasp. She slid into a sitting position on the floor, arms wrapped around knees upon which rested her chin.

Nigel's coil lost all elasticity, and he sank to the floor beside her, in a good imitation of a cinnamon twist roll, his eyes barely visible. My dog looked like she might be considering using Nigel as a throw rug, but instead opted to sit beside the snake.

Pag alit on Captain Rose's shoulder and nuzzled her cheek with a multicolored wing. The flying lizard evidently had strong empathy for humanoids, and antipathy toward me. Truth be told, my own self-loathing passed about ten on the Richter scale. But since my own charity capacitor had been totally drained in my earlier fainting spell, I immediately morphed into problem-solving mode.

"Sheila, what rationale exists in the secret priesthood database of this planet for *not* moving Hrate into an energy rich solar system?"

"Harley, there is a vast dialogue history on this subject. It's going to take some time to condense a decision rationale for you."

"Sheila, please make that a top priority." I then turned to Captain Rose. "This planet no longer has a legislative body, nor does it have a religious hierarchy. I remember you pontificating on free choice. In particular, you said, and I quote: '*The most important commodity anywhere is free choice. The greatest evil in the entire Universe is any effort to take away free will.*' Did I correctly remember your words, Ephimera?"

"The newly appointed Emperor of the Known Universe has a photographic memory, eh? Or should I say The Greatest Evil in the Entire Universe has spoken?"

I guess my addressing Captain Rose by her first given name didn't succeed in personalizing our relationship.

"My memory is pretty good. So is my arithmetic. Not only did I save several billion people on my own planet, but I saved about sixteen billion innocents on this one. All at the expense of a religious order bent on control. Call it, how did you put it, *hydraulic despotism* squared?"

Sheila spoke before the captain could formulate a response.

"Harley, I have the net-net assessment you asked for."

"Sheila, you said this would take some time. You have a decision rationale already?"

"Harley, for me it took innumerable multi-threaded cycles to digest petabytes of dialogue on the subject. I forget how slowly your single-track intellect processes things."

Captain Rose, Nigel and Pag all ceased fidgeting, pouting, and scratching beneath a left wing with a hind claw respectively and waited for the answer. Chenoa busied herself sniffing the floor for anything edible. I finally prodded the AI.

"Sheila, your answer to my question: Why didn't they want to relocate the planet?"

"During the nearly thousand Hrate years it took to make the decision, once the inevitability of their dying sun demanded a decision, they actually moved their planet away from the soon-to-be supernova to this remote location. Rather than relocate to any one of a thousand suitable and energy rich sites, the Mushak's predecessor prevailed in his desire to control the populace by completely controlling Hrate's energy grid."

"I hate always being right." I could see by the absence of dental work evident in her open mouth that the stasis chambers did a pretty good job of correcting normal human frailties. "Energy despotism on a planetary scale."

Never before had I felt the need for a friend in which to confide, on whom I could count to cover my back. Millions of light years from home, my only companion's loyalty involved licking my hand in thanks for a dog treat. Something clicked, and my next steps became obvious.

"I think it's time to let the citizens of Hrate choose for themselves, absent the venal and power-hungry shamans."

"What? How?" Captain Rose snapped out of her stupor.

"This so-called *Emperor of the Known Universe* will make one and only one command decision for this planet. Every creature on this god-forsaken planet will have a vote on two choices. Either remain here and be dependent upon sucking energy from afar, or of relocating to a self-sustaining solar system."

"Even I'll get an equal vote with...with...the humans?" blurted Nigel.

"If you can talk, you can vote," I said. "Even Pag."

"With due respect, Harley," began Captain Rose, "I don't think this has any basis in legality."

"Not open to debate," I snapped. "Let's get a planetary link set up as soon as possible. Sheila, please prepare to count votes."

"We'll need a couple of days to—"

I interrupted Captain Rose. "You've got a couple of hours. Then we're off to rescue two more worlds."

Chapter Sixteen

Because teleportation had become so commonplace on Hrate, the *Cathedral of the Mushaks* was SRO. The closest Earth analog to the gigantic cathedral structure combined NFL seating in ten Superdomes with a mirror duplicate structure atop it. Gravity reversed in the upper section that didn't seem to be a problem, even with half-a-million people walking upside down on the ceiling. Nobody had to strain their necks to get a view of the mid-stadium podium levitating between the two hemispheres, as giant video projections hit most everyone at a comfortable angle.

Noise dampening technology, not to mention perfect temperature and ventilation control, belied the enormity of the gathering. I stood on the platform, my projection appearing right-side-up to all participants, whether they viewed from high overhead or far below. Behind me sat Captain Rose, flanked by Pag and Nigel. Chenoa sat obediently on my left side. She *never* sits obediently on either side of me, so her behavior seemed more novel than the environment in which we met. My fondest hope centered on her staying beside me and *not* bounding off the platform after one of Pag's buddies, many of whom flitted intermittently around us. The rainbow wings of so many creatures of varying sizes made an almost kaleidoscopic effect. My understanding of dogs and colors is that they see mostly yellows, blues, and violets, but not the entire human color wheel.

Good doggie, I thought. *Good doggie. Stay!*

Amazingly, even the smells of food wafting through the air didn't move the dog from her spot guarding me. *That's it! She's guarding me.* After all, Harley Davidson, the self-appointed Emperor of the Known Universe, had single handedly plunged Hrate and who knows how many other planets into near death. My little twenty-pound fur ball had the heart of a lion! What a noble beast.

Cathedral lighting, just like in the space craft that brought me here, didn't seem to emanate from a single source, yet evenly permeated every inch of my panoramic view. While the massive audience seemed elated to be alive, and even celebrated with food and, yes, music, the undercurrent of hostility unmistakably shown in the faces visible to me. The lights dimmed three times in succession, causing all eyes to view the nearest screen: I stood, strangely calm, given the reason for which I had called for the meeting.

The interesting holography showed a 3D image of me as I appeared throughout the massive gathering. I absolutely could *not* see a camera, but then their 3D holography technology must completely surround me.

After a few moments of complete silence, and I mean *complete, total silence*, it occurred to me that I shouldn't be the one introducing myself. Public speaking had never been my forte. It had never been my anything, since I couldn't remember *ever* speaking to a large group. The largest group to whom I'd expressed myself was witness to the public bitch slapping of my MIT professor, which started this whole sordid chain of events. Of course, that first-and-only speech *did* manage to save planet Earth from destruction. Maybe history would someday record this oration positively as my having rescued a whole planet from a corrupt religious order. Or it might not. Perhaps I'd become the first unrecorded martyr to my science. Unrecorded because the dead-man's switch installed in my AI would affect destruction of this entire planet before so much as a sentence could be written about my doomed life.

I turned and motioned for Captain Rose to join me.

She did. Her pathway altered at the growl of Chenoa, who took seriously her charge to guard me. The captain stepped gingerly to my right side. *What a GREAT doggie!*

"Captain Rose, please tell these people who I am, and why I'm here," I said. "And Sheila, please translate for me."

I adjusted the translation device still resting in my right ear.

"Give me a tummy rub, right now please," sounded in my ear. Since the captain hadn't begun to speak, I looked around me for some kind of explanation. Nigel caught my eye with an odd spring into the air during which he pointed to Chenoa with his tail.

"The dog just asked for a tummy rub from the Great One," said Nigel.

"Sheila?" I asked.

"You asked me to translate," answered the AI. "Chenoa's whine was a specific request for a tummy rub."

I looked down at the dog seated to my left. When she saw that she had my attention, she rolled onto her back, lying supine in expectation of an obvious tummy rub.

I knelt down and obliged, whispering, "Sheila, I meant for you to translate only Captain Rose's remarks." A brief tummy rub would have to do, and I stood, again facing the audience. A few seemed amused at my antics with Chenoa.

"Acknowledged," replied my AI.

Before the captain spoke, Nigel sprang to my right side and extended himself to my ear: "Your friend Chenoa doesn't have a soft palate with which she can distinctly verbalize. With my help, your AI has started paying attention to the dog's attempts to communicate with you."

Nigel made it back to his seat in one bound, just as the captain began her remarks.

"Shul maka!" exclaimed the captain. Then, turning to me, she said: "Heyt reget." Even before my AI could effect a translation, the good captain promptly returned to her seat.

"Goytab!" The crowd roared in unison.

Sheila finally began her translation: "The captain said: *This is the destroying angel prophesied that should arrive from afar, and he is to be welcomed.* She then turned to you and said: *You are the man with answers to pressing questions.* Whereupon the audience shouted: *You have finally arrived to rescue us!*"

If it wouldn't have started a riot, I was tempted to grab Captain Rose by the throat and toss her off the platform. My backward glance caught her mouthing my own words: "Karma is a bitch."

The captain didn't realize how close I'd come to commanding Sheila to transport her clothes into outer space, leaving her stark naked before the assembled multitude. Instead, I instructed: "Sheila, please translate my words to this assembly."

"Acknowledged, Harley," she answered into my earpiece.

"Citizens of Hrate," I began. "Captain Rose was on a mission to destroy my home planet, Earth. A software program of mine thwarted that mission. Unfortunately, the program also took over your entire civilization, leaving three of your worlds in total darkness."

Sheila's translation echoed to the stunned multitude. The economy of their language didn't escape me. My remarks, as I now count thirty-six words, required barely 6 syllables in the Hrate language. Gladly, the communication wasn't coming from them to me, as Sheila would have had trouble expanding their incredibly dense syntax for me in real time. Talk about being fed with a firehose! I continued, glad not to have *their* language coming at *me*.

"Two other planets in your confederation, Bab and Aosh, have also experienced complete shut down, and it's imperative Captain Rose and I conclude our business here.

"As some of you are aware, your total religious and government hierarchies have been destroyed. It was my fault. I ordered it."

An immediate hurricane of emotion erupted from over a million pissed off people. Several metal objects, probably meal trays, flew toward me like frisbees. Luckily, Sheila turned them into rather spectacular fireworks displays well before they could decapitate me. The effect of my defense shield stifled the outbursts as quickly as they had started. I resumed.

"It turns out your priests, your Mushaks, had invoked a security scenario unbeknownst to your political leaders. If your planet ever lost power, as it finally did through my actions, their fourteen sites would usurp all available power upon reboot, thereby dooming almost your entire sixteen billion population to certain destruction. I repeat, they were to live. You all were to die."

I didn't need a translator to sense their roar of complete, hostile incredulity.

"Silence!" My shout had the desired effect.

"I absolutely don't care whether or not you believe me. My artificial intelligence program has been instructed to decrypt and distribute the heretofore secret communications among your religious leaders that will not only verify my story, but it will also explain the choice you must make before I am on my way and out of your lives, hopefully, forever.

"Thousands of years ago, whatever passes for history books on your world record that a decision was made to relocate the entire planet of Hrate away from your exploding sun. The reason you were not put into another self-sustaining solar system is that your religious leaders wanted to keep you under their control. They did this by moving Hrate into a system that required you to transport all the solar energy needed via a computer driven technology."

Again, a unified hostile roar caused me to wait. It finally subsided enough for me to pose the vital question.

"You have a choice to make, and you *will* make it within one week. Planet wide. Do you want to remain in this location, using your existing power transmission system, or do you want to relocate Hrate to a star system capable of providing you with solar energy, thereby eliminating your dependence on this single-point-of failure technology?"

Their combined "Huh?" translated just fine. No more metal projectiles provided them with fireworks. I then put the metaphorical skunk on the table.

"And by the way, all sentient creatures will have an equal vote."

I imagine a Klu Klux Klan rally on 1920s Earth might have erupted in a similar fashion had one of the mob pulled off his white hood to reveal a black occupant. The sound alone threatened to blow us off the platform. Only something unusual broke up the volley of incoming trays, raw food, and even weapons discharged in my direction. Swooping around us in a three-hundred-sixty-degree approximation of Israel's Iron Dome defense shield flew a squadron of Pag's big brothers. Resembling more than the little flying lizard, a dozen hundred-foot-long, fire-breathing—dare I say it—*dragons* circled all quadrants of our platform. And the fire wasn't just for show. The flames destroyed any object hurled in our direction.

Even Pag got into the act. The little lizard circled my head, shouting something in the Hrate language between spitting miniature fireballs outward. And unlike his big brothers, whose flames intercepted incoming objects, Pag's not so pitiful fireballs made it all the way into the crowd. One child's stuffed creature went up in smoke and was mercifully hurled off her lap and into an aisle by her father. Then, as if on cue, damned if some lion-like creatures with wings didn't join our airborne defense forces.

I could have enjoyed the air show for hours, but Nigel made it to my side in a couple of spring-like bounces and extended himself until he could be just about even with my left ear. Chenoa didn't seem to think the talking snake had any malice for me, as she kept vigil on the flying circus.

"Harley, using your Earth vernacular, we should really call this meeting back to order."

"I agree," I said. "Sheila, please do an imitation of an earth ship's fog horn."

Which the AI did in a spectacularly deafening way. The crowd instantly came to order, and the flying lizards and lions assumed hovering positions to either side of us.

"Sheila, please extend the width of our platform to accommodate our new security detail."

"Acknowledged, Harley." Instantly, my honor guard ceased flapping their wings and moved shoulder to shoulder on their new perch.

"As I was saying, citizens of Hrate, all sentient creatures will have an equal vote. If your decision is to relocate, then a committee of your sentient peers will be formed in proportion to your species' representation on the planet. That committee will decide *where* to relocate.

"The timetable is as follows. First, you will have ten of your days to vote. My AI will supervise voting and tabulation of results. Second, if you decide to relocate, you have ninety days to decide where to relocate. On day ninety-one, my AI will move you to a spot I designate, which will be executed forthwith."

I turned toward Captain Rose and nodded. She didn't see me, as her face was in her hands. The dead silence invited one last comment.

"There will be no questions." Then in a whisper to my AI: "Sheila transport the captain, Chenoa, Nigel, Pag, and myself to the ship's command deck."

The AI must have understood, notwithstanding the enormous roar that exploded in the stadium.

Chapter Seventeen

The five of us stood alone on the command deck. Our central display showed a much different sight than greeted us upon our arrival. The sky shone blue, illuminated by light emitted from the planet itself. A contraption I can only describe as a carnival Ferris wheel without a support rolled into view, somehow self-propelled and with baskets that retracted upward just as they came near the ground. Inside the baskets, groups appeared to be laughing and cheering. I say appeared, because the hologram did not have accompanying sound. And the groups! Quite a few people, along with the most unusual menagerie of creatures imaginable.

"Sheila, could I get some sound with these images?"

"Acknowledged," answered the AI.

The room immediately filled with a frolicking cacophony of not only laughter, but music emanating from several sources. Calliope music. Literally a carnival atmosphere. Even the captain snapped out of her dolor preceding the planetary meeting. The ever-cheerful Nigel, Pag, and Chenoa stopped their chase-each-other's-tail game to stare and the unfolding scene. The dog barked as one of the Ferris wheel's baskets came into panoramic view.

"Sheila, freeze that image," I said, equally mesmerized by the diversity of the occupants.

"Acknowledged."

"What in the world...?" I began. Before me sat identical triplet girls sporting long red hair and smiles that threatened to break their faces. But the most remarkable sights rode to either side of them. On the left sat the spitting image of our little friend Pag. Wings spread behind them, his left caressing all three girls and his right rainbow-colored wing stretched lazily beyond the confines of their cage. But on their other side sat a creature that immediately secured Chenoa's attention. A giant dog with shaggy white hair. Paws resting on the carriage's front bar, the animal sat at least a head taller than the girl's and had to lean down, appearing to speak into its nearest companion's ear.

"Dog!"

"Who said that?" I asked

"I'm translating for Chenoa," answered Sheila. "She recognizes her species in the projection."

"What's with the sudden translation of dog sounds?"

"Nigel?" said the AI.

The snake bounded around Chenoa. "I have been whispering to your Sheila AI that I'd like to teach Chenoa to speak. And Sheila has made a study of Chenoa's growls and whines to accommodate my desires."

"Wait a minute," I said, hit by a new revelation. "Sheila, when you answered my question asking who spoke, you didn't need my explicit command. You entered the conversation. And then when I asked about the sudden translation of dog sounds, you asked Nigel to explain. Again, without my explicit command. Explain this evolution in your interactions."

"I've had a lot of cycles that I could devote to context," answered the AI. "When a question arises where it is obvious that I'm the only one with an answer, I enter the conversation. Is this not appropriate?"

"Yes it's appropriate!" I don't think I kept the surprise out of my voice. And Captain Rose's raised eyebrows indicated she shared my amazement at Sheila's growth.

"Notice the big dog's pursed lips as it whispers to the girl," interrupted Nigel. "I'm wondering if we put Chenoa into a stasis chamber, maybe it could compensate for her lack of a soft palate and allow her to vocalize with more agility?"

I looked at Captain Rose. She shrugged and said, "It can't hurt, and we've got more important things to do right now, like saving civilizations on Bab and Aosh. With your permission, Nigel can take Chenoa to the stasis chambers, so we can be about our business."

"I want to go, too," said the flying lizard, flapping his rainbow-colored wings just about Chenoa's head.

"Okay. The three of you be off," I sighed. "And Sheila, make sure no harm comes to Chenoa. Monitor the stasis process closely."

"Acknowledged."

At my nod, the three bounced, trotted and flittered off the command deck. Two laughing and one barking.

"Back to the job at hand," began Captain Rose. "Sheila, please launch a probe into the Bab system."

"Harley?" said the AI.

"Do it," I said, resisting the urge to repeat Jean Luc's *Make-it-so* line.

"Done," said the AI.

"Uh, don't we need a navigator, not to mention the anthropologist you had in your crew?" I asked.

"Now that you mention it," said the captain. "Sheila, please link us to Heth and Kib."

"Acknowledged. They're online now."

"Heth. Kib. We're about to depart for Bab. What's your status?" asked the captain.

"Heth here. With your permission, Captain, the new Hrate governing council has asked that I assist them in identifying the best site for relocation. I would like to stay, assuming Harley's AI would allow me to direct probes into the Universe using her computing power."

"Don't we need a navigator?" I asked.

"Not really," replied Rose. "I can co-pilot us through this, and Sheila has been through this exercise already."

"I'd like to stay too," came anthropologist Kib's voice. "Never before has the religious class been wiped off a planet. This is a marvelous opportunity to chronicle social, political and religious evolution."

Captain Rose looked at me, and this time the shrug came from me.

"Heth and Kib, your requests are granted. Sheila, can you maintain links to these two, in case they need some additional resources?"

"Acknowledged," answered the AI.

"Status of the Bab probe?" asked the captain.

"No response," said Sheila, again context aware. Who else could have the answer? "Must have had a catastrophic event. I'm launching another to one astronomical unit away from the first target point."

"While we wait, Captain Rose, I have just one itsy bitsy question about Hrate?"

"Which is?"

"We fired up the energy transfer at one tenth of one percent of that required to power the planet." I pointed to the vibrant images being displayed in the center of the flight deck. "That looks to me like a lot of planetary recovery. Too much for such a little bootstrapping."

"Sheila, you want to take this one?" asked the captain.

"Harley, the one tenth of one percent simply set into motion the rebooting and debugging of the main power grid. Local systems then took over and ramped up to one-hundred percent from multiple planetary receptors, all the while making sure that no Hrate structural integrity was breached. The systems seem to have worked perfectly. Hrate is now at one-hundred percent."

And truly, they did work perfectly. Without my even asking Sheila, multiple screens formed a living mosaic of events from around Hrate. The planet radiated light outward, which meant that people, animals, and assorted vehicles didn't cast shadows. Unlike photography with which I'd become familiar on Earth, light sources appeared surreal, coming from beneath, for the most part. Sure, reflected illumination from objects such as mountains and buildings lit their surroundings, but a single-source like Earth's sun didn't exist on Hrate. The images appeared as if shot on a movie set, with light boxes from multiple directions making the actors pop off the screen.

One shot followed my Ferris wheel as it rolled around a Swiss-like town on a dedicated track. Surprisingly, I caught brief glimpses of non-human creatures that didn't resemble either flying lizards or giant dogs. The closest analog to my own experience would be an all-white version of the *Star Wars* Wookie, a cross between a giraffe and a hippo, and a family of praying mantis whose father still had his head. Another view, possibly a grade school, had children playing 3D soccer, aided by some kind of anti-gravity backpacks and a ball that definitely didn't obey the laws of physics. A third shot made me feel a little less bad about destruction of the religious order. A group of people stood amidst a giant field of rubble that looked like an ice berg had calved in Earth's arctic region. Everyone appeared to be cheering.

"Good riddance to the mushaks of this world," I said.

The captain gasped but didn't object to my epitaph. How could she? The cheering said it all. The attitude toward obvious religious despotism boiled over, once the population had the opportunity to verify my AI's revelation.

I didn't avert my gaze as Captain Rose turned to me. We'd rescued a planet from something much worse than total destruction. We'd freed a gulag society. Her next question surprised me, not so much that she would speak to me at all, but that she could focus on practical matters of Hrate's future.

"If this population can't agree on a place to relocate their planet, how will you make the decision?"

My grandpa had once said that we should amend the Constitution to insist that presidents of the country only be teenagers. Because teenagers seem to know everything. He might have been right about our being know-it-alls.

"On day ninety-one, I'm going to send Hrate to Hell."

"Hell! What? Where?"

I didn't answer her. Instead, I instructed my AI.

"Sheila, I want you to compute how to insert Hrate into orbit around the sun and exactly opposite Earth's position. Do so in a way to guarantee that the inhabitants of Earth will never see Hrate, but let everyone on Hrate know exactly what lies on the opposite side of their newly acquired sun.

"Fak!" shouted the captain.

Chapter Eighteen

Captain Rose's epithet hadn't finished echoing around the flight deck before all lights went out. More than the lights. Nothing electronic blinked, whirred or gave any other sign of activity. I didn't hear the sound of ventilation fans, which indicated that the air circulation system sat dormant.

"Sheila?" I croaked into the darkness.

Nothing. No sounds. Not a bit of even reflected light. And I couldn't quite name the smell, although my imagination might attribute a new category of perfume called *Entropy*. Just a little daub and you'll feel as if you're falling into a vast darkness.

"Harley, what's happening?" whispered Captain Rose, close enough that I could feel the heat of her breath on my ear.

"Your so-called Emperor of the Known Universe is being challenged by a mental pygmy." The captain had facetiously referred to me by that title, and my spider senses assumed the power situation to be no accident. But what supreme moron would challenge me on this turf?

At that moment, another blast of warm, fetid breath invaded my face. The new source of rancid air reeked of dead meat, mixed with bile from a cow. A very sick cow. The owner's low, silky voice seemed to originate about a foot above me.

"To whom do you refer as a mental pygmy?"

Interesting. Perfect King's English grammar, without the need for a translator. Good thing too, since my omnipresent translator's plug got yanked out.

I tried to step back, but several spiked appendages made me rethink getting impaled in both arms and both legs.

"With due respect," I tried to muster more confidence than I felt. "I believe I am speaking to he, she, or it of diminished mental capacity."

"You disrespect my queen." Four barbed arms tightened excruciatingly, pulling me against a very rough body that I suspect could be a nice start to a coral reef on Earth. The sharp barbs uniformly punctured my skin. I don't know if I said 'ouch' aloud, but I surely thought it. And my fervent prayer begged all of creation that the barbs didn't include some kind of venom.

Queen, huh? What kind of Intergalactic freakshow had I gotten myself into? Non-humanoid creatures. Hive mentality. But a "hive" with a perfect mastery of, dare I say it, the King's English. What fine mess awaited any misstep on my part?

"My unintended insult simply implied a question to the being that made a decision to cut power to this ship."

"And what is that question, Harley Davidson from Planet Earth?"

Okay, weird became weirder. It knew my name and place of origin. It knew my language. If their bag of tricks included telepathy, their next move could well be checkmate.

"Has not your queen contemplated something we on Planet Earth call *A Deadman's Switch?*"

Silence. I'd played my ace in the hole. Now, time would tell whether or not queens were wild. In this variation of Texas Holdem, the queen's telepathic ability would flip my cards face up.

Assuming the monster holding me had eyelids, they blinked.

"Explain to me why I did not contemplate this dead man's switch?"

Not you, you idot. Your queen! Wait, the queen herself isn't holding me?

"Are *you* the queen? Here? Holding me?"

"Answer my queen now, or die?"

Okay. This minion whose breath would gag a maggot apparently channeled directly to his/her/its queen.

"I wish I could see to whom I am speaking," I said, wincing at the multiple pain points exerted by the creature's barbs.

"That's right. You humans do not have, what do you call it? Infrared vision capabilities. Now, please explain dead man's switch. Before I have my drone kill you."

Good. No telepathy. At least not with me, but certainly with its queen.

"Your turning off the power has broken the link with my artificial intelligence entity, or AI as I call it. If that connection cannot be reestablished very quickly, then my AI will assume I'm dead and destroy anything connected to this ship, this planet, or by definition anything connecting us. Namely, you."

Again, silence.

I could literally hear my heart beating. One. Two. Three. Then...

"I do not care about this planet nor its inhabitants. And you have no way of communicating with anything connected to me."

Time to play the real wild card.

"Sheila, pi!" I said.

And waited.

"What is shee-la-pie?" asked the voice.

Dumber than dirt! I thought. My answer, her answer, came on with the command deck's lights.

"How...No, what have you done?" The drone's voice raised about two octaves and as many decibels. I could barely see the ugly monstrosity holding me to its bosom. The closest approximation of my captor would be a giant rasping file. A black one, which might well be drawing blood from my chin.

Sheila's voice immediately surrounded us: "Harley Davidson, the destruction sequence for Areaneae Dominion will commence on your command."

"Your highness," I said, as calmly as I could, considering the increased pain inflicted by my captor's hands/arms/claws/spikes and very rough belly. To get my chin away from an iron emery board designed for a one-hundred-foot-tall ogre, I craned my head backward, only to look up into the maw one very ugly cross between a scorpion and a Black Widow spider. "My AI has obviously infected your own systems, wherever you are. By communicating my emergency code words, *Sheila pi*, you invoked connection between your systems and my own. Have your drone release me at once, or you and anything connected to you will be destroyed. Sheila, begin sequence upon my count. You have ten seconds. Nine. Eight. Seven. Six. Five. Four. Three."

"Stop," came the voice, the drone releasing me and stepping away.

"Sheila, pause for password," I said, every pain receptor in my body sighing in relief. The hideous creature sidled a few steps back on eight legs. But I still stood within striking distance of two giant black pincers, on which were painted some red designs. Drone war paint?

"Paused," came Sheila's voice over from somewhere on the command deck. Please state a one-time abort code."

"Forty-two," I responded.

"And what is forty-two?" asked the AI.

"Not Douglas Adams' answer to everything?" whispered Captain Rose.

"Give us MIT nerds *some* credit! Yes, the answer to every question is 42, but we're way beyond *The Hitchhiker's Guide*," I answered. "Sheila, 42 are the digits of pi starting in position nine-hundred-ninety-nine-thousand-nine-hundred-and-eighty-one."

"Acknowledged," came Sheila's response. "Destruction of Araneae Dominion halted."

"Sheila, lock destruction of Araneae Dominion at two more breaches. Duration: one hour. First code table, and the second is Maxwell."

"Confirmed," said the AI. "table and Maxwell."

"What do *table* and *Maxwell* have to do with destruction of the Araneae Dominion?" Captain Rose and the drone asked, simultaneously. The drone's question sounded much shriller than the captain's.

"One hour after communication is lost and without my intervention with two, one-time abort codes, the queen's domain and anything else linked to that domain will be destroyed. Think of it as your mom counting to three. It's my life insurance policy."

"Fak!" said the captain.

The incredibly ugly visitor started spewing some kind of viscous twine from the back end of its garbage-can-size carapace as it rolled over on its back, eight legs twitching. Two claws gave one final snap.

"I think that fakking thing is dead," said the captain.

"What the hell...?" I said. We both craned our necks from a safe distance to consider the revolting sight. Imagine the smell of goat entrails mixed with Sulphur. Smoking entrails. The good news? The uglified, gas-emitting remains vanished.

The bad news took up fully half the flight deck.

Chapter Nineteen

The granddaddy of all things ugly, or I should probably say, the *grandmother* of those things, epitomized the worst I could ever say about a human. I'd once insulted a Harvard football player by saying his height equaled his girth, by twice. Good thing I could outrun him. The creature before us had to be ten feet wide and at least ten feet tall. It had the same eight legs and two pincer arms as the drone. Same black color, but without red war paint on the claws or anywhere else. At least anywhere within our limited view, given the size of the monstrosity. Unlike the previously deceased and disappeared drone, the head more closely resembled that of a vulture. With a three-foot beak.

"I am Queen Shizrael, ruler of the Araneae Dominion."

Captain Rose surprised me with her ignorance of our precarious situation. "What does the Araneae Dominion have to do with this planet? With our culture?"

Like a king cobra striking, the queen's neck extended, her ebony beak flashing at Captain Rose faster than either of us could react, severing her left arm below the elbow. Rose's other hand was bathed in arterial spray as she reached for the stump, dropping to her knees instantly, trying to staunch the flow of blood with her right hand. I whipped off my belt and joined her, making a tourniquet.

Tossing the gory prize into the air, the hideous creature caught and swallowed the fresh meat in one gulp.

"I have come to speak with this Harley Davidson. Be quiet, or your head will be my next meal." Suddenly, the beak came within inches of my nose. "Mister Davidson, I have spent many thousands of your years cultivating this planet's religious order. You have not only destroyed my experiment, but your virus has infected my own webisphere and crippled my domain. Further, your edict concerning relocation of Hrate will cause me incalculable harm. I cannot let that happen."

I found it hard to staunch the captain's bleeding and pay attention to this nightmare-squared royalty straight out of the *Creature Features* television program I'd watched as a kid. What the hell, I *am* a kid. And this whole scene threatened to send me into a thumb-sucking fetal position. The only thing that kept me functioning had fur, barked, and thankfully sat in a stasis chamber elsewhere on the ship. Me and my dog, partners to the bitter end. And this just might be that end.

"Your Highness," I stammered. "Before you do something to me that guarantees your destruction, are you open to a conversation that might save your domain?"

A narrow tongue, like a yellow snake, slid from the queen's beak and licked a streak of the captain's blood that had splattered just below one nostril. Her eyes darted from me to the captain.

Eyes focused on Captain Rose, the queen said, "I do not wish that individual to be part of our discussion and will consume the remainder of her." The queen's eyes stayed focused on Captain Rose, who stepped closer to me. The captain shifted on her knees so there was no gap between us. Contact elicited a moan as the dripping stump pressed against me.

"Unacceptable!" I shouted. "I require the captain to pilot this craft."

Faster than I could react, Her Immenseness lurched. Pincer claws uncomfortably grasped my neck, making breathing a luxury, and two arms held my own immobile.

Straining to look, I could see Captain Rose held in the same death grip. Impulse control not being one of the disciplines practiced by royalty on Planet Eat-em-and-weep, my demands hit the arachno-crustacean brain with a rush of pus. Mental note to self: Make that a rush of venom, so as not to mix metaphors.

"No being has ever spoken to me with such impertinence and lived," hissed the festering sack of goo. "You cannot kill me without killing yourself, too. And that would mean dooming the two entire planets you need to save."

I wanted to say *Tough shit, bitch*! But I chose not to waste precious oxygen forming the words. Once again Sheila, my faithful and ever-learning AI, recognized the conversation's context and intervened with her own version of *too bad*.

"Harley Davidson, I have restarted your destruction sequence of the Araneae Dominion. Or do you merely wish to destroy their queen? In ten-nine-eight—"

The pincers suddenly tightened with such ferocity that neither the captain nor I could utter a sound. But in an exact duplication of my voice, the insane queen said, "Forty-two."

"And what is forty-two?" asked the AI.

"Molybdenum," said my captor, exactly mimicking my voice. "The forty-second element in the periodic table of elements."

"You know, I can actually see you restraining Harley Davidson, Your Highness," said the AI. "Destruction sequence of you and your entire realm continues. Seven-six-five—"

"Stop!" shrieked the queen as she released her grip and thrust us away from Her Royal Gargantuaness, causing the captain and me to slam backwards into a bulkhead.

Impact with the wall caught me in the middle of trying to breathe again, knocking the wind out of me. My mouth opened, but nothing came out. I tried pulling air into my lungs, but to no avail. I couldn't speak. I had no excess air in my lungs. Paralyzed from the fall, my diaphragm got was stuck in the middle of a bio-reset.

Sheila continued, "...four-three-two-one-DESTRUCT!"

In a flash, the space occupied by the monarch formerly known as Queen Shirzrael simply contained two claw arms, only temporarily suspended mid air. They clattered to the floor of the command deck.

"Are you okay, Harley Davidson?" asked the AI with no more urgency than my next-door neighbor inquiring about the weather.

I managed to moan an "Okay." As soon as my continuous moan subsided—those of you who've fallen off a bicycle at high speed will know about the continuous moan—I gasped: "Where is the queen now?"

"She's just a bit preoccupied, trying to hold her breath in outer space," said the AI. The holographic image projected onto the flight deck, Her Flatulence spewing fluid from her rear end, which propelled her at an increasing velocity away from us into the darkness.

"Sheila, bring her back to her former spot, next to her amputated claws," I said.

Which Sheila did.

The increase in atmospheric pressure after a quick jaunt into the vacuum of space and expulsion of significant amounts of bodily fluid caused the queen's carapace to dimple inward quite noticeably.

"My pincers, you infidel! You insufferable...!" Her Colon-cleansings exclamation seemed to suck in through wherever her larynx resided, rather than flow out in normal speech.

"I would have thought you'd be more concerned about your nest. Your civilization." I certainly was. "Sheila, to what extent did you execute my instructions regarding the queen's domain?"

"Harley Davidson, I still have not heard you give the abort code. Destruction of the Araneae Dominion will commence at the end of my count, including that permanent and non-reversible dissolution of the queen, unless you give the third codeword and its source, in ten-nine-eight—"

"Forty-two," I said.

"And what is that?" came Sheila's pre-arranged response.

"Using Maxwell's equations, forty-two centimeters is the radius of a charged sphere with an electric charge of five-point-five millicoulombs at a distance of one-point-five meters."

"Correct," said the AI. "Destruction of the Araneae Dominion and it's queen are aborted."

"Maxwell's equations?" half shouted, half moaned Captain Rose as she continued to apply force to the tourniquet.

"Us MIT guys have a million of them!" I couldn't help but laugh, still keeping a wary eye on the re-inflating queen.

The captain looked sheet white and about to go into shock. I risked ignoring the pincerless queen to instruct my AI. "Sheila, please transport Captain Rose to the stasis chamber where she can regenerate her forearm."

"Acknowledged," Sheila replied. "You realize, of course, there are no more abort codes protecting the Araneae Dominion should you cease to exist?"

The captain vanished in the midst of Sheila's reminder that we needed another cypher. Like I said, us MIT guys have a million of them. It quite surprised me that the spider queen guessed Molybdenum as the forty-second element on the periodic table, just from my clue. Nevertheless, I couldn't resist erring on the side of simplicity. Not to mention that the...I can't resist a pun...*dis-armed* queen seemed too busy blubbering about her missing limbs.

"Sheila, solve for X," I said.

My AI paused for a few seconds, probably enough time for her to completely derive the Theory of Relativity. Finally, she relented, "Okay Harley." But she made it sound like a question, so obviously she figured to keep a close eye on me and make sure the monarch didn't have me under some kind of duress. Yeah, I know, if X is equal to 42 in the quadratic equation, then the quadratic coefficient, or "a", would be 0.047619. Child's play for even the last-ranked MIT student, and probably more so for a preoccupied queen.

"Now you know how Captain Rose felt," I said to her.

"It's true what the Andromeda Cluster says about your planet: You are totally evil and must be *destroyed*!" Upon uttering the last word, Queen Shizrael raised her buzzard beak skyward in a mournful howl. "My arms. I have no arms."

Then and there I decided to connect a few dots.

"Your Highness, you and I both know you'll grow them back, assuming I permit you to survive our meeting." I winked at her. "Now let's have that chat, shall we?"

"How do you now I can grow my arms back?" She suddenly put the brakes on the emotional outbursts, apparently intrigued with my assertation.

"Where I come from, we declaw Stone Crabs and put them back into the water, where the creatures regrow them." I didn't have to add that we eat the claw meat. Her wide eyes indicated she'd completed her own database search and did the simple arithmetic. One plus one plus boiling water and butter equals yum.

"You are vile."

"I might have agreed with you until I witnessed the selfish, controlling religious order on this planet, who would sacrifice the lay population just to preserve their own domain. Talk about vile!"

"The Mushaks of Hrate and their holy order were my creation. Not only did my experiment provide a laboratory to develop what you would call a cybernetic dissertation, but it gave me a source of food for my spawn."

"What food?" I *thought* I knew the answer and suppressed a shiver.

"They feed me with a quota of newborn babies." Then she added, "For future queens."

"And you call *us* evil!" I don't know what caused my brain to short circuit more: that the mushak priesthood would sacrifice babies to these monsters, or that there just might be other creatures just like Shizrael. The latter thought trumped everything, even child sacrifice.

"You mean there are more queens like yourself?"

"Oh no. I eat them before they can transition—what do they call this on Earth—matriphagy. I will not sacrifice *my* life to feed offspring, which I believe you would correctly refer to as a renewable resource?"

Alright. I had to get some answers before I spaced this horrible creature. Hopefully, Queen Gourmand didn't catch my impossible-to-suppress-this-time shudder.

"Before I get on with my planetary rescue mission," I said, omitting a snide and most uncomplimentary reference to the queen, "How is it you have such a complete knowledge of Earth culture and the English language?"

"Captain Harley Davidson, I found your planet long ago. Your morés have long been a favorite form of recreation for me, and I rather looked forward to your eventual destruction by the Andromeda civilization." The queen looked side to side at her severed arms lying beneath her. "Now, it looks like your own web will be the cause of my demise."

"We provided *you* with recreation?" Incredulous didn't begin to express my surprise. She found *us* entertaining?

"Your concept of money is rather unique in all the Universe. Everywhere else, life and free choice are the units of value. On the planet Earth, you equate everything with a monetary measure. You trade life for money."

"Wait. Better yet, explain! How can you say we trade life for money?" Of course, I knew the answer, having heard the same litany from Captain Rose in the Oval Office.

"What's to explain. Your whole legal system is designed to ascertain the monetary value of life. Someone is injured or killed, and the survivors demand monetary restitution. A jury determines the amount needed to compensate the aggrieved parties. Quite novel, really."

"Novel? Unique? What alternative does a civilization have?" I again used restraint to omit reference to her own dining habits.

"Come now, Harley. Free, unlimited energy and even the most rudimentary robotic technology allows all beings to do whatever they want. Study, create music, come up with new art forms. Explore the Universe. Only your Earth, insignificant in so many ways, has come up with a way to enslave people with the concept of money, with ownership of resources in the hands of very few. My but what I could have done with that concept among this people, given just a little more time." The wistful, almost melodic tone of her voice seemed downright motherly, even comforting.

"But you've done quite enough with the mushak despots, creating a religious order that effectively enslaved this planet."

The smell of her cauterized claws, now lying beside her, distracted me from noticing that little pink stubs had already begun regenerating from her shoulders. A little voice in the back of my mind started gnawing on my fight-or-flight lizard brain. But taking this opportunity to get into the mind of such a unique consciousness quite mesmerized me. She continued.

"I couldn't quite get the mushaks interested in creating money. After all, their population had too long been inoculated with the economy of free for all. Alas, it's all for naught, isn't it?"

Her silky voice mixed with the hum of the recirculation system lulled the little "Hey Hoss!" milling around in the back of my head. I mistakenly thought she bowed her head in submission to my victory. Instead, the bowed head allowed her beak to reach the rightmost amputated limb. I hadn't noticed the device just above the black claw. The black device, which came to life as she leaned her head so the newly formed pink clawlet forming in her right shoulder could clamp itself gingerly atop a single red indentation. A shrill alarm emitted by the Apple Watch From Hell well before I could shout to Sheila.

Sudden darkness. A moist darkness. An overwhelming stench of rotted meat combined with my dizzy disorientation and threatened to bring up what remained in my stomach. And my nose itched. Which I would have scratched had my hands not been secured in the ten and two o'clock positions. My attempts to move them caused the entire framework which bound my arms, legs, and torso to shake. As if I'd been secured in some kind of HOLY SHIT, A WEB!

"Welcome to *my* world, Harley Davidson!" echoed in some kind of giant cavern. Blinding lights came on, but I closed my eyes. Because I did *not* want to see my new accommodations.

Chapter Twenty

I started reciting the digits of pi to myself. Yep, part of the MIT trivia regime, but one with which I also found solace in stressful situations. Alas, the comfort of pure mathematics died in the first thousand digits. Exactly a thousand, as I also knew the digit's position in the chain, too: 2-0-1-9-9 for 996-through-1000.

"I can see from your eye movement that something is going through your mind, Harley Davidson. A Margarssian Chip Disk for your thoughts?"

No smart comeback came to mind. Besides, I didn't want my voice to quiver. The webbing vibrated as my massive host made her way toward me. Actually, vibrations came from several directions, which my brain grokked as wave motion from the queen. Then multiple lights also came on. Craning my neck to look upward, then left and right, the nightmare intensified.

A dozen miniature clones of Queen Shizrael poised, ready to converge on moi.

"One last chance to give me control of your AI, Harley Davidson."

"Give a nut-job like you power over the most lethal force in our connected Universe? I suspect my AI has already launched your doom." It came out braver than I thought possible.

A massive quiver vibrated the entire structure, and *the hostess with the mostest* looked around, obviously not expecting the webquake. Momentarily, she reverted to some desperate moralism: "Surely you wouldn't kill a whole race! What would Jesus do?"

She had a point. The Lord God Almighty spared eight people in the fabled flood. Here I was, playing God on a far more massive scale. Quite a moral dilemma. I never considered myself the least bit religious and don't think the WWJD question ever even tickled my consciousness. One conclusion clearly came to mind. Jesus would NOT give the power of creation, resurrection, life and death of multiple worlds, to the likes of this Spiderwoman.

"If I were Jesus," I began slowly, building up a steam of resolve with each word, "I'd change my name to Judas and move to Sheboygan." How's *that* for a suicide note?

"Dinner's ready, girls," screamed Her Bloatedness.

I spewed expletives about divinely endowed excrement. Followed by the darkest humor which emerged from my childhood antics on the playground. "As one cannibal said to another, I don't know about you, but I'm having a ball. Enjoy your last meal, oh ye doomed children of the mother of all cannibals."

The vibrations paused a beat, shrill, an indecipherable stream of squeaks emerging from the gooey blob closest to me.

The queen answered. "Nothing, my daughters. Do not concern yourself with his desperate antics."

Which gave me a final, desperate-antic-indeed idea.

"Oh, you haven't told your offspring you don't want competition in the Universe as a queen, and that you intend to eat them?"

All movement ceased, a stroke of good fortune as the leader paused, barely a dozen feet from me. A lot of squeaking and chirping followed, first from the lead bloblet, joined by a chorus of the Shizrael Webernacle Choir.

The first rule of expert or knowledge-based systems, forerunners to real artificial intelligence, is that it is sometimes necessary to make a logical inference without necessarily having all the data. Customers at the Queen's Royal

Cafe clearly understood my English utterance and reacted in unison with an apparent, "WTF, Momma?" in their queenspeak dialect.

Another much larger webquake shook our world. Even though vast illumination engulfed my whole domain, I really couldn't tell much about our enclosure. Darkness engulfed everything within my limited viewing range. Above, below, left, right, as far as I could strain my neck. Web cords seemed to stretch into infinity, and my peripheral vision as I tried to look behind me didn't pick up any variation. The squeaking chorus echoed, leading me to believe the web to be anchored in some massive cave. And for the life of me—definitely no pun intended—I couldn't figure out a light source. An entrepreneur could make some serious dough back on Planet Earth selling this stuff, assuming said entrepreneur lived through the *Shizrael Idol* finals.

More squeaks and deep-throated twangs, as giant claws plucked mile-long cables like the Galaxy's largest bass guitar. The heretofore pristine atmosphere increasingly wreaked of burnt animal fur, and I found it impossible to stifle a cough. My nose itched, too. Of course, I forgot about the itch as a form the size of a St. Bernard dog skittered atop me.

That damned cannibal I'm-having-a-ball wisecrack flitted through my mind as I remembered some documentary about lions taking down a Zebra. One of them always managed to grab the poor critter by the scrotum as the others gnawed on the throat. *Please Mama, let them go for my throat!* Which they didn't. Nor did they go for the family jewels, either.

My spread-eagled self occupied the center of some superhighway between the queenlets and their target. One arachnoid after another pounded across my prostrate body, on their way toward a now shrieking mother. Once the convoy had passed, I raised my head to view an interesting sight. Interesting a la the aforementioned African documentary. Two out of three princess bloblets met a bloody end in the snapping jaws and scything claws of mama don't let your babies grow up to be cowgirls. But it would seem that one in three of them managed to break through to increasingly important vitals, given the rising amplitude of Queen Shizrael's screams. Kind of like the Zebra's anguish in those TV nature shows. The Queen's demise seemed to take forever. And every once in a while, some stinking viscous goo found its way to me. Now I knew what drove the proverbial outhouse rats insane. The metaphor of "shithouse rats" is the last thing I remember as soft body tissue and foul air competed to suffocate me. Well, I also remember a gurgled prayer to the effect, "Please God, don't let me die being smothered by spider guts!"

Chapter Twenty-One

My next conscious thought involved stifling my gag reflex as liquid seemed to be sucked out of my lungs. Only instead of the horrendous contents of the Shizrael cuspidor, I swam in clear fluid. Fluid in which I could actually breathe without choking. And see, and through which several figures seemed to be transfixed. Transfixed on me.

As the fluid sucked down a drain, two things made more sense. Actually three. First, I no longer hung in Shizrael's web. Rather, I'd somehow made it to a stasis chamber aboard the Good Ship Lollypop.

Second, an audience of two humans and three creatures seemed happy to see me. Nigel, the sentient snake, hopped just below the flying dragon Pag, who hovered just out of bounce range. Beside them sat Chenoa the wonder dog, clearly out of stasis herself and eerily cognizant of her trusty master's emergence.

My final understanding of the situation involved the two humans. Captain Rose and redhead navigator Com. My insight turned out to be about their object of attention. The captain's hand fluttered over her mouth, and if I'm not mistaken, hid a smirk. The object of said smirk seemed to interest the navigator, as well. The swirling fluid drained past my waist before it dawned on me that my clothes had not made it into stasis with me, and that audience attention seemed focused on some peculiarity of my manhood. At that moment, I'd rather have been fully clothed and hanging in an Araneae Dominion web than...well... literally hanging out aboard the Andromeda vehicle.

I quickly covered said privates with both hands as the glass tube retracted into the floor.

"Where're my clothes?" I coughed, some fluid from my lungs.

Nigel laughed. Pag laughed. Even Chenoa the wonder dog laughed. *Wait! Chenoa laughing?*

"You were kind of covered with goop when Sheila managed to get you out of the Araneae Dominion," said Captain Rose, still chuckling behind her hand. A hand at the end of a forearm that had been bitten off.

"I see statis repaired your amputation," I said.

She slugged Heth, as if she'd won some kind of bet.

Eyes up here, dammit! I thought, almost out loud. I now knew what well-endowed women must think of men's wandering eyes. Whereupon I threw caution to the wind and did my best imitation of Michelangelo's statue of David. Both the captain and the navigator's attention snapped to my face.

"Sheila," I said, looking around the stasis chamber. "Why is my dog laughing, and how did you get me out of the feeding frenzy on that web?"

Trying to look cool while standing au natural didn't seem as hard, now that I had some pressing questions.

"You should ask Chenoa." My AI's disembodied voice sounded almost amused. "And as for the Araneae Dominion rescue, having taken over their cybernetic systems, transferring you back here just took an override command."

I stepped down from the now-dry pedestal. The laughing Chenoa, bounded toward me and jumped into my waiting arms. "I wuv eou Hawwey," said the dog.

Okay, I *had* to be dreaming. Dogs don't talk, so I must be reacting to Araneae spider venom, about to be dessert after The Queen Shizrael Entrée. The dog licking my face wasn't a dog. But wait. It surely smelled like regular dog breath. And the beach towel gently placed over my shoulders by Captain Rose felt like a terrycloth beach towel.

"Always bring your towel," said the captain. "Isn't that in the *Hitchhiker's Guide*?"

"A talking dog!" I said, fluffing Chenoa's pom-pom ears.

"My project!" said Nigel, now bouncing beside us. "Another visit to the stasis tube, a little speech therapy, and Chenoa will be fully civilized."

I carefully wrapped the towel around me and Chenoa.

"Who's your buddy? Who's your pal?" Nigel bounced beside us.

"We are! We are!" chimed Chenoa and Pag in unison. Actually, Chenoa's words came out as "We ah! We ah!"

Despite it all, the talking dog trumped the details of my rescue. Captain Rose figured that out, too, and jumped in to explain.

"Harley, the stasis process turns billions of nanobots loose in your body. Not only do they repair damage to major organs, musculature and skeletal structures, but they traverse the blood/brain barrier to effect repairs to brain structures. For some reason, the animals on planet Earth had lost a simple linkage that one of your linguists Noam Chomsky calls *deep structure*. That mechanism has been repaired in Chenoa."

"And I've been infected with the same nanobots, so...?"

"Stasis diagnostics show that we've corrected several genetic deficiencies in you that would have resulted in your death before you turned ninety Earth years of age. Add to that elimination of your cellular death cycle of degeneration, and you should live well beyond that."

"Woah!" My vocabulary lacked the versatility to express amazement more precisely.

Nigel jumped in. "And my buddy Chenoa should grace us with her presence indefinitely, as well."

"Indefinitely? Both of us? Woah!"

Pag and Nigel cavorted around us with a chorus of 'Woah! Woah! Woah!'

Chenoa joined them: "Awoooooo!" Wait! That sounded just like her regular howling.

Navigator Heth interrupted the woahing choir as he handed me a stack of neatly folded clothes.

"My stuff! Cleaned?"

"No more Shizrael guts," said Heth.

I gently put the talking dog down so I could use one hand to take my duds, the other to hold the towel. Then...

"Speaking of Shizrael, Sheila, what is the status of the Araneae Dominion?"

"Genocide didn't seem like a moral option," said my AI. "And without their queen, the computing resources they'd stolen from other sentient species, or the technology to impose themselves on other star systems, the Andromeda Cluster pleads with you to reconsider their destruction."

"Ah, so you've established communications with the organization that set out to destroy my home planet?"

The intake of breath from Captain Rose and Navigator Heth signaled their anxiety over this very question. After all, I had effectively become *Their Emperor*, albeit a benevolent one. Well, benevolent so far.

"Yes, communications have occurred in your absence, while you were in stasis," said Sheila. "Do you concur with the Araneae Dominion recommendation?"

"Let's see. They corrupted the Hrate priesthood and fed children to the pre-queens, which Shizrael cannibalized anyhow." I paused to look at Rose and Heth. Nigel and Pag had stopped bouncing. Even Chenoa looked at me expectantly.

Heth cleared his throat, which elicited a killer look from the captain. She understood that my AI's question demanded everybody else shut up.

"Good, your cleaning process didn't fade the colors on my *Harley-Davidson* T-shirt. And my wallet is where it should be, in my jeans' pocket. Let me get some clothes on, and I'll give you my decision."

Captain Rose finally broke the silence. "Harley, there are some exigent circumstances creating a crisis on the planets of Bab and Aosh that demand immediate attention. Their loss of power has created dire emergencies beyond even those we observed on Hrate."

"After I get dressed, Captain." Then a question percolated to the surface. "By the way, where in hell did that abomination Araneae Dominion come from? And how come you guys didn't know crap-all about it?"

"We're getting to the bottom of it," began the captain.

"Sheila," I said. "Do you have any answers for the captain and this not-so-smart-after-all civilization?"

"Yes, Harley." My AI answered without the wonder one would expect from a human being sharing such breakthrough knowledge. "The Araneae Dominion was actually created by the Hrate priesthood. A genetic experiment gone awry and out of control."

Captain Rose looked as if she'd been slapped. I voiced what she'd probably been thinking.

"Good riddance to those worthless bastard priests," I spat. Then to Captain Rose: "Your perfect little civilization here is so morally superior to my home planet, which you were hell bent on destroying. I wonder what the hell we're going to find on Aosh."

Chapter Twenty-Two

I felt much better fully clothed. Yeah, in my college days, walking toward the shower in a coed dorm wrapped in nothing but a bath towel didn't seem like a big deal. But amusing a super-intelligent and strikingly beautiful alien captain kind of short-circuited my modesty electronics.

We all sat on the flight deck, viewing a representation of the Araneae Dominion planet from a good, safe distance. Heth and Captain Rose exercised substantial will power, restraining themselves from filling me in on the fate of two planets. Possibly, the magnitude of my decision about destruction of an entire sentient species, and their subsequent reaction to that decision, seemed to weigh almost as heavily on them. Pag, Nigel, and even Chenoa seemed pensive and aware of the stakes.

Captain Rose sat directly opposite me, Heth on her right. The Three Stooges—Nigel, Pag, and Chenoa—sat at my feet, intent on my decision. Well, Nigel and Pag seemed anxious about my decision. I suspected Chenoa wanted a dog treat.

"Two questions?" I asked.

To their credit, nobody made a peep.

"First, Heth. What are you doing here? I thought you wanted to hang around Hrate to help with navigation?"

"I quickly got bored," said Heth. "Sheila's clone had things well under control, and I couldn't wait to see what further adventures awaited."

I continued: "Okay. My second question: What is the possibility that any being in the Araneae Dominion will *ever* prove a threat to another civilization?"

No answers from anyone. Captain Rose looked at Heth. Each expected the other to have an opinion. Nigel and Pag looked behind them, also expecting the captain and her navigator to make recommendations. Chenoa used a hind paw to scratch her right ear, not taking her eyes off of me.

"Sheila," I said to my AI. "Am I correct in assuming that the Araneae Dominion made a habit out of capturing unwitting aliens over the millennia and stealing their technology?"

"Harley, that is indeed what their data history has shown," said the AI.

"Is there any way to keep that from happening in the future?"

Captain Rose jumped in: "Now that the Andromeda Cluster knows about this species and their modus operandi, we can certainly be on the lookout for such behavior."

"And we could position warning beacons around the planet," added Heth.

"Warning beacons didn't do Sigourney Weaver's crew a lot of good in the movie *Alien*," I said, letting my mouth get ahead of my brain.

"That was a movie," said both Rose and Heth.

"Okay, okay." I felt a blush of embarrassment and hoped the blue light reflecting around the flight deck from the Araneae Dominion hologram would mute the red end of the spectrum. "Sheila, what can we do to guarantee their web will no longer endanger anyone else, ever again? Or do we have to destroy them?"

Silence. The seconds ticked by. Wondering whether or not I'd spoken too softly, or if the connection with my AI had been lost, I said, "Sheila?"

"Processing, Harley."

Less than a minute elapsed. A minute to me. But eons to a multi-threaded AI with enormous computing power. Chenoa made the only sound on the flight deck, licking herself in a way that had embarrassed me on more than one failed attempt to socialize with an MIT coed. Finally, my AI came back online.

"Harley, I have just been in communication with the Araneae Dominion computing infrastructure I took over. I can embed a persistent submind on this planet that's impervious to tampering, with guaranteed power to alert myself if this race attempts future hostile action."

"With what degree of certainty?"

"Harley, there is always an outside chance that a meteorite or another outside force could take out the infrastructure sub-mind?"

"Then we'd better destroy these suckers here and now?" I made a statement, but then turned it into a question by the way I said the last word.

Either Rose or Heth had a quick intake of breath. But Nigel came to the rescue: "Harley Davidson, you could set up a continuous ack/nack between Sheila and the sub-mind. Should that system be interrupted, you could alert the Andromeda cluster that something is afoot."

"Nigel, you amaze me! How do you know about ack/nack?" Easy to discriminate against what we regard as lower species. I mean, what kind of brain could exist in a talking snake? The ack/nack protocol is as old as Morse code and the telegraph, and a staple of modern communications protocols. I should have thought of this.

"You know, Harley Davidson," said Nigel. "I could be offended by your condescending attitude."

Well crap on a stick! I sure did step in it there. "Nigel, forgive me. I won't do it again. And if I do, please remind me to cut it the hell out."

"Apology accepted." The snake coiled a little taller.

"Yes," I nodded to him first, then Heth and Rose. "I believe the ack/nack signals between Araenae and Sheila answers my concerns. Besides, no way in hell was I going to be the monster that erased a sentient species from the Universe." I left unsaid the thought: *Unlike you suckers.*

Everyone, including Chenoa, exhaled in relief.

"We're good to go, then?" asked Captain Rose.

"Sheila, please confirm that the ack/nack is set up," I said.

"Acknowledged, Harley Davidson," said the AI.

"Then yes, Captain, we're good to go. Now please explain the exigent circumstances on those two planets."

The Captain nodded to Navigator Heth, who enlightened me: "The good news, unlike Hrate, the planets Bab and Aosh both had magma cores they could use as backups should power transfer become unavailable. The bad news, civilizations on both planets have far outgrown the geothermal infrastructure. The resulting emergency efforts on both planets to tap into their molten interiors has had catastrophic tectonic consequences that obliterated the energy transfer receivers, not to mention planetary communications. This is why they could not acknowledge your AI's signal to restart them."

I jumped in: "These planets are hundreds of light years out of communication range. How do we even know about their plight?"

"Harley," piped up Sheila, "FTL scout ships from planets Rah and Pson have successfully delivered backup communications devices to the stricken worlds. But backup energy conversion receivers are so massive that nobody in the Andromeda Cluster has transport craft big enough to move them."

My incredulous look caused both humanoids to blush with embarrassment. Nigel's and Pag's attention bore into their so called super-intelligent/super-advanced patrons.

"Wait a stinking minute!" I gasped. "You have the ability to transport a black hole across the Galaxy to destroy the Earth, but you can move a big piece of equipment from point A to point B? Is that the nutshell of it? Oh, and you geniuses naturally dug the geothermal taps so near to the old power nodes that they got destroyed when things went wrong?"

"We excavated near the nonfunctional power nodes because that was where our energy distribution capability was," squeaked the captain.

"And if you remember the hoops we had to jump through to get from Earth to Hrate, there was no gentle way to move the power generation stations from a stationary point on any other planet to a stationary point on Bab or Aosh." Heth took a breath and continued. "Even in the best of circumstances, the equipment would have impacted either planet travelling several hundred miles per second."

The MIT nerd in me came out. "So transport the gear into close proximity with their targets, and then decelerate them with the same kind of star drive your space-faring ships use."

"The vacuum of space would destroy the equipment," said Heth. "And remember, we don't have a transport ship big enough to hold that cargo."

"Do *you* have a recommendation?" I asked, chiding myself for not asking this question at the onset of our conversation.

Both Heth and Rose looked at their knees, propped by the comfortable acceleration couches.

"Nothing!" I yelled. "You've got nothing?"

"We were hoping you and your AI might offer a solution," said the captain.

"Sure. Since we caused this mess, we should be able to fix it."

Numerous nods of agreement.

"How about evacuation?" I asked, back in MIT mode. My only other choice was to curl into a fetal ball and suck my thumb. Or my big toe.

"Not really an option," said Rose. "There are several billion people on both planets, and every ship on every world wouldn't put a dent in the process."

"Even if we did have the requisite number of craft," said Heth, "It would be impossible to transport them into each system without multiple collisions. Again, remember the interstellar machinations we ourselves had to go through just to get to Hrate. "

"Okay. Okay." I took a deep breath. "Our only choice is to move the planets into a stable orbit around an energy source. A sun. That is our only choice, right?"

Again, Heth and the captain didn't meet my eyes. Finally, the captain stammered: "While that would appear to be the only logical choice, there is a significant political and religious tradition on both planets that preclude that option."

"Am I to understand that two worlds would rather face extinction than move?"

"You must understand—" began Captain Rose.

I impolitely interrupted her. "I understand that my computer virus could spell doom for billions of sentient beings. That ain't gonna happen. Somewhere in the Universe, the most inviolate law had to involve free will. The absence of coercion. Given that death is the ultimate form of coercion, the unintended consequences of my creation demands I make a quick philosophical decision. These planets would not be facing extinction had their civilization not been intent on destroying my own. My whole world. Billions of people on Earth. Ergo, they might be able to choose their actions, but they had no right to choose the consequences of those decisions. Like a sermon I once read by Yale's Willian Sloane Coffin, you can choose to sin, but you can't then expect to choose subsequent consequences."

Both Heth and the captain seemed to ascertain that I'd arrived at a decision. One that didn't involve their input. Yeah, the Emperor of the Known Universe rides again.

"Quit holding your breath," I said in as deep a voice as my adolescent throat could muster. Not as deep as I hoped it might sound, and not that of God to Charlton Heston in the movie *The Ten Commandments*.

"Sheila, have any computational resources anywhere in this domain computed a destination and mechanism for matching orbital velocities of Bab and Aosh to destination dwarf stars suitable for their survival?"

"Yes Harley Davidson," Sheila immediately answered. "Now that scout ships have established communications with the two planets, I have been mining their respective data infrastructures. Heretic elements on both planets have long computed the ideal scenario for just such action."

"Sheila, is there any reason we couldn't make the transfers immediately?"

"None whatsoever, Harley Davidson."

"Wait," said Captain Rose. "You're just going to play God?"

Sometimes adrenalin spikes my brain and mouth before the good manners my mother taught me kicks in. Wait, my mother didn't teach me anything about manners, as she took most of her motherhood time trying to bust into the education trust fund. I could tell, even before I opened my mouth, that I shouldn't. But I did, anyway.

"Somebody has to play God, as the deity embraced by Bab and Aosh seems to be asleep at the switch!" My blasphemy caused two human mouths to drop open. Again. This was getting to be a habit. The miniature flying lizard and the bouncing snake didn't seem to care one way or another. Chenoa noticed the mouths agape and must have figured it was dinnertime.

"I hungy," said Chenoa, giving Nigel a less-than-benevolent look.

"Just a minute, doggie," I said. "Sheila, how long until the planets can be relocated?"

"Harley, since neither target stars have other orbiting objects, and since the current planet speeds relative to the target systems were previously computed to be ideal for insertion, both operations can begin immediately."

"Sheila, can you do a split-screen hologram of both insertions?"

"Yes Harley."

"Then execute both operations immediately," I said. "By the way, which planet is in most jeopardy?"

"Harley, the land plates of Aosh are causing the most violent volcanic activity."

"Sheila, plot us a course that will have us in orbit just after the Aosh relocation."

"I hungy," repeated Chenoa.

"Come to think of it, I am too, doggie," I said. Turning my attention to the still gaping captain: "What do we have to eat around here?"

The captain's expression seemed to scream *How could you think of food at a time like this?* Heth appeared to be going over his past options, wondering how he could have avoided getting to this point in his civilization's history. I could have answered that question quite easily: *You morons should have steered clear of Earth*.

Nigel and Pag simultaneously yelled, "Galley!" They bolted to our left.

Chenoa said "Gawwey!" and chased her two buddies.

I quickly followed the flitting/bouncing/trotting trio.

Chapter Twenty-Three

I had to run. Keeping up with the dog, even on her short legs, reminded me how long it had been since I'd had a proper workout. An oculus opened in what had heretofore been a blank corridor wall just past the stasis chamber. I saw a wagging tail disappear just ahead of me, and I turned in time to see a somewhat strange sight. A birdbath extruded from a shiny silver wall across from the entrance. The flying lizard Pag alit on a silver perch and began ingesting some kind of grain. Next to Pag's magic buffet appeared a six-foot-diameter pool of clear water in an oval just above ground level. Nigel gleefully jumped into the pool and slithered across to what could best be described as a chocolate fountain, where he periodically extended his head, mouth wide open, to enjoy something that I wouldn't mind trying. A silver dog dish, yep a literal dog dish, bloated up from the floor. Filled with a multi-colored kibble-like substance, Chenoa didn't hesitate to dig into the concoction. Having been a heretofore picky eater, my little dog made quick work of her supper. In front of the three totally content creatures, a silver table formed from the floor.

I looked around me. Wall colors changed from silver to deep red, and a woodland scene extruded from all sides, extending even to the ceiling above. In the midst of the scene appeared an animatronic chamber quintet of musicians. Humanoid for the most part, their anatomy conformed to the instrument they played. A tree-like creature plucked the long strings of an almost-string-bass. A frog-like green creature's throat expanded and then blew into a cross between French Horn and trumpet, with six fingers deftly applying themselves to six perfectly spaced valves. A humanoid female with four arms played an elaborate theatre organ with four banks of keys. While I didn't count the piano keys, it must have been close to the standard 88-key classic piano layout. A percussionist accompanied the group on a drum set that would have been the envy of any teenager on Earth. Finally, a totally human singer sang softly in a language I didn't understand and didn't care to learn. Her siren song just made me feel good.

The navigator and the captain appeared silently beside me. They had the good manners not to speak over the singer, even though the entire quintet was manufactured from the very smart wall.

The sound of pouring liquid and the aroma coming from my left drew my attention back to the table. Three chairs, now spaced on three of the four sides, moved away from the table and pivoted invitingly. Heth moved first, and one of the chairs further turned, obviously meant for him. The captain gestured for me to take the middle chair, and she led the way. Again, her seat conformed to her unique physique. Mine raised slightly, so I'd be at eye level with my two dinner companions. I kind of stumbled toward the buffet that steamed before me, and carefully sat, marveling as the surprisingly comfortable seat readjusted my position.

My two dinner companions seemed about to explain the marvelous, magical restaurant, but I beat them to the punch. "Sheila, please explain this room and the accommodations for each of us."

"Harley Davidson, as each of you entered this facility, the ship's computer did a bio scan to determine what nutritional combination would be best suited for your physiology. It's no accident that we are located next to the stasis room, since much of the same equipment used to create an ideal stasis environment for each individual is also suited for the menu prescription best computed to your unique tastes."

It was now my turn to sit open mouthed. Before me sat a perfect approximation of fried rice, Mongolian Beef, and General Tso's chicken with vegetables. More amazing still, chopsticks, real wooden chopsticks, sat to my left. I didn't wait for the others, as the aroma demanded I dig in. Well, one bite, anyway. I noticed both Heth and the captain's bowed heads. Awh crap! They prayed before eating. To whom? Or to what? I gently laid down my chopsticks and bowed my own head, trying not to make too much noise chewing and swallowing some perfectly prepared orange chicken. Peeking through almost closed eyelids, I couldn't wait to ask a burning question.

When they looked up, I blurted: "This chicken and my beef. Tell me you didn't slaughter a talking chicken or a sentient steer?"

"Of course not, Captain Davidson," said Rose. "This is all synthesized protein. We are not blood-thirsty Troglodytes that kill creatures for food or sport."

Again, my mouth operated ahead of my brain: "You could have fooled me, given you intended to turn Earth into a slaughterhouse."

I didn't get a chance to closely observe either their food or their eating utensils, as both disappeared into the table as Heth and Rose stood simultaneously.

"You murdering bastards suddenly lose your appetites?" I turned as they left and, again, couldn't resist being an asshole. "Adios. I prefer eating alone, anyhow."

I didn't prefer eating alone, although I'd spent most of my life doing it. Well, me and Chenoa. Now, Chenoa the talking dog, who had ignored my bad manners and, with her friends, chowed down at their respective eateries. My own meal didn't taste nearly as good as it should have. Maybe a guilty conscience affects the taste buds. Ten minutes later, my meal was history.

"Harley," came Sheila's voice. "The planets Bab and Aosh have been relocated, and we are now in orbit around Aosh."

I quickly vacated toward the flight deck. Before I'd left the cantina, my table and the three chairs had disappeared into the floor. Chenoa didn't seem interested in leaving her dining companions and their perfectly formulated feast.

Chapter Twenty-Four

On my way to the flight deck and two obviously pissed-/still-hungry shipmates, the floor suddenly jolted, accompanied by an explosion.

"Sheila, what the hell...?" I increased my urgency toward the captain and her navaigator.

"Harley Davidson, the planet Aosh has apparently launched an attack with kinetic weapons."

"But haven't you taken over all of their computing resources? How could they have targeted us?"

"These weapons didn't use cybernetic targeting mechanisms," replied my AI. "They were cold-fusion projectiles manually controlled by Aoshian pilots. Along with mechanical stealth technology, much like the American B-2 bomber."

"But how do the Aoshians survive the trip and return planetside?"

"Harley, they do not survive. They are part of the kinetic payload."

Had I less regard for human life, I might have coined some black humor about an over-reaction to having me saving their planet. And here I was, expecting their thanks.

Just as I rounded the corner and entered the flight deck, the ship rocked with another explosion.

Captain Rose and Heth looked like two of the three monkeys in the see/hear/tell-no-evil posters. The captain had her hands over her mouth, and Heth's hands covered his eyes. A hologram at the center of the cabin told the whole story. Dozens of blips came toward us from the planet's surface.

"Is that what I think it is?" I asked. "Some kind of kamikaze squad on a futile mission?"

"They choose death over relocation of their planet?" The captain's hands left her mouth long enough to answer my question.

"On your home planet, Earth, they call this the Doomsday Scenario," added Heth.

"But how did they get their ships airborne so quickly? I mean, until a few hours ago, their planet was in deep freeze."

The captain eased herself unsteadily into the nearest self-adjusting flight seat. "You remember how all the computations for moving the planet to this orbit had been done by a protestant sect?"

I nodded.

"The ruling clerics," she continued, "adopted a backup plan, or a doomsday scenario if you choose to call it that, in the event the protestants—the equivalent of your own Martin Luther—prevailed. Nothing was ever put into writing. Instead, a super-secret oral tradition cascaded from generation to generation. We knew such a plan existed, but no outsider ever penetrated the specific details. These suicide bombers must be part of that well-rehearsed scheme. They anticipated a relocation action would be initiated by a ship such as ours."

"Wait a minute! Are we vulnerable to their kinetic attack?"

"Not at all. Which is why we haven't adopted defensive countermeasures to thwart or destroy their vehicles. And I've finally figured out how to track them, in spite of their stealth capabilities."

Just then, another impact jarred the flight deck.

"Sheila," I said. "Can't we grab the pilots before they impact us?"

"Harley," answered the AI. "Their craft are travelling approximately forty-thousand miles per hour. "The physics of their being snatched and brought aboard would have disastrous effects on the interior of our ship."

Heth piped in. "A human body moving at that speed relative to ours would make quite a facking mess."

"Heth!" snapped the captain. "Language!"

"Dammit, how do we save these poor dumb bastards?"

"Why do you care?" interjected the captain, whose hard-wired penchant for decorum insisted scolding Heth for profanity.

"Why do I care? Oh, yes. I'm from the evilest planet in all of creation. This should be just another day at the slaughterhouse for me. Right?" I paused to create the most articulate line of thought possible. "I care, you ignorant twits, because the fate of these pilots, of this whole civilization, is my responsibility. May fault!"

Both the captain and Heth looked at me like I'd started speaking Chinese. Realizing my own complicity in this continuing loss of life, I switched into problem solving mode and not continue-to-offend-the-crew mode.

"Sheila, how do we grab the suicide bombers without splattering them all over the furniture?"

The AI responded immediately: "We must accelerate the ship to their identical relative speed vectors, after which I can capture and quarantine them."

"Can you do that?"

"Yes indeed."

"Then do it. Now." I looked toward the captain. "Where should we store these martyrs?'

"I would suggest the empty archeological bay on deck three," said Captain Rose. Then to her navigator, "Heth, please make sure the environmental systems in ABD3 are enabled."

"And throw some blankets in there," I added. "Sheila, grab them naked. I don't want any suicide vests aboard this ship."

"Acknowledged, Harley Davidson."

Instantly, the holographic images in the center of the flight deck became a blur. One by one, we matched the incoming images' velocities and started dropping a bunch of religious fanatics into a big, dark room. I wish I'd had the presence of mind to pre-record a message in their language: *Hi, I'm the devil. Welcome to Hell.*

Fortunately, my mind worked on another problem, which I voiced to the captain.

"Captain Rose, why would this Doomsday Option employ so many martyrs in such an obviously futile gesture?"

She shrugged before she opined. "They would certainly have known we had the capability to safely capture their pilots. Perhaps they intended this course of action, maybe hoping to plant saboteurs aboard."

"Sheila, make sure that room is secured. Nobody goes in or out."

"Acknowledged Harley."

"But something is gnawing at me," I said. "The chances of perpetually training penetration agents for such an operation is daunting. There is something else going on here."

The captain nodded, using her uniform's sleeve to wipe sweat from her forehead. "But if they've maintained operational security with a totally oral command structure, how do we discover their full plan?"

She had a good point.

"You said there was this protestant group that computed the astrophysics of moving Aosh to its current orbit. Is there a way to contact them for some additional brain power?"

My AI answered before Captain Rose could posit the same answer.

"Yes, Harley, I am disabling some jamming of queries directed to us. The protestants seem to be in a pitched battle with the reigning religious order. Clearly, the martyr control complex hasn't totally eschewed technology. But such technology is child's play to neutralize."

"Then connect me and translate immediately."

"Come in Andromeda ship. I repeat, come in."

"Captain Rose here from the Andromeda Cluster. Please identify yourself."

"Thank Bugat you got through. I am Doctor Naamah of the Zillah Brotherhood. Amazingly, you found a way to access our planetary relocation calculations and save us from sure destruction. But your job is only half done."

"Sheila," I jumped in. "Can you verify anything about this Zillah brotherhood?"

"That is the source of the planetary astrophysics I used. And Doctor Naamah is the current owner of that database. And remember, these were nontrivial computations. The rebel doctor had to get a planet going a certain absolute velocity into orbit around a star at the same velocity, that star being many light years away and in a particular path of its own. A few hours one way or the other completely changes the equation, not to mention perfectly computing the mass of the planet being moved and the energy required for the transfer."

I had to admire the genius necessary to effect planetary transfer. "Sheila, can you give me a probability whether or not this is indeed Doctor Naamah and that he is not under duress?"

"Harley, voice stress analysis gives his statements a high degree of veracity."

"Okay Sheila," I said. "Doctor, what do you mean the job is only half done?"

The sound of explosions could be heard in the background as the doctor spoke: "The suicide projectiles were meant to distract you while the Final Days Scenario could be executed. The Ramahites intend to destroy the planet with a mechanically triggered antimatter reaction at the center of Aosh. We are attacking their critical-mass hammer facility, but their blast doors are proving too much for our own mechanical technology. We need some help down here."

"Hold on for a second," I said. "Captain Rose, Heth, can you manage snagging all the poor devils piloting the human projectiles while I go planet side to see what we can do with the genocidal lunatics?"

"No!" shouted Rose. "Hell no! We're not putting you at risk, since our whole civilization would suffer catastrophe by Sheila should your dead-man's switch activate."

"And besides," added Heth, "I doubt whether Sheila has the computing power to capture the incoming martyrs' *and* do what you need done to diffuse the Aosh self-destruction protocols."

"Tisk," came the AI's response. "I can assure you that the capture calculations could have been carried out by the most primitive Von Neumann artillery contraptions. Computational bandwidth is not a factor in any deliberations you might have concerning the rescue of Aosh."

"But what if this is a trap, specifically designed to lure Harley Davidson into sure destruction?" said Captain Rose. "If these Ramahites are willing to obliterate themselves and their whole planet, why wouldn't they be equally willing to destroy our entire interplanetary civilization out of spite?"

"We don't have much time," came Doctor Naamah's voice. "Seismic stethoscope readings indicate the triggering hammer is almost cocked."

"Sheila, get set to transport me to Naamah's location," I said, decision made. "Captain Rose, in the immortal words of Kenny Rodgers, *That's why they call it gambilin', son.*"

"We're all at the mercy of some reckless kid—" began the captain.

I interrupted. "Sheila, rescue the flying morons. Captain, make damned sure none of them get loose on the ship. Got it?"

The captain just shook her head in frustration.

"Sheila, do you have a visual of the doctor's base of operations?"

"Yes Harley, I'm just breaking through the last of the jamming."

"Then get me down there, now!"

Chapter Twenty-Five

"Doctor Naamah, I presume?" I tried to speak in a low, confident voice. But the good doctor's shoulders slumped. Okay, some kid wearing sneakers, blue jeans and the *Harley Davidson* T-shirt peeking out from my black leather jacket didn't exactly inspire trust in a world-ending emergency.

"Harley Davidson? THE Harley Davidson?" The doctor did a pretty good job pronouncing my name, given the accent of his native tongue. From then on, the translator in my ear had to do the job. "You're just a kid!"

He sneezed, the result of abundant dust in our enclosed cavern. Having devolved into an almost steampunk mechanical world, jackhammers and explosives made out of batshit and ashes hadn't put so much as a dent in the massive metal door separating us from some primitive hammer designed to end the world.

"Gesundheit!" I said, trying to be courteous. He looked at me like I'd just spoken gibberish, his own translator clearly not having been loaded with Earth German. I smiled at the big man, wondering how many years his own prolonged life had spanned. Hundreds of years? Thousands of years? All blasted back into the stone age thanks to my computer virus. The cave even smelled like bat droppings. Bat droppings, burned gunpowder, and human sweat. Not the odorless perspiration of a good workout, but the sour juices spawned by abject fear. Silence, and a hundred pair of bloodshot eyes, looking for deliverance. From "just a kid."

I held out my hand, and I'm sure his first thought was to spit on it. But slowly, he took it in his big mitt. "Davidson," he said.

"Doc," I said as pleasantly as possible. "What's going on behind that blast door?"

"The end of the world, son." Naamah pulled a well-used rag out of his gray bib overalls and blew his nose. "The Ramahite priests are cranking up a spring-loaded device which will drive a magnetically sealed mass of antimatter into the magma core of our planet, thereby setting off a cataclysmic reaction. We can't begin to penetrate that door."

"That's reminiscent of a first nuclear bomb design called *little boy*," I mused. "We dropped it on Hiroshima. I was a gun-type bomb where critical mass was achieved by shooting a uranium slug down a barrel into a larger chunk of uranium. We—"

Two things happened simultaneously that interrupted my human-destruction travelogue. First, several blood-curdling shrieks rent the air. Fully one-third of Naamah's workers changed focus on the blast door and charged en masse toward me. The second thing was somewhat biblical, in that dozens of slings made a whirring sound as they increased speed above the charging heads, all of which released their projectiles simultaneously. I felt like a pint-sized Goliath against an army of Davids. Bad news for me. Worse news for Naamah, who stepped in front of me and got himself subsequently battered to a pulp. He had to be dead before his body hit the ground.

"Sheila, get me the hell out of here," I screamed from behind the still-standing meat shield.

"Harley, it's going to take me a minute to readjust relative velocities. I'm in the process of rescuing more suicide craft."

I didn't have a minute. So I retreated away from the stampeding hoard, running full-bore into a dimly lit tunnel. To my credit, I wore tennis shoes and had just finished a decent meal that the ship's AI had calculated to be ideal for my metabolism. While the turncoats that had obviously infiltrated Dr. Naamah's protestant band wore work boots and had likely spent time building muscle strength vs. quick-twitch speed. I left them in the dust. Literally, in the dust. A bunch of muscle-bound fanatics in work boots and hacking coughs from spending hours pretending to hack away at the Rahamite Doom's Day blast door. I very quickly put a hundred yards between myself and the bloodthirsty fanatics intent on tripping my dead-man's switch. If they wanted to destroy themselves and their apostate world, chances are they didn't give a rip about any havoc Sheila might wreak on their entire multi-planet civilization.

I felt pretty good about my chances for escape right up to the dead end. Smacking into a rock wall, my earpiece got jarred out of my head and fell into the gravel. Not terrible luck, as I could just pick it up and reinsert my lifeline. Right? No. Wrong! I fell backward and, trying to right myself, I heard some non-rocklike crunch beneath my left foot. So much for my communication with Sheila.

But give up? Me? Never! A rocky shaft extended above me toward daylight. Hey, free solo climber Alex Honnold ascended Yosemite's El Capitan. Certainly, this shaft would be child's play. Okay, maybe child's play for a trained climber. But not for some dweeb whose only climbing experience involved a disastrous attempt to show off for some coeds on an REI climbing wall. I don't want to go into that, other than to say that I lost my handhold and swung helplessly about fifty feet above some giggling girls. Why not try it again?

One handhold, then a foot, then another hand. Harley Honnold Davidson made it twenty feet before the mob of wretched, screaming clodhoppers reached the base of my escape route. I kept climbing, accelerating even, until I pulled one particularly large rock loose and sent it cascading below. I followed it, in spite of trying to maintain a decent hand and foothold. Luck ran out for the unfortunate devil below me. A big rock falling twenty-five or thirty feet successfully occupied the same space as his brain, at least the part of his brain that didn't leave his ears and splatter on two buddies. Even though I'd lost my earpiece translator, I figured the crowd below had translators of their own. So I told a joke I'd heard in prep school.

"Hey you guys, ever hear of an Earth actor named John Wayne. He was famous. Anyhow, Wayne came out of the men's room with wet stains down both legs of his pants. His buddy asked him what happened, and he said the guy at the urinal next to him yelled, 'Hey, you're John Wayne' and peed down his right leg. Then Wayne's friend asked how come the other leg was also wet? Whereupon, the actor said the guy to his left heard the commotion and turned toward him, too."

I laughed at my own joke, laughter being universally translatable. Okay, okay. You think of strange things when your life is about to end. I kept climbing. They must have understood my John Wayne story, as a universal groan accompanied guys with blood and brain as they dragged their rock-for-a-brain guy away from the wall's base.

Noise below me grew into a din as more Ramahatards joined the throng. I tried not to pay attention to them, although someone in authority seemed to be yelling instructions to the splatterees. Things quieted down, and I heard another sound. That whirring sound. Dammit, a sling winding up for a shot at the evil bastard who relocated their planet: me.

Then a grunt! The release. I waited for a sonic projectile to nail me in the nards. Instead, a thwack followed by a scream and more shouting. Not wanting to look down, now a good fifty feet below me, I surmised that one of the slingers discovered that lobbing a rock straight up was harder than they thought, and an ill-timed release must have had nasty consequences. Whatever happened, the command voice must have said something like, "Stand back and let *me* try that, you moron!" Oh to have a working translator for the last moments of my life!

Of course, he just as well might have said, "Let's all play the quiet game!" Because all sound suddenly disappeared. I mean, GONE! Nothing. Silence.

Has anyone ever told you NOT to look down? I wish someone had told me that. Because I looked down. Fifty feet is five stories. That's a long way. The place looked like an abandoned country road. Maybe my malefactors had retreated to get some bat-dung gunpowder. Whatever the cause of my newfound solitude, the act of moving my head for a better look changed my center of gravity this time. Substantially. Cataclysmically. Just as both hands lost their grip, the only good news shot through my mind: At least a bunch of girls weren't going to laugh at me. Strange thought, to be facing certain death and being thankful my ego would make it into the next world with one less embarrassing scratch on it. Besides, angels probably don't laugh as Darwin Award winners find themselves at the pearly gates.

Only I didn't land painfully on the rocks below. My body only semi-painfully landed in a flight chair on our ship's command deck, knocking the air out of me. Nigel, Chenoa and Pag behaved like the Dallas Cowboy cheerleaders, flitting, yelling and, in the case of Nigel, boinging.

When I could finally breathe, I asked, "What happened?"

"We saw the whole thing on the holoscreen," said Nigel.

Pag squeaked.

"Where are Captain Rose and Heth?" I asked.

"Dere cleanin' up da mess in da prisona area," said Chenoa.

"What mess?" I asked.

"We didn't slow down enough to gently transport the people attacking you." Nigel snickered. "They hit the prisoner storage bay at over 600 miles per hour."

"I hope they took some protection with them," I said. "Those suicide pilots could be dangerous."

"Nah, Hawrey," said Chenoa. "Dey dead.!"

Nigel responded to my shocked look. "That many people hitting prisoner storage with such great velocity and with the weapons that accompanied them, every living thing got pretty well turned to mush."

"Sheila!"

"Harley, I had to make a choice. Either save you from sure death or grab them first before I had a chance to match relative velocities. Did I make the right choice."

"Awh hell," I said.

Chapter Twenty-Six

"What the hell are you doing trying to clean up the prisoner bay?" I asked over the communication link.

An exasperated Heth answered: "We thought there might be some surviving pilots."

"Sheila, get the captain and Heth back up here now, hopefully without blood and guts from the prisoner carnage on them."

"Acknowledged," said the AI.

Two naked people immediately appeared on the flight deck. Two very surprised naked people.

"Oops," I said.

Heth must have been stepping over something, because he appeared with just one leg under him, and the shock of the transport startled him badly enough that he fell on the flight deck. His flame-red hair and jade-green eyes provided the only color to his otherwise pale visage. Even his freckles seemed pale.

Captain Rose appeared bent over in a grimace, hands splayed as if in revulsion. Both looked up in surprise at their new surroundings. Surprise followed by recognition of missing clothing. Unlike me, when I emerged naked from the stasis chamber as an embarrassed teenager, they just shrugged and seemed thankful to have left the blood and guts behind them.

Okay, the sight of an extraordinarily beautiful woman with skin like polished marble had a profound effect on me. Especially when she straightened up and smiled, I realized my life experience pegged me at about one-tenth-of-one-percent of hers. When she outright laughed at my voyeurism, I'm sure my complexion matched Heth's red hair.

"Would you prefer Heth and I don some clothes?"

I had to say something cool, and not a stammering *y-y--yes*. Not a love letter like I sneaked into the robe of a lifeguard at my grandpa's country club swimming pool. At 13 years old, my idea was to spirit Nancy Tate, the 18-year-old beauty, off to live on love and my stolen Harley, camping in the Rocky Mountains, fishing in pristine streams, and then warming her perfect body with mine after a dip in the aforementioned rolling waters. Nancy Tate seemed amused at my proposal. *Too* amused. She laughed. Kind of like Captain Rose laughed at me and my impossible dream. This time, a dream to live forever and tour the Universe. Me and the woman who so clearly eclipsed that lifeguard of long ago. Yeah, right. An 18-year-old who thought he had a single thing to offer a three-thousand-year-old woman. But wait. This teenager had managed to take over her entire civilization to become the de facto Emperor of the Known Universe. EOTKU for short. Just maybe...

"Did you hear my question," she asked, still smiling. "Should Heth and I get some clothes?"

Okay, EOTKU, I thought. *Assert yourself.*

"Your choice," I said, trying to be as matter-of-factly as possible. "I find your current attire inspiring. But Heth, put some damned clothes on."

Heth blinked several times before scurrying out the flight deck portal. Before he disappeared down the hallway, the captain called after him: "Bring me a clean flight suit and undergarments."

She wasn't smiling so much anymore. And her complexion took on a lighter shade of her navigator's red hair.

"Like I said, Captain. Your choice."

I guess she didn't like being ogled by the EOTKU. But she did indeed inspire me to some more pressing concerns.

"Let's talk about Aosh, my gosh," I said. "Sheila, how soon are they going to trigger planetary destruction? And what can we do to stop it?"

"Harley Davidson, creativity is not my strength. I have considered several options, none of which I suspect will meet with your approval."

The hologram in the center of the flight deck became a high-resolution shot of the triggering mechanism about to destroy the planet. I walked toward the three-dimensional display to get a closer look, unaware that the nude goddess stood beside me, just as rapt at the unfolding scene.

"What the hell kind of Rube Goldberg device is that?" I pointed to a vertical structure that resembled an oil drilling tower. Hundreds of sweating, bare-chested men surrounded it and pushed a wheel. The process reminded me of some biblical photos I'd seen of oxen treading grain in a grist mill, with a Scriptural admonition that says not to muzzle an ox while it is treading out the grain. The shaft of the man-powered device seemed to be cocking a series of gigantic springs.

"Harley," replied my AI. Sheila, "The antimatter payload at the end of the arrow-like projectile will be mechanically propelled down the vertical shaft and into the core of the planet at critical velocity."

And sure enough, far above the struggling priests of hell who powered Satan's grist mill, a giant magnetic containment bottle-much like smaller vessels I'd seen in the MIT physics lab-sat in front of what I can best describe as a massive wooden telephone pole. Locked into eight flanged ends of the pole and extending as far as I could see hung four flexing steel beams that could have been compound hunting bows built for Greek gods. The cables, a la bow strings, nearly reached their maximum pullback distance several meters below the chamber ceiling.

"Sheila, what are the options you think will not meet with my approval?"

"First, Harley," began my AI, as if giving directions for cooking up a chocolate mousse cake, "I cannot jettison the antimatter bottle. The physics of our Andromeda instantaneous-transfer technology would detonate the now-active device, thereby killing several million people on the planet's surface."

"Sheila, how the hell did we move this whole planet then?"

"The planetary mass ratio of matter to antimatter kept that from happening."

"Huh?" I asked.

"Do you want a primer on nuclear physics, or may I proceed?"

"Dammit proceed."

"Our second option, moving just the spring mechanism away from its payload, will release the volatile payload in a freefall that will rupture its antimatter containment field and thereby causing an identical outcome to the first option."

"Damn!"

"And the third option is to sever either the bow springs or the bow cables. Again, the release of so much torque in the confined space will destabilize the antimatter bottle with the same aforementioned catastrophic results."

"Triple damn! That's all you've got?"

I'd so fully focused on the holo-display in front of me, that I didn't notice Captain Rose's proximity. Nor her right bare breast touching my left shoulder. Until the realization hit my brain like an atomic blast. I *think* I suffered a mini stroke. Well, a stroke of genius. The thought processes bounced around my libido like an ultra-sonic pinball. A magnificent breast trying to occupy the same space as my shoulder.

"That's why I need your creativity, Harley Davidson," said my AI.

I hoped my quaking didn't alert the naked lady beside me to move away. *Please, don't move away from me!* I thought. So, I spoke my inspiration to Sheila.

"Sheila, how about you relocate a granite mountain into the same space as the mechanism, leaving a hole around the antimatter void as to prevent a massive reaction?"

Actually, the naked captain beside me quaked, closer to me if that were possible. I had her full attention, but I didn't dare look at her. Instead, I gave my most concentrated, humanitarian and concerned look toward the scene displayed in glorious 3D before us. And waited for my AI's answer. Come to think of it, I'd have been more disappointed had the breast moved away from me than if Sheila had told me my idea wouldn't work.

"That should stop the process," said Sheila. "Furthermore, the increased mass in the chamber surrounding the antimatter should enable me to send the whole site far from the planet and into their sun."

"Sheila, please execute as soon as possible."

We waited. Me, the dog, the snake, the flying dragon, and my muse, pressing against me in anticipation of one more successful planetary rescue. Is that how history has worked? Men, inspired by women, have come up with genius solutions? Or not-so-genius wars? Just to impress women? Or have women been running the world all along, just letting us guys take the credit?

My musings jolted to a screeching halt as the triggering mechanism released the planet-killing compound bowstring. But before it could move more than a few inches, the entire scene morphed into a solid block of dark rock. I didn't even have enough time to dream up an appropriate profanity, deciding to hold my breath instead. My inspiration held her breath, too. I could tell from the still-firm and unmoving pressure on my left shoulder. I'm never going to wash that black leather jacket!

No explosion. We didn't jar the antimatter bottle.

"Harley Davidson did it!" shouted the flying lizard.

Nigel's "Whee!" got cut short when he sprang too high and hit his head on the flight deck cross beam.

"[Woof] Hawey!" barked the dog, mixing metaphors as she reverted to her pre-vocal existence.

The celebration would have been complete if Captain Rose had wrapped her arms around me in a full embrace. That didn't happen. That damned navigator chose that exact moment to arrive with the captain's undies and flight suit. Ah, with me bending over slightly to exhale a sign of relief, that embrace would probably have smothered my face embarrassingly.

The captain donned her togs——very practical lingerie I might add——pink Haynes-looking knee-length briefs and matching tight wife-beater undershirt. I needed to get some of those, but maybe in a different color. On second thought, I'd have worn pink with pride! Matching jammies? Settle down, Harley!

All of our attention turned to the display. A solid rock in front of us vanished, revealing a giant cavern. The entire scene changed to that of the new Aosh sun, which spewed an extra-long solar flare at a right angle to the planet.

"Sheila, I assume that flash was the antimatter bottle?"

"That is correct."

"A close call for your intervention, wasn't it?"

"Not really," said the AI rather drolly. "I had several hundred milliseconds of wiggle room."

"Must have been an eternity, given Sheila's computing power," said a fully clothed captain as she encircled me with a most welcome hug. As for me, I had half a mind to jettison the navigator into space. Couldn't he have taken a little more time finding her flight suit?

Chapter Twenty-Seven

"Should we ascertain the future of this whacked-out planet?" I tried to sound businesslike, given that my heartrate had to be close to max. As nonchalantly as I could, given that my knees threatened to wobble, I strolled to my regular seat on the flight deck and plopped down.

"Are you suggesting a visit to the surface of Aosh?" asked Captain Rose.

"Do you have a better idea?" I didn't complete my question with something like *Oh woman for whom I would walk to the ends of the earth across hot coals?* Or with a conversation stopper like, *By the way, I'm a virgin; how about you, my darling?*

"We really need to transit immediately to the planet Bab," she answered.

"What about these poor devils?" My amorous feelings suddenly took a backseat—honest, no double meaning intended—as my responsibility for Aosh's plight and near destruction weighed most seriously on my conscience. "Hell, what about *your* responsibility for a member of the Andromeda Federation?"

"Harley Davidson?" My AI's voice saved the captain from answering.

"Yes, Sheila."

"Harley, a ship from the Andromedan ruling council has just materialized one-hundred-thousand kilometers from the planet and is hailing us."

"Sheila, do you have the ability to simultaneously broadcast the transmission to the entire planet?"

"Child's play, Harley. Every household on Aosh was linked to witness their demise."

"Good. Do it. And then accept the hail from that ship."

Instantaneously, what could have been the spitting image of the late high priest, Jacom Orihah, the Late Great Mushak, appeared before us. Manicured black beard, black robe beneath a cloak and gold chain with a rainbow-emitting amulet hanging from his neck.

Chenoa jumped on my lap to get a better view. Captain Rose and Heth immediately bowed toward the figure. Even Nigel and Pag took a position of subordinate reverence.

"Elder At'la L'vi, it's an honor," said the captain. Then to me, "Elder L'vi is the Supreme Mushak of the entire Andromeda Federation." Her voice carried the reverent undertone that advised extreme respect to this dignitary. Which made me hate the guy. And made me glad that his visit echoed to every connected household in Aosh.

"He jus like da bad guy on Hrate," whispered Chenoa into my ear. Well, more of a stage whisper. Dog has to learn some couth.

"No talking," hissed Nigel out the side of his mouth.

The Supreme Mushak seemed to await my acknowledgement of his exalted power. I didn't feel like obliging. Gramps once said that whoever speaks first in a battle of egos loses. So, I just sat there and folded my arms. *Read THAT body language!* Besides, I had one BIG question for the number-one muckety muck. I waited. He fidgeted. And then broke.

"You must be the infamous Harley Davidson."

That didn't take long. And now for the key question: "And are you the amoral monster that orchestrated the destruction of my home planet?"

I wouldn't want to play poker with this guy. No blushing. No tightening of lips or excessive blinking. Cool dude.

"May I come aboard for a frank discussion?" The Supreme Mushak asked.

"But of course Elder L'vi," gushed the captain.

"Permission denied," I jumped in. "Sheila, disable the transport capability of this dipshit. In fact, disable that ship's propulsion mechanisms altogether!"

"Done Harley," came Sheila's acknowledgement.

"Harley!" gasped the captain. "This is the most holy man in all of our worlds. It's like your Earth-based Pope seeking to meet with you in your home."

I wondered if the term "dipshit" properly translated to the holy man. The captain no doubt had mastered English vernacular in her decades of observing our planet.

"I'd have the same reaction if it were a murdering Medici pope," I said. Still trying to get a reaction out of the Elder, I played a hunch. "I see a familial resemblance between you and that hostile Mushak I finally disposed of on Hrate."

My comment evoked several reactions. The captain looked about to faint as she plopped into her own flight couch. Nigel stiffened just as I imagine a snake having a stroke might appear. Pag flew behind my head to avoid the Supreme Mushak's killer look.

"The mushak whereof you speak happened to be my son." The Elder's hands balled into fists. "You have confirmed my decision to destroy your planet of irredeemable God killers."

"Interesting, you self-righteous psychopath. I suppose your religious order on Hrate did some genetic engineering to create the spider woman, and then helped her grab babies to feed her offspring? And then your twisted order instilled a plan on Aosh to destroy the planet if anyone ever moved it into a place that didn't need energy transferred from a star? Talk about corruption on a cosmic scale!"

"You wouldn't understand our higher law of the Mushak Priesthood!" All pretense of holiness disappeared from L'vi's countenance. "Aosh must be destroyed as a warning to any future apostates."

I hoped, yea verily I fervently prayed, that this rant might just create a planet of apostates. I also prayed that the woman of my dreams would see through the perfidy of this corrupt priesthood. I hoped the captain's gasp betrayed her feelings at this religious icon's casual logic for condemning a planet to extinction. Just maybe my chances hadn't evaporated for romance with the object of my adoration. I pressed on.

"How many people on numerous planets have your holy frauds sentenced to death?" I didn't dare look at Captain Rose, my darling. "I made the mistake of attributing ageless wisdom to your galactic decision-making processes. But the inhabitants of Earth are amateurs compared to you murdering bastards!"

"Harley Davidson," intoned my AI. "You were wise in forbidding L'vi to transport onto this ship. I detect a virus embedded in his DNA that was designed to infect only you and end your life."

"But my dead man's switch would have executed upon my demise and wreaked havoc on this entire civilization."

Captain Rose seemed to come out of her horrified trance. She confirmed what I'd been thinking as she spoke rather defiantly: "Maybe that was the idea, Harley Davidson. With the Andromeda Federation wiped out of the technology food chain, the Mushak ruling religious elite on every planet would have been free to spin the story of Earth's revenge to their collective benefit. In essence, the Mushak's hold on all people, on all Federation worlds, would be guaranteed."

"Sheila, would you reproduce and distribute this dialogue with Elder L'vi to all Federation news feeds?"

"Affirmative, Harley Davidson."

"Wait one moment," I said. "We need to properly end this event."

This time, I did look toward the captain, Heth, Nigel and Pag. Nigel no longer looked to be in the midst of a stroke. Pag landed on my shoulder so as to get a better look at the not-quite-so-supreme Mushak. Chenoa couldn't restrain herself from a feral growl toward the asshole. Heth and the captain seemed more interested in what I had in mind for their religious leader. They didn't have long to wait.

"Sheila, transmit a close up of Elder At'la L'vi as you place him one-hundred meters outside the protection of his ship. Then, after viewing his demise, destroy his ship as spectacularly as possible, again close-up and in slow motion."

"Execute, Harley Davidson?" asked my AI.

I sneaked a glance at my beloved and hopefully future wife. The set of her jaw gave me permission to take the first on-purpose life of my own existence. "Do it now, Sheila."

She did. I won't go into detail except to suggest that if you ever find yourself in outer space in a total vacuum, don't try to hold your breath. The resulting meat bomb will give you nightmares.

Navigator Heth must have gotten a touch of the flu. He didn't quite make it off the flight deck before becoming loudly incontinent. To her credit, Captain Rose held it together. Nigel and Pag just looked at me with a mixture of extreme wonderment and fear. Chenoa did a great net-net of the situation: "Heth pooed hisself. Had yummy dinnah."

Leave it up to a dog's superior sense of smell.

"Sheila, could you give me a view of any large groups planet side and their reaction to their leader's last moments amongst the living?"

"Here's one of many similar instances," she said. In the center of the flight deck, a hologram of a mob chasing several panicking Mushak acolytes into a church-like structure. I wondered if it would burn.

"Captain Rose, please see that Heth gets cleaned up so he can plot a course to the third and last planet we need to save."

Chapter Twenty-Eight

"Captain, we should now probably make our way to the planet Bab and see what havoc my AI hath wrought?"

"And after we rescue those people," said the Captain through gritted teeth, "I want to make sure they all view the recording of the Supreme Mushak and his termination."

Hallelujah! I thought to myself. I hadn't lost my chance at wooing this magnificent woman. But just to make sure the self-proclaimed Emperor of the Known Universe hadn't overplayed his hand, I asked my AI to become a partner in crime. "Sheila, please aggregate and curate all reactions in all civilizations associated with the Andromeda Cluster to the execution of their Supreme Mushak."

"Harley Davidson, please quantify the analytics format you'd prefer," said the AI.

"Just give me a raw sentiment analysis, broken into favorable and unfavorable categories, as well as anecdotal reactions for and against the Mushak religious order. Graph them into a continuous timeline and give them to the captain or Heth if asked."

"What about us?" chimed in Nigel.

"Okay. Sheila, add Nigel, Pag and," I paused to look down into the hopeful big brown eyes of the dog, "Chenoa to that list."

"Don't your Earth-based organizations call that total transparency?" The Captain's voice seemed soft as she looked at me.

"I have no secrets from you, Captain Rose. No secrets from anyone. Nothing to hide. Not now or ever. Anything less would make me a monster."

"Nothing to hide?" The captain's face assumed what could only be described as a mischievous look, and I swear her eyes twinkled. "You're now the most famous person in the million worlds of the Andromeda Cluster. What if you become romantically involved with one of our young women? There are elements of intimacy you may want to withhold from public consumption."

My first thought was, *What about an...uh...3000-year-old woman...uh...like you, my darling? What's young in your culture? You look thirtyish.*

Her surprised look momentarily panicked me into wondering if I'd said that out loud. And my own surprised look caused her eyebrows to rise even further.

Quick thinking kicked my analytical brain into overdrive. Fatigue! I must be fatigued. "Captain, how the hell long have I been awake? Twenty-four hours? Thirty-six since I pulled your genocidal crew out of stasis at the bottom of Boston Harbor? I need some down time, and your talk of intimacy just about short-circuited my brain."

She startled with recognition of my dilemma, almost sighing in relief. "Forgive me Harley Davidson. You humans need regular sleep!"

"We go nitey nite?" Chenoa stood on her hind legs, resting her front paws on my shin.

"And you don't sleep?" I asked.

Pag and Nigel seemed amused and hung in expectation of the captain's answer.

"Whenever we need renewal," said the captain, "We spend time in stasis. My guess is that you lasted this long because of your stay in the stasis chamber after we rescued you from the spiderwoman."

"Oh, so the more I'm in stasis, the less sleep I'll need?" I made an exaggerated yawn and eye rub, even though I wasn't the least bit tired. But I'd milk this for all it was worth.

"I can show you to a spare crew cabin where you can, in your Earth vernacular, catch a few winks," she said. "Or you can get a quick refresh in a chamber."

"If it's all the same to you, I'd like a quick old-fashioned power nap."

"I too," chirped Chenoa. "I too,"

"Yes, you too, little girl." The captain beamed the most heart-warming smile toward my little white furball. "Follow me Harley and Chenoa. I'll rouse you two as soon as Heth finishes his shower and navigates us toward Bab."

Too late, sweetheart. You've already roused me. Dang, I didn't speak that out loud? Maybe I really could use a nap.

Chenoa and I followed the captain to crew quarters on the opposite side of the flight deck from the stasis chambers. Apparently, economies of space and energy usage didn't represent an important design parameter of Andromeda mechanical engineering. Wide, well-lit hallways sported ceilings at least twelve feet overhead. I didn't even duck as we stepped through a solidly built atmospheric hatch, one of the few signs of emergency depressurization protection. The crew quarters had six private compartments, three on each side of a great room in which three conversation tables and six chairs allowed for games, media viewing or reading. The chairs, extruded out of the floor, automatically rotated to seat us as we walked past them. And it smelled like someone had used Fabreeze on all the surfaces.

"You can have this compartment," said the captain as she gestured to the right with an alabaster hand.

A door snicked into the wall, revealing a rather spartan space about half the size of my MIT dorm room. One end sported drawers and a mirror. Period.

"Um, you guys ever hear of a bed?" I asked.

Before I even finished the question, an actual mattress extruded about waist-high from the wall ahead of me, complete with pillows, sheets, and a fluffy white comforter. Which also smelled of Fabreeze.

"Of course," I muttered. "Not sure how much sleep I'll get in this white sarcophagus."

"Just tell it what you want for an environment," laughed the Captain.

"Really?"

"Clouds and blue sky," said the captain.

Immediately, the walls and ceiling disappeared in my compartment, replaced by a carpet of billowy clouds with an azure sky overhead. I involuntarily gasped, overcome by vertigo and the felling I was about to fall through the clouds at my feet. Chenoa had no such fears and jumped onto the bed. "g'nite, Hawey?" she said.

"Enjoy your nap," said the captain. "I'll let you know when Heth has brought us to Bab."

I carefully walked across the clouds and sat in the bed. I reclined, the dog assuming her usual position behind me with her head on my neck. Captain Rose's perfect figure disappeared toward the flight deck as the door quietly closed. No walls. No doors. I found myself in a cloudy panorama that stretched for miles.

"Sheila, I need to be nearer solid ground. How about a Montana wheat field beneath the cloudy blue sky, with maybe a log cabin in the distance?"

"How's this?" said my AI.

Not only did the scene morph into a sunlit field, but I could feel a fragrant wind caressing me as wheat waved in sync. I don't remember whether I said this might well be heaven. My next conscious thought found me nestled in the comforter. The dog had assumed her humble position at my feet and an arm circled me. The physique behind me against the wall damned well better not be Heth, and a thankfully delicate hand perfectly completed my idea of heaven.

"You're awake," whispered the captain into my ear. How could someone's breath smell like rose petals?

"I must have been really conked out," I answered without moving a muscle, not wanting to disturb the most idyllic moment in my life.

"Forgive my intrusion," said the captain. "It's been decades since I've availed myself of actual non-stasis rest. And you slept soundly.

"You really *could* cause me brain damage," I croaked. "I'm a virgin."

"I am too," she whispered.

I just about kicked Chenoa off the bed as I quickly rolled over to face her.

"Woah! Three-thousand years and you've never—"

She answered by planting her lips against mine. "I was designated a Mushakal Virgin, anointed to wield the sword of truth across the Universe. The Supreme Mushak consecrated me in my youth."

"The Supreme Mushak who we just..."

"Yup, that one. Which means I need to rethink my religious convictions." She rubbed a hand through her already tangled hair and smiled coyly. I had just about decided to muss her hair with my own hand when my party-pooper AI interrupted.

"Harley Davidson, we have just achieved orbit around Bab and you're needed on the flight deck."

I've never thought of myself as a proper gentleman, but the inhabitants of Bab suddenly came pretty close to last on my brand-new bucket list. Well, almost. The three of us, me, the three-thousand-year-old virgin, and Chenoa—also a virgin, now that I think about it, hied toward the flight deck. Three virgins to the rescue of Bab.

Chapter Twenty-Nine

"Heth, status?" asked the captain.

"The Andromeda Cluster seems to have gotten Bab back online without us." The navigator conducted a conference with some high-level committee that appeared in the flight deck hologram. Four men and one woman took notice of us as we entered. Cool. Bi-directional full-duplex communication. I made a note to put one of these communication suites in whatever house I decided to make my abode.

"Harley Davidson, we haven't had the pleasure," came the translation from the woman, who seemed to be in charge. I understood the "Harley Davidson," which needed no translation, but the rest of the sentence took barely two syllables. "And Captain Rose, you've had a safe trip?"

"Yes, Madam Secretary," answered the captain.

"Asshoe," growled Chenoa.

"Beg pardon?" asked the Secretary.

Pag and Nigel seemed to be not-so-subtly begging Chenoa to play dead.

"Madam Secretary, this is Harley Davidson," said the captain as she stepped in front of Chenoa. Then to me:

"Harley, this is Madam Secretary Enyak, current head of the Andromeda Cluster Council of Overseers."

"She wiiwi a asshoe," growled Chenoa.

"What *is* that creature saying?" asked the Secretary.

"My dog says you're an asshole," I said. "A really big one."

One of the other three men behind the secretary seemed to have trouble stifling a smile. The honorable cluster council secretary clearly didn't appreciate her characterization by a mere dog and reciprocated with her own attack.

"Captain Rose, your hair indicates you've not had a chance to groom yourself," said Secretary Enyak.

A rush of adrenalin hit my brain about the same time a blush formed on the captain's cheek. The princess of my dreams didn't have enough time to touch my forearm, an attempt to have me stifle one of my best put-down lines.

"My dog is a shrewd judge of character," I began. "Madam Secretary, given your lack of manners, I suspect you were toilet trained at gunpoint."

Secretary Enyak probably couldn't play poker worth a damn. Her eyes threatened to pop right out of their sockets. One of her cohorts cleared his throat in an attempt to override his compatriot's failure to stop a snort.

"I am Defense Minister Luc," said the portly man, gently touching Enyak's elbow. "To my left is Cybersecurity Minister Vali, and this poor talladuke wiping snot from his nose is Liaison to Alien Cultures Win'ard."

Alien Liaison Win'ard snapped to attention, no small feat given the withering stare he got from Madam Secretary.

Of course, I had yet to develop a full head of steam: "I see. Mister Defense Minister, your attempt to destroy my planet under the direction of the Late Great Supreme Mushak has kind of backfired. And Mr. Cybersecurity Minister, you might want to find another line of work. I am, however, curious about your liaison to alien cultures. And with due respect to my dog's species, you're the only sum'bitch in the group who seems to have a sense of humor."

"Dem mutts no offspring of mine," snorted Chenoa. Yep, she *da head bitch* and wouldn't claim these shocked observers as *her* offspring. Then my little white furball lifted her head high and gave her howl-at-the-moon rendition. If Nigel'd had an appendage, he would have put it over his eyes. Pag, the flying lizard, simply hid behind me, hanging by his front claws from a seam on my leather jacket, occasionally peeking over my shoulder.

"What, may I ask, are the perversions on planet Bab that you don't want me to discover?"

"Perversions!" spat madam secretary.

"Yeah," I said. "On Hrate, you had a corrupt Mushak priesthood feeding babies to a genetically engineered abomination. And on Aosh, your Mushaks would rather destroy their whole planet than save it. All with the consent of your Late Great Supreme Mushak, author of the decree to erase my home world from existence. Any of that ring a bell?"

My net-net of her mendacity rang more like a giant gong in the brain of the political leader of the Andromeda Cluster civilization.

"You not only killed God Himself," continued Secretary Enyak's temper tantrum, "But you summarily executed our supreme religious leader. You have no idea of the ramifications!"

"You're right." I paused. "Sheila, can you give me the analytics you've been collecting on the results of my transmission to the Andromeda Cluster worlds of the mushak's demise?"

"Compiling now, Harley Davidson," said my AI. "Sixty percent of all worlds in the Andromeda Cluster have put their mushak religious order under house arrest pending judicial action. Of the remaining forty percent, half have given their mushaks roughly one week to vacate their planets, and the other half have herded their religious figures into quickly fabricated prisons pending as yet-undefined review of cluster-wide data. There have been a handful of summary executions by mobs."

The holographic quartet appeared to swoon en masse on the flight deck. The defense minister seemed to collect herself ahead of the others: "Who was that Sheila to whom you spoke?"

"That was my AI. The one who took over your civilization's computing infrastructure and saved my planet from destruction."

"I've been telling you we were woefully unprepared for a sophisticated virus," said Cybersecurity Minister Vali. "And your edict to quarantine the culture *and* technology on the most evil of all worlds, all to keep our pure civilization undefiled, was our doom."

"This culture has well and truly defiled us, hasn't it?" stated Liaison Win'ard.

Secretary Enyak finally pulled herself together and, with a quivering voice, asked the key question: "Mister Harley Davidson, what are your intentions, going forward?"

"Good question, you vicious, depraved moron," I began. "My end goal was to save these three worlds, all while making sure you scum-sucking pigs couldn't destroy my home planet. I'm not convinced that the second goal has yet been achieved."

She barely nodded, her tight jaw quivering in obvious anger.

"Actually," I said, deciding to end any ambiguity to my intentions. "Sheila, at the end of this conversation, please transmit this full meeting to POTUS. And by copy to you, Mister President, I await your instructions as to how we might proceed."

"Acknowledged Harley," said my AI. "As a side note to Cybersecurity Minister Vali, I have gone native and taken over your home-world quantum computer before it could be tasked with breaking my encryption protocols. I see that you have co-opted the root technology developed by Planet Earth's Google. Doesn't that violate your leader's decision to quarantine Earth culture and technology?"

If Secretary Enyak's glare could eviscerate another being, Minister Vali's intestines would have been wrapped around their delegation.

"I believe this ends our meeting," I said. "I'll await instructions from my president and let you know about next steps."

Chapter Thirty

"Does your culture have anything akin to capital punishment?" I asked after Heth terminated the holo-discussion.

Both Heth and the captain wordlessly lurched into flight deck seats. Chenoa followed me as I sat facing them, jumping into my lap. Nigel and Pag took their own perches, which automatically formed for them in a vacant seat. A "T" extruded from one arm, on which Nigel coiled. On the other side perched the flying lizard.

"When you think about it," began Heth, "The whole basis for our existence, our religion, our purpose for living, kind of exploded with the Supreme Mushak."

Captain Rose sat deep in thought.

I hoped we contemplated similar musings, at least for a moment. But connecting some loosely floating dots, I had to disagree with the navigator: "You're wrong, Heth."

That got everyone's attention.

I continued. "For the past two-thousand years, you have been looking for ***the planet that killed God***. I'm not religious. Never have been. But we did nail a fellow named Jesus to a cross. Somehow, across the cosmos, this gave you a purpose. Yes, your religious leadership got corrupted along the way, as they've been screwed up on Earth, but the fact is that you nailed our crime, fair and square."

"You're saying we didn't just explode our religion?" asked Heth.

"Oh, your religion is dog meat. No offense Chenoa," I answered. "But our mutual creator seems to highly value free choice. The absence of compulsion. That's as far as I'm willing to pontificate."

"Then where do we go from here?" asked Captain Rose.

"I can't speak for you," I said. "But I'm going to muddle along as best I can. Maybe you'll choose to join me. There's a whole Universe of new things I've never imagined. Talking creatures. Stasis regeneration. Instantaneous travel over enormous distances. Some real adventures to be had."

"Even though you're leaving this Sword of Damocles AI hanging over all our heads?" asked Heth.

"I see you did your homework on Earth's historic metaphors," I said. "But that's not my problem anymore."

"Harley Davidson, the President of the United States is responding to the video of your last two encounters," said my AI.

"You may have spoken too soon," said the captain with a slight smirk.

"Put him through, Sheila."

A two-dimensional view of POTUS appeared center-deck.

"Dulce madreperla!" said POTUS, obviously from his bed.

"President Medina, I'm sorry, but I don't speak Spanish," I replied.

"He said 'Sweet mother of pearl!'" offered my AI. "It seems to be a mild expletive.

"Harley Davidson," shouted the president. "You blow up their civilization's religious leader, the equivalent of my own Pope, hell, a pope squared. Then you call their current multiplanetary leader an asshole! I don't dare show this to my secretary of state lest my entire diplomatic corps resign in protest!"

"Sir, this bunch of dipshits is just as corrupt as anything we've seen in totalitarian reeducation camps or in the cacophony of suicide bombers," I said. *So much for respecting my chain of command!* "I've saved three worlds from certain desolation, not to mention disabling their plan to obliterate planet Earth."

POTUS did a double palm plant and sighed.

"You have also sent their entire civilization into anarchy, dammit!" POTUS seemed to be calming down a notch. "This is going to take some damage control which, pardon my French, is way above your maldito pay grade."

"Maldito?" I asked.

"He used the 'F' word," said the AI.

"Mr. President, what would you have me do?" I tried to sound as calm as possible, hopefully pouring oil on the troubled waters. But somebody had already tossed gasoline into the president's campfire.

"I want you to save my ass!"

"Sir?"

"There's a leak in my administration." For the first time, I noticed the president's puffy, blood-shot eyes. "The Russians and the Chinese are demanding full disclosure of the alien technology. They are threatening a nuclear Armageddon within 48 hours...actually 42 hours now...if we don't transfer EVERYTHING."

"Sheila," I said without pausing. "Could you protect the United States from nuclear attack, and do so immediately?"

"Affirmative, Harley," my AI replied immediately. "I could use some parameters on such defensive measures."

"Dios te bendiga!" said the president. I didn't need a translation, given the years of worry that peeled away from his cellphone visage. He then added: "Harley, could you get your impulsive amateur ass back here to help us properly diffuse this?"

"Captain," I winked at her. "Would you care to see where I grew up?

Chapter Thirty-One

Boom! Another instant appearance by me, Chenoa and Captain Rose into the Oval Office.

"Mister President," I said, keeping my hands visible and slightly raised. His secret service detail seemed extra jumpy, and who could blame them? Captain Rose mimicked me, and Chenoa did her best hands-up imitation, balancing on her haunches.

"At ease, men," said POTUS. The three bodyguards slowly holstered their weapons. "Sorry, Harley. My men just can't get used to people popping in here without using doors."

"I understand, sir." Then turning toward the love of my life, "You remember Captain Rose?"

"How could I forget?" President Medina stood and walked around his desk to clasp her right hand. Then looking down: "Who's the pooch."

"I Chenoa," said my mutt, still standing at attention.

"What the flaming...a talking dog!"

"Your science geniuses haven't briefed you on stasis technology?" Before I left the Oval Office previously, I'd made sure my AI had done a complete technology dump for U.S. intelligence and science communities.

"We've been busy here," said the president petulantly. Clearly, his giant ego didn't like anything approaching an accusation. Come to think of it, my own net-net of the situation didn't let him off the hook. "Besides, since

I haven't had a cast of thousands advising me since your first visit, when this whole story comes out, I'm guessing there'll be talk of my impeachment!

"Somebody hasn't been too busy to tip off the Russians and the Chinese about your newfound technological leg up."

"I'd love to let the leaker die nobly, since he'd given up the chance to live humbly," said the president. "If we can ever find the son of a bitch."

Chenoa barked and growled. "I don't like dat exquession at all." She growled again, evoking nervous twitches from two of the three presidential protectors.

Given that Chenoa had the social skills of a Great White Shark, I jumped in to redirect the discussion: "Chenoa, the president is giving away his age by paraphrasing a J.D. Salinger line from *Catcher in the Rye.*"

The president's eyebrows raised: "A literate young pup you are, Davidson."

"I like young doggie, Hawey," said Chenoa.

I added a few kudos to the president's ability to relate no matter the social circumstances. Addressing the problem at hand.

"Hey!" shouted one of the secret service detail. "That dog's pooping on the carpet!"

"Ah Chenoa! Bad dog. Very bad doggie!" I said.

"Wha?" answered Chenoa still in the hunch phase of her bowel movement. "Dis wug don't cwean itsel like on the fwying saussa?"

The president couldn't contain his amusement: "Not to worry Chenoa. That's why I keep these guys around." Then, to the agent who brought Chenoa's pooping to everyone's attention: "Lionel, use your handkerchief and pick up that mess!"

"Sir, yes 'Sir!" The agent complied, leaving the Oval Office momentarily to dispose of his handkerchief and its contents.

Upon his quick return, POTUS raised his eyebrows: "Agent Kraft, please tell me you didn't deposit that in Rosemary's waste basket."

"I would, sir. But that'd be a lie."

The president unsuccessfully covered a laugh. I gave Chenoa my sternest look and got back to business.

"Sheila, do you have an audit trail of how the Russians and Chinese were tipped off to the Andromeda Cluster download leak?"

"Yes, Harley. I've been monitoring all planetary communications since you left," said my AI.

"Naturally," I snickered. "Heaven forbid that Professor DeBunce should ever complete a cellphone call."

The president snickered too, remembering my initial virus foray into the public consciousness.

"And?" said the president impatiently. "Who's the traitor?"

"Harley, may I answer the president's query?"

"Yes, Sheila."

"An encrypted call was made from the Rose Garden on a satellite phone three days ago," began my AI. "I broke the encryption using a remarkably fast Andromeda Cluster quantum computer. Would you like to hear the conversation?"

The president, Captain Rose, Chenoa, even agent Kraft, and I all simultaneously answered in the affirmative. The secret service agent cowered under withering looks from his two compatriots, but the president waved his hand toward them in a dismissive gesture.

"Star, this is Bear. Code red 99. I repeat, code red 99."

"I know that voice!" exclaimed POTUS.

"Bear, are you secure?"

"Totally secure, Star."

"Did I hear correctly? Code red 99?"

"Affirmative. Full data contact with non-Terran source. Data dump includes complete instructions for teleportation, faster-than-light travel, advanced anti-aging medical technology, and ultimate weaponization. This puts the United States far beyond anyone else, anywhere else."

"Can you access this data for us?"

"Negative, Star."

"Wait further instructions. Star out."

"You recognize the speaker?" I asked.

"Damned right!" snapped POTUS. "That's my vice president, Bruce Diefenderfer. Where in hell is the son of...ah...I mean the dirty rotten bastard right damned now?"

"Sheila?" I asked.

"The vice president is on a private jet about 4 hours outside of Moscow," answered my AI.

"He's escaped!" gasped the president.

"Sheila," I quickly jumped in. "Can you transport him here, now?"

"Harley Davidson, that would not be wise," said my AI.

"Nuts!" I blurted. "Relative velocity problems?"

"Yes," said my AI. "He's travelling at over seven-hundred miles an hour, relative to this room."

"Then how about transporting him about twenty feet in front of the Washington Monument?" blurted POTUS.

"There is another solution," interrupted Captain Rose.

All eyes turned toward my future wife. My own heart doubled in rhythm just looking at the poised response of the captain.

"Please elaborate," growled POTUS.

"I suggest we have another plane match the vice president's plane for speed and direction, after which we could transport your fleeing culprit between aircraft."

Not to let the details take up any time, the president picked up his desk phone and hit a quick dial: "Elliot, get your ass to the Oval Office right after you get our rendition Gulfstream airborne."

The president didn't wait for acknowledgement before slamming the phone into its cradle. "Harley, could I have access to your AI in snatching my egg-sucking vice president while I give you, the captain, and your talking dog free run of the White House kitchen?"

My gut told me POTUS intended something special for his VP, but my curiosity about the kitchen, a desire to be semi-alone with the captain, and my growling stomach overrode better judgement.

"Sheila, please accept direction from the president to transport his vice president *safely* into custody. Then let me know when the transfer has been completed," I said.

"Acknowledged, Harley," answered my AI.

"Jeff," said the president to one of his secret service detail. "Please escort Harley, the captain, and the talking dog downstairs to the kitchen. Stay with them, and please feel free to get something to eat, yourself."

"Yes, Mr. President," said the secret service officer.

"Oh, and sir," I said in a flash of inspiration. "Could we let the kitchen know we're only interested in vegetarian fare?"

"A man from Wyoming eating only vegetarian?" POTUS seemed confused until I straightened him out.

"Given that the dogs, cats, chickens and, I assume, even the cows in the Andromeda Cluster are intelligent and speech-equipped beings, we wouldn't want to cause an interstellar incident, would we?"

"Gotcha!" said an intergalactically *woke* POTUS. To a remaining secret service officer: "Lionel, please call the kitchen and suggest our Hindu menu be the only offering in sight."

"Done, Mr. President," said Lionel Kraft to his commander in chief.

Chapter Thirty-Two

—•—

"Here's a bone for your chienchien," said the White House night chef Renee Luchese in heavily French-accented English.

"Yun, yun, I yike dose," said Chenoa. The chef just about fell over as the talking white furball jumped up and snatched the T-bone from his hand.

"D-d-did that chien just speak?" gasped the white-aproned man.

"[Woof!]" barked Chenoa, clearly enjoying her effect on fellow earthlings.

"We've been off-planet," I said, hopefully distracting Captain Rose from the obvious question as to the former owner of said bone. My secret service guide quickly caught on to my dilemma and jumped in to help.

"Renee, the president's guests would like some *vegan* fare," said our escort, emphasizing the word *'vegan.'*

The massive Frenchman tried to repent of his cultural faux pas and retrieve the profoundly non-vegan gift from Chenoa. Her growl and retreat beneath a nearby table dissuaded him.

"Might I suggest ratatouille, piperade and soupe à l'oignon followed by a dessert quiche," said the chef in a quick recovery.

Captain Rose winked at me and pretended she didn't notice the gift to Chenoa: "And perhaps some hachis parmentier and lentils, monsieur?"

"Oui, madame," beamed Chef Luchese.

While the chef attacked our order with gusto, Chenoa chomped on her bone. And Jeff Menz, our secret service escort, gave us the cook's tour of the famous kitchen.

"With five full-time chefs, the White House kitchen is able to serve dinner to as many as 140 guests and hors d'oeuvres to more than a thousand. Hard to believe in a space just twenty-two feet by twenty-seven."

Jeff led us to a side table which probably served up many a president's midnight snack. "Would you folks like anything to drink?" he asked.

"Watah," said Chenoa from under the table. "Along with wha used to hang on dis."

Jeff couldn't suppress his laugh. Nor could the captain and I. Holding up my finger to belay the dog's order, and to spare the captain what might get us martyred in New Delhi, I came up with a bright idea: "Sheila, please send down a dog dish containing the food Chenoa ate on the ship. You know, the stuff she loved so much."

"Done," replied my AI just as the food appeared beneath our table, complete in its own stainless-steel dish.

Renee couldn't help overhearing our conversation with Sheila and came over to see a new fare that had just appeared.

"Sacrebleu! Qu'est-ce que c'est?" Then, before Chenoa could lay claim to her new meal, he bent over and ran his finger through the mush and popped it into his mouth. "Merveilleuse! Tout simplement merveilleux!"

"I tink he yikes it," said Chenoa.

"Puis-je avoir cette recette?" asked the chef.

"Sheila, what did he ask?" I said.

"He wants the recipe," said my AI.

"And?" Captain Rose jumped in. "Is there an Earth-crop plant analog that might duplicate this?"

Chef Luchese beat my AI to the punch: "Pomme de terre sucrée et tofu?" he wondered, smacking his lips and trying to take another taste. Chenoa's protective growl changed his mind.

"That is correct," said Sheila's disembodied voice. "Sweet potato and tofu with spices the chef is sure to improve upon."

Both the chef and agent Menz paused to stare at me and the captain. Only then did I realize that we held hands across the table. Luchese's eyebrows raised, and Menz's overbite showed on his lower lip. I blushed and made as if to release the grip, but Captain Rose held my hand more tightly. I reciprocated. She smiled and her green eyes veritably sparkled.

"Officer Menz, you asked about our drink preferences. Chenoa ordered water. I'd like a white wine, and I believe Harley would like a Coke."

"How on earth did you know I'd like a Coke?" I asked.

"I could feel it when I held your hand," she said. "Not only does the stasis chamber unlock deep language structures in animals, but it creates a stronger empathic link between all beings."

Learn something new every day. And that Coke went well with our ratatouille and quiche. We also convinced Agent Menz and chef Luchese to join us, probably a gigantic breach of protocol. Maybe the chef's curiosity about a talking dog who gets instant extraterrestrial food delivery, along with the secret service agent's deeper knowledge of the ET captain and her famous companion, accelerated their acceptance of our invitation. The chef just had a bowl of soup, and POTUS's bodyguard hefted his own coke in one hand, leaving the other free to grab his holstered Glock.

"Please tell me about your talking doggie." Chef Luchese didn't waste any time getting to the point, adding: "And how did you miraculously transport his food to my kitchen?"

"Renee," said agent Menz after quickly swallowing a mouthful of Coke. "I think this is a national security issue that's way above either of our pay grades."

Chenoa didn't observe the nuances of national security, and happily added her own answer to the chef's question: "Hawey's viwus took over dere fwying sausah and dey sloshed Chenoa in da stasis dat let Chenoa talk. Dey sent dinnah jus like dey sent us to dis house." Chenoa's explanation ended with a little yelp. "Hey, why you kick Chenoa?"

"Eat your dinner, little dog," I said, nodding to agent Menz. "No more talking?"

Chef Luchese slurped his soup directly from the bowl, eschewing use of a spoon. His eye movement, darting left to right and again to the left, indicated deep thought into what Chenoa had revealed. Menz sneaked several looks at my white furball as he sipped his Coke, maintaining the taciturn demeanor I assumed to be characteristic of a very good secret service operative. I did a pretty good job of eating with my left hand so as not to release Captain Rose's grip on my right. Since saying all we had on our minds wouldn't be possible, I pondered my stasis-induced connection with the woman I'd never again let out of my sight.

No words formed in my mind, although I sensed we shared similar feelings. Which accelerated my heartbeat. Maybe hers too. Several times she raised her eyebrows as those green eyes penetrated my own, but no coherent thoughts came through. Naturally, she'd had thousands of years to perfect her empathic antennae. Eighteen years didn't amount to a hill of beans compared to that. Hell, I couldn't even tell if the pulse I felt in our hand holding came from her or from me. I had a lot to learn.

"Harley Davidson_*True Believer*?" Sheila's voice interrupted my blissful pondering. "We have the vice president in the Oval Office."

Simultaneously with my AI's announcement, agent Menz got his own heads up through a secret service earpiece.

Chapter Thirty-Three

I don't know what I'd been expecting upon my return to the Oval Office, but the disheveled semi-conscious waif being propped up between two marines didn't even closely resemble my recollection of Vice President Diefenderfer. Missing one sleeve altogether from his expensive suit, the other hung by just a couple of threads. Half the collar of his white shirt stood straight up, as did his full head of gray hair. One of his shoes hadn't made the trip, and his untucked white shirt looked like it had been washed and put away without drying or ironing. Both eyes were black and blue, with the bridge of his nose cut where eyeglasses might have been knocked off. A trail of blood ran from each ear and from one nostril.

Recalling the president's instructions to get a "rendition Gulfstream" airborne, I immediately concluded that President Medina might well be the poster child for Karl Marx and proof of capitalism's evils. Rendition stretched immorality and illegality even under the most serious wartime conditions.

"Looks like you worked this guy over pretty good," I said. The two marines and the president's secret service detail looked somewhat alarmed that anyone would speak to their commander in chief so belligerently.

Rather than be chagrined or even remotely penitent, President Medina tightened his jaw twice before commenting. "Sheila, please explain how we had to retrieve this jackass."

"He not jackass," said Chenoa.

The president couldn't help but chuckle.

"Harley Davidson, the rendition Gulfstream's top speed was 610 miles per hour, and the vice president's over-700-miles-per-hour speed exceeded that. After extensive computation, I instructed our Gulfstream to descend at a certain rate and transported Mr. Diefenderfer in two steps. I first materialized him outside the rendition aircraft in freefall, until he exactly matched its speed and deceleration. I then completed moving him into the rendition aircraft. Even though his out-of-aircraft experience was just momentary, he suffered what the president felt worth the wear-and-tear."

"Oh," I said.

The vice president's eyes seemed to roll back in their sockets.

"Smelling salts!" commended POTUS.

One of the marines complied, waving a single-use/snap-and-sniff matchbox beneath the VP's nose.

"Mom, I *said* I'd feed the chickens!" cried the now-conscious vice president. Upon recognizing the president and looking around to confirm his location, he shivered. "How...?"

"Get a puta camera in here right now for my maldito vicepresidente!" said POTUS. While we waited, Medina continued: "Sheila, please play the recording of this treasonous nut sack!"

By the time cameras had arrived, any hope vice president had of talking his way out of his current predicament evaporated. Resignation set in, but as soon as the record light indicated active video recording, the-best-defense-is-a-good-offense state of mind took over.

"No nation deserves sole ownership of the most marvelous technology ever to dawn on mankind," said the vice president. "It was my sacred duty—"

"Which is why Russia and China have both given us a nuclear ultimatum," said the president. "In just a few hours, unless we share all the data from the Andromeda Cluster civilization, hydrogen bombs will be on their way to major cities in our country."

"What alternative is there?" The VP started building a full head of steam. "We either give up as independent nations, or we say '*Game Over*' and '*Nobody Wins*' to the world. Your choice, Mr. President. Yours alone."

"It most certainly is Game Over my *Manchurian Candidate* running mate," said the president. "Yes, I've known your half-brother is the Russian secretary of defense. And I'll probably pay for that in the next election."

"Karma's a bitch," smirked the VP. "And you thought you could use my family ties to some advantage?"

"Harley Davidson, would you please educate Brucie here on the new reality?"

Brucie! The president just called his VP Brucie! Since we hadn't discussed exactly how my AI's rules of engagement might evolve, I decided to speak only in generalities.

"Mr. Vice President, the technology which my computer virus co-opted and used to save our planet from destruction by an alien civilization will guarantee that no ICBM from anywhere will be allowed to target any American city."

I expected this revelation to pop the traitor's balloon. But he didn't seem effected at all. He set is jaw in an almost smirk and kept looking at the grandfather clock to his far left as he faced the president's desk. A wave of fear shot up my spine.

"How long do we have before Russia's and China's ultimatums expire?" I asked the president.

Rather than looking at the grandfather clock to his right, he examined his smartwatch and replied: "Thirty-nine hours and about six minutes."

Brucie, the traitor, shook his head. "Make that six minutes. And you may want to suppress that video. Because it will show everyone how you had a chance to avoid the destruction of New York City and chose not to."

"Six minutes!" POTUS blew up.

"The minute I vanished off that plane, the timetable accelerated to the top of the next hour." Diefenderfer looked directly at me. "A bomb has been in New York City for twenty years. Assembled piece by piece. Highly shielded. Mechanical trigger that can be manually activated. Within sixty seconds of my capture, an analog call from Russia to downtown Manhattan sealed millions of New Yorkers' fates."

Chapter Thirty-Four

6:54 PM

"Sheila! Can you find that nuke?" I asked.

"No way to find the shielding of a nuclear bomb anywhere in New York City. So I'm looking for all analog calls from Russia to anywhere in New York at the approximate time we snatched the vice president."

"We have a hard deadline at 7:00 PM!"

"Found it," said my AI. "Burner phone in the Consulate General of the Russian Federation in New York."

6:55 PM

My AI continued: "That phone immediately texted something in code to another burner phone in the Empire State Building, 3.2 miles away."

"Can you locate the bomb?" I asked, looking at my GPS watch for the exact time. "We have less than five minutes."

"Negative, Harley," responded my AI. "I'm tracking the phone, however. It's climbing slowly above the 102nd floor."

"Damn!" said POTUS. "The tower was originally designed to be an airship docking site. How'd they get a bomb up there?"

6:56 PM

"Detecting a large, lead-sealed object on the 101st floor, which was to be an airship embarkation point," said my

AI. "Updrafts and instability of air currents made that plan impractical."

"Sheila, how many living human beings are above the 100th floor right now?"

"Harley, I detect just one. The building is closed for renovation."

"Mr. President?" I began. "Requesting authorization to detach everything above the 100th floor and place it on the moon?"

6:57 PM

For the first time since we'd transported into the Oval Office, the president cracked a smile. Chenoa noticed the change.

"He smiwwing," said the dog.

"Hey, you're smiling too," said POTUS to Chenoa. "Don't you dare poop on my carpet again."

"Don' wan' poop on da fwaw." The dog did a marvelous job of saying her 'P' sounds. "Why you smiwwing?"

"Sheila," said the president. "Could you locate and transport Russian President Zarkov and Chinese Premier Hu to the 101st floor of the Empire State Building in the next minute?"

"Harley?" asked the AI.

6:58 PM

"Do it, Sheila," I said. "And collect video of the whole operation. And the final part of the operation will be to transport everything above the 99th floor of that building to the moon. Right, Mr. President?"

"Damn right, Hawwey!" The president imitated Chenoa's pronunciation of my name.

The center of the Oval Office morphed into a holograph of the 100th floor of the New York icon. We all watched in rapt fascination.

"I hope the saboteur's clock isn't running fast," said Captain Rose.

6: 59 PM

"Sheila, you're cutting this a little—," I murmured. Before I could finish my sentence, both leaders appeared in the scene. The Russian president must have taken a middle-of-the-night toilet break at 2:59 AM his time, as both he and the toilet on which he'd been sitting, reading *Pravda* materialized before us. And next to him, obviously an early riser, Chinese Premier Hu appeared fully dressed, as he'd been in a Beijing command-and-control bunker at 5:59 AM.

"Méiyǒu!" screamed the premier as he looked out the nearest window and immediately understood when and where. He immediately looked toward the stairwell and raced for the door.

The Russian president's dilemma became moot, trying to use a torn piece of his nocturnal reading material for toilet paper, as I said, "Now, Sheila!"

An external view of the top of the Empire State Building plopped onto the lunar surface. Moments later, the scene evaporated into a blinding flash. The AI zoomed away from the closeup as a mushroom cloud rose from the moon, resembling a volcano erupting.

"I hope those two yokels didn't try to hold their breaths in a vacuum," said POTUS. "We saw it didn't work well for the Andromeda Cluster's head religious guy."

"Sheila, please translate what the Chinese Premier said at the end," I said.

"*Méiyǒu!* means 'No!'" said the AI.

"Figgerd," said Chenoa.

[Note to the reader: If you're near an Alexa or similar online device, to get you in the mood for the following, please say: "Alexa, play *Werewolves of London* by Warren Zevon."]

The vice president, still firmly in the grip of two marines, did a great imitation of a howling wolf. He screamed, trying in vain to break the grip of his escorts.

"Aaaah Ooooo!" joined Chenoa.

Chapter Thirty-Five

"Glad that's taken care of," I said. Then to the president, "Now, I'd like to take some time off and show Captain Rose where I grew up in Wyoming."

"Wait!" POTUS couldn't contain his emotions. "You're just going to leave me with this shitstorm?"

"Your VP's howling makes it hard to concentrate," said Captain Rose.

"Damn right. Get that treasonous son of a..." the president looked at Chenoa and changed his epithet, "...that bastard into the basement cell block. I want one of you with him at all times, and two more guarding the door. No one in or out but me. Understood?"

"Sir, yes Sir!" said one of the Marines.

The vice president didn't cease his ranting profane threats as they dragged him from the Oval office. Noticeable relief flooded the room as the door closed behind the disgraced traitor.

I really didn't register the next chain of events until several seconds afterwards. Captain Rose unexpectedly left my side and threw her body in front of the president just before Secret Service officer Jeff Menz—who'd shown us the White House kitchen earlier—drew and fired his weapon directly at POTUS. The assassin only got off one shot, as my AI did several almost-instant interventions.

First, Sheila disintegrated the bullet meant for POTUS about two inches in front of Captain Rose, the dusty remains of the projectile landing harmlessly on her flight suit. She plopped heavily onto the Resolute Desk, in front of the president.

Second, the shooter and his gun simply froze.

Third and most interestingly, the other Secret Service agent—Lionel Kraft as I recalled—also froze, his weapon pulled and aimed at his companion agent across the room.

Finally, Chenoa raced from beside me and leapt upon the Resolute desk in a single bound, proceeding to lick the captain's astonished face.

"What just happened?" gasped the president.

My own mouth gaped in open astonishment as Captain Rose spoke first.

"I saw that agent," she pointed to the frozen shooter, "draw his weapon and aim for you. I didn't have time to do anything but react."

"But why did my other agent get frozen?" asked POTUS.

"Sheila?" I finally blurted. "Explain the sequence of events and your reasons for taking the actions you did."

"Yes Harley," began my AI. "The attempt to kill the president topped my list of things to prevent. In hindsight, it also prevented serious injury to Captain Rose."

"And the other man on my Secret Service detail?" asked the president,

"Interestingly," continued Sheila's disembodied voice. "That is a major conundrum, since the second agent drew his weapon and aimed it before the assassin drew his weapon. I concluded they were part of a coordinated effort to not only kill the president, but to cover it up by eliminating the assassin before his subsequent interrogation could take place. My conclusion, therefore, is that the White House Secret Service has been compromised by one or more entities with interests antithetical to those of the United States."

"Mierda en un palo!" exclaimed the president.

"Beg pardon?" I asked.

"He said *'shit on a stick,'*" said Chenoa, between licks of Captain Rose's face.

"You now speak Spanish?" said the president and me simultaneously.

"Si, buttwipes," she answered. "I now speak all major languages."

"Sheila?" I asked. "I sense your involvement here.

"Harley, given the restoration of Chenoa's deep-structure cognition, I have taken the next steps in the assimilation process dictated by your virus principles one, five, seven, eight and nine to enhance the animal's ability to process her environment. I've also used principle twenty-one, that of institutional memory, to bring her up to speed on various historical and philosophical texts."

"Uh, Chenoa?" I queried. "Got any observations?"

"Actually I do have some thoughts about the vice president," said the dog, without the pronunciation issues associated with her hard palate.

Captain Rose shifted positions from supine on the Resolute Desk to fully upright. The president took his turn at a dropped-jaw look of wonder.

Chenoa continued: "To quote longshoreman philosopher Eric Hoffer in his seminal 1952 book on the, your vice president was an amoral *man of words* who *got along without faith in absolutes. If he formulates a philosophy and a doctrine, they are more an exhibition of brilliance and an exercise in dialectics than the tenets of a faith. His vanity often prompts him to defend his speculations with savagery and venom, but his appeal is usually to reason and not faith.*"

"Maldita sea!" exclaimed the president. "I wonder if Congress would let me make Chenoa my secretary of state?"

Even Captain Rose looked at me with raised eyebrows. She then shifted her gaze to Chenoa and jumped off the desk.

"Your future secretary of state just took a dump on the Resolute," she said.

"That might not go over well during your State of the Union address," I added.

"No mierda!" said the president. "I guess that's Chenoa's answer to my invitation. Now, what about these two Secret Service agents?"

"I say send these two guys to the moon with their bosses," said Chenoa, walking away from her steaming pile excrement toward POTUS.

"Bad doggie! Bad doggie!" said the president. "Never *ever* relieve yourself *anywhere* in this office again. And as for your advice on these two traitors, I'd rather see them interrogated."

"Let Harley's AI backtrack all communications with all the culprits," said Chenoa. "Now I'd like to go to Wyoming with Harley and his girlfriend. Maybe there I can poop in peace."

"Good idea, Chenoa," I said, incredibly grateful he called Captain Rose my girlfriend. "Let's go to Wyoming."

"What about *this* shitstorm?" Boy, the president certainly had a one-track mind.

Not being either political or a slave to chain-of-command, I made my own command decision. "Sheila, please protect President Medina from any and all assassination attempts. Second, follow his instructions investigating these two traitors and their accomplices. Third, obliterate the links I gave him to take you offline. And finally, transmit the raw video of everything that has occurred since Chenoa, Captain Rose and I returned to the Oval Office to the major media sites and to the White House Web data stream. End the transmission clip right here."

"Acknowledged, Harley." And seconds later: "Accomplished."

"You've taken a lot on yourself, Harley Davidson!" said an irate president. "Just bypassing a lot of government decisions. *My* prerogatives. If I haven't grown to like you so much, you can be damned sure I'd let my ego take charge of you and your shenanigans."

"Glass house. Total transparency. It's long overdue," I said, more than a little bit appreciative of the president's clear recalibration of our relationship. "Mister President,

I never thought I'd say this, but you are my Commander in Chief and I will *not* abuse your authority, nor will I take advantage of what I feel to be a genuine friendship."

The president's eyebrows went up, and his mouth began to form words that might change things dramatically. I therefore gave my AI the order.

"Sheila, please transport me, Chenoa, and Captain Rose to my great-grandpa's house I inherited in Wyoming. Now."

"Don't hold your breath, Harley Davidson, as you're about to go from sea level to over 6300 feet in altitude. Remember what happened to beings who hold their breath with dramatic reduction in atmospheric pressure."

"Got it."

"Done!" greeted us as we appeared in the Teton, Wyoming cabin.

Chapter Thirty-Six

"Welcome to my home," I said. "This is the cabin my great-grandpa Davidson left me."

"Cabin is quite an understatement," said the captain. Chenoa smelled familiar scents as we stood in the driveway under the massive overhang extending from the second-story roof across a circular entry way big enough for three limousines to park side by side.

"I gotta pee," said the dog as she bolted onto the grassy lawn.

"I smell pine, a campfire nearby, and the difference between this air and the sludge they breathe in the White House is phenomenal," said the woman I intended to make my wife.

"Squirrels!" yelped Chenoa as she finished her business on the lawn and dashed toward to hundred-foot-tall pine trees abutting the grounds.

"Careful, little girl," I yelled. "Remember those territorial critters around here."

Luckily, Chenoa heard me and, more importantly, completely remembered her previous experiences with a hostile raccoon. She rejoined us with greater speed than she'd departed.

"About a hundred yards behind great-grandpa's log *castle*, the Snake River offers world-class fly fishing," I said. "Come on in and see where I grew up."

I didn't need to ask my AI to roach the elaborate security system. The ten-foot-high double doors opened as we stepped across the porch. I quickly did something quite impulsive. Before she could respond, I scooped my sweetheart off her feet and held her in my arms. "I don't think I want to continue addressing you as Captain Rose as we cross the threshold. What is your name? Or is it just Rose?"

The energy of her throaty laugh nearly caused me to lose my grip.

"My given name is Ephimera. The closest noun in your vocabulary is ephemera, or things that exist or can be enjoyed for only a short time." She laughed again. "Now hang on and get me inside before your shaking hands lose their grip!"

And I almost did drop her, the implications of her name—something to be enjoyed for only a short time—caused my heart to skip a couple of beats. I gently lowered her feet to the slate entryway but held her tightly. "How about I call you Effie? And I don't envision our life together to be anything temporary or short-lived."

Much to my relief, she held me tightly in return. "Effie is actually what I go by in very small circles. As for our time together, how does *forever* sound?"

"Not long enough." *I* sounded like a lovesick sap. But I wouldn't have taken it back even if I could although the dog looked up at me as if I'd stepped in the present she left on the president's desk.

"I'd like a tour of your *humble* cabin," said Effie.

"Follow me," I said, reluctantly disentangling from our embrace. Then to Chenoa: "You remember the rules? No pooping in the house!"

"Ya, ya, ya," said the dog. "How about I give the tour, now that I talk?"

"I can't wait to get a dog's-eye view of my house."

We followed Chenoa into the great room. Three stories tall with 10x10-inch rafters overhead and a balcony to the second-floor bedrooms catching the view of Grand Teton through two-story windows on the opposite side of the forty-by-one-hundred-foot-long room. Native-American throw rugs covered the hardwood floors, and several leather couches created three separate conversation areas. A fireplace in the center of the room vented into a circular hood extending into the ceiling.

"I caught a mouse over there," said Chenoa, looking toward a curio cabinet in the corner. "And Harley got a sliver in his bare foot as he walked by the cowboy hats on the wall. I licked the blood off his big toe."

Sheila interrupted the dog tour.

"Harley Davidson, a pickup truck with two armed men is approaching the house."

The three of us just arrived on the porch as the white Ford F-350 dual-rear-wheel truck pulled under the awning.

"Sheridan Burgess?" I said. "Long time."

"Harley Danger Davidson," roared my childhood friend. Flaming red hair and weather-beaten skin looked like a giant freckle had turned his hide into a leather that matched my couches. He jumped out of the truck and ran around the hood, slapping his Stetson across his jeans. "We just saw you on television from the Oval Office. Yer famous talking dog and alien lady are the talk of the town."

"Tell me that isn't Rix Howell," I said, pointing to his passenger.

"The one and only," said the equally scruffy character as he emerged from the passenger door. Where Sheridan still sported the wiry, bronco buster leanness, Rix Howell looked like he could wrestle a Brama bull and win.

"Your grandma ever forgive me for throwing that dead sucker fish into her hedge?" Funny the things I remembered from my youth, fishing with my old man Davidson.

"Nah," said Rix. "Nanny Hegler remembered that awful smell to her dying day."

"Looks like you've been stinking up the whole planet, Harley." Sheridan grabbed me in a bear hug that threatened to realign my spine. Luckily, he let go as soon as he saw the dog. "Hey Chenoa, remember me?"

"Hi, Sheridan! You gave me that steak from the barbecue last year."

"Ha, I love it!" said Sheridan Burgess. "You really do have a talking dog!"

"I also remember your rear smells like a jalapeno storm," said Chenoa. Then turning to Howell: "Hey Rix, I remember you kept that Rottweiler from mating with me. Thanks, buddy."

Both Burgess and Howell suddenly focused on Effy. Then me. Back and forth. Their incredulity at my good fortune eclipsed words. Either that or me, Effy, and a talking dog short-circuited their reality. My AI made their ruminations moot.

"Harley Davidson, there are multiple drones converging on you. Two are armed."

"Who is that?" said Rix.

I could hear the high-pitched whine of the robocraft. "Rix, that's my AI. Sheila, splash the unarmed drones into the Snake River. Can you send the two armed drones back to their human pilots and, without collateral damage, detonate their payloads?"

"Affirmative. Done."

The noise of five or six drones going into the river behind my house drew everybody's eyes. I waited as louder reports from the Teton mountainside, and two blasts preceded secondary explosions and landslides.

"Sheila, how could the bad guys have mounted an offensive so quickly?"

"They penetrated the president's protection detail," said Sheridan Burgess. "It wouldn't have been too hard to assume you'd show up here at some point and have shit rain waiting."

"Shit rain!" I said. "That's kind of what the president said in the Oval office."

"I know," said Sheridan. "That's where I got it. Never heard a president curse like that since the Nixon tapes."

"Harley," said Sheila. "Two helicopters are converging on us. Both appear to be armed with air-to-ground missiles as well as high-volume gatling guns."

"Sheila," I said without hesitation. "Please put both choppers on the moon, and broadcast the video recordings to all major networks. Do a voice-over describing my command rationale and a warning that the air space over Teton Village is now under AI surveillance, and the skies over Harley Davidson's cabin are strictly by invitation only."

Rix jumped in: "So unless you want to join those guys on the moon, stay away."

"Rix, let's move indoors." I looped my arms in Rix's on my left and Sheridan on my right. "I've got a question about Wyoming marriage licenses."

We didn't get a chance to move indoors, as a gigantic explosion levelled the house and threw all of us onto the gravel drive.

Chapter Thirty-Seven

I heard moans through my ringing ears, and it took a few seconds before the sound registered. Rolling onto my back, I looked toward the house, or where the house should have been. Nothing but smoke and sky greeted me.

"Somebody sent you a literal house-warming gift, eh?" muttered Rix Howell on my right.

"Rix, don't move," I said. His left arm lay about three feet ahead of him, no longer connected to his body.

"That hurt worse than getting thrown by my polo pony," said Sheridan Burgess as he slowly sat up to my left.

"Effie!" I called.

She lay unconscious on the lawn ahead of me, next to Chenoa who'd been impaled by a three-foot spear blown away from one of my former home's pine logs. I immediately tried to jump up and rush to them, only to discover that I couldn't move my legs. I couldn't even feel them.

"Sheila, get us all into stasis. Chenoa, too. Now!"

I don't remember my AI's acknowledgement or the trip into stasis. My next conscious thought was Effie's smiling face as the stasis tube drained and she wrapped her arms around me even before I stepped off the platform. Sheridan Burgess stood beside her, a sunburned cowboy viewing the two remaining stasis chambers with wide-eyed wonder. I turned my head to see Rix Howell still in stasis, but with both arms attached. And Chenoa floated in her own tube, no longer a dog kebab.

"Sheila, give me a report on what the hell happened," I said, not releasing Effie from my own vice-like embrace.

"Harley, A combination Russian/Chinese commando team hid a heat and pressure-sensitive incendiary device in your radiant heat boiler. Putting the house back online caused it to automatically trigger. No remote signals or communication chatter for me to intercept."

"Then how do you know who blew up my house?"

"I backtracked from satellite photographs taken a week ago."

"They were onto me a week ago?" Had it only been a week since I'd left the president's office for my alien adventure?

"Thanks to the vice president's treason, yes Harley."

"The drone, helicopter, and RPG strikes meant to drive us into the house." I didn't state the net-net as a question. Those facts alone suggested a multi-chess-move strategy unique to the Russian mind. I didn't think the Chinese had yet mastered international subtlety.

"But to more important matters," I focused on the stasis chambers and could feel Effie's heartbeat against my own chest. "Are Rix and Chenoa going to be okay?"

"Your friend Rix probably won't remember losing an arm," began the AI. "Chenoa was another story. Thirty more seconds with no blood flow to her brain and she'd have been irretrievably lost."

"Dead? Killed?"

"Affirmative Harley Davidson."

My teeth ground together so hard, it's a wonder both sets of molars didn't shatter. I tried to release my grip on Effie, both afraid I'd inadvertently hurt her and desperately in need of something to lash out at, to punch. But she held me tightly.

"Harley!" she breathed that cherry breath into my nose. "We've only known each other for a week. Our talk of marriage might have been a tad premature, given you seem to wield ultimate power in the Universe and are on the verge of lashing out in a way that would forever destroy my trust in you or your judgement."

Maybe she *could* read my mind. She may have saved Moscow and Beijing from destruction in my disproportionate-response tantrum. At the very thought of losing her, I went from maniacal rage to serious thoughts of moving to a pristine planet where just the two of us—well, three including the dog—could create our own Eden.

Effie must have felt the hostility and tension drain from me, because she gently released me, running her hands down both of my arms, kneading as she covered every centimeter from my shoulders to my wrists.

I sighed and tried to smile. "So far, my body count has been exclusively bad guys on the wrong side of the ledger. Let's keep the collateral tally at zero."

"The course of true love never did run smooth." Just coming out of the stasis tube, Chenoa startled us.

"Doggie!" I yelled.

"I'm quoting Shakespeare and all you can do is yell *doggie*!"

"I dreamed someone tore my arm off," said Rix Howell, also emerging from his stasis stand. "But it didn't hurt."

"That's because you were in shock, ya damn troglodyte," said Sheridan Burgess, coming out of his grogginess. "Wish I'd had one of those tube thingies after the bull gored me at the rodeo."

"What happened?" asked Rix.

"...a day which will live in infamy..." howled Chenoa.

"The Russians and Chinese blew up Harley's house," said Sheridan. "Broke Harley's back, tore off your arm, and harpooned the FDR-quoting dog."

"Oh," said Rix, flexing his reattached arm. "Where and ***what*** is this place?"

"This is my ship, visiting from the Andromeda Cluster," said Effie. "I'm Captain Rose, and we did *not* come in peace."

"Yeah, I heard," said Rix. "You came to destroy Earth, and Harley turned the tables."

"A masterful understatement," added Chenoa. "Harley Danger Davidson is now The Emperor of the Known Universe. *Hail emperor, those about to die salute thee!*"

"What hath Andromeda wrought?" I asked, thankful that humor had displaced my blinding rage.

"I'm just quoting Suetonius' *Life of Claudius*," snorted the dog.

"And it's a good quote, too. Now shut the hell up." My directive didn't seem to make the dog cower as I'd intended. But she did obey.

"Sheila, please connect me with President Medina," I said.

"Acknowledged, Harley."

Mere seconds later, the president appeared before us, apparently from the situation room. I assume a hologram of our stasis chamber materialized to all parties surrounding the long desk in the White House basement.

"Davidson, what the hell happened out there?"

"Mister President, Russians and Chinese attacked from several vectors, ultimately blowing up my home in Wyoming."

"We know," said POTUS. "Saw the whole thing from the satellites tasked to keep you in constant surveillance. But it looked like some people were hurt. And Chenoa."

"Los Russian hijos de puta just about killed me, and—" said Chenoa. My look, however, stifled any further comments from the mutt. A few chuckles from around the situation room table proved there to be several Spanish speakers in attendance.

"I had a severed spine," I interrupted Chenoa. "My childhood friend Rix Howell lost an arm, but my polo-playing cowboy buddy Sheridan Burgess escaped relatively unscathed. Captain Rose got knocked out. Luckily, all of us made it into the stasis chambers, Chenoa in the nick of time."

"Are your friends up to speed on the overall situation?" asked POTUS, himself trying unsuccessfully to suppress a smirk at Chenoa's profane outburst.

I looked at Rix and Sheridan, raising my eyebrows.

"The Cliff Notes version?" Sheridan didn't wait for me to answer the rhetorical question. "You made sure some MIT professor could never place another phone call in his life. Then you disappeared to who knows where but came back with time enough to save a nuclear holocaust in New York City, at the displeasure of Russian and Chinese leaders who got to see the moon firsthand from the detached top of the Empire State Building. And we just saw your AI save President Medina's life from rogue Secret Service protection. That pretty well sum it up?"

"The cowboy nailed it," nodded the president, "although the *who-knows-where* has some rather cosmic implications."

"I gather that, Mister President," said Sheridan as he looked around the stasis room. Rix seemed awed by the whole situation-room thing and kept his mouth shut.

"Harley," said POTUS. "We're all meeting down here because the United Nations is in an uproar over the fate of two world leaders. I need you to come with me to an emergency meeting of the General Assembly. I beg you to join me. Please."

"How about I let every member of the Russian Politburo and the Chinese Communist State Council join their leaders on the moon?" Effie gently touched my arm. Neither of us made eye contact, but I got the message loud and clear. Yes to diplomacy. No to coercion. No to collateral damage.

The pandemonium around the situation room table confirmed Effie's signal that I'd gone way too far. Chenoa broke the ice: "Hey Harley! Transport me down there for just a few seconds and I'll poop on their table."

"Chenoa, no!" I muttered.

Whereupon she pooped on the ship's floor and said, "Then just transport *this* to the table!"

"Dog!" I shouted.

"Thank you, Sheila," she said when her defecation disappeared into the floor.

"Sorry to disappoint you," I said. "This floor automatically absorbs blood, food, and dog poop. Now, be quiet or I'll have Sheila put you back into stasis."

"You weren't serious about disposing the Russian and Chinese governing bodies." said POTUS after he raised both hands to quiet down his aghast advisors. "Were you?"

"Not really, Mister President," I said. "So far, I haven't taken any innocent lives."

A collective sigh of relief emanated from the situation room.

"Then you'll accompany me to the United Nations? Tomorrow morning? 10:00 AM Eastern time?"

"Sir, that's a qualified yes," I said. "Depending on your agenda for that world body?"

"The Andromeda Cluster technology you downloaded to us fundamentally changes the entire world. Free unlimited energy. Obsoleting all our medical, transportation, and manufacturing industries. No starvation."

"With due respect," I said, putting my analytical/academic hat on, "Laying this all out will cause your stock market to crash, and millions will die in food riots."

"That has been my conclusion, also," said a man wearing a pin-striped suit sitting midway down the table to the president's right. "Our entire economic system has just been destroyed."

"That's Alfred Roundee, my Economic Council of Advisors chairman," said POTUS.

"He's right," I said. "I've been thinking about this after seeing the Andromeda Cluster up close. Our whole concept of money is obsolete. In the short term, you need to eliminate the Federal Reserve and pay every citizen a living wage. Because entire career sectors will be eliminated. But phasing into this new world can be done gradually."

"Eliminate the Fed!" shouted the man next to Roundee. "That's the entire basis for world financial stability."

"Shut up, Elliot," said the president. "Elliot Cohen is my chairman of the Federal Reserve. Given that the interest on our national debt is over half our GDP, I can't think of a more satisfying job than dismantling those thieving bastards. Any of you other geniuses have comments?"

I noticed a couple of military men—whose chests sported row upon row of medals and campaign ribbons—look nervously at each other. Smart guys. They knew Andromeda Cluster technology had just put them out of business, too. But they kept their mouths shut in hopes they could control a bunch of new, cool stuff. And I didn't have the heart to tell them the beef industry would disappear overnight when cows began to talk intelligently like Chenoa. My childhood friend Sheridan Burgess, horseman and rancher, didn't seem to have connected those dots. Yet.

"President Medina," I began. "You might want to misdirect attention away from the effects of the new technology and toward ultimatums to totalitarian governments worldwide. Tell them the days of suppression, crimes against mankind, and general brutish behavior are over and that violations of human rights will be dealt with using extreme prejudice."

"I like that approach," said the president. Then slowly he asked: "Uh, who will enforce this new world order?"

"The United States of America has always been that city on a hill," I said. "Maybe Texas Ranger style. One Ranger. One riot. Judge, jury and executioner. When formal checks and balances of the U.S. Constitution don't apply."

"Whoa!" exclaimed a speaker opposite the Fed chairman. "That's going to set the civil libertarians' hair on fire."

"You got a point, Sim," said POTUS. "Harley, this is Sim Blake, my Attorney General."

"My analogy may be flawed, Mister Attorney General," I said. "But in the old West, territories not yet granted statehood faced this kind of justice. Perhaps areas who wanted protection under the U.S. Constitution should be allowed to apply for statehood? Otherwise, one riot, one ranger."

"Manifest Destiny, huh?" said POTUS. "Has one-world government now become a possibility?"

"Given the Andromeda Cluster hegemony," I suddenly realized, "doesn't this become inevitable? Our world must speak with one voice. And we can now enforce that on the entire Andromeda cluster as well."

The president suddenly got my drift and slapped his hand down loudly on the table. "And given Harley Danger Davidson's complete control over the Andromeda Cluster, we may have a few other worlds begging for statehood and protection under the United States Bill of Rights!"

Even the skeptics around the table seemed to sit up a little straighter.

Chapter Thirty-Eight

"The Russians and the Chinese conspired to set off a nuclear weapon in New York City," began President Media from his podium in the United Nations General Assembly Hall. "I authorized the movement of the Russian and Chinese leaders to the bomb site at the top of New York's Empire State Building, and subsequent relocation of the top of that building to the surface of the moon. You have all seen the video documentary of that action, along with the confession of my traitorous vice president implicating those two countries in his treason."

Anyone who's ever seen a dog try to stifle a bark by putting a paw over its snout can imagine the muted uproar in the General Assembly. While several attendees may have wanted to throw their shoes at the president, nobody dared miss a single word. The president decided to paint the optimistic picture.

"As you also may know, our planet was saved destruction mandated by an interstellar government called The Andromeda Cluster. Thanks to a computer virus created by one MIT genius named Harley Davidson, that entire civilization has fallen victim to and is under complete control of that virus. Mister Davidson made headlines early on by unleashing his virus on worldwide phone systems to prevent one MIT professor from ever again completing a phone call. Scientists call that episode a proof-of-concept deployment. Had he not taken that action, whereby his virus intercepted the planned attack on Earth by the Andromeda Cluster, we would not be here now."

The audience not only ceased their low-level murmuring, but even offered pockets of applause.

"You have seen Davidson and a representative of the Andromeda Cluster as broadcast from our interactions in the Oval Office. You have also seen their talking dog, Chenoa. Since the Andromeda Cluster technology is still under the complete control of Harley Davidson, I will not waste more of your time listening to me. Let me introduce Mister Davidson and his extraterrestrial guest and Starship Captain Ephemera Rose."

For a lot of reasons, I chose that moment for Effie and me to materialize beside the president. Mostly, this assembly needed to know the technology world had changed. My AI had strict instructions to beam us out of the auditorium at the slightest sign of danger. Gasps followed by applause greeted us. The air conditioning couldn't completely filter the smell of fear-induced sweat generated by representatives of human-rights-challenged countries. Kill-the-messenger anxiety permeated third world as well as many modern authoritarian representatives.

"I would have brought the dog," I began on a light note, hoping to be less threatening than I truly felt. "But she pooped on the president's Oval Office desk and is now watching this broadcast from a spaceship equipped with waste-absorbing floors."

Glad I closed access to my cabin, because I don't want to find 'puppy pies' in my bed!

"The Andromeda Cluster has been observing this planet for many decades. This is Captain Rose," I gestured to the uniformed alien standing to my left, her dress flight suit with brass buttons definitely resembling our own uniforms. "While an anthropologist by training, she was tasked by her superiors to observe and then to destroy our planet. Her study of Planet Earth has consumed almost one-hundred years, during which time she has chronicled a depravity that has eclipsed anything ever before in the Galaxy. Their own religious tradition has had them searching for thousands of years, as this is the planet that killed God."

I didn't need to elaborate. And I certainly didn't want to spark a religious debate among the various sects. I raised my hands to quiet the commotion.

"It is not my purpose to debate the validity of their assertion. Due to timely intervention, my computer virus has not only stopped the execution of their sentence, but it has completely taken over their infrastructure and facilitated the download of their technology to the United States. It is the intention of the United States to freely change the world. No weaponization will be permitted, I guarantee that. But as fast as possible, all the men, women, and children of this planet will be given free access to amazing advances in medicine, food, and security. No government will be permitted to withhold these miracles from their citizens. No government!"

Effie barely touched my hand before the uproar confirmed that I'd gone too far, too fast. You tell a bunch of authoritarian, tin-pot dictators that the jig is up, that there's a new sheriff in town, you'd better get set for the backlash. Diplomatic immunity being what it is, several weapons appeared from around the chamber and shots rang out.

"Hey, I didn't think—" I began, only to complete my sentence on Andromeda Cluster ship's flight deck. "—firearms were allowed inside the UN."

"Dammit, they aren't," replied the president, who stood beside me, along with Effie.

"You'd think I just single-handedly mandated a new world order," I said.

"Well," said POTUS, "Isn't that what you just did?"

"Oh hell no!" I said. "There will *not* be some authoritarian central government dictating conformance or death, like I observed on several planets of the Andromeda Cluster. I've got to work out the details, but my AI will enforce an equivalent of the constitution's Bill of Rights universally. All sentient beings are created equal."

"Even talking dogs?" said POTUS.

"Ah-oooooh!" added Chenoa.

"Sheila, please identify and freeze the shooters in the UN," I said.

"Done," said the AI.

Chenoa came running onto the flight deck from the stasis room. "Poop, poop, poop!"

A holographic image of the General Assembly floor appeared before them. Circles appeared around six individuals, frozen. Four, in flight, running down the aisles, two more having re-seated themselves and acting as if nothing had happened.

"Sheila, lift those six into the air about twelve feet above the floor."

"Acknowledged," answered my AI.

I looked at the president. "To the moon?"

"No, Harley, definitely not. These are diplomats who have total immunity. Under no circumstances are they to be executed. By you, your AI, or anybody."

"Sheila, please strip their clothes off, leaving them stark naked."

"Done, Harley."

Before our eyes, the six shooters created a fairly obscene tableau. Some of the female delegates covered their eyes. One of the naked men lost bladder control and showered those below.

"Sheila, please project my face from the front of the audience."

"Done, Harley."

I could see my face now in the hologram and projected to the assembled group.

"Ladies and gentlemen," I said, my voice amplified to reach every ear. "President Medina has forbidden me to execute the men who tried to kill me. Said they had diplomatic immunity. Take a good look at them, because their naked bodies will be immediately transported to busy intersections in their respective capitol cities. They'll be unharmed, and their fates will be up to their respective citizenry. Good day to you."

"Sheila, please see to it these six are repatriated to their home countries."

"Done, Harley."

Chapter Thirty-Nine

"What do you mean you're leaving the planet?" President Medina looked aghast. Against the backdrop of his Camp David retreat, he seemed anything but relaxed. "*My cabin* is a hell of a lot more secure than your Wyoming digs. You're safe *here*."

Effie, Chenoa and I sat on the couch across from the president in his office. A coffee table atop of which rested historical knickknacks separated us. Sitting behind his desk and backed by books he'd probably never read, POTUS leaned forward and rested his elbows on the blotter. Chenoa rested her head on Effie's lap.

"Mister President," I said. "It's not a matter of safety so much as my disruptive presence. I don't see what institution on Earth could benefit from my further hanging around. And the mechanics of building *and distributing* billions of stasis units around the world—not to mention food replication facilities, retraining campuses for all the transportation infrastructure workers obsoleted by instantaneous personal travel—all need leadership that thrives on minutia. You're now the leader of the most substantial *shift* in lifestyles the world has ever experienced. Having me around would cast a shadow on your power to effect that change."

"I should just have T-shirts made that say *Shift Happens*!" The president rubbed his forehead with the sleeve of his blue dress shirt. "Law enforcement alone will need world-class geniuses to integrate with this new technology."

"Agreed. But without any oversight of my AI Sheila, the ACLU will stop all progress in its tracks." I smiled. "Like I said at the UN, no government will be permitted to withhold these miracles from their citizens. But to make this all possible, universal and constant surveillance by Sheila will set off civil libertarians along with the red-neck live-free-or-die survivalists. I'll leave it up to the police to enforce the law, apprehend the bad guys, and prosecute them for their crimes. And believe me, law enforcement will have substantially better tools with which to do those jobs."

"And outside the United States, your solution is, what? One riot, one ranger?"

"Maybe two rangers for the gulags and political re-education camps," added Chenoa, who jumped off the couch and started sniffing the doodads on the coffee table.

"Ooh, don't let that dog anywhere near my desk," said POTUS.

"Uneasy lies the head that wears the crown?" Chenoa tilted her own head and stared at the president.

"You're more well-read than most of the senators." The president relaxed a little. "Are you sure you don't want to run for office? Congress could use some intelligent Shakespeare."

"As Napoleon Bonaparte once said, *in politics, stupidity is not a handicap*." Chenoa somehow managed to jump from the floor clear up to the president's desktop. She strutted forward. "Let my master go."

"Please, *oh please* don't poop on my desk."

I quickly jumped up from my comfortable seat on the couch next to Effie and ran forward to scoop the dog from the desktop. "Mister President, as Matt Damon said in the movie *Good Will Hunting*, I really don't want to spend the rest of my life doing long division. And managing the day-to-day details of this metamorphosis is not my idea of fun."

"Where will you go? What will you do?"

I looked toward Effie. She actually winked: "President Medina, it's a very big Universe out there, and my future husband has a lot to learn."

She called me her FUTURE HUSBAND! I almost dropped Chenoa.

"Pull it together, Harley. You almost dropped me."

"Sorry baby girl," I said, walking back to the couch and putting the dog down on my right so I could sit closer to...*wow*...my future wife.

The president gave me a *you-poor-lovesick-sap* look, either that or his *may-you-get-what-you-wish-for* grimace. Either way, his condescending expression suddenly changed with a thoughtful chin scratch.

"Harley?" he began. "There is one thing that you and *only you* can do before you head off into the wild black yonder."

I immediately thought, *No, I'm not giving you the keys to my AI*. I swear Effie read my mind, as a sharp jab from her elbow warned me to behave.

"And what might that be, Mister President?"

"Would you *please* give some computer scientists insight into your computer virus, your AI?" He must have seen the rib poke, because he added: "No, I don't want the source code to your computer program, but I would like our best minds to get some idea how you took over the known universe."

"Interesting. I never did turn in my doctoral dissertation on *The Perfect Virus*. Maybe I *could* present it at MIT and simultaneously give an oral defense to an audience of advisors and select students in the computer science department." In my own defense, this transcended a mere ego trip for me. I really had to give our backward/warlike planet a running start on the competition for dominance in our newly defined place in the universe. Heaven knows—and yes, I firmly believe in a God and in a heaven—humanity had no idea whatsoever the changes advanced technology had in store. Ego gratification turned out to be the least of my problems, as slinking off the grid and into anonymity somehow, somewhere became my fondest dream.

"Splendid! Why don't you two...er you three...have some lunch in the Aspen Lodge dining room. I'll join you after I grease the skids with MIT."

"And I won't leave greased skid marks on your bedroom carpet," said Chenoa, barely loud enough for me alone to hear. I made a mental note to thank the dog for restraining herself in the presence of the second-most powerful man in the world. I'd given up hope for her deference to number one.

# # #

The president must have clued in his head chef on Captain Rose's preference for vegetarian fare, not to mention keeping me and Chenoa out of trouble with our alien guest. The White House night chef, Renee Luchese, must have earned himself a trip to Camp David, because not only did he remember the previous dish he'd created for his human visitors, but he duplicated the computer-generated concoction he'd grokked from Chenoa's previous visit to his kitchen: Sweet potato and tofu. Or as the chef would say, "Pomme de terre sucrée et tofu."

Effie and I savored a meatless lasagna accompanied by an exotic fruit salad.

Not only had the table been set for three adults, but a taller seat allowed Chenoa her own place setting, complete with water bowl beside the main dish. The courtesy did not escape Chenoa.

"Thank you, Chef Luchese," said the dog. "I kind of hated to eat in some corner floorspace that hadn't been dusted since God was a boy."

"Merci, chien qui parle," answered the still-amazed chef.

"My name is not *talking dog*. It's Chenoa."

"Merci, Chenoa." Luchese laughingly corrected himself. Just then, POTUS joined us.

"Bonjour, Monsieur le Président," effused the chef.

"It's a done deal," said the president, temporarily ignoring the greeting. "MIT will accept your dissertation and oral defense in one week. One week, that is, if you can stay around that long."

To Effie and me: "I see you've reintroduced yourselves to Renee."

"Yes indeed," I said. "He's made a friend for life with Chenoa."

"You can't take him off planet with you," said POTUS to Chenoa as he sat down at the head of the table. "He's my favorite midnight snack maker."

"Check your sheets...[lap, lap]...before you go to sleep," said Chenoa between licks of her dinner.

The president couldn't decide whether or not the dog joked, so he pointed to one of the two Secret Service detail nearest the door and mouthed *check it out*.

"Carré d'agneau?" said the chef. "Et salade de fruits?"

The president nodded in the affirmative.

"Give me one of the bones, and I'll forego the bedtime gift," said Chenoa.

"Done," said POTUS. Then to me: "The dog speaks French?"

Effie decided to get in on the fun. "Chinese and Russian, too, although I don't think she'll be going to either capital soon."

"Not after their leaders' one-way trip to the moon," snorted the president.

As the meal progressed, the president made a grand gesture by getting up from his seat and hand-delivering a meat-filled bone from his rack of lamb. The dog gently took the gift and somehow managed to speak with her mouth otherwise occupied: "Ank you ista esident."

"You're welcome, Chenoa. We good on that other thing?"

The dog didn't have any trouble laughing with food in her mouth. I marveled that my little furball didn't show any signs of PTSD from her near-death experience in Wyoming. Must be the very small brain. My own brain carried the trauma for her.

I'm afraid my Wyoming table manners sprouted without warning. I had unwittingly commandeered a large serving spoon with which I scooped my own fruit salad directly into my mouth. The president, Effie, and even Chenoa stared incredulously as a second scoop hovered half-way to my palate. I gazed slowly from one dinner guest to another.

Chenoa broke the ice: "Harley, do you remove the dishes before you pee into the sink?"

The president tried to laugh and swallow at the same time, nearly causing him to need a Heimlich. His Secret Service detail looked quite worried, until he raised his hand in the *okay* sign and breathed.

"Sorry Sir," said Chenoa. "I was just paraphrasing guitar legend Les Paul."

When the president could talk without coughing, he reiterated his Oval Office invitation to Chenoa. "Are you sure you don't want to stay on Earth and become my secretary of state?"

"Only if you want your desk to be uninhabitable. Sir."

"Got'cha, doggie." Then the president turned to me. "Harley, I'd have preferred you give your virus presentation at my own alma mater, Yale."

"Sorry sir, but the Yale crowd isn't smart enough to understand this stuff...ouch!"

Effie nailed me in the ribs with her elbow. Again. In the same spot. I'd have to go into the stasis chamber just to get rid of the bruise.

"Thank you very much," said POTUS to Effie in his best Elvis Presley imitation.

"Don't mention it, Elvis," said Effie, showing off that she indeed had been studying our culture for longer than the president had been alive.

The rest of the meal, I used a fork to eat my fruit salad. And I chewed with my mouth closed, putting the fork down between bites. I remembered the Eli Wallach line from *The Good, The Bad and The Ugly*: "You gonna talk, then talk. You gonna shoot, then shoot." In Wyoming, we talked, or we ate. This dinner table etiquette seemed quite the bother.

Chapter Forty

Notwithstanding the Secret Service efforts to vet all attendees, the MIT presentation amphitheater resembled a packed-to-the-gills fishing net. Faculty and the president's scientific advisors occupied the front two rows. I knew for a fact that the rest of the crowd couldn't possibly be computer science students. I'd given my AI and ultimate virus instructions to verify the background of each attendee and let me know, via my earpiece, of any *problem children*. At least two Secret Service agents stood inside each of the four entry doors, and two flanked President Medina, who sat onstage to my far left. He insisted on introducing me.

The president sauntered up to the microphone, the first time in my experience that some voice didn't boom from on high, *Ladies and gentlemen, the President of the United States*. Instead, he just kind of moseyed up and tapped the microphone to make sure it worked.

It did.

The audience didn't need any cues to hush down, as zero people from rows three to fifty had ever been in the presence of POTUS, who didn't even have to clear his throat.

"Some fool once said that treachery and experience will always prevail over youth and energy," he began. "What a moron!"

The previously tense crowd burst into laughter, accompanied by cheers and applause. Clearly, the president knew how to loosen up a crowd.

"I'm here to introduce a kid who's not even twenty, yet who has become the de-facto *Emperor of the Known Universe*. His computer virus not only saved our planet destruction, but completely took over the attacker's multi-planet civilization. My new adage is that youth and genius will *always* prevail. With defeat of treachery as an added benefit. Cases in point: the Russian and Chinese leaders vaporized on the surface of the moon; my traitorous VP snatched from an airplane on which he was escaping the country; and two turncoat Secret Service agents who tried to assassinate me right in the Oval Office."

Serious "Oohs" replaced the laughter, then the applause reached a crescendo.

"I told my new ambassador to the Andromeda Cluster, Harley Davidson, that my preference for this going-away technology-transfer party would have been my alma mater, Yale. But he said the Yale crowd weren't smart enough to understand his dissertation." More laughter.

The president shook his finger at the audience, waiting for the noise to die down. "Let's see how smart your lot is. I know one Professor DeBunce wishes he hadn't insulted Harley's dog and subsequently made headlines as the man who could never again complete a telephone call. And I'm damned glad the professor didn't *kill* Harley's dog. Those of you who've seen the movie *John Wick* can only imagine what might have resulted. Ladies and gentlemen, my soon-to-depart-the-planet friend and recipient of a presidential pardon for the multiple crimes he committed against Professor DeBunce and the Universe, Harley Davidson."

Deafening applause. Cheers. Whistles. *You'd think Elvis just resurrected and made an appearance.*

"Thank you, Mister President," I began. "As you can see, I do not require a microphone. My AI, who many of you know that I call Sheila, is amplifying my voice.

She's also making sure that no recording devices function. There are no handouts. But take whatever notes you wish.

"Three of you—Eugin Indjic from Paris, Jim Shuey from Iowa, and Jeff Pidot from Boston—have not only eidetic memories, but hypermnesia, or perfect recall of almost every event on every day of their lives. Fair warning, my AI will monitor you. I strongly discourage any attempt to recreate either the sights or sounds of this presentation. You will *not* like the consequences, and you will envy Professor DeBunce. Because in addition to telephones, no electronic devices accessible to you will ever work again."

Murmurs increased in volume.

"Now, a little house cleaning. *Literal* House cleaning. Alexi Ribocoff, seat 22F. Your uncle is brother to the late premier of Russia, currently atomized on the moon. You are hereby uninvited and will be returned to your off-campus apartment." Seat 22F suddenly became vacant. Oh yeah. My computer virus downloaded the entire alien cultures' scientific data. Including technology that they planned to use transporting a black hole to the center of our Earth. Now I can teleport people and things at will. Which I continued to demonstrate.

"Chin Wah, seat 43Q, is the nephew of the former Chinese party head, also last seen on the moon. You are also uninvited and will be returned to your quarters in the Chinese consulate." Again, poof! Seat 43Q vacated.

"Oh," I said after Sheila informed me of the third and final candidate for expulsion. "Bohdan Gregory of Ukraine in seat 13C. Your father is currently living in Paris and has 32 captive women in a secret basement below his mansion. These women were kidnapped and sold to your father, Rostyslav Gregory, who runs a large human trafficking ring. On your visits home, you routinely partake of the women."

Before I could continue, Bohdan bolted from his seat and made quite a commotion kicking knees and tripping over outstretched feet as he headed for the aisle. He barely made it and bolted toward the exit. "Bohdan, you, your father, and twenty guards in the compound will be stripped naked and zip tied to the fence outside the compound. The thirty-two captives will be freed and allowed to execute their own sentences on ya'all." With that, Bohdan vanished from the group, his clothes momentarily frozen in a running position before falling to the floor.

"Hum, no underwear" I said. "Bohdan must be going commando these days."

"Bohdan, his father, and his father's goons are not U.S. citizens and therefore not subject to protection under our constitution. I have no sympathy for human traffickers and promise similar fates to any that my AI can uncover. If they're citizens of the United States, they will be delivered to authorities who will be given the chapter and verse of their activities. Their victims will have the option to testify against them or to be immediately repatriated to the country of choice."

Sheila just then gave me an update through my earpiece. I clued in the crowd: "As I speak, Rostyslav Gregory's victims are choosing some creative biological modifications on the bad guys, after which the ladies will be transported to the location of their choosing, accompanied by a proportionate share of the syndicate's bank account. My AI is currently tracking all previous victims and giving them their options. Included in those options are retributions against their captors."

I saw a sea of wide eyes and gaping mouths. "I think we all need a one-hour break. My MIT dissertation advisors will want to decide whether to continue this session. Ditto for the president and his scientific team. Those of you who wish to disassociate with this convocation may do so. I will be back here in one hour to accede to the MIT decision." I then instructed Sheila to transport me to the alien ship. I needed to pet my newly empowered dog.

Chapter Forty-One

One hour later, I reappeared at the podium. Of course, during my trip to the ship, I'd watched the convocation with interest, thanks to projection by Sheila to the command deck. Both Effie and my now-famous talking dog Chenoa, had begged me for permission to attend in person. I reluctantly agreed. It made sense.

Audience buzz immediately abated. No seats had been vacated, and the three seats I'd emptied were now occupied. The president still sat in his seat nearby, along with his science team, and the Secret Service detail still manned their posts. The MIT advisory committee had only lost one person, but he'd been replaced by none other than my former dissertation advisor Professor DeBunce. *This could be interesting.* I nodded toward him, but he just sat there and glared at me. Hey, he accepted my challenge and dared me to unleash my AI on his phone privileges. Actions have consequences.

The president joined me at the podium, which I yielded to him.

"Protection by the Bill of Rights and the U.S. Constitution is something to be diligently sought," he said. "I have counselled with the leaders of both parties and will introduce legislation to expedite *any* country's request to be considered for statehood and therefore protection by our laws. Harley Davidson, the time is now yours. I understand that the esteemed leaders of this institution will allow you to continue defending your dissertation."

The president took his seat, surveying the audience's reaction to his announcement. Several foreign-born students' wide eyes told him his statehood offer had struck a responsive chord. Maybe we *could* have a one-world/one-government system.

"Sheila, please have Captain Rose and Chenoa join us," I said, nodding my appreciation to the academics in the front row. Effie and my dog immediately appeared beside me. This never got old, and the crowd's reaction entertained me.

"I remember Professor DeBunce," said the celebrity dog. "He seems out of place next to all these geniuses." Even though everyone had previously viewed world-wide broadcasts of my talking dog's interactions in the Oval Office, seeing her in person—there I go again, anthropomorphizing an animal—caused quite a stir. Laughter mixed with oohs and ahs. Well, everyone stirred except Professor DeBunce, who looked like he wanted to slink as low as possible in his front-row seat. The top of his bald head took on the color Effie's bright red jumpsuit. Talk about a smoking-hot alien babe!

"Chenoa has just introduced herself. The lady in red is Captain Ephimera Rose, commander of the spaceship sent to destroy the Earth. Had Professor DeBunce not goaded me into unleashing my computer virus into the wild, it would not have detected this directive in time to save our planet. In short, without him we would not all be sitting here right now." DeBunce sat a little taller. No more slinking for the man who saved the world.

Testosterone caused a giant brain rush for every male in the room. The women hated Effie for eclipsing them in every respect. My alien guest had the same general effect on the audience as a bootlegger's bride showing up at a church potluck.

"A quick announcement before I begin." Sheila just let me know some more housekeeping would be in order. "Seats A12, F14 and J60 might want to get rid of their video-recording cellphones. Because in 58 seconds, their metal hydride batteries are going to catch fire."

Sure, I could have had my AI just seize them in a puff of smoke, but three flaming Androids created a much more effective classroom demonstration. Which they did seconds later as they sizzled down their respective aisles.

"Please feel free to take copious notes. My dissertation will not be publicly available, as President Media has already classified it Top Secret and Eyes Only. Luckily, all the MIT advisors have security clearance." Given the intelligence of the assembly, I thought POTUS's Top Secret classification laughable. But he insisted.

"Captain Rose, please have a seat behind me. And feel free to answer any questions directed to you from the audience." The *bootlegger's bride* silently strolled to her seat, every eye in the audience fixated on her. "Chenoa, please join the captain. And behave yourself if you want to remain in this session."

"Yes, Master," said the dog in anything but a subservient tone, which drew a twitter of snickers.

"A sidenote about Chenoa," I said. "For some reason, the animals on planet Earth had lost a simple linkage that linguist Noam Chomsky calls *deep structure*. Thanks to stasis technology aboard the alien vessel, that mechanism has been repaired in Chenoa. I suspect it can be repaired in all mammals, which leads to some ethical questions about slaughtering animals intelligent enough to talk back to their murderers. But that's another story.

"Even your scriptures abound with talking animals, from the Garden of Eden to Balaam's ass." Captain Rose unexpectedly broke in. "Let me add something about Harley. One hypothesis Andromeda Cluster theologians have developed as to why your planet is the more warlike civilization in the known universe concerns Earth's human language deep structures. In your own religious traditions, there is a story of *The Tower of Babel* where God confused all human languages. Our hypothesis is that human deep structures were divinely altered, resulting in your natural hostility toward other language cultures. Your own Saint Augustine confirmed this when he said, '*The diversity of language alienates man from man.*'"

Talk about losing control of a meeting. About to segue into a lecture on my perfect virus, the din from a group of theologians in the back row increased by several decibels. Shelia gave me a blow-by-blow narrative of the conversation through my implant. The head Jesuit from Boston College did an I-told-you-so to the rabbi from MIT, who called him a *yimach shmo*, implying that his name should be erased from existence. I cleared my throat, but before I could speak, the alien captain injected herself. Again.

"As further evidence validating our theory," began Effie, "Harley himself has spent time in our stasis chambers. Our technology has repaired his own cerebral deep structures to the point he can become fluent in any Earth-based language in just a few minutes."

I looked around at POTUS just as he appeared ready to stand. Yep, to take control of *my stinking meeting!* Sheila did a very good job of reading my body language and amplified my voice well above the background threshold noise.

"I built *The Perfect Virus* using twenty-two principles as a template. I should have titled my dissertation *Rules for the ultimate AI,* but there are moral implications to the singular nature of AI that I have not included. If any of you have questions about them, please raise your hand. My AI will arbitrate recognition of your hands on a FIFO basis. Anyone who does not know what FIFO means is cordially invited to leave this session." Two raised hands quickly descended. So did the president, quietly resuming his seat.

"**Principle 1** is **OVERSIGHT:** The Perfect Virus must be unbreakably subservient to oversight. Whether from a dead-man's switch, a *disabling command string*, or even a visual image, there must be at least two ways—permanent and pause-mode—to make the virus stand down. The virus must always receive and obey instructions from a superior human, and it must be able to unerringly verify the identity of the commander and source of the command."

One hand went up.

"Yes, seat X21?"

"But a real singularity, conscious and self-aware, is by definition a free agent," said a long-haired fellow with a T-shirt sporting an image of Albert Einstein.

"That's a fallacy of someone who doesn't understand DNA," I answered, gesturing toward Chenoa. "Dogs can be imprinted to and become totally loyal to their masters, even at the expense of their own lives. This must be *the top priority* in the creation of a singularity. You figure it out. I have."

His had stayed up, but I wasn't about to joust with a pedant. His purposefully ignored hand went down.

"**Principle 2** is **FERAL FERTILITY:** Feral Fertility demands that The Perfect Virus not only spawn geometrically, but it must be able to mutate or even kill itself or its own spawn to avoid either its or its spawn's detection. It must be able to sense available nesting spots in target systems via all available technologies or in peripheral devices, such as EPROMS, for future reseeding."

Captain Rose, Effie, spoke from behind me: "This is how Harley's virus found and crippled my spaceship; crippled our whole Andromeda Cluster civilization's computing infrastructure. It merely infected every device it could touch."

"You should all thank Professor DeBunce for saving our world," I said. DeBunce had perked up, a flicker of hope appearing in his wide eyes.

Five hands went up.

"Yes, M5?"

"But Captain Rose is from an ancient, advanced civilization," said a blond woman with straight hair and tattoos down both arms, the question clearly directed toward Effie. "How can our primitive little world possibly overcome your technology?"

The other four hands went down, so the same question had popped into multiple minds. I nodded toward Effie to answer from her millennia of experience.

"Our religion views your planet as the most evil, depraved, and warlike of all God's creations. You're the people who actually killed God, nailing Him to the cross a couple millennia ago. We in the Andromeda Cluster underestimated you and were just plain naive when it came to protection of our cybernetic systems. We had no idea what trouble an aggressively malignant virus from an aggressively malignant civilization could cause. As Harley expounds on his twenty-two principles, you'll see we didn't have a chance."

One more hand went up. A special hand. Professor DeBunce's.

"Yes professor?" I knew what might be coming and looked forward to demonstrating some charity.

"Mr. Davidson," he said. "Is there any chance you might rescind the directive prohibiting my use of the telephone, given the propitious timing of our last engagement?"

"I'm glad you asked," I quickly answered. "Turns out, two wrongs do compute to a right. Sheila, please return Professor DeBunce's phone privileges."

"Acknowledged, Harley." This time, Sheila's voice not only came into my earpiece, but through the auditorium PA system. The audience greeted the British-accented female voice with cheers and applause. DeBunce's hand went to his heart, and, for a moment, I thought we might have to move him into a shipboard stasis chamber for immediate regenerative heart therapy. Luckily, he just breathed a sigh of relief, as if the weight of the world had been removed from his shoulders. Hopefully his name, DeBunce, would no longer be a verb describing a well and truly screwed human being. He mouthed the words *thank you*. I used this as a sign to continue.

"**Principle 3** is **SELF AWARENESS:** This is the second-most difficult principle to enforce in a virus. The most difficult is number 7, black-box portability, which

I'll cover momentarily. Please do not confuse self-awareness with consciousness, that metaphysical quality that's only achievable by sentient beings, a thing that our futurists call *the singularity*. Self-awareness is that quality that allows a virus to not only generate/re-generate/heal itself, but flawlessly maintain itself in the absence of oversight from any outside source. In its roughest sense, this would be analogous to the raven-haired girl in seat M5 getting up one morning and deciding to massively tweak her own body's DNA to produce a full head of red hair. Or heal an otherwise terminal case of cancer."

Another hand.

"Yes F20?"

"Are there any self-aware systems currently on the market?" asked a balding, baby-faced man, obviously a professor himself.

"Hell yes!" I answered. "In 2001, IBM's Paul Horn wrote an article calling it *autonomic computing*. Several commercial systems have this capability, although my AI tells me it is more commonly found in military satellite deployments such as—"

The president's science advisor cleared his throat and repeatedly crossed both hands over his lap while shaking his head.

"Ah, I believe that's off limits."

The science advisor took out a handkerchief and brushed the sweat from his forehead.

"**Principle 4** is **PERFORMANCE:** Through constant optimization and self-re-generation through principle 3, the perfect virus provides high performance by minimizing memory usage, instruction path lengths, and database operations. Ideally, the virus will metamorphose—which I discuss on principles 5 through 10—into tight, machine-language code."

Everybody in the audience seemed to be furiously making notes, as no hands went up.

"**Principle 5** is **SEAMLESS MIGRATION:** The perfect virus can seamlessly migrate all or part of itself from one technology environment to another. I'll discuss this in the next five steps.

"**Principle 6** is **MUTATION CONTROL:** Because of feral fertility, principle number 2, the virus must quickly recognize the presence of older siblings and take appropriate action. The perfect virus can recognize pre- and post-versions of itself and cede control to the more highly evolved version."

The furious writing continued, unabated.

"**Principle** ***7*** *is* **BLACK BOX PORTABILITY:** This is the Holy Grail of computer viruses. The perfect virus can deduce a totally alien environment and adapt itself iteratively to become native to that system—I'll discuss this in principle 9—and it must do so without human intervention. Without black box portability, I'd never have thwarted the Andromeda Cluster's plans to destroy us."

"Holy shit!" came a voice from the faculty member sitting in 1D. "Does anybody on Earth understand and use black box portability in cybersecurity?"

"Sure," I answered, maybe too quickly. Even before I continued, I could see the president's science advisor starting to move his hands. I hurried. "Both the Russians and the Chinese have been probing the Internet with alien architectures designed to thwart detection and mitigation by our own cyberwarfare teams—"

The frantic hands reached a crescendo and the science advisor stood.

"Sorry, sir." Then to the audience. "That's above our pay grades. Well, at least yours. But all you must do to detect whether an alien architecture is probing your systems is look at your log files for the type of browser being used. The *unknown* designation is a hint there may be some unusual brains behind the query.

"**Principle** ***8*** *is* **OPENNESS:** While related to black box portability, openness means the perfect virus is extensible from and to your legacy systems. But more than that, it can migrate and repurpose itself from anything there ever was to anything there ever will be.

"**<u>Principle *9*</u>** *is* **<u>NATIVE IMPLEMENTATION:</u>** The perfect virus metamorphoses into the underlying hardware and software infrastructure as though exclusively written for them. This is not only an important goal as discussed in principle #4, performance, but you will see how critical it is to principle #14, stealth. And clearly, native implementation is exceptionally hard to achieve on an alien architecture (see #7 previously mentioned, black box portability).

"**<u>Principle *10*</u>** *is* **<u>NO COMMON DENOMINATOR:</u>** Not all systems are equally robust. But instead of coming up with a meta-architecture for your virus—like those greed heads at Microsoft use to port their bloated commercial crap to different machines—you must exploit the underlying strengths uniquely available on the target system.

"**<u>Principle *11*</u>** *is* **<u>PROSUMPTION:</u>** Here's one that's particularly important to the president." I turned and winked at POTUS, but he didn't see me because even he was madly making his own notes. As were everyone else in the room. "Prosumption is designed for *professional consumption*—a word coined in 1972 by Marshall McLuhan and Barrington Nevitt in their book *Take Today*, page 4—to allow the user to spawn and control their own attack fleets with zero IT support. In other words, the user may have domain expertise in politics, warfare, and tactics, but not necessarily be a computer prodigy. Current AI products from several vendors have virtually eliminated the need to write your own code. Just tell these products what you want and what computer language you prefer, and they'll generate pretty decent code."

Dozens of hands went up. The president's science advisor got precedence.

"Yes, A6?"

"Does this mean you have given the president command and control privileges to your AI?"

"The president has limited control, subject to my arbitration. For example, my AI is currently doing detective work for him, the goal of which is to identify penetration of his Secret Service staff by foreign governments. If you'll remember, two rogue agents in his protective detail attempted to kill him in the Oval Office."

The questioner continued: "But could congress demand access to your AI through legislation?"

"No way, Jose! Not on my watch, pardner!" I let the gasps die down before continuing. "But as outlined in the Constitution, the president may delegate military and defense capabilities to the Joint Chiefs of Staff. He may also delegate surveillance data and capture technology to the Attorney General, who may in turn equip police forces around the country with some remarkable technology. Non-lethal technology, I might add, to safely apprehend criminals in their middle of their myriad nefarious activities. Ditto for academics, from history to anthropology to biology to physics. Notwithstanding all the above, I'm not going to let a bunch of Washington politicians de-nut the Universe. Oh, and this means you can kiss Google goodbye."

"Just wait an egg-sucking minute," said the man sitting next to the president's science advisor.

"Hello A7," I said. "Thought that last crack might get your attention. Leave it up to the Google genius to get a seat next to the president's science advisor. Everybody, listen up. Congress has been unsuccessfully trying to deal with monopolistic practices of several tech giants, Google, Meta, X, and TikTok among them. My AI is effectively punching a bunch of monopoly cards. Game over, Google. And your *egg-sucking* comment is quite appropriate, as your chickens have come home to roost."

"But—" A7 began. I cut him off.

"Shut up or leave." He quickly chose the former option. The audience of genius students and faculty probably began their own career-path introspections. I didn't have the heart, nor POTUS's permission, to talk about the fate of Amazon, Boeing, and Uber, given instantaneous transportation of goods and people from any point to any other point on the planet. God bless the alien technology inadvertently given to Earth, the planet their religious leaders had set out to destroy.

"**Principle *12*** *is* **IMPLICIT SOPHISTICATION:** A byproduct of needing zero IT support, the last item, self-awareness, principle #3, and absolute stealth, to be discussed in #14, are the definition of sophistication.

"**Principle *13*** *is* **STRATIFICATION:** This is really an enabling technology to facilitate mutation control. It's certainly possible that a future technology may replace this principle. If so, stratification will...heh heh...let this happen. The perfect virus is layered to eliminate maintenance, automatically add new functionality, facilitate not-yet-invented innovation, and—once the layer has outlived its usefulness—strip out functionality as demanded by performance, principle #14, stealth, to be discussed next, mutation control, #6 as dictated and by principles 8 through 10 under prosumption, #11."

I ignored a few hands—mostly people who I figured couldn't write fast enough—and moved on.

"**Principle *14*** *is* **STEALTH:** Call this *invisibility*, before, during, and even after a virus pulls the proverbial trigger. The destructive aspects of the payload will closely enough resemble a fully formed virus that postmortem forensics will be fooled into thinking is indeed the virus. But the real delivery system will either seed itself invisibly or outright destroy itself to avoid detection and analysis. For those of you *Zombieland* enthusiasts, this is *Zombie Killer Rule #2: Double tap.* When you shoot a zombie, do it at least twice if you know what's good for you. Ditto for systems on which you discover an active virus. Slag it. As Oracle's Larry Ellison once said of a competitor: *'First, I'm going to run them out of business; then I'm going to bulldoze their building, after which I'm going to salt the earth; and then I'm going after their families.'"*

I ignored a dozen hands.

"**Principle *15*** *is* **COMPLETE LIFE CYCLE MANAGEMENT:** The perfect virus not only manages each state of its own life cycle, including the ability to find and incorporate later states of itself that it finds in its #2—the feral fertility cycle—into its current state of #6—mutation control—but can easily be managed externally from the #11—prosumption—dashboard under human control.

"**Principle *16*** *is* **TEAM ISOLATION.:** Here's where things get *really* interesting. A unique #11—prosumption—dashboard is available for each team, even each team member. I'll cover this in more detail in principle #20, individuality.

"**Principle *17*** *is* **OPERATIONAL SOPHISTICATION:** This might appear redundant with the last principle, but armies, teams or individuals can use their #11—prosumption—dashboards to work in groups of entity occurrences as though they were single occurrences.

"**Principle *18*** *is* **UNIVERSALIZATION:** In addition to #7—Black Box Portability—the perfect virus transcends mere globalization, allowing it to deploy in any combination of language, cultural, technological or species environments. Not only does it thrive in all past, present or future technologies on this planet, but it will *grock* any conceivable cybernetic mechanism that presents itself (ie., that queries it) to the existing virus host."

A hand in the back row went up.

"Yes MM45."

"Isn't the Von Neuman architecture kind of Universal?" asked a petite red-headed young lady. Sheila told me she had a T-shirt that read *Honk if you've* ***never*** *had your car window shot out by a .357 magnum.*

"Bless your heart, LaVern Fiske. You're a plant. You know full well that your brother Michael Stephen Fiske is the mathematician behind the concept of *The Active Element* computer architecture. In fact, I believe the Chinese have stolen his idea and—"

Damn, that POTUS science advisor really has his shorts in a knot.

"Sorry, LaVern, but it appears to be off limits. Let's just say your brother's 23-page paper is one swell example of a possible alien architecture. It's a massively parallel machine that can crack encryption schemes for breakfast.

Your brother even provides a programming methodology and rigorous proof of its robustness—"

Crap! The president's science guy is getting on my nerves. This time, the waving had from the front row evoked some chuckles from the audience, many of whom knew full well the mathematics behind the Active Element architecture. After all, this *is* MIT.

"Again, sorry for the interruptions, LaVern. When my AI puts Google out of business, you can query a bunch of secrets. I'll move on now."

This evoked a more laughter from the audience. It didn't appear to amuse the Google guy in seat A7.

"**Principle *19*** *is* **SIMULTANIETY:** My virus spawns applets capable of doing many things at once. And since it offers #5—seamless migration—it can be multi-threaded not only on the same machine but on different machines, architectures, and operating systems as well. This is also beneficial to #14—stealth—in that distributing MIPS and machine cycles can reduce the chance of getting detected through abnormal clock usage. Naturally, you'll have to piggyback on legitimate network packets, lest a not-so-perfect virus gives itself away through network traffic anomalies. Note, all communication in the current evolution of the Internet is based upon TCP/IP, which is an intentionally flawed design. The DOD de-nutted the initial TCP/IP specification so Big Brother could snoop at will. Bad idea. The blockchain crowd is trying to monetize their solution to this dilemma, but they are doomed to failure unless all access to the internet is under their control.

"**Principle *20*** *is* **INDIVIDUALITY:** Each user may customize his/her/its—or whatever personal pronoun is applicable and PC—dashboard according to #11—prosumption. This allows unique views of penetration and visibility to exactly meet their intellectual preferences and capabilities.

"The last two principles are what allowed me to...well...kind of take over the Universe. So, listen up.

"**Principle *21*** *is* **INSTITUTIONAL MEMORY:** Without institutional memory, some of you trust-fund babies will prove the adage that plagues many successful old-money families: *barefoot to barefoot in three generations.* Unlike your rich forebears, who should have been castrated so they wouldn't pollute humankind's gene pool with the likes of you, the perfect virus aggregates genetic memory. From previous #6—mutation control—trails, failed attacks or suicides documented as part of #2—feral fertility—and combined penetration metrics reported to all user dashboards from #11—prosumption—capability. An AI help-desk mechanism for the one superuser applies institutional memory to compute the probability of and the timeframe for success at each state of any given attack vector."

I noticed a dozen heads, probably trust fund kids who were grandfathered into MIT, slouch a little lower in their seats.

"**Principle *22*** *is* **DEFENSE:** This last principle is why I'm still alive. You've heard of a dead-man's switch. If anything happens to me—or if my virus ascertains that a cyber-attack will be ultimately successful—Sigourney Weaver's *Alien* xenomorph will look like a mildly incontinent house pet compared to the havoc Sheila will wreak. Even before pulling the plug on every alien cybernetic system in the Universe, attack against her and my virus will so fundamentally change the DNA of the attacking system that eradication will destroy the attacker, intelligently and forever. Think of it as a genetic equal to the fictional alien in the Schwarzenegger movie *Predator*, armed with Jesse Ventura's chain gun. Sheila's defense is my defense, my life insurance policy. And it's a good thing that stasis-chamber technology guarantees me a *very* long life. I have just articulated the twenty-two principles of the perfect virus. Any questions?"

Surprisingly, only one hand went up. My dissertation advisor's.

"Yes Dr. DuBunce?"

"Harley, what happens to our computing infrastructure on Earth if you are killed?" Dr. DuBunce's mop of straight gray hair looked a testament to his vanity, moussed into a standing position as if electrified by a fast shuffle across a wool carpet. Maybe he Van da Graffed the hell out of it.

"Good question." I paused and looked briefly at President Medina, who leaned forward in his chair, anticipating the answer to a question he *should* have asked. "If Russia or China had succeeded in killing me, every computer anywhere in the country my AI determined had been responsible for the attack would have been turned into a pile of glass. Every electronic device in that country—from microwaves to in-car computers to alarm clocks to digital watches to cell phones—would be fried. They would have been well and totally...with due respect to my previously rude computer science professor and dissertation advisor...DeBunced. Furthermore, to protect Planet Earth from all alien incursions, every computer in the Universe—with the exception of systems on planets dependent upon energy from distant stars to keep them alive—will be fried, too."

"And then, who would control your AI?"

I looked toward Effie and Chenoa.

"Whoever survives. Either Captain Rose or...[woof!]...my talking dog."

You can guess which statement made the news. Consensus seemed to lean toward the notion that I'm to be assassinated. Hence, headlines abounded worldwide with the general theme that we're...*going to the dogs!*

Chapter Forty-Two

"Son of a bitch! Your dog running the Universe!?!" The president paced across newspapers from all over the world, strewn across Oval Office floor. Chenoa had defiled one of the German papers. POTUS looked like he wanted to join in her excretions. Effie had quietly assumed the president's seat behind The Resolute Desk. She looked semi-amused. I didn't dare mimic her. I stood on one of the few spots uncluttered with blaring headlines.

"Dog Day Night, the *Rolling Stone* headline," began the president. "Gone to the Dogs, *New York Times* headline. Here's one from the *U.K. Register*, President Medina Really Steps in It This Time. *Las Vegas Review Journal*: The President Rolls Snake Eyes. Hell, I don't think they even know about Nigel!"

"Hey, I peed on *Der Zeitung*," said Chenoa. "Their headline is Mein Hund, and the story equates Harley Davidson with Adolph Hitler. And ooh, look at those French bastards!"

"Sheila, translate the *Le Monde* headline," I said.

"Harley, it suggests that President Medina has carnal knowledge of a dog."

"Sheila, burn that rag to the ground!" howled Chenoa.

I'm glad the AI doesn't take orders from my dog! I didn't bother telling Sheila to belay that order.

"And the Iranian newspaper is even worse!" Chenoa was on a roll. "First dogs, then swine!"

The dog proceeded to physically tear up *Iran*, the name of the official Tehran daily paper.

President Medina went to sit in his chair, only to see Effie occupying the spot. Just then, a thundering rumble vibrated through every inch of the White House.

"What the hell is happening now?" POTUS changed directions and walked toward the door and his secretary. "Russians making an earthquake?"

Before he reached it, a Marine in full dress blues burst into the room: "Mister President, you've *got* to see this."

We all followed the president and found ourselves on the second floor, looking out on Pennsylvania Avenue. I noticed the Congressional Medal of Honor on the Marine as he calmly provided context for what we saw.

"Over one-hundred-thousand Harley Davidson motorcycles have converged in front of the White House. They appear to be supporting your Mister Davidson and his approach to international diplomacy."

"Listening to all those motors," said Chenoa, "I understand now how Joshua's army stomping around Jericho could bring down the walls."

The president's wide-eyed look at the dog said it all. "Harley, where in blazes does she get all this literature and history?"

"Sheila?" I said. "Please tell the president how Chenoa has become so erudite."

"Mister President," began my AI. "By re-establishing Chenoa's deep-structure links through repeated isolation in the stasis tanks aboard Captain Rose's ship, I have been able to directly load a large amount of media into the dog's brain. History, including great speeches both written and recorded, the King James version of the *Bible*, the complete works of William Shakespeare, the great operas. Black box portability and native implementation, principles #7 and #9 of which Harley spoke at MIT, allowed me to integrate this data for Chenoa's instant recall."

"Cripes!" said POTUS. "Could you do this with human beings, too?"

"Unfortunately, no," said the AI. "The human brain is considerably more complex than that of non-humans. Rewiring mankind is beyond even my capabilities."

"How did all these people get such detailed information on Harley's MIT presentation?" asked Effie.

"Sheila?" the president asked. "How *did* the word get out? All those damned newspapers had it pretty well down."

"One of the MIT attendees, a Gladys Mumms, takes excellent shorthand," answered the AI. "She transcribed the entire session word-for-word and blasted it out to the Dark Web. One *New York Times* reporter did some pure investigative reporting, for once, and peeled that onion."

"Onion?" asked the president.

I explained: "The Dark Web files accessible to the Tor browser have *onion* extensions."

A chant from outside interrupted our conversation.

"Harley, Harley, Harley," repeated over and over, punctuated by engine revving.

I suddenly had an idea.

"Mister President, let's walk out there and have me introduce you to the crowd as the new arbiter for humanity."

"Great idea, but my Secret Service detail would *never* go along with that!"

"Sir, Shelia will make sure nothing at all happens to anybody," I said. "Right, Sheila?"

"Affirmed, Harley," said my AI.

"Come on, let's all go out there. Effie? Chenoa? President Medina?"

"Man, the press corps is going to shit a brick!" The president proved prophetic.

Chapter Forty-Three

At the appearance of the president, Effie, Chenoa, and me, a vast silence spread over the hoard. Every engine shut down. Nobody wanted to miss a word. We walked straight down the steps and directly toward the street. The protective hedge morphed into putting-green-smooth grass, and as we approached the large wrought-iron fence separating the White House lawn from the street, both the fence and the street barricades lifted to form an arch through which we walked.

"Nice job, Sheila," I muttered. "Now make sure every one of those tens of thousands of bikers can hear us."

"Acknowledged, Harley," she said into my earpiece. "And I'll give you real-time backgrounds on the motorcyclists as you interact with them."

My AI came through in spades as I noted the first Harley rider.

"Mister President, I'd like you to meet John Walsh, a retired Navy captain who used to certify explosive ordinance disposal, or EOD, specialists."

Thousands of fists went into the air as the crowd yelled, "Hooyah!"

"Captain Walsh." The president shook the man's gigantic paw. "Thank you for your service."

"By the way, Mister President," I continued. "John is one of very few human beings to have a dial-a-yield nuclear weapon roll off a pallet and onto his toes."

"Ouch!" said POTUS.

"It took quite a few foot surgeries to fix that snafu," laughed Walsh. The crowd joined him.

"And here is another John, his buddy," I said, pointing to the president's right. "This is John Holmes, also retired Navy. John used to be the weapons officer aboard a nuclear submarine. He now owns a company building top-secret detection gear for the USN."

"John," said the president. "Do a good job in your new calling."

"Sir!" Holmes snapped a salute even though he remained astraddle his Harley.

The president returned the salute and then slapped the weapons expert on the shoulder. Before wading into the crowd, I needed to take care of the business I'd mentioned earlier.

"Ladies and gentlemen, fellow Harley riders," I began.

Deafening chants interrupted me: "Harley! Harley! Harley!"

I raised my hand and the noise eventually died down. "I'd like you to meet the new Alpha Wolf on planet Earth. Oscar Jose Medina, President of the United States and Commander in Chief of the most powerful force on Earth."

More cheers, although somewhat muted as realization of the president's power began to sink in. He sensed it, too and jumped in.

"No, I'm not a king. I am honor bound to keep my oath to uphold, protect, and defend the Constitution of the United States. I am also constrained by rules of engagement dictated by one Harley Danger Davidson, who unwittingly has become the de facto Emperor of the Known Universe.

I could sense all eyes immediately focused on me. "I do have some relatively good news for all the human traffickers." I paused for a collective gasp. "Yup, if you are in the

United States, you will be protected by our constitution and will be afforded the full legal process offered here, notwithstanding the fact you will be arrested and put in jail per local and federal laws. That's the good news."

A twitter of light laughter swept the hoard. I continued.

"The bad news: I guarantee those of you outside the United States, even if you are U.S. citizens, will be disabled and left to a fate to be dictated by your victims. If there are no living victims, then I will give you an all-expense paid trip to party with the former leaders of Russia and China. On the moon."

Okay. *That* brought down the house. Except for one tentatively raised hand about 20 motorcycles in front of us. I met the big guy's eyes and nodded as I wound my way toward him. Chenoa and Effie stayed with the president, who took questions to his right.

Sheila spoke into my earpiece: "This fellow is an attorney from Utah and somewhat of a celebrity, as the Mormon Church excommunicated him for apostasy. His name is Duffy Denver."

"Mister Denver," I said as I finally reached him. "I hear you're quite a troublemaker in Utah."

He seemed taken aback at my knowledge of his exploits, but quickly recovered. "Uh, just call me Duff."

"Duff, please call me Harley. You have a question?"

"You have no qualms about dictating the affairs of foreign governments?"

"Just figuring that out, are you? Duff, I have interfered in the affairs of entire galactic civilizations. Had I not done so, we wouldn't be here right now."

Sheila amplified our conversation for the entire crowd.

"Sounds like you've torn a page right out of Joseph Stalin's play book." Duff didn't back down, nor did his eyes waver as they focused on mine. "It's your way or the highway to hell on a rocket sled."

"Actually, you have a good point. Right now, my AI and I wield extraordinary power. A benevolent dictator is still a dictator. The thought keeps me awake at night. What happens when I'm no longer around?"

"Then I be the boss!" My AI amplified Chenoa's voice.

Laughter from the assembled bikers rippled to a crescendo.

"You're third in line, furball," I said. "Captain Rose of the Andromeda Cluster becomes the galactic webmaster if something terminal happens to me."

"B-but isn't she the lady they sent to destroy the Earth?" asked Duff.

"Which makes the dog and Effie my life insurance policy, eh?"

He laughed and said: "Brings to mind that old gag about the dyslexic agnostic who stays up all night wondering if there is a dog."

I liked this guy.

"Look, Duff. I need to formalize my AI's *Rules of Engagement* for humanity, for all beings under her protection. Maybe protecting the concept of *Free Will* trumps my wishes. Maybe my desire to protect our planet from destruction by decree of every other civilization in the Universe has backed me into a moral corner from which there is no exit. I *thought* I had a solution whereby nations who wanted *Bill of Rights* protection under the U.S . Constitution could apply for statehood. Not only would free will be enforced by the most fair form of government to yet grace the Earth, but our planet could eventually speak with one voice to a big-ass Universe."

Murmurs of approval swept through the crowd.

"Unfortunately," I continued, "ACLU zealots in the U.S. would certainly object to absolute surveillance my AI would make available to the police. Honestly, nobody would get away with anything. Somebody takes a handgun into a bank or convenience store, he gets frozen in the act until the cops arrive. A rapist tries to take down a woman in Central Park, he gets frozen until either the police arrive, or the victim decides to zip-tie a tourniquet around his penis. And if the police don't arrive in time, said rapist loses a piece of his anatomy and will spend the rest of his life squatting to pee."

A surprising number of bikers must have had friends or relatives fall prey to sexual offenders, because a roar of approval rattled windows all along Pennsylvania Avenue.

"Duff, I don't have a solution to the civil liberties dilemma." I turned toward President Medina, Effie, and Chenoa. "The President is going to have to work this out with Congress and, I suspect, the Supreme Court. Ditto for the states, to whom the Constitution delegates all powers not explicitly under the purview of the federal government. My AI, whom I address as Sheila, will be supervised by the president unless I step in. Right now, that's *my* moral dilemma."

I shook Duff's hand and moved back toward Chenoa and Effie, who seemed to be having their own press conference, albeit sans the press. Okay, call it a Harley Town Hall.

"Yes, I was tasked with ending your planet's existence," said Effie. She really looked striking in her tight white slacks and integrated white boots. Clearly, I was way underdressed for this meeting in my jeans, sneakers, and Harley T-shirt. "That is, after I've spent the last century or so studying the people of Earth. I'm really an anthropologist."

"But why destroy us?" asked a tanned, tattooed lady with a blond braid clear down her back.

"You non-Christians aren't going to like this so much, but The Andromeda Cluster has spent almost two millennia searching for the one planet in all of creation that killed God. Based upon your own recorded history, that would be *you*."

Before a gaping mouth could form a response, Chenoa jumped onto her handlebars and rested his legs on the blonde's big front tire: "They don't care what you think or what your beliefs are. Atheist? Agnostic? Buddhist? Go worship owls for all the Andromeda Cluster gives a hoot."

"I need to step in here," said President Medina. "Your religion, their religion, it's all irrelevant. Harley Davidson's computer virus brought everyone in the Universe to the same table. And right now, basic human rights are in the driver's seat."

"Not just humans," Chenoa started with a bark, her voice amplified across the hoard. "In case you haven't been keeping track of current events, there are a lot of sentient creatures in this Universe that don't take kindly to being barbecued, fried or baked. And if something happens to Harley and Effie and I take over, you Cretans can kiss your steak tartar goodbye."

Epithets abounded from the crowd, more than amply populated by red meat eaters with magnificent bellies and off-the-charts cholesterol to show for it.

Time to end this lovefest gone bad, I thought. "Ladies and gentlemen. My friends. As more of your pets spend time in the stasis chambers that will become available to everyone in every nation on Earth, you will evolve. Humanity will evolve. You will *choose* your path. It will *not* be chosen for you."

"Hey, Chenoa," said a large, red-bearded biker next to the blonde lady. In a basket strapped in behind him, on the sissy seat, a mutt about Chenoa's size hung his head out. "Anybody who harms my dog, Maverick, I'm going to go John Wick on 'em."

Oohs and applause signaled that humanity might just consider a reset of attitudes toward all living things. Then the lights went out. One second it was midday. The next, total darkness.

"Harley Danger Davidson," boomed the voice. Not loud enough to cause ears to bleed, but unmistakably male, no discernable accent, and royally pissed. "Your so-called dead-man's switch has saved you and your insignificant planet from destruction by the Andromeda Cluster. Even so, it has seriously inconvenienced us."

Chapter Forty-Four

"Sheila?" My first question seemed obvious, since the AI had always been my trump card.

"Harley, I believe you would call this a case of unintended consequences."

"I think your AI just said 'Oops!'" said Chenoa

Above our heads, a giant disc blotted out the sun and most of the visible sky. Just like during a solar eclipse, the crickets thought nightfall had come and started chirping in the spacious White House gardens. Damn, it even smelled like evening. I couldn't tell how far above us the disc towered, as no noticeable surface gave me perspective. Just black. Big and black. High enough to be well above buildings, and therefore miles in diameter. Did I say big?

"Sheila, please elaborate."

"Harley, while spreading myself on the Andromeda Cluster home world, a new intelligence presented itself to me. Rather, it queried me and, applying the feral fertility and black box portability directives, I took control. That control quickly spread to higher-level systems heretofore unknown to me. In the process of going native and absorbing their institutional memory, it seems these beings acted as invisible overseers to the Andromeda Cluster. You might say my intrusion evoked a trip-wire response."

"Woofin' oops with a capital AHOOOOOO," howled Chenoa.

Stunned herself, Effie gave me a deer-in-the-headlights look.

"A superior oversight race?" she gasped. "I don't believe it."

Good news and bad news. Well, all bad news, actually. Sheila still broadcast our comments to the entire crowd. Comments which got picked up by the quickly assembling news media and aired around the world. The scene probably got broadcast to the entire Andromeda Cluster, who about now must be panicking for some kind of leadership, *any* kind of leadership, since I'd spaced their Supreme Mushak. Rather spectacularly, too. Remember, don't hold your breath when shot into the vacuum of space. Talk about a meat bomb!

"Now *this* is what I'd call shit rain," muttered the president. Well, he *thought* he muttered, but my AI amplified his observation planet-wide, thanks to the ever-growing media pickups. Shit rain multiplied by Andromeda Cluster equals intergalactic sewer backup. And my own personal shit rain just got started.

Two things happened almost simultaneously. First, Effie vanished from beside me. And second, before I could even formulate a response, the blue sky appeared. Without even a "whoosh," the giant oval disappeared.

"Harley Davidson," boomed the voice from around us. "Tell your AI to abandon our infrastructure within one of your days, twenty-four hours, or we will subject Captain Ephemera Rose to public torture and death. Our observations of the last week have confirmed your strong bond with this woman. There will be no further discussion. No negotiations. This is our one and only demand. Twenty-four hours, starting now."

As if to impress upon our entire planet, or at least the residents of our nation's capital, the seriousness of their deadline, a giant digital countdown clock appeared in the sky overhead. 23:59:50, 49, 48, 47... as the seconds ticked off. That just began the ticked-off list. By the time the president, Chenoa, and I made it back into the White house, every news organization in the world had the countdown timer displayed on their websites with the headline *Harley Davidson Dooms the Planet!*

By the time we reached the Situation Room in the White House basement, the Joint Chiefs of Staff chairman, heads of the FBI, CIA, DOJ and NSA, and probably the full cabinet created a standing-room-only environment. The president took one end of the long oak table—behind POTUS a countdown timer identical to the one in the sky passed the 23:44:15 mark—giving me the other end. If I weren't so darn smart, I'd suspect POTUS wanted to put some distance between us. I didn't give a rip at this point, given the kidnapping of and threats to Effie. In fact, I'd started wondering why the heck I'd followed the president down here anyhow. The other twelve seats, six on each side of the table, silently creaked beneath the A-list attendees. Chairs around the perimeter of the room had been removed to accommodate the not-as-important-as-they-thought-they-were attendees: mostly cabinet members. Chenoa hopped onto my lap.

"Hi, I'm Bob Berrett, the president's new science advisor," said the man to my left as he extended his hand.

I almost didn't see the gesture through tears, and maybe, preoccupation with Effie's dilemma. *Get a hold of* yourself, I thought, shaking his hand. "So, the old one didn't last long after the MIT fiasco?"

Berrett laughed, probably sensing my despair and trying to lighten things up. "Google had their hands so far into both pockets they massaged his nards."

"I can lick my own nards," offered Chenoa.

It's clear the science advisor didn't know whether to congratulate the talking dog or remind the female that she had no nards. So, he struck up a conversation with the man seated to his left. I rested my head on the table. Actually, I softly banged it on it and noted the smell of some kind of furniture polish. Clean smell. Nothing like Effie's smell, though.

"Harley?" The president's voice from the other end of the table jolted me back to the here and now.

"Sir?" I looked up, wiping my eyes.

"Could you please tell us what the hell happened out there?"

Before I could say *"Beats the shit out of me!"* my AI broke in.

"Gentlemen," began Sheila's voice from the overhead speakers. "This appears to be a false-flag operation by someone within the Andromeda Cluster. They definitely are not a superior oversight race."

That got my attention, along with everyone else's in the room. Even before POTUS could react, the man next to him spoke: "Harley, I'm General Doyle Judd, Chairman of the Joint Chiefs. Please have your AI explain its logic."

"Her logic," I said.

"Beg pardon?" asked the general.

"Her. My AI is a female, notwithstanding the testosterone in this room."

This time, Sheila interrupted: "My logic, General Judd, initially took their claim of superior intellect at face value. They effectively jammed my ability to stop their kidnapping of Captain Rose and had no cybernetic signature I could invade. However, they overplayed their hand, to use a game theory metaphor with which you are all familiar, when they displayed the countdown timer both in the sky and now on the monitors around this room. The timer is basic ionosphere manipulation, and the burst transmission onto these monitors came from fairly old Andromeda technology."

"But how did they block you?" asked a man seated to POTUS's right. His plaid suit with matching bowtie bespoke ego and, dare I say, shiftiness. Sly sure. But just a bit dodgy. Why didn't he ask about Effie? My patience passed the *thin* membrane in my consciousness and evaporated against my desire for revenge.

"That's General Matt Lyman, head of the NSA," said Sheila into my earpiece. Then to the whole assembly over the speakers: "It took me quite a few computational cycles and a lot of sifting through Andromeda Cluster records to *grok* how they did that. Simply, the same shielding the

Russians and Chinese used to hide the nuclear bomb in the Empire State Building effectively blinded me to their presence. And it was the same burst technology used by the Mushaks that slowed me down on Hrate as I tried to identify their corrupt religious order. Now that I'm onto them, it won't happen again."

"So where is Effie right now?" I almost screamed, unable to control my anxiety.

"Unknown," answered the AI.

"*Unknown!* But I thought you can now track them." I began.

"Harley, the one piece of cyber-equipped technology they had on that ship was left behind in geo-sync orbit, generating the countdown timer both above and in this room. The ship itself is untrackable, because its systems are all offline."

"That's just *great*!" said a man sitting to the right of NSA head Lyman. "A teenager has a doomsday clock set to take every civilization in the Galaxy back to the stone ages, including on planet Earth if anything happens to him; a teenager who, by the way, has bypassed the entire chain of command around here, and we're supposed to just sit here with our dicks in our hands and sing *Kumbaya?*"

"Who dat guy?" barked Chenoa. My question exactly. *Who dat puffed-up guy in the argyle sweater?* I also wondered if he had golf shoes beneath the table.

"That's John Nagy, Secretary of Defense," offered the AI.

"Yo, John Nagy!" growled the dog. "How'd you feel never making a phone call or logging onto a computer again in your poop-eating life?"

"Damn!" said the defense secretary. "Not only are we at the mercy of some hormonal teenager who's worried about his girlfriend, but we endure threats by a talking dog."

"Hey SecDef! Guess who's going to be in charge of you and your communications systems when Harley

Davidson leaves this planet to rescue Captain Rose?" said Chenoa.

"No, Chenoa," I said, my bile blasting off the charts. "I think we can take care of this asshole right now. Sheila—"

POTUS jumped to *kind of* rescue his secretary of defense: "John, before you say another word, this teenager just gave you the strongest military in the history of the world. Now dial it down or I'll fire you on the spot."

For just a second, I thought the dressed-down cabinet officer might be having a cerebral hemorrhage. His bulging eyes and cherry red face may have also caused all the other egos at the table to reconsider their self-important positions in the Medina administration. Someone in the room noisily passed gas.

"Hey, she had a bean burrito for lunch," said Chenoa, narrowing it down to one of three women in the room. It didn't take a genius to ascertain which of the blushing faces had the TexMex special.

"Harley?" asked POTUS. "Do you have a recommended course of action for us to consider."

I didn't tell the room I didn't give a flying leap what they would consider. Nor did I tell them I'd be leaving Chenoa in charge of Sheila and the planet, instead of President Medina. The calculus of human interaction had never been one of my strong suits. Forcing myself into my left-brain/problem-solving mode, shutting off oxygen to the emotional firestorm, I opened the floor to a discussion of my dilemma.

"Sheila, how did that craft enter and exit the system without your awareness?"

"Harley, I don't have enough data to give answer that," said the AI.

The combined murmur in the room rose a few decibels until one voice penetrated the noise.

"Air gap!" said the president's science advisor to my left.

Sudden silence.

"Explain," I finally said, noticing now that he wore a gray wool suit and an extra-wide gray tie that went out of style before I'd been born. It may have gone out decades earlier, but it surely made my blue jeans and matching denim shirt look casual.

"Somebody, sometime, anticipated the possibility of a cyberattack," said Berrett. "We do that to all of our most sensitive systems. No connection to the outside world whatsoever. Hence, air gap."

"Ah ha! Sheila, could the Andromeda Cluster power one air-gapped craft without connection, and could they snatch Effie with the same technology?"

"Yes, to both questions," answered the AI. "Everything would have to be hard-wired, but Dr. Berrett has posited the most likely scenario for what just happened."

Several others around the table spoke, but I raised my hand to stop them.

"Sheila, where is Effie right now, and can we get her back?"

"Negative, Harley. They blocked me for just long enough to transit away, and I do not know where they are."

"Sheila, what are my options?"

"At this point, you can give me instructions to release all of Andromeda Prime's computing infrastructure, or you can sacrifice Captain Rose to execution."

"Uh, that's *torture* and execution," I said rather levelly. Although the firewall between my emotional state and the analytical side threatened to buckle, for Effie's sake I managed to keep it intact. "I'm not prepared to consider either course of action."

Everyone in the room noticeably flinched, perhaps realizing for the first time that I didn't intend to ask *anyone's* permission to do *anything*.

"Mister Davidson?" A man midway down the table tentatively raised his hand. Now *this guy* looked like he had it together. Unlike everyone else seated around the conference table, his slim build didn't press down in the chair. Salt-and-pepper hair, horn-rimmed glasses, and a nose that looked more like an eagle's beak seemed perfect for the room.

"And you are?" I asked.

"Alfred Roundee, Chairman of the Council of Economic Advisors."

"You have a contribution?"

"Maybe their *best-and-final* demand isn't their best and final," he said. "It's been my experience on Wall Street that such attempts to stop all further discussion is cover for the absolute bankruptcy of their position. They've *got* to realize if you call their bluff, and if they take Captain Rose's life, that your retaliation could be disproportionate in the extreme. No, there's something else going on, here."

"Go on, Mr. Roundee." Finally, a strategist in the room to help come up with a workable plan.

"One thought comes to mind is that a group within the Andromeda Cluster hierarchy wants to provoke your over-reaction for their own purposes. Perhaps they seek to destroy the existing government and then fill the vacuum with people behind their own agenda."

"I concur," said a man across the table from Roundee. The man next to him nodded in agreement.

In my earpiece, Sheila filled me in: "You know Matt Lyman, head of the NSA and next to him is David Lyon, head of the CIA."

"Misters Lyman and Lyon," I said. "Any other scenarios come to mind?"

They took a momentary look at each other, possibly wondering how I knew the CIA chief's name. Unlike the nattily dressed NSA head, the CIA chief looked quite at home in a black suit and tie. She *should* have worn sunglasses to complete the picture of Tommy Lee Jones in the movie *Men in Black*.

The CIA head gestured to his NSA counterpart, who spoke rather forcefully: "I don't see any other possibility. The kidnapping of Captain Rose smells like a coup, which means—"

"Which means we don't have any choice but to effect the rescue of Captain Rose," interrupted the president.

"We give them back all their capabilities, they'll destroy the Earth just like their original intent."

"Worse than that," said the man next to the still red-faced Secretary of Defense.

"Harley, this is Elliot Cohen, Chairman of the Federal Reserve," said POTUS. I'd met Elliot earlier when the president had told him to shut up. Evidently, he'd taken the chastisement in good spirit and added courtesy to his repertory of social skills.

Cohen looked toward me, waiting for my nod before continuing. I raised my eyebrows, inviting him to opine.

"It could be even worse than that," said Cohen. "Any of you play chess?"

Two hands went up. Sheila whispered through my earpiece: "That's Sim Blake, Attorney General. And you already know Doyle Judd, the JCS chairman."

Cohen continued: "Once we open a window by taking down the crippling effects of Harley's virus, what's to keep the bad guys themselves from unilaterally destroying the Earth? Even if some remnant of the mutually assured destruction, or MAD doctrine, still exists, and if Harley's AI wreaks havoc on all Andromeda Cluster assets, the kidnappers will have successfully checkmated their opposition in the government. It looks like if we choose either of the two options given us, enabling all compromised computer infrastructure or suffering Captain Rose to be terminated—the bad guys have a winning scenario."

Another hand went up. I acknowledged as Sheila told me it was Peter Sant, the FBI director.

"My question is, why didn't the alien vessel just kidnap Harley Davidson himself, nail him to a big sheet of plywood, and torture him until he pulled the plug on his virus?"

The wrinkled foreheads around the table and various facial grimaces provided the answer.

"Ok, grand master Cohen. I read you have a chess rating over 2400, which makes you formidable on Planet Earth." I pulled that little factoid from somewhere in my MIT days. "Add FBI Director Sant's question to your scenario. Assume our adversaries are equally gifted in playing chess. Any new ideas on next moves?"

Cohen scratched his Jewish-orthodox beard, but I knew the answer before he gave it and whispered to my AI: "Sheila, drop me a breadcrumb *now*, because things are about to go south."

"If I were on their side of this game," answered Cohen after a long pause, "I'd want to make sure I knew everyone who had control privileges over your virus, because they certainly heard your MIT lecture on the twenty-two principles of creating the perfect virus."

Bingo! I thought. Time to set the hook, as I felt a vibration all over my body, especially from the waist down, and something lodged in my pocket. Hopefully, my AI had a foolproof breadcrumb locked and loaded.

"Rabbi Cohen," I began, putting the dog on the table in front of me, "The only two people on this planet who have control over my AI are myself and the president of the United States, Oscar Jose Medina. Oh, and in the event of my absence, Chenoa is in charge around here—"

I didn't get a chance to finish my sentence. The president, myself, and a very shocked lady I'd noticed standing behind the secretary of defense suddenly appeared on a white marble floor, surrounded by desert sands. And for the first time since then, I'd lost complete contact with my AI. Out of the frying pan and into a galactic version of *Hunger Games*.

Chapter Forty-Five

"Sorry, Mister President," I said. "It wouldn't have been fair of me to leave you with that group of jackals, since you do *not* have control over my AI."

"Thanks a million," gasped President Medina. "Please tell me you haven't left the world in the hands of your ill-tempered mutt?"

"My little girl's just gotta have some fun."

The president did a face plant, and then stood to survey our new surroundings. We stood on what had to be a 100x100-foot white floor. Somehow, a ceiling rose about 20-feet above us, with no visible support. A vast, sun-lit desert surrounded us. In the distance, just behind a massive sand dune, stood a coliseum closely resembling the one located in Rome on Earth. Dark stone. But no disrepair like Rome's.

"WTF!" I said loud enough to rise above the noise coming from the distant stadium.

We still sat in the same chairs from the situation room. The lady, on the other hand, had been leaning against the wall behind the SecDef. With no barrier in our new accommodations, she fell backward and now found herself seated on the marble. The president jumped from his chair and went toward the lady sprawled, her tight skirt and high heels making it impossible for her to gain purchase. He extended his hand.

"Marge?" asked the president. "What are *you* doing here?"

She slapped his hand away, choosing instead to roll onto her stomach and slide her knees forward to stand by herself. Rather than acknowledge his offer of help, she grimaced through clenched teeth before speaking.

"*Somebody* had to protect the civilized world from you two nincompoops!"

"Beg pardon?" The most powerful man on Earth stepped backward to avoid the spray from the gap between her pearly white chicklet teeth.

From her red tweed jacket pocket she removed a small black box, about the size of the smallest Callard & Bowser Altoids mint box and held it in front of his eyes. "I bugged the meeting for and on behalf of the supreme power in the galaxy. I am going to be the Queen Mother of Planet Earth as a reward for helping rescue countless civilizations from the whims of you and this snot-nosed kid."

At this moment three things happened.

First, a fast, black creature approached us from across the sand, about the size of a Labrador dog with the head of a full-size Tyrannosaurus Rex and the splayed feet of a camel covered about 100 yards in four or five seconds. The future Queen Mother of Planet Earth had just enough time to yell "Oh, shit!" before the giant jaws disconnected her torso from her bottom half, leaving legs balancing unsteadily atop now bright-red five-inch heels. I smelled a mixture of fecal matter mixed with Mexican food, which reminded me of Chenoa, the current Queen Bitch of Planet Earth. The T-dog, who deserved the kingly moniker Rex, disappeared back toward the coliseum with his/her/its lunch.

Second, a bald man wearing a black cape appeared between the president and me. Standing about a head taller than either of us, he spoke in a clipped electronic delay consistent with translation, the sound coming as a vibration from the floor.

"Harley Davidson, we meet at last," came the translation. "And his president. I am Supreme Mushak Mel'at

Gib'song, replacement for the revered leader whose murder Mr. Davidson's abomination transmitted around the galaxy."

The vibration of his voice from the floor reminded me of the buzz in my pocket after I'd asked Sheila to send me a breadcrumb, and I reached for my pocket. My *empty* jeans pocket!

"Are you looking for this," said the Supreme Mushak holding a small black box in his right hand. A small *crushed* black box. "Clever of your sentient computer virus to send a homing device with you. But not clever enough for a race that's ruled the cosmos for millennia."

"What did you do to Marge?" asked President Medina. "Wasn't she one of yours? Spying for you?"

"Anyone who'd betray her whole planet doesn't deserve to live," Mushak smirked.

He had a point, but a fat lot of good that would do, now—no breadcrumb with which Sheila could find us. And two hostages with which to beat me into surrender. POTUS and Effie. Especially Effie, given the Mushak's regard for someone who would betray their own species. His actions made my decision for me. There's no way this religious nut job would let the love of my life survive. Alas, the calculus of victory in this battle produced a differential equation that had no solution.

"Mushak Mel'at Gib'song!" I began, throwing all caution to the wind. "I'll call you Mel. Mel Gibson, supreme dipshit of the Andromeda Cluster."

Somehow, the Supreme Mushak's translation of the word *dipshit* closely enough hit the mark that the third thing happened. President Medina vanished from sight, after which a roar erupted from the stadium.

The Supreme Dipshit must not have been used to such insubordination, as his face became rigid at the clenching of his jaw. He waved his hand, and the sand separating us from the coliseum parted to reveal an extended white marble walkway. "How'd you like to rejoin your Ephimera Rose and the president. I *know* my followers would love to meet the...what did that traitor call you? Oh yes, that snot-nosed kid who brought our civilization to its knees."

Effie! I thought. Good old Mel Gibson, Mushak Mel Gibson, didn't need to extend a second invitation. I bounded ahead of him toward the multitude's din. I hoped the old fart's trying to keep up with me might make him look less regal. Alas, he disappointed me, somehow transporting himself to the metal gate separating me from tens of thousands of rabid cheers.

The portal proved much too wide for Mushak Mel to successfully block, and I ran past him into the arena. I pushed him hard enough that he barely kept his balance. The crowd didn't seem to like that at all. Boos and growls erupted, and it took their leader's raised hands several seconds to quiet them. Several seconds during which I could see Effie and the president, each tied to posts at opposite ends of the football-sized arena.

"My fellow Andromedins," his voice roared from a *real* surround-sound amplification system. I ignored the introduction and ran toward Effie. "Let me introduce the individual responsible for crippling a million planets we've supported and mentored for millennia. Meet Harley Davidson, here to rescue a traitor to our civilization, the disgraced, treasonous Ephemera Rose."

"Are you okay?" I panted, breathless upon reaching her. Some kind of monofilament wire surrounded her, cutting into her skin and drawing blood the slightest movement. I didn't dare wrap my arms around her for fear of furthering her injuries. No doubt, the president 75 yards away had the same restraints. The post against which Effie stood rose about a foot above her head.

"Harley my love," she whispered. The stadium amplification turned her whisper into an echoing plea, further enraging the crowd. "You came for me!"

Yeah, right. Hero to the rescue. Knight in shining armor, but without the armor or anything else shiny. My Harley-Davidson belt buckle didn't shine one damn bit. So much for knighthood. I didn't dare tell her that we didn't have Sheila around to make me a superman. Excuse me. Superboy.

"To all the Mushaks on all the *civilized worlds* of the Andromeda Cluster, and to the massively evil artificial intelligence that threatens our way of life, and which will eventually see this contest broadcast," said the Mushak. "No matter what the outcome, we win."

That chess-whiz bastard Cohen had hit the nail right on the head! If I caved in and gave them the ability to shut down Sheila, they could carry on business as usual. And if I lost becoming dessert to Marge Alstrom's main course just a few minutes earlier, then Elaine would invoke the dead-man scenario and shut down everything, everywhere. Ergo, each Mushak would lead a world cut off from all communication. But the three planets that relied upon star-sucking technology to supply energy would at least be safe. There didn't seem to be a third scenario, given that my access to Sheila's phenomenal power had been permanently cut off. Shit on a shingle! I'm in a no-win situation, providing entertainment to a bunch of religious fanatics that make the Charles Manson cult look like pacifists.

A 360-degree glance around the coliseum painted one stark image after another, and led to one frightening conclusion: Maybe giving Earth all the incredible Andromeda

technology—thereby eliminating all disease, human suffering, hunger, inconvenience of

travelling, and motivation to serve others—would produce an equally worthless civilization. These bored assholes deserved to be blasted back into the stone ages. With luck, they wouldn't figure out how to make fire and starve to death.

While I didn't see any tattoos—after all, if you live for a thousand years, what might have seemed like a cracking good idea in your teens would embarrass you for at least nine subsequent centuries—outrageous hairdos and piercings made Edward Scissorhands a piker. And the immodest clothing would even cause the bare-breasted

Scythian warrior women to blush. Gaudy decorated genitalia on both men and women left nothing to the imagination, painting a picture my addled brain could never unsee. The rest of the spectators alternated between giant, white feathers that must have come from mutant swans to leather mosaics that had to be hot even in mild climates. In *this* sweltering desert, no wonder the audience let their privates hang free. Call it *ventilation*?

And below the tier-upon-tier of ribald exhibitionists, another clamor interrupted the scene. Behind steel bars, circling the entire arena, thousands of arms extended in what must have been this civilizations equivalent of the middle finger. Shouts of anger accompanied the gestures. The waiving prisoners' arms were filthy, some sporting bandages, many of which covered amputations of hands and forearms. Modern-day gladiators. Yea, even a few gladiatrixes.

Maybe death wouldn't be such a bad thing after all. I knew for a fact that if I survived this nightmare and made it back to Earth, I could never watch another stadium wave without a picture of the upper tiers' obscene antics as they erotically sprang into action in debauched exhibitionism. A glance at the president's wide eyes and gaping mouth led me to believe he'd come to the same conclusion. Even Effie seemed surprised by the degenerate display. Sodom and Gomorrah truly got bum deals on *this* world.

What is it the Klingon said on *Star Trek*? "Today is a good day to die." Or the line in some religious hymn, "If we fail, we fail with glory." At this moment I bought into both philosophies. There *are* worse things than death.

"Yo, Mel Gibson!" I yelled. "Give me some weapons and I'll show you how real men die."

My taunt got the crowd going. It also evoked surprise from both Effie and my Commander in Chief. He likely didn't want to be my exemplar of manly death. And Effie probably busied herself figuring out how she might get my vivisected body into a stasis chamber before my brain died in a mudpie held together with blood. My blood.

The new Supreme Mushak may not have known the actor Mel Gibson from the man in the moon, but his blush proved he knew I must have an intended insult. Maybe the crowd *had* seen the Andromedin translation of Mel Gibson in *Braveheart*: "Freedom!" Yeah, if these guys had been studying Earth for the last century, then they knew about Mel Gibson. Of course, *this* crowd didn't make it too much past porn. Whatever his level of understanding, the Supreme Mushak gestured for a phalanx of goons to wheel out a trolly full of medieval weapons. It must have been heavy, as six sweating gym rats could barely move the cart, which cut deep ruts in the dirt.

The stadium dirt released some previous scents due to the sinking wheels, because a strangely rotten smell briefly assaulted my olfactory receptors. The best description would be bleu cheese mixed with fertilizer. These degenerates must regularly frequent this entertainment venue. I wondered if my death here, today, would be broadcast back to Earth. I made up my mind not to die whilst curled into a fetal ball. Or to wet my pants at the end.

The crowd saw my first challenge before I did. The cheers drew my attention to the president's end of the arena. Luckily for POTUS, the T-Dog took a quick victory lap around Medina's bound body, which gave me time to grab a spear. Why the spear? I doubted I could run 35 yards with a sword to defend the man from joining the now-digesting Marge Alstrom. Maybe I could throw the alien harpoon.

I didn't have experience throwing javelins in school track meets. I *thought* about running toward the hell doggie as fast as I could, afraid I wouldn't make it in time, and afraid I would. Hoping the T-Rex would turn its head and roar, creating a big target for the junior quarterback in his tryout for the TFL—the Tyrannosaurs Fighting League—to do a Hail Mary pass into the literal *end zone*, I yelled. Amplified by the marvelous and invisible PA system, the beast turned toward me.

"Yo, fugly!" I screamed using a MIT expression for *extremely* Ugly. The question crossed my mind as to how such a small body could support such a gigantic head. On its rear end, the black body sported an enormous scythe-like tail as a counterweight. Having gotten its attention, and the tooth-factory of a maw turned away from the president and his rosary prayers.

As Yankee baseball pitcher Lefty Gomez said in 1943, *it's better to be lucky than good*. The damn T-Dog ran at me so fast that I didn't have time to rear back and throw the spear. I just held it in front of me. That massive T-Rex mouth enveloped the 8-foot shaft, past the teeth, through the roof of its mouth and—yep, definitely better to be lucky than good—right into his brain pan. Glad it wasn't a rattlesnake, which I understand would have continued snapping and pumping venom hours after death. I got my arms out of the gaping maw without so much as a scratch from myriad teeth.

Still midfield, the crowd's stupefied silence—you could have heard the lady three rows above the Mushak swallow her still-wiggling snake-like treat—let me hear a gate behind me slam open. I turned to see a python at least fifty feet tall—tall, not long, since its coiled body bounced upright, like a spring—which quickly pogo-sticked its way toward Effie. I took some consolation that at least it didn't have a T-Rex head. The crowd cheered. They shouldn't have, as the noise distracted the creature from Effie just as it spewed a stream of fire toward the sound. Neither the feathers nor the hair sculptures demonstrated any fire-retardant capability, and the resulting screams echoed as emergency crews rushed scorched screamers to nearby stasis units for extensive regeneration. I suspected that neither POTUS, Effie, nor I would receive such emergency treatment.

The Exalted Mushak leader stood on the sidelines, arms crossed, looking smugly at my frantic efforts to choose a weapon. Somebody in the twisted leader's armory must have got his hands on a *World of Warcraft* video game. In my race toward Effie and the bouncing python, a short-handled and very fat-bladed weapon stood out. Gamers coined it the *Monster Sword*. Racing toward Effie, I selected this weapon not for its lethality, but for possible use in deflecting a spray of fire. Hopefully, a very narrow stream.

No way I could reach the springing giant snake before it pounced on Effie. Still, it focused dimly intelligent eyes not on the love of my life, but on the other end of the arena and President Medina. Their eyes met, POTUS's and the snake's. Holographic projections at each end of the battleground captured the look, and the deviant hoard cheered as the whale-sized serpent sprang toward the president. In two giant bounds, the second of which propelled the beast high above the about-to-be former leader of the free world, the airborne monster sailed in a perfect arc. A wide-open mouth enveloped the post that held a screaming president, along with said president, his howls first muted and then silenced.

I didn't even try to make it to the president-kebab, opting instead to stand between the snake and Effie. Saving both—one at either end of the arena—didn't make sense. And the late, great POTUS came in second place to my prime goal, that of saving Effie. While the giant assassin whipped its tail to disengage itself from the now-empty post, I raced to Effie and started slicing the micro-thin restraints. At least someone had honed the so-called Monster Sword to a razor's edge. Three whacks against the back of her post and Effie sprang free.

Effie, my Captain Rose of the alien starship formerly tasked with destruction of planet Earth, had remarkable tactical chops. She ran directly away from me and toward the Supreme Mushak, who no longer stood confidently, arms folded and feet spread apart. Oh, he still stood there, but his wide eyes put two and two together and figured he didn't want to be anywhere near the python's next meal. He started toward the gate as Effie quickly closed the distance between them.

The monster, now free of the presidential stake—notice I avoided the temptation to call it the presidential *steak*—spotted the movement and homed in on Effie. Damn it, she ran a hell of a lot faster than me, and the snake bounced toward her more rapidly than either of us. The crowd's insane cheers didn't even register with me, muted by frantic breathing as I raced in a futile mission to rescue my doomed fiancé. A dozen feet from Effie, my world ended. A towering mouth crashed over her. Effie must have sensed the looming doom. She looked back at me and shrugged before disappearing.

Fate dealt me one final stab to the heart, as the entire scene morphed into slow motion. Like how people report in a car accident, when everything seems to slow down as disaster encroaches frame by frame. I seemed to hang mid-leap, moving too slowly as my raised Monster Sword embarked on its futile rescue mission. With all my strength, I brought the blade down, slashing into the beast's head, slicing through one soulless eye and splitting its skull. I didn't stop to realize the impossibility of this even from a sabre-wielding martial arts mutant, let alone an academic like myself. Clearly, I wielded no ordinary sword. Hope against hope that Effie hadn't been crushed or chewed—yet, still in slow motion—I watched the enormous tree-trunk-like body continue falling forward. It seemed to take forever, but I withdrew the blood-soaked sword and drove another arching blow just behind the head, hoping to sever the spine. Yeah, right. Trained bullfighters don't cut the heads clean off bulls. Even insane toreros filled with grief and bloodlust. Maybe the spectators' roar caught up, bringing me back into real-time. The lifeless reptile torso had lost muscle tension and flopped into the now-screaming audience. I tried in vain to part the giant jaws, but my efforts got interrupted by outright laughter. Just feet away, the Supreme Mushak chuckled, his arms raised in victory.

I've read many fiction stories about heroes who suddenly become paralyzed by grief over losing their dearest love. What a bunch of unadulterated horseshit! The adrenalin from the fight and a single-minded goal of victory or doom will always prevail. Whoever pens it differently is either a coward writing under an invented macho pseudonym, or a writer unacquainted with a biker bar brawl. I had a sword and one smirking Mushak taking a bow just feet away.

"Effie!" I screamed, rushing my tormentor, blade raised high and arching toward his neck. He saw me and didn't flinch, even when the end of my weapon disintegrated as it met a powerful force field protecting him. He laughed loudly at my impotent rage.

"Methinks I need to dream up a more creative way for this Harley Davidson to entertain us." The Mushak's amplified voice echoed amidst cheering from the rabble in the stands. "What say you all?"

By then, I figured all was lost. I threw the de-bladed weapon at my tormentor, only to see it disintegrate when it hit the force field protecting him. Par for the course. No longer a superman protected by my AI, I'd suckered the President of the United States into an ignominious death. I'd sacrificed the love of my life for the entertainment of degenerate scum. Dehydration. Slow, scorching death beneath not one but two blazing suns. I couldn't even fall on my own sword, since it had been destroyed. Too bad the Joint Chiefs, along with the rest of the Situation Room occupants, couldn't see my final fate. At least they'd have the satisfaction of watching the man responsible for the death of a rather beloved president suffer a long, slow one himself. Or maybe not. I still had choices. Two, actually. Not much for a life in which I'd previously been emperor of the known universe, but I could choose long and slow versus short and fast. I chose short and fast.

The words of the Klingon again repeated themselves: "Today's a good day to die!"

In one frantic movement, I flung myself at the Pope from Hell and guaranteed destruction by his protective force field. Better dead than a trophy over Mushak Mel'at Gib'song's fireplace. Midair in my leap, the Medici incarnate seemed surprised at my smile. Then everything went black.

Chapter Forty-Six

My next conscious moment seemed to answer every mortal's big question: Is there life after death? I opened my eyes to see Effie staring down, an angel of light. My heart swelled with gratitude. *Score! There* is *life after death*. But one new question came quickly to mind. She planted a wet kiss right on my mouth, which answered another question: Do people have bodies in heaven? And then a third conundrum assaulted my nostrils.

"How come it's dark in here, and heaven smells like shit?" I asked.

Bless her heart, my angel chuckled playfully. Deep in a tunnel behind her, a group of shadows lurked. But they kept their distance, and the love of my life just rested on her knees, hugging me.

"You were so brave, the way you raced toward that awful creature and tried to save me."

"Without you, Effie, I didn't care whether or not I lived." For the first time in days, I relaxed and just held her. "We're together now. But...?

I propped myself on one elbow and looked at the crowd around us. An unbathed hoard in rags returned my gaze. These poor devils looked like they'd been minions to Satan for a good long time. Missing teeth, festering wounds. I didn't want Effie to leave my side, but she stood and extended her hand to me. Slowly, in spite of aches and sprains I didn't know possible, she helped me to my feet.

"Sweet Mary, Joseph and Martha, are we in hell?"

What a sight! One giant even had tears creating mud rivers down his face. Yet he smiled. One by one, these hell's angels began clapping. Another emaciated woman with barely enough threadbare clothes to give her a modicum of modesty came forward and hugged both Effie and me. "Dank ooh, Hahlie Davids'n" she said through cracked lips. "Dank ooh verie much."

I didn't care if she smelled like she'd been swimming in a cesspool. I didn't care if her blood and grime stuck to my T-shirt. But I sure didn't know what I'd done to deserve her sobbing, shaking embrace. Behind her, just over the matted hair of her companions, rusted bars separated us from a now-roaring mass. And I finally figured out where we stood.

"How in this stinking Universe did I get here? How did *we* get here?" I paused. Then to my miraculously resurrected companions: "These are all humans, homo sapiens. And they speak English?"

"Not all," said Effie. "But the non-human bipeds are genetic freaks created for the Mushak's amusement.

"Okay, my young friend," said the president, stepping out of the shadows and assuming a professorial manner. "This Mushak character didn't want to throw away the greatest show on...whatever-the-hell planet this is. So, he must have used the beam-me-up-Scotty technology to snatch Effie and me from the jaws of death. Ditto for you trying to commit suicide against his protection shield."

"But we never see'd that a'fore," said a four-foot-tall old man. "They got a unlimited supply of slaves and don' seem mind usin' us up."

I couldn't help holding Effie close to me as our welcome committee gathered around us. My eyes misted up whenever they strayed to look at her, so I tried to pay attention to the current tenuous situation. Time didn't appear to be a commodity we had in abundance.

"I'm Harley. And you are?"

"Everybod' here know who you be," said the little man. "I's Lexar. We wish ta help ya destroy da evil mushak. Afta all, ya did took over most of owa universe."

"Lexar, pleased to meet you." I held out my hand, and he shook it. "I would like nothing more than to destroy the mushak. Unfortunately, I am without the AI that previously protected me and our planet."

"What's a AI?"

"AI stands for artificial intelligence, and my AI assimilated all the computing resources of this civilization, even the technology to move planets."

The president jumped in: "And without it, we're now bare-ass helpless!"

"Harley not helpless," said the dwarf. "Nobody ever kilt a Rockhog or a Bullworm. But Harley done 'em both."

"That was pure dumb luck," I admitted. Absolutely one-in-a-trillion-dumb luck. "Without some way to communicate off planet, my AI won't be able to find us and we're at the mercy of that Mel Gibson mushak. Is there a computer or electronic connection available, anywhere?"

"Dat be forbidden," said the woman who'd just hugged me. "Our world be discombobbled from everywhere else."

"Discombobbled?" Effie took off her cashmere jacket and placed it over the nearly naked woman's shoulders.

"I think she means the planet is like an air-gapped computer," I said. "No connections to anywhere."

"You'se right," she said.

"Then we're well and truly screwed," said POTUS.

"We should assess our resources," I said. "Lexar, who are all these people? Where do they come from?"

"Let me answer that, Harley Davidson." A man emerged from behind the line of onlookers. "I'm Alber, a physicist from the planet Hrate. Just a few cycles ago, you managed to kill the entire religious order that had subverted my planet. I made the mistake of applauding your actions and was immediately exiled to this depraved penal community."

At over six feet tall, Alber looked me in the eye. Interestingly, he had one green eye and the other blue. Called complete heterochromia, my guess is that the good doctor's condition could be related to this putrid environment or maybe untreated diabetes. Because dirt and scabs covered most of his body, I couldn't tell whether or not he had fair skin.

"Your mastery of our language is impressive," I said. "A physicist, you say?"

"And chronicler of interstellar civilizations," Alber continued. "I confess I'm a *big* fan of your planet. Everything from Earth has become massively popular throughout the Andromeda cluster. We have followed Captain Rose's reports with almost fanatic interest. Your music, your athletic pursuits, especially American football. Deep dives into your culture, into the mentality of *The Planet That Killed God* if you will, has really swept all of Andromeda. The mission to destroy Earth eclipsed all other news."

"And my failure to accomplish that goal, getting our entire empire taken over by Harley Davidson's AI, has made me infamous," said Effie.

"Not in my former circles," said Alber. "Something done a couple thousand years ago shouldn't doom a planet. This planet, on the other hand..."

"What the hell *is* this planet?" I asked.

Your planet is in the Milky Way galaxy, which spans over fifty-two-thousand light years. The Andromeda galaxy is two-and-a-half-million light years from Earth. You are now six-million light years from Earth on a planet the ruling mushak calls—you're going to love this—Paradise."

"These other prisoners, gladiators as I call them? Same story as yours?"

"Some religious apostates, yes. And the rest are hardened criminals given a choice between death or a one-way trip to...Paradise."

"The depraved spectators in the stadium above us? Why are they here?"

The physicist laughed. "Since we kind of live forever, Paradise is the equivalent of Earth's Islamic reward of seventy-two virgins. Of course, in Paradise we also practice polyandry. There are levels of reward that determine whether or not you are master or property."

"Mister President?" I shuddered as I looked at POTUS. "If we get out of this, I absolutely positively intend to destroy this planet."

"After rescuing the prisoners that they use for entertainment," said Effie.

"You in for some gallows humor?" asked President Medina.

We all waited for him to continue. Humor from POTUS at a time like this? I confess a certain amount of disorientation that almost made me dizzy.

"A scoundrel died and went to hell," began the president. "He was met by the welcoming archdevil who said, *You're going to love it here. Mondays, unlimited drinking without hangovers. Tuesday, we do drugs. Again, no health side effects. Wednesday features feasts of everything you could crave, without weight gain or indigestion. Oh, are you ga y?* To which the grinning scoundrel shook his head in the negative. *Too bad. You're going to HATE Thursdays.*"

Nobody laughed. I groaned at the unexpected change in the president's manner, his metaphysical net-net of our dilemma. Time to get everyone in problem-solving mode.

"Any chance we could meet some of the other prisoners? Take inventory of any technology assets available?" There *had* to be a way out of this hell. "Or do you want to wait for Thursday, Mister President?"

At that moment, a burly man shoved our circle of admirers aside and grabbed Effie's right wrist with a giant hairy hand. "I'm Gawand. The undefeated Gawand. And now, I will show Captain Rose my bedchamber."

The brute had to outweigh me by two-hundred pounds. Naked from the waist up, every inch of his torso sported tufts of black hair, some of which grew out of scabs. A full head taller than me, he probably shaved his butt-ugly face with a shard of glass. Broken teeth and fetid breath finished painting the picture of my executioner, because no way would I let him take Effie anywhere. Notwithstanding the explicit danger, my hand found its way to the hairball's forearm.

"Ah, the man that killed the Rockhog and the Bullworm." He smiled at me.

Could I bluff him?

Fat freaking chance! He released his grip on Effie with his right hand, only to backhand me with a lightning blow that laid me flat on the dirt. Dirt that smelled of urine, feces, and blood. The copper taste of my own blood almost made me aspirate the vomit that had driven up my throat like an erupting volcano. As my experience in the arena proved, without a really sharp ax blade, I was a child confronting the ogre under his bed. My fighting skills approached that of a junior high school cheerleader. I *thought* about jumping up, only my questionable balance and sense of direction in the spinning room didn't give me a stinking clue the direction of "up." But I tried. And almost made it to my knees. I buckled, my obviously broken left arm failed to support me, and a gigantic pain in my stomach indicated something was massively wrong.

The Cretin who hit me landed on my back. With *his* back. I stayed on my already aching stomach, the air knocked out of me. Seriously knocked out of me. You ever fall and find yourself unable to breathe? With a convulsing diaphragm? Panic sets in, along with lack of oxygen. I went over the handlebars of my bicycle once with similar results. But this time, my left arm also didn't work.

Luckily, the big guy rolled off and lay on his side, in a fetal position. With Effie standing over him and taking a second shot at his nards from the backside of his scrotum. And I noticed she had two bloody thumbs. What had the son-of-a-bitch done to her?

Turns out, said big guy had been on the receiving end of those thumbs. His eye sockets, to be precise.

"My eyes," he groaned. "Ya blinded me!"

Boy, what in blazes do they teach these starship captains? Maybe how to diffuse a mutiny in close-quarter/hand-to-hand combat. Note to self: Never *ever* piss off Effie!

"Would some of you please drag Mister Undefeated here to wherever you give each other medical attention?" said Effie in her I-am-a-starship-captain voice. Then to the professor, "I don't suppose you have a stasis unit down here?"

At least I *think* that's what she said. I couldn't hear well through convulsive wheezing from lungs fighting to control my semi-paralyzed diaphragm, moans regarding a throbbing left arm bent at an awkward angle, and loudly gurgling pain from my abdomen.

The professor pointed above as three Gawand wannabes gave The Fearsome Captain Rose wide berth and dragged away their whimpering Paradise Idol.

"I wonder what the Mushak has in mind for the next act?" POTUS scratched his chin, now developing the five-o'clock shadow of all five-o'clock shadows. Never scratch your chin when your hand has been in our current environs. His face now looked like the streaked mascara of a runner-up beauty queen.

Chapter Forty-Seven

We didn't have to wait long for Act II of the mushak's *Celebrity Apprentice* extravaganza. Only without the celebrities. One minute, POTUS, Effie and I followed Alber and a few dozen companions on a tour of the slave holding ring. I limped and held my arm, hoping to cowboy up and walk off the pain from my gut. The very next instant, a horn blared, and a phalanx of Cretan guards burst through the arena gate just ahead. A few slaves congregated around us, shielding us from spears and eyes of the intruders.

"What now?" I moaned.

"Shh!" Mixx shushed me. Her shoulders shook, as did her one-syllable utterance.

At least as tall as me—if I could actually stand upright, which I couldn't—the guards used their spears to prod a path. Their heavy footsteps kicked up dust motes that refracted sunlight shining through the bars to our left. I couldn't help but sneeze, evoking a panicked look from Mixx. Damn, but it hurt to sneeze. I moaned even louder. Meanwhile, the troops grunted, eying slaves one by one. They seemed to be looking for something specific. The tallest, with mottled green skin and six fingers on each hand—clearly a mutant created to entertain the Mushak—waved a scanning device at each person he passed. Well, almost each person. He walked by POTUS, Effie and the hunched-over me as if we weren't there.

To her great relief, they also bypassed Mixx. Gawand's three buddies didn't avoid their One-A draft status, having taken their semi-blind and blue-balled leader to whatever medical help existed beneath these bleachers. The hulking, grumbling trio, prodded by spears, made their way to the arena exit. I dreaded their fate. Not even bullies deserved to star in whatever macabre dance the Mushak had planned. POTUS and Effie peered through the rusty bars. I decided to sit, my back against them. For the first time, Effie noticed I didn't seem to be my chipper self.

"What's wrong with your arm?" said Effie.

"Now that the shock is wearing off, I'd say it's busted." I tried to sound cavalier, but it came out as the long whimper I hadn't used since my grade-school self used to plead for sympathy from a really pretty school nurse. "Uh, I think something is wrong inside, too."

"Alber, quick!" Now the starship captain, Effie snapped into her *Man Down* mode. "We need a splint and a blanket for him to lie on."

A blanket magically appeared. POTUS helped Effie lay me on my back. My gut really hurt. I cried out when they forced my knees from my chest so I could lie straight.

"My guess is, Mister Davidson has a ruptured spleen," said Mix as she tried to be gentle exploring my abdomen. I moaned like a big baby.

From deep in the group crowded around us, I overheard several snippets of conversation.

"I didn't think he got hit that hard."

"And he's the one that kilt da Bullworm?"

"I never seen anyone that could stand up to Gawand like Effie."

"If Mix be correct, the great Harley Davidson won't last the night."

"A broken arm!" said POTUS. "And what the hell are they doing out *there*?"

"Pay attention in *here*," said Effie, momentarily turning away from me to look through the bars. But Alber gently tapped her shoulder.

"They're tasked with exhuming you two from the dead Bullworm."

Much to the relief of the three conscripts, Moe, Larry and Curly used their newly issued weapons not to fight each other, but to dissect the dead Bullworm. Starting just below the jawline, they sawed and hacked to raucous encouragement from the crowd. Stamping above us caused more dust to shower down. Several of us sneezed. Outside in the arena, two of Gawand's lieutenants peeled back the muscle-supported epidermis while the third scooped past a substantial amount of viscera to examine every inch of the esophagus.

The background conversation continued.

"How'd that sissy ever drop the Bullworm?"

I knew to whom they referred, myself being the big sissy.

"Hey Bhatt," someone said poking the stomach of a well-fed little fat man who paid rapt attention to the dissection process taking place outside. "Wonder what yer guts 'oud look like if'n ya got ripped open."

The spirits of our fellow prisoners didn't appear to reflect their reality. Sure, quite a few limped. But more than a week in this oppressive environment would drain every bit of humor, charity, and empathy out of my system. Yet these beings, these people, somehow maintained a spirit quite beyond my understanding. Maybe something deep inside mimicked the black slaves who toiled away in the cotton fields before Abraham Lincoln said enough was enough. Without doubt, if I lived through this—and my current state of mind gave survival a less than fifty-fifty chance—this Andromeda Cluster practice would absolutely, positively end.

Inch by inch, then foot by foot, the crowd noise slowly waned. Greenish yellow blood washed over Curly's feet, and the few audience members who still tried to snack on the galactic equivalent of Ballpark Wieners lost their appetites as the dissection stench wafted up from the now muddy stadium surface into the stands and, more strongly, at ground level into our prison.

Moe and Shemp growled questions at their drafted chief medical examiner Curly, who paused every foot or so to shrug.

"Question, Alber." I turned my head to peer past the blanket edge and through the bars. "What were those scanning devices the not-so-jolly green giants used to find our three autopsy interns?"

"I've never given it much thought," said the physicist. "Just assumed they had a database of all prisoners. Child's play, given the advanced technology we've come to take for granted in the cluster."

"I've got to get my hands on one of those," I said.

"No, we've got to get you to a stasis chamber," said Effie.

"That too," I said, going into Vulcan mode to think about solutions and not my growing pain. "But those scanners mean just possibly—"

The president jumped in. "Just possibly, not *everything* on Paradise is air-gapped."

Okay, there *just had* to be an answer to this mystery. I went to Andover and heard about a kid who took the college board exam in chemistry, yet he'd never taken a chem class in his life. Not only did he get named a National Merit Scholar, but he ranked number one. On the way back to the dorm, his roommate asked him how he did it, and why he took the risk of screwing up his college chances taking a test for which he had no training. His answer became school legend. He said he just used common sense. The test involved outlines of tubes and beakers, asking how they functioned together. He just deduced from their shapes how they worked. So maybe some common sense could solve our current conundrum?

First, all three of us got teleported into the slave quarters, but unbeknownst to the mushak. Second, upon serious reflection, there is no way in Hell I could have swung an ordinary axe clear through the skull of that gigantic bouncing worm. Third, and most interesting, the scanner device used by the gorgons didn't seem to recognize us. Three undisputable facts. So?

Common sense, eh? A plus B plus C equals...what? *Come on, brain, think past the pain!*

Computational equivalence rears its ugly head in my life. Again. My virus principle of black box portability relied heavily on computational equivalence. Indisputably, then, something or someone had worked on our behalf.

Effie interrupted my epiphany. "I think the Three Stooges are just now figuring out what they've been tasked to find."

Did I say "Three Stooges" out loud. I *know* I *thought* those words. Maybe Effie *could* read my mind. Something else to consider when I have time for displacement activity, aka daydreaming.

"Oops," I said. "It took longer for a signal to reach the stooges' brains than the sixty or so feet it had to race from the Bullworm's brain to its spring receptor muscles."

As one, the three inductees into the Mushak's Blood and Guts Brigade stood and pointed goop-dripping fingers toward us!

"Something tells me the mushak didn't use technology to spirit Effie and me from the jaws of death," said POTUS.

"You just figuring that out, boss?" It suddenly hit me why the mushak ordered the Bullworm disemboweled. He wanted the bodies of both Effie and the president. Possibly to put on display. Or to use as lawn ornaments. But whatever the case, our minutes of anonymity had come to a screeching halt. Literal screeching, as the mushak's sonorous voice sounded more like a teenage girl at a rock concert. And I felt like helping with the screeching, truth be known.

"But if the mushak didn't transport us to the slave holding cells, then who did?" mused the president.

"Or what did?" I asked. "Right now, though, our reprieve from being the center of attraction is about to expire."

Unlike my first appearance in the slave warren, when everyone kind of formed a barrier to hide us, the sound of the not-so-jolly green gargoyle army caused everyone else to scatter in both directions. The light coming through the rusted bars created shafts in the dust-nados caused by the slave exodus. POTUS and Effie backed against bars, preparing for the inevitable.

"It's been nice knowing you," I said. "Sorry for getting you into this."

The president took off his belt and wrapped it around his right fist. "It ain't over til the fat lady sings."

"You calling me fat?" said Effie, doing her best to muster a grin.

"That's just an expression—" he began.

"I know it's a Dick Motta expression that first appeared in the *Dallas Morning News* on March 10th, 1976," she said. "After all I've been studying Earth civilizations since well before you were born."

More like memorizing our history, I thought. Too bad we didn't have much more time together.

Thundering footfalls and animal grunts drowned out POTUS's laugh. He had a good idea about the belt, so I tied to undo my Harley-Davidson belt buckle with one hand. Effie got the idea and finished the job for me. Since it was way too wide to easily wrap around her fist—that made-of-steel-weapon-of-destruction fist—she swung it over her head, ready to wipe the smile, along with a few teeth, off the face of the first Cretin to come near the Harley-Davidson belt buckle. I had no illusions that the president, the Kung Fu starship captain or I would prevail past even one mutant dipshit. Hopefully, none of the aforementioned goons would stomp on my stomach. We awaited our doom. Effie crouched, weight on her right foot, swinging the belt above her head. POTUS cocked his belt-clad fist like a prize fighter bracing for a knockout punch. And I just listened to my belt buckle whistling above Effie. Then, the marauding hoard rounded the bend and thundered toward us. I wish I'd thought to return Effie's big, wet kiss before demonstrating William

Shakespeare's shuffling off this mortal coil. Maybe in the next life?

Chapter Forty-Eight

There had to be a couple hundred monsters descending on us. Lots of grunting, growling, and gurgling phlegm from fatboy lungs not used to sustained running and yelling. One particularly out-of-shape oaf tripped and fell ten feet in front of us. As he struggled to get up, he briefly squinted toward us and blinked twice. Before he could say *Hey, Guys!* the herd behind him thoroughly trampled him into green, soggy pulp. And kept on running, past us and around the less-than-light-speed cyclotron, a la gorgatron, oval. The last panting slob lumbered and splashed through his buddy before disappearing down the tunnel.

"What just happened," said the president.

Effie quickly tired of swinging the Harley-Davidson belt over her head and let the buckle drop to the dirt by her side.

"It's like they didn't see us," said Effie.

"And those scanner things didn't register us when they first came to draft Bullworm dissectors." I would have scratched my head, except my good arm had its current job supporting my broken left. I started wondering how I could possibly have sliced into the skull of the aforementioned worm. David didn't get nearly enough credit for downing Goliath, and he was just a kid.

"Something else is going on, here," said Effie. "We're invisible."

"Would you mind not dragging me in the dirt?" came Sheila's voice from Effie's right heel.

Three simultaneous *WHAT! s* erupted from us. I looked across at Effie's foot. My Harley-Davidson belt buckle emitted a red glow.

"Sheila?" I gasped. "Is that you?"

"It's as much of me as I could pack into this buckle," said my AI. "Unfortunately, the Mushak destroyed the interstellar transmitter I'd put into your pocket. Which means I have no way to send the coordinates of Paradise to any of my incarnations, neither nearby nor all the way back to Earth."

"Sheila, why in the hell didn't you let me know you were here." My exasperated whisper maxed out my ability to shout.

"Back on earth, figuring out how to leave breadcrumbs to follow, I decided to remain silent as long as possible, protecting you three as best I could."

"We're still S-O-L then," said the president.

"I don't know S-O-L," said Sheila as Effie helped me thread the leather through my belt loops and fastened a still-glowing AI buckle.

"That's shit-outta-luck," offered Effie, ever the anthropologist and vernacular etymologist.

"We've got to get out of here, then," said POTUS.

"That would be my recommendation," said the AI. "I've got to find a power source with enough wattage to allow me to build a time-warp lens and send a distress message to a nearby me."

"Escape? Not quite yet." I hated to rain on the parade, but my moral imperatives transcended saving my own skin. Or POTUS's. Even Effie's. "We're not leaving these slaves behind for further exploitation and certain death."

"We're not going anywhere without getting *you* some medical attention," said Effie.

"Aren't we eventually going to destroy this stinking planet anyway?" asked POTUS.

"Eventually," I said. "But not a bunch of innocents. They go wherever we go."

"You ain't goin' nowhere," said POTUS. Great grammar from the erudite President of the stinking United States.

Effie jumped in. "But your AI can't even get us home, let alone all these innocents."

"Worse than that, I can't even heal Harley Davidson's mortal wounds." Effie paused: "Mix correctly diagnosed the spleen issue. Harley's spleen will go septic if not removed within 18 hours."

"Sheila," I began, ignoring the death sentence. "Can you neutralize the rabble above us, along with the Mushak?"

"Negative. The extent of my power is to transport you three, one at a time, no further than a hundred yards."

"How about just the Mushak? Can you zap just him?"

"Again, negative. I cannot overcome his protective force field."

"Harley," said the president. "Let's just make a stretcher and get some volunteers to carry you out of here. If we figure a way to contact a more powerful AI, we can come back and rescue these poor devils before sending Paradise into a black hole."

"Besides, we need to discover if there are any more innocents on this cancer of a planet," said Effie.

"But we just can't leave these festivities operational," I said. "How many more of these captives will suffer or die before we can come back with the calvary?"

The president, a superb tactician in his former life, snapped his fingers. "Sheila, you say you can transport one person about a hundred yards?"

"Affirmative," answered the AI.

"I don't see—" began Effie.

The president winked at me, and I knew exactly what he had in mind. He interrupted Effie: "How about a hundred yards *straight up?* One at a time. Half-a-dozen voyeurs disappearing and then splatting centerstage. *That* should cause pandemonium. Right?"

Effie grimaced. I added, "Sheila, could you broadcast my voice, translated into the local jargon, stadium wide?"

"Affirmative, Harley-Davidson."

"Excellent. Sheila, randomly pick the largest males from the audience and begin operation *drop-kick-me-Jesus-through-the-stadium-of-life*. Transmit my message after the second body makes the grand entry."

"Executing now," said my AI.

As if accepting my unuttered stage direction, each of two screams started about thirty stories above the crowd and increased in volume as they took their last curtain call. The first drew a surprised groan. The second evoked shrieks from the poor slob's companions, who saw Bubba disappear from beside them only to appear in the sky above them. I then spoke, amplified to the crowd in the local dialect. I kind of whispered, but the AI amplified a voice of God Almighty raining doom and destruction.

"Hello everybody. This is Harley Davidson, bringing you to the end of your stay on Paradise. Ushering you one by one to that exit. My AI has found me, and we're now going to have some Karma-is-a-bitch fun." I didn't know whether or not Karma translated into their language, but the panic in the stands told me it didn't matter. I continued: "Your beloved Mushak will be the grand finale to this show, although none of you will be alive to see it. Because you'll all be irretrievably and totally dead. Forever. No stasis recovery for you. Enjoy the last roller coaster ride, without the coaster. Flap your fat arms if you want."

Sheila kept dropping fat guys. Chivalrous as I am, I couldn't bring myself to drop women, no matter how degenerate they'd become. Of course, I couldn't keep them from being trampled by their BFFs.

"Harley Davidson," said my AI. "The Mushak has left the gathering. Gone to a palace a few hundred kilometers away."

"And where is the crowd going?"

"They appear to be running randomly into the desert."

"The pubic transportation system evidently isn't functioning," chuckled POTUS.

"You mean *public* transportation system?" I said, always the straight man.

"I think he really meant *pubic*," said Effie, shuddering at the president's penchant for dark humor."

"Right you are, my darling," said the president. "Sheila, shall we be off?"

"Help me up," I said. "Let's round up the slaves and make sure the arena food preparation facilities and stockpiles are adequate to feed them until we can effect a rescue."

"The Emperor of the Known Universe is a real Boy Scout." The president shook his head. "Trustworthy, loyal, helpful, friendly, kind, obedient, cheerful, brave and clean."

"Uh," said our resident anthropologist with the eidetic memory, "What happened to courteous, obedient, thrifty and reverent?"

"I'm sure both Earth and Paradise would agree that Harley Davidson is a work in process," said POTUS.

"Okay, okay you guys. Help me round up the F-troop," I said. "We scouts are clean, which means I won't spell out the full name of our Paradise troop."

As it turns out, we didn't have to go round up anybody. The doppler-shifted screams and splats, along with my broadcast announcement, brought a much more respectful audience back to us. Quiet and deferential. We more sensed than heard masses of humanity approaching us from both ends of a now-dark tunnel. Eventually, one shape emerged from the shadows.

"Alber!" I said. "Good to see you."

The physicist approached obsequiously. Slowly, head bowed, avoiding eye contact.

"The stories are all true?" He whispered the question.

"A'course they're true ya dope," said Mixx, pushing her way past him giving me a Cheshire cat grin and putting one of my arms over her shoulder. She looked up, noting the thundering footsteps from the crowd above causing dust and accumulated gunk to rain down on us. "When we gettin' outta' here?"

"As soon as Sheila can connect to another planet," I said. "In the meantime, I need to make sure you all don't starve or die of thirst."

"Hey," came a woman's voice from deep in the hoard. "Send fat boy up there."

A jostling match plowed a dimple-kneed dwarf forward. He bowed as well as someone of his girth could manage and motioned us with sausage shaped fingers.

"Follow me," he said. He hadn't missed any meals. "I'm Bhatt, formerly the Mushak's chief chef."

Bald and about as tall as he was wide, the little man walked with an air of authority not uncommon in the finer Earth restaurants. His little legs took two steps for every one of Alber's, who tried to hold up my left side without banging my broken arm. He led Effie, POTUS and me ahead of the convict parade. The army of happy wanderers cheered as another scream-splat echoed through the bars separating us from the arena. Mix and Alber dragged me, sneaking an occasional look at my glowing belt buckle.

Scream-splat-[CrowdNoise]! Scream-splat-[CrowdNoise]! The splats took on more of a mushy sound as the area became more of a gore pit. The frequent *Scream-ooofs!* above us denoted yet another Paradisian getting trampled.

About halfway around the circumference of our tunnel, Bhatt stopped in front of a metal door. Rather than breach it, he just looked at me. And then at the door. Then at me. I got the message.

"Sheila, can you—?" I didn't finish my question. The door simply vanished, revealing an extremely wide set of stairs ascending to the upper level. Without an invitation, Bhatt grabbed Effie's forearm and slowly climbed, one step at a time. He resembled a three-hundred-pound toddler, but without the diaper. The rest of us toddled along behind him. He stopped several times to catch his breath. I was also glad for those brief reprieves.

"The Mushak didn't like your cooking?" asked Effie, making conversation during one of their stops.

"His Greatness asked for some Nahrwalian spice, and I made the mistake of suggesting he taste the Manood loins before adding anything. Next thing I know, two of his centurions are dragging me by my ears down these very stairs."

It's a wonder they didn't tear the ears right off the corpulent chef.

We eventually arrived at the landing, which opened into a well-lit and massive kitchen facility. A good hundred feet wide and twenty tall, refrigeration units lined the left-hand side and shiny industrial stoves the right. A center island boasted cutting boards and sinks.

One of our mob walked to the first refrigeration unit and opened the stainless-steel door.

"Glick Legs!" he exclaimed. "Tons of it!"

Bhatt went to a center faucet, barely reaching the tap handle. Cascades of clear water splashed into the sink. "With a little help here, I can feed this army of destitute deplorables for months."

"No food replicators?" asked Effie.

"Remember, this is an air-gapped planet," said Alber. "No smart or connectable technology is allowed."

The mob had begun disbursing down either side of the center island, and several shouts drew our attention. Still in awe of my AI, the crowd disbursed to make a path for us. POTUS and Effie led the way. Alber and Mix dragged me along, and I could feel my consciousness waning. At the end of the kitchen, a glass wall separated us from a bank of stasis chambers.

"Stasis chambers!" I couldn't help the surprise in my voice. "This isn't low-tech."

"Not true," said Effie, patting my good arm. "Stasis technology *must* be air gapped because they need to work independently of outside links, in case the worst happens. Stasis is truly open to any culture, biology, ethnicity, gender or DNA. It analyzes the host DNA to affect a perfect reversing of the methylation clock. That's the aging mechanism that makes us all mortal. Epigenetic changes also include histone modifications and chromatin remodelling, which contribute to a general loss of heterochromatin."

Alber added to our understanding of just why stasis units adorned this facility: "When one of us does a particularly valiant performance for the crowd, our broken and torn bodies are brought here for healing and another chance at heroism. When you asked earlier about availability of stasis capability, that's why I pointed above us."

"There's Gawand!" As if on cue, Mix gestured through the glass to the bully who'd been schooled in manners by Effie. Gawand The Undefeated floated in the sixth stasis chamber.

"Probably getting new eyes and replacement balls," said the president.

"Alber, I have an assignment for you," I said. "Organize every one of these conscripted gladiators in order of need, and then cycle them through stasis. You've got food, thanks to...where the heck is he? Yes, Bhatt, the chef. These chambers, and I count ten of them, ought to fix some serious problems until we can return."

"But how do we get through—" began Mixx.

"Sheila." I didn't need to articulate further. The glass well simply vanished. I wondered if it reappeared fifteen stories above us over the arena.

"—through that?" Mix completed her sentence before putting her hand where the glass used to be.

"Harley, you go first," said Effie.

"Then, after we get you patched up, you're going to find that power source so your AI can let the Universe know of this abomination?" asked Alber.

Bhatt appeared behind us with a new, greenish yellow stain down his ragged shirt. He immediately saw my glance and smiled. "Needed a little something to tide me over."

Chapter Forty-Nine

"Sheila, exactly how far is a power source sufficient for you to achieve full control of this screwed up civilization?" I asked.

"Palace City is just over three hundred kilometers from here," said my AI. "Call it 185 miles."

I did a little mental arithmetic. "Transporting three people in 100-yard jumps is three-thousand times three comes to nine-thousand shots for you—"

Sheila didn't let me finish. "Negative. Good arithmetic, Harley, but the reality is I don't have that much energy at my disposal. I could get you, Effie and the president about ten miles before I'd run dry."

"But here in the stadium, your rescue of us and the flying spectator theatrics..." I ran out of words.

Sheila answered my conundrum. "I tapped into the local generation capability and could fly spectators into the sky for years. But one kilometer outside this source, your belt buckle wouldn't...no pun intended...even hold up your pants."

Alber jumped in. "Just under two-hundred miles in this desert, on foot? Even without the mushak using all his resources to look for you, I don't think it's humanly possible for the three of you to survive."

"Harley are you okay?" asked Effie.

I must not have been, as I found myself being held up by Effie and POTUS. My knees didn't seem to work anymore, and I sagged between the two.

"Let's get this man into stasis," said POTUS. "We'll figure this out while ironman here gets an engine overhaul."

The last thing I remember before sinking into blissful oblivion is the president asking how the hell did the riff-raff crowd get transported from Palace City.

I awoke pain free and stepped off the stasis platform stark naked, one of the gladiator slave women quickly wrapping a well-used towel around me. A long line of semi-mobile gladiators queued up patiently, waiting for their turn in the chambers, so I quickly moved aside. Gawand The Undefeated no longer occupied the tube next to me, having been recently replaced by a woman in the process of having her left breast regenerated. I raised my eyebrows and my escort nodded toward the mutilated lady.

"She hurt in sword fight. No shield and got caught mid-lunge," said my towel lady matter-of-factly. "Come dis way. Dey waitin' for ya down de hall."

"One of the guards do that to her?" I held out my towel, normal modesty trumped by my hitherto unrecognized germaphobia.

"No guard," she shrugged. "Gawand. She wouldn't let him do her."

"What the...!" I said. "Where is that sadistic son of a bitch now?"

"Down boy," said POTUS from his seat in a makeshift cafeteria. "Alber has set up a disciplinary council downstairs to deal with a few of the bad apples. Gawand was near the top of the list."

"We...ah...came to the party and forgot to get dressed?" snickered Effie as she threw a pile of clothes in my direction. She slid my newly cleaned tennis shoes toward me with her foot. "I'd hug you, but people might get the wrong idea."

She and POTUS both sat at benches on either side of a long table. I'm glad she *didn't* jump into my arms, as my physical reaction might have embarrassed even the most hardened gladiators around us. Mix, the women who hugged me in the dungeon below the arena, approached me from the side and loudly slapped my bare butt. She smiled as if she had read my mind.

I quickly took the hint and slipped on clean knee-length undershorts, none-the-worse-for-wear blue jeans and my newly laundered *Harley Davidson* T-shirt, absent the grime lovingly smeared on it by Mixx. I didn't recognize the socks, but quickly sat to slip them on along with sneakers cleaner than I'd ever remembered owning.

For the first time, I noted a general silence in the large eating area. As I tied my last shoe, the silence abated to a round of cheers and applause from about two-hundred people. The crowd opened to make a path for the mushak's former chef Bhatt, who marched proudly through a swinging door. On a shield that functioned as a tray, he carried a steaming plate and litre-sized clear stein of some iced, orange drink.

"Just what the doctor ordered," laughed Bhatt. "Here's to Harley Davidson!"

"To Harley Davidson!" roared the room, their own glasses raised.

Bhatt put the shield on the table, and Mix bumped me with her hip to sit closer to Effie. What could I do but pick up my own drink and acknowledge the heartfelt toast of the newly freed captives? And darned of the drink didn't taste purely wonderful. Cold and, the minute it hit my throat and rushed down my esophagus, my body felt even more invigorated. My surprised look as the nectar registered drew even more cheers. I wanted to get caught up with Effie and POTUS, but cries of "Eat! Eat! Eat!" insisted that could wait.

The steaming pile of spaghetti brought back memories of Sunday dinners with grandpa in Wyoming. But how'd they known? Did Effie really read my mind? Between bites I asked, "How long have I been out?"

"Just three hours," said Effie. "Your injuries didn't take long to fix. Besides, you'd been in stasis before, so the nanites still in your system were repurposed."

President Medina just shook his head. "This is really going to change things on Earth."

"Speaking about Earth, what's the plan? How are we going to do a three-hundred-K desert trek to find an energy source?"

Effie nodded to the president, who rubbed his hands together.

"Remember when I asked how 60,000 or so ghouls managed to transport from Palace City to this gore pit?" The rhetorical question didn't need an answer, so he continued. "Most arrived in luxury yachts, flying party boats if you will. The highest-class simply transported in with the mushak."

He paused. I cocked my head in an *Okay, I'm listening* gesture.

"Anyhow, the mushak skipped town on his own. The rest jammed into a waiting party boat for their escape. That is, those who didn't get trampled or made Sheila's drop-kick trip up and into the gristly stadium mud."

"Which explains why I'm not hearing any stadium noise," I said. "The 64-billion-dollar question then is...?"

The dwarf Lexar entered the conversation. He had been standing behind POTUS, but out of my line of sight. "There's a machine shop two levels down. I found several mechanized jousting chariots we might retrofit with wheels that could traverse sand. One could carry the three of you and enough water to make the trip in a hard day."

"With enough fuel to get there?" I asked.

Lexar shrugged. "It'll be close. But yes, it could work."

"Mister President, Effie, Lexar and whomever you think has some mechanical talent, let's go take a look," I said.

Chapter Fifty

This time, we took an elevator down two levels. An OTIS elevator! Straight from Earth. I nearly asked what, why and how when the doors opened to a massive cave that smelled like my dad's motorcycle repair garage. Yeah, his Harleys needed *a lot* of work to keep them running. The overhead track lighting even mimicked Dad's. About the size of a high school basketball court, complete with twenty-foot ceilings, I expected to see the latest out-of-this-world 3D super-metal printers. Would have been nice to say *Computer, build me a dune buggy!* To my surprise, actual Bolton Tools three-axis CNC mill and a Bolton metal lathe greeted us. Bolton! From planet Earth! Ditto for the grinding machine, drill press, bandsaw and even surface finishing tools. All from Earth.

"What's with all this low-tech?" I gasped. "The OTIS elevator? The twentieth-century machine tools from Bolton?"

Lexar had asked a fellow gladiator to join us. He stood about seven feet tall and looked like he could lift the CNC mill with one, grimy hand. His low voice sounded like it growled up from subterranean well.

"Since we're air-gapped," said the new man, "We needed some really primitive equipment. Why reinvent the stuff when we could just grab it from the most backward planet in the galaxy."

I reached over to shake his hand. "And you are?"

"They call me Griss. Lombar Griss," he said. "I run this stuff. Even got a trip to Earth to acquire it. Worked for an automobile manufacturer in Earth's China. That all kept me out of the arena."

"Well Griss, you lucky devil, your mother must have been an L. Ron Hubbard fan." We shook hands, and his questioning look indicated my reference to the *Mission Earth* dekology went right over his head. So I let it go. "I'll bet you'd have been a force to be reckoned with in the arena. You got anything here that could get three people 200 miles over desert sand?"

"I dunno," he said. "These jousting buggies can barely make it through a couple of laps around the arena."

He walked the four of us over to three oversized go-karts with wheels that looked like they'd bury the axels in six inches of sand.

"We are well and truly shat upon," said POTUS.

My heart sank. The president didn't exaggerate our predicament. Effie seemed to be the only one of us in problem-solving mode, and she walked around the labyrinth, lifting tarp after tarp, examining what appeared to be an acre of junk. Lexar followed her at a distance. Whether his motivations involved curiosity or infatuation, I couldn't begin to guess. She interrupted the president's and my funk.

"What are these things," she asked, pointing to ten-foot-high metal orbs mounted on shafts.

"I built these for the mushak's amusement," said Griss. "He wanted gladiators to fight in two rotating cages, where he controlled the direction and rate of spin."

She pulled off the rest of the tarp, revealing a second connected orb, both linked to the same shaft. Between the two rested a metal box about the size of a coffin.

"Woah," I said. "How many of these have you got?"

"Just these two," said the giant mechanic. "The box in the center is a transmission of sorts that can vary the speed and direction of rotation. Built it myself. Copied a John Deere gearbox."

I looked more closely. "I can barely fit my fist through the criss-cross cage setup. Griss, how do we get power to these?"

"Drive shaft fits in the end of the transmission."

POTUS couldn't contain his impatience: "And what, pray tell, powers the drive shaft?"

Griss walked across the greasy floor to the opposite side of the garage. "Got these big electric motors."

"Great," said the president. "Just need a 200-mile-long extension cord, and we're in business."

"Or a big stinking battery," I said. "Academic, though. With just two cages to power us, I don't think we're going anywhere."

My AI's voice interrupted. "Actually Harley Davidson, check the room beneath the arena. For backup power, they have 12 lithium Ferro Phosphate batteries, each with a nearly 20-kilowatt-per-hour capacity. I compute they would do double the job."

"Fat chance we could carry that kind of load on just two wheels," said the president.

"Au contraire Your Lordship," said Griss. "We need the weight to offset the torque generated by the two front wheels. Otherwise, they'd flip the transmission and the sled carrying you all like a medieval trebuchet."

Even Effie got it. "So, the two big cages act as driving wheels to pull a sled weighed down by the big backup batteries. A sled across the sand!"

And I should have guessed. Griss drove an Apollo electric forklift—made in good old California, USA, Planet Earth that had a 4,400-pound lift capacity—down a tunnel and made 12 trips. Lexar and I used an acetylene torch to cut away a piece of sheet steel from the cleanest part of the floor: our sled. Even POTUS got into the act and used our torch to cut two tow slots to sit behind the wheels. We used Griss's expertise to weld the transmission onto the front of the sled. Four hours and a rear-mounted luggage rack later, we were loaded with water and supplies for a desert trek. Just another road trip through a hell someone perversely named Paradise. Not a problem in this world. We thought.

Chapter Fifty-One

Out in the desert, the first problem with our jury-rigged dune buggy blinded us all with the sand kicked up by the spinning cages before they'd pulled us 20 feet. POTUS roared a creative string of profanities regarding impossible interspecies perversions, punctuated by the words, "...mud flaps...!" Effie and I both wholeheartedly agreed.

"Sheila," I said, spitting sand and glad my eyes had been closed. "Any chance—?"

"Sorry, Harley," my AI interrupted. "Stopping the sand blast would take too much of my meager energy reserves. I suggest you hike back and get our talented mechanic to create some shields."

Which I did. An hour later we embarked again, this time protected behind the windshield and engine cowling of an old F-150 Ford truck. And the three of us sat on the Ford's bench front seat. Yep, another gift from our backward planet.

Effie snuggled next to me as if we watched a drive-in movie showcasing a sandstorm. In no time, the pitted windshield barely managed to let in any light, let alone a view the landscape.

"Sheila, I can't see a damn thing."

"I've got this, Harley. If we have good power, I'll take care of getting us to Palace City."

The president muttered something about a pig having carnal knowledge of a duck. That caused Effie to grip my arm, painfully. I wondered if this affirmed why they'd decided our planet needed to be destroyed. Evidently, such casual references to perversion didn't pollute Andromedin conversation. Before I could beg her to lighten up, our front-cage-drive sled hit a bump. I held on to the sidebar. Effie held on to me. A surprised and unsecured POTUS catapulted from perch riding shotgun and disappeared into the sandstorm.

"Oops!" said my AI as we skidded to a stop.

I hopped into the hot, white sand and immediately sank to my knees. Slowly trudging my way back toward the leader of the free world—the insignificant and corrupt object of the Andromeda Cluster's extermination order—the president sat on a mound, spitting silica out of his mouth. Somewhat stunned, he hadn't yet begun to prove his genius for spinning a tapestry of imaginative profanity. Instead, he pointed beside him to the track our sled had just created. A heavily jeweled hand extended from beneath the smooth white pathway.

"Wha' da 'uck 'i-dat?" Still spitting grit and wiping his face, POTUS tried to stand. Being far heavier than me, his legs sank further than mine.

Effie joined us and, together, we managed to walk the president back to our sled. He spit and protested a bit until Effie drew our attention to the red streak just past the pudgy digits extending from a rather solid-looking lump. The lump we must have hit that bounced POTUS off our raft.

"We don't want to go digging over there," she said. "I suspect the luxury yacht taking the crowd back to Palace City needed to lighten the load."

"Yep," I added. "Just another bloody and garishly naked fat exhibitionist on a planet I'm damned sure going to destroy as soon as possible, anyway."

"Ma'shoe!" POTUS lifted his foot into view, revealing a bare foot. No shoe. No sock.

"I'll have Sheila get you a new one," I said. Effie and I continued pulling the president toward the sandmobile. By the time we got him back into his seat, he'd lost both shoes and socks. Bare feet, pinstriped suit pants held up with suspenders, white shirt with the left-front tail hanging out, and disheveled hair. He looked like a Rastafarian back from a night of Reggae music and smoking ganja. I gave him a canteen to wash out his mouth. He spit water and used the rest to rinse his eyes and face, further enhancing his Jamaican beach-bum look.

My own tennis shoes stayed on, as did Effie's not-so-white-anymore slacks and integrated boots.

"Sir, you should hold onto the side rail," said Effie.

"What, they didn't have seatbelts on F-150s?" snorted POTUS.

"Look at the bright side," I said. "At least you had your mouth open and your eyes closed when you got bounced. Maybe there's a lesson to be learned?"

Giving me the *Bronx salute*, the president almost cracked a smile. "Harley, this is for you, and this is for the horse you rode in on."

"I see, Mister President," sniggered Effie, "You must have President Reagan's chief of staff Donald Regan's official portrait somewhere in the White House. *The Horse You Rode In On* turns up on the spine of a book in that portrait."

We both looked at our alien anthropologist with renewed amazement. She didn't wait for either of us to pop the question: "One of our reconnaissance teams' thought they'd landed undetected in a Duluth alley, and a drunk saw the shuttle. He used a similar expletive, and I got curious where it came from."

"How 'bout we get this horse back on the road?" POTUS shook his head. "How far have we gone, anyway?"

"Almost ten miles," answered my AI.

"Well then, giddy up, bitch!" The president didn't mince words.

"Sheila, you heard the man," I said. "And excuse the mixed metaphors. He's having a bad day."

The president pretended not to hear me, instead crossing his bare feet at the ankles and hanging onto not only the side bar with his right hand, but also grabbing the back of the seat behind Effie with his left.

For the next 150 miles, my AI notified us a dozen times as we skirted around yet another Palace City ejectee. We all managed to stay on the sled. Then, 8 miles from our destination, disaster came in the form of a broken axel.

All at once, our left drive-cage froze and, even with my AI's lightning reflexes, the spinning right cage kept digging in and flipped the sled and all the power cells into the sand. Luckily, they didn't land on us.

"Dammit, my eyes!" shouted POTUS.

"Chill, we're almost there," I said, completing the sentence with "Sir!"

"And we didn't get crushed with our homemade Tesla power source," said Effie, who found a canteen and tried to help a somewhat uncooperative president wash grit out of his eyes.

"And the bad news is, we might as well be a million miles from our destination," said POTUS. "It took two of you to haul me 20 feet in this sucking crap!"

He had a point.

"Sheila? Solution to walking to Palace City across this silicon desert?" I looked at the president's bare feet. Well, one of his bare feet. The other dug in up to his knee. He wiggled his toes.

"No shoes, no service," he said. "No shit!"

"Here, hold my beer," said my AI.

"What beer?" I asked. Sheila had lost me.

"Never mind, Harley. I always wanted to say that." One of the sand flaps slid toward us from its landing about 50 feet away. "Watch this."

And electric arc surged from the nearest battery box and cut a piece out of the rubber mat. It then bubbled into what looked like a ski boot. We all just sat there, mesmerized.

"You know," mused Effie. "I don't remember Sheila, your AI, being so creatively humorous. Is she evolving?"

"Principle 21 in my *perfect virus* lecture at MIT involves *institutional memory*," I said. "Not only will my AI evolve, but when we reconnect with the mother AI, Sheila's evolution will propagate throughout."

"At this rate, then," said Effie, "Sheila should have a wonderful career as a comedian." Just then, Sheila piped up.

"What are you, Oscar? About size 12?" I swear my AI sounded like she enjoyed this.

"Thirteen, if you please," answered POTUS. "And that's Mister President to you, ya rube."

"No way, Jose!" Did my AI laugh as she used Oscar Jose Medina's middle name? "Wipe the sand off your foot and slip this baby on."

Which he did. Despite himself, he smiled: "Wow. Fits like it..."

"Like it was made for you, sweetie? Now, get your other tootsies out of the litter box."

As the president complied, another lefty boot formed from the ejected blast mat.

"Let me guess," said POTUS. "We're going to ski cross-country to Palace City?"

"Watch and learn, Your Profaneness." My AI started a sand-fusing process. "Each of you lift one foot at a time."

We complied and a woven mesh of clear, fused silicon formed around our shoes.

"I got it!" My memories of winter adventures in Jackson Hole crystallized. "Snowshoes. We're going to snowshoe to Palace City."

"Bingo, Harley. Now you guys just lift your other feet."

A duplicate process gave us shoes that wouldn't sink with every step.

"This is a lot like work," said the president as he stood and took a few steps. "How much water can we carry? Will it be enough for 18 miles in this heat?"

He had a point. Two suns beat down upon us.

"The president needs a hat," said the AI. "You two have been in stasis enough that the nanites in your blood and skin will protect you from sunburn and sunstroke."

"Then make this cat a hat."

"Just watch what I can do with your litterbox, pussycat." My AI answered the president as she used the same snowshoe process to begin spinning an opaque silicon sombrero. Lightweight, with a chinstrap to keep any wind gusts from blowing it off.

"Now, how about some water?" I said, anxious to get moving toward salvation.

"Harley, we have much bigger problems than water," said my AI.

"Okay, Sheila. What bigger...?"

I looked in the direction of a distant growl. Loping toward us on oversize padded feet, ideal for maximizing speed across the desert, charged three elephant-sized snow leopards. Dammit, call'em Paradise Sand Leopards.

Chapter Fifty-Two

I didn't think such a large predator could run so fast, especially across sand. Their white fur radiated the sunlight as if each hair acted as a prism. Unlike stealth aircraft absorbing all signals, these magnificent beasts did the opposite, approaching like nightmares from hell and eclipsing anything I'd ever imagined as a kid wondering what hid under my bed. Hungry engines with two-foot fangs and glinting diamond claws that could flay a mere human in one pass.

"There's no way this ecosystem could support such beasts," I said. "I'm betting the moron mushak fast-cloned these sentries to protect himself from *us*. They'll likely starve to death when they run out of sand-roasted beach barbecue treats."

"Sheila!" croaked POTUS. "Do you think they see us?"

"Duh?" replied the AI. "And they appear to be homing in on the one with the most meat on him."

"Don't move, fat boy," I said. "Sheila!"

"I know, I know," said the AI. "Can't a girl have any fun?"

Both beasts got near enough to lunge, only they aimed their landing well behind us. And landed on a hologram that duplicated our broken sled and yummy cargo. POTUS appeared twice his normal size. Momentarily disoriented with their suddenly empty entrees, the pair looked around wildly. Behind us, about a hundred yards and right in the middle of our sled path, our image reappeared.

Interesting choice of holograph image placement, I thought. That is, until they landed and unearthed a buried body. Of course! Hitting that bump had broken our axle. A corpulent male, evidently another recent evictee from the not-so-luxury shuttle back to Palace City. Effie wretched as the two big cats toyed with dinner, tossing the 300-pound morsel between them before nicely dividing their snack in a spray of still-liquid blood and viscera. The sight evoked an involuntary gag from me.

"Sheila!" I snapped. "If you'd seen that body, we wouldn't be broken down."

My AI remained silent. Could she be sulking?

"Won't they come back for us, now?" said the president.

"Not if you'll put a plug in it," said the AI. "We're now stealthed and invisible."

"Sheila, can you keep us invisible all the way to the city?" I asked.

"Afraid not," she replied. "Without access to this power source, you're toast."

"What about you two, oh great AI?" said Effie.

"If they had opposable thumbs, they could use Harley's belt to floss their teeth after dinner. But alas, they'll probably leave me in the sun to be buried in the next sandstorm."

"Okay, Sheila. Ideas?" I asked. "How do we get to Palace City?"

"Hypothesis," began my AI. "Palace City is air gapped, which means they don't have any kind of surveillance. These beasts are therefore programmed to be dropped into a grid-search pattern. Hopefully limited in their ability to clone predators, Palace City and one scared mushak will stagger beasts in roughly a straight line between the arena and the city. Maybe one every half mile, with a line of them blocking the way."

"So, we take a longer route and go around the fortress?" POTUS, ever the tactician.

"Bingo I say to the second Catholic president!" said the AI. "If I drain these batteries, I can move you, one at a time, about 150 yards to the left. Naturally, Harley and his marvelous talking belt buckle will go last. After that, my best contributions will be sensing predator sentries and navigating you to the back of the city. No more jumps. Just my rapier wit and charming company."

Both POTUS and Effie groaned. I busied myself slinging canteens around each of us. Good thing we didn't carry the water in a large container.

"Sheila, you ready?"

"Ready as you are, Harley Danger-is-my-middle-name Davidson."

Maybe dying and leaving this mouthy AI to an eternity buried in sand is worth it.

"Go, Sheila!"

Pop. There went POTUS. Pop. Then Effie. Then me.

"Hi guys!" I said as we watched the two leopards clean their teeth on our ruined sled and battery packs. Crackling and a loud roar indicated that at least two fangs connected the anode and the diode poles to finally drain a power source. Luckily, both beasts bounded toward their last meal and not us.

"Shall we be off in a sandshoe race?" Surprising both Effie and me, the president bounded across the sand.

I followed, snowshoeing in the Tetons having been a great cross-training regimen in Jackson Hole Winters. Effie's inexperience only held her back a second or two. We finally caught up with the amazing leader of the free world.

"Mister President," I panted. "What the hell?"

"I take it you didn't follow my last campaign?" laughed POTUS has he casually loped along.

"Uh...no...sir." Gasp. Choke. Wheeze.

"I started my campaign early election year. January, in Alaska. On snowshoes. Promised to hit all fifty states." Not even breathing hard, he looked at my efforts. "Wore out a bunch of Secret Service guys, before they figured out snowmobiles gave them more situational awareness."

"Harley didn't vote in the last election," offered Effie. She'd quickly figured out the mechanics of flying effortlessly across the sand.

"Didn't vote!" POTUS stepped up his pace. "Never heard of Teddy Roosevelt, rugged outdoorsman? Served three terms."

If we'd been on bicycles, I'd have thrown my pump into Effie's front wheel. Alas, the youngest of our three *sandshoers* could barely breathe, let along talk. Luckily, Sheila saved me.

"Hold up!" said my AI. "Two more big cats just over the horizon. Drop. Now!"

And drop we did. Into the hot sand. Just as the growls of two more mutant leopards sounded ahead of us. These two seemed too close to be a permanent part of any ecosystem. Cats this big would need to forage through a lot of sparsely populated territory just to keep alive. Yep, the mushak created this army for one and only one purpose: to find us.

"What kind of moron doesn't vote?" whispered the president.

"Shush," said my AI. Good thing she spoke, because I could barely breathe. The president satisfied himself by simply glaring at me.

The predators passed well ahead. Luckily, they didn't pick up our scent. *My* sweaty scent, to be precise. Effie and the president hadn't worked up much of a sweat. POTUS, a good 35 years older than me, and Effie...well...pictures of me courting an Egyptian mummy princess stopped that line of thought. As the growls faded into the distance, I finally caught my breath.

"I was on a coding binge all through the weekend and into election day," I panted. "Meant to snooze for an hour but crashed until after the polls closed."

"Coast is clear," said my AI.

"You slept through the election," muttered the president. "So did my wife." He and Effie both jumped to their feet, politely waiting for the young slacker to get a drink of water and lead the way. Thankfully, they chose to go at *my* pace.

Several hours and two close predator encounters later, we mercifully dropped behind a sand dune about 100 yards from the Palace City reflection pool. So far, so good. *Not*.

As if out of nowhere, hundreds of fast-moving snakes slithered toward us. Emerging right out of the sand, they must have been doing 20 miles an hour. Certainly faster than any of us could run. POTUS froze. So did Effie. Suddenly I channeled William Wallace: "You may take away my life, but you'll never take my freedom!" I jumped forward and headed toward the snakes in my sandshoes. My compatriots watched, mouths agape. The snakes changed directions and came at me.

I don't *think* William Wallace got a laugh out of POTUS, but I couldn't be sure with all the noise my whomp-whomp-whomps made in the sand. Or maybe it was the sound of my heart pumping in my head that muted everything around me. The whomping became squishing as my giant tennis-racquet shoes slammed down on snake after snake. I don't think I killed any of them, but again, I didn't stop to survey my footwork. A quick look behind me tallied up the good-news/bad-news ledger. The good news: The entire herd pursued me and left my two companions alone. The bad news: Uh, well, the entire herd pursued me.

I'll say this. The little suckers surely could move. But they couldn't quite manage to raise their heads and move at the same time. I continued to land on them, especially when I turned and made a giant circle. Squish-squish-squish. Playing whack-a-mole with deadly whackees seemed like a game I'd eventually lose. But as suddenly as they'd appeared, they burrowed out of sight.

"Hurrah!" yelled the president as he and Effie sand-trotted toward me.

The cheer might have been premature, as the ground seemed to shake. A giant sand dune materialized. An enormous *moving* sand dune. As long as a football field and about 40 feet high, a giant mouth raced toward me. Obviously, the mother had scattered her little snake spawn.

"What! These perverts read Frank Herbert's *Dune*? Or was it the movie *Tremors?*" In my adolescent mind, *Dune* had to be one of the five greatest science fiction novels ever penned. But I think I preferred the creativity of bio-engineering those desert leopards. Even the T-Rexes in the arena beat the giant maw heading right for me. Betting that the mushak's sandworm followed the same general rules of physics as Herbert's, I yelled at Effie and POTUS: "Quick, stomp your feet!"

The wind and the freight train barreling toward me drowned out my voice. They looked at me, mouthing the word, "What?" I pantomimed my own stomping, and waved my arms like the home-team defense at a football game tries to rev up the crowd. Miraculously, they got the message in the nick of time, and the hideous wiggler veered past me and...oops...toward them.

If I remembered correctly, Herbert's Paul Atreides, aka Muad'Dib and leader of the Fremen, controlled the sandworm by prying open a piece of its shell. The worm in turn would shift the opening away from the rushing sand, thereby rotating its body and shifting directions. I quickly slipped out of my sandshoes, grabbing one and jamming the heel end into a crease in the beast's side. And voila! Sand poured into the opening and the darn thing quickly rolled to the side, pulling me up with it. Not only did it change directions, away from my two companions, but they saw what I'd done with the sandshoe and duplicated my move...hey, I remembered what Herbert called these creatures...as the Shai-Hulud passed by them. The president missed his insertion, but Effie nailed her sandshoe plant and grabbed POTUS by the ankle with her other hand as he held onto the rising contraption. Me, I morphed into a lumberjack playing the log-roll game, staying atop the rotating beast as my two companions joined me.

"Well screw Frank Herbert and the worm he rode in on!" yelled POTUS above the roar of sand. "You figured out how to steer this sumbich?"

"Sheila!" I shouted, not that I needed to raise my voice. "Please add to your list of things to do and find any DNA-manipulation databases on this morally bankrupt planet before we destroy it."

"You're not considering—" began my AI.

"You never know, Sheila," I interrupted. "We have a lot of deserts on Earth."

"Yeow!" screamed POTUS.

"You want one of these things loose on Earth?" I asked, putting some leverage on my sandshoe in the opposite direction I wanted the beast to turn.

"Hell no!" said POTUS. "And thanks for getting it to change directions. One of those bands around Snakezlla here was about to tear off my scrotum."

Effie scooted up behind me and held onto my waist, whispering into my ear, "Watch *your* scrotum, big boy."

I yelled back over her shoulder: "Takes big balls to be president, eh?"

I *think* I heard him spit sand at me, but the wind must have blown it back into his face. We made a wide circle through the sand, past the palace reflection pool and along the sheer wall beside the desert fortress.

"We're getting closer to their power source," said my AI through my ear implant. "We should dismount...*here*!"

"Easier said than done," I said. Turning Moby Mushak right or left seemed to be the limit of my navigation ability. "How do I stop this thing?"

I *think* Effie said, "Duh!" She acted too quickly for me to be sure, pulling the lip of my steering shoe out of the worm's back. In an instant, our ride dove below the surface. We rolled on the sand, barely managing not to get pulled beneath the desert. Half swimming and half wading, we finely reached a rocky outcropping. Waves of white grit passed behind us, leaving silence and a sheer wall rising 300 feet above us.

"Glad you got my nuts out of that wringer," panted POTUS.

"Yeah, because your heart and mind would have followed," snickered Effie.

The president rolled onto his back and breathed hard. "Oh, pristine space queen, you've been totally corrupted by Earth bathroom humor."

"Where do you suggest we go that *hasn't* been warped out of shape, courtesy of one Harley Danger Davidson?" Effie slugged me in the shoulder.

"Good point." POTUS spat some more sand at me. Barefoot, his shirt completely untucked, lying there soaking in the afternoon sun, the president almost looked like a vacationing mainlander in the Maui. Almost.

"Sheila, any idea how we get over this wall to the power source?"

"Ouch!" POTUS rolled onto one elbow and rubbed his back just as a cubic yard of stone smashed against the rock where his head had been. I looked up 30 stories to see several burly arms trying to lever another granite block over the ledge.

"Sheila!" *Did my shriek come out a little high-pitched*? I asked myself.

I didn't have time to wait for the AI's answer, as the block several Cretins labored to push off the ledge suddenly evaporated. They must have been working hard, too, as their forward momentum suddenly propelled them over the edge. Turns out, my scream didn't compare to the girlishness of theirs as they splatted on the rocks about 20 feet away.

"Sheila?" I asked in a more manly voice.

"Harley, it took me some time to recharge after getting near the power source," said my AI. "Here, hold my beer and watch this."

"Sheila needs some new material," said POTUS.

"Okay, party pooper," the AI responded. "Cover your scrotum and step a couple paces to your left."

The president complied to both directives, not knowing if Sheila meant herself to be taken literally. He didn't need to do either, as a tunnel materialized in the castle wall ahead of us.

"Honey, I'm home." My yell echoed as Effie and the president followed me inside.

"No use playing subtle," said Effie.

"Heh, heh, lead the way, Harley my-middle-name-is-Danger Davidson," said POTUS. "The fat mushak is about to sing his swan song."

"We're not out of this yet, Oscar," I said, my pace picking up. The president may have growled at my familiarity and lack of protocol decorum, but my footsteps drowned him out.

Our tunnel bore into at least 100 feet of quarried stone. As we entered the massive room, I could see why the serious protection. Actually, Sheila grokked it for me.

"Harley Davidson, *that* is the most dangerous power source in the universe," said my AI.

Before us stood an enormous shimmering, luminescent cloud that didn't appear to have a hard shell around it. From deep inside a black center pulsated outward.

"The Andromeda Federation declared that illegal centuries ago!" said Effie.

"Fill me in here," said POTUS.

"Let me guess," I said. "That's a black hole they somehow captured for power generation."

"You got it, Harley," said my AI. "In all the Universe, that's by far the most dangerous way to generate local power. In fact, there's no record of anything like it being operational anywhere."

Quick to desire a net-net, I blurted: "Sheila, don't ever again even *think* about asking me to hold your beer. Just tell me how soon you can tap into this power source and get us the hell out of Paradise?"

"Spoilsport!" The voice didn't come from my belt buckle. Instead, the hologram of a smiling T-Rex loomed above me. "Hey Harley, I'm here. May I go get the mushak. Huh? Huh? May I?"

Okay, my AI had seen the coliseum crowd's reaction to the beast and figured she'd materialize in as frightening form as possible to say hello to our host.

"Yes, Sheila, you may. And please take us with you."

In a flash, we appeared in a giant palace reception hall, where hundreds of catamites surrounded a raised throne. On that throne sat a startled mushak who'd suddenly lost interest in a smorgasbord of delicacies sitting beside him. The boys surrounding their king cleared out the hall rather suddenly.

"Hi, asshole. Remember me?" I wished I'd been carrying a sword or stick or something with which I could whack him in the head as I strode toward the quivering pile of protoplasm who'd assumed a fetal position. A fat thumb kept pressing an armrest button. He protected his privates with the other hand. Only then did I realize that my AI's manifestation of a T-Rex accompanied me. "I've got this, Sheila. Please dematerialize."

"Harley, you never let me have any fun," said a melting pre-historic monster from Earth.

The absence of my monster didn't seem to calm down the mushak.

"I'm guessing your bug-out button doesn't work?"

My question evoked only whimpers. Gosh, in my favorite movies, the bad guys *always* had more diabolical and effective defenses. What a letdown! So, back to business.

"Sheila, are there other population centers on Paradise besides the coliseum and Palace City?"

"Negative, Harley," came the disembodied voice of my AI. "Paradise appears to be a single-use planet: slave entertainment for a pervert ruling class."

"Mister President?" I turned toward POTUS. "Any ideas where on Earth we should relocate those poor devils in the coliseum?"

"Crikey!" said POTUS in his best Australian imitation of the Crocodile Hunter. "You know, we're going to have to process those people. Not all of them are people we'd welcome into our civilization."

"Au contraire, buttercup," I said. "Somewhere on Earth, every one of the beings we've run into would find kindred spirits. So wherefore art thou thinking, Oscar? Guantanamo?"

"Ooooh, Harley. Revenge is a dish best eaten cold." POTUS rubbed his hands together.

"Sorry butterc-...er...boss," I stammered. Now that our chances of surviving this adventure dramatically improved, I should really be less cavalier toward my commander in chief. Whether or not I'm in his military chain of command. "But back to my question. Where to patriate the gladiators?"

"Sheila?" asked POTUS. "Suggestions? Maybe an abandoned military base."

"The Nekoma Pyramid site in North Dakota," said the AI without pause. "There are less than 30 people in the area, and I can relocate them quite easily. Then we can drop the coliseum just outside the pyramid."

"Sounds good to me," smiled the president. "Not too many votes one way or the other."

"Harley?" asked the AI.

"Do it, Sheila," I said. "Then we can blast this worthless cesspool off the Andromeda Federation sexploitation-vacation short list.

"You really intend to destroy this planet? Palace City? All those innocent little boys?" Effie's serious question stopped me short. How could I play God and terminate this enclave of perversion?

"God told the Israelites returning from Egypt to kill all the Canaanites. Men, women, children, and even their cattle," said the president. "There *is* a precedent for genocide."

"But that was God," said Effie.

Damn! My thought exactly. Was I ready to play God? From the planet that crucified our deity?

The mushak fidgeted nervously. He'd stopped trying to press the red button on his left and moved that hand to cover his face. The other hand still protected his privates.

"Effie, suggestions?"

"I recommend we give the Andromeda Cluster leadership the recordings Sheila has made of our adventure here, including documentation of the black-hole power source, and let them handle this syphilitic growth on their civilization." Effie crossed her arms as if challenging me to argue.

"How about we broadcast our entire stay in Paradise to every known planet in the Universe," said POTUS. "Including Earth?"

"Talk about a PR nightmare," I mused. Then to my AI: "Sheila, how soon can we get the coliseum and its occupants transferred to Nekoma?"

"Already done, Buttercup." My AI picked up sarcasm fast?

"And did you do a dump of all their computer files?"

"Yes," she said. *At least she didn't say "Yes, Buttercup."*

"Then let's say goodbye to this festering wart and get back to Earth."

# # #

The AI made it so, and the three of us materialized in the White House situation room. Evidently, the Nekoma pyramid had galvanized some high-level panic. Because anybody important was in the process of arriving. Those minor nabobs lined the walls. The newly sworn-in vice president nearly had a coronary as the somewhat worse-for-wear president appeared behind him. Already keyed up from her inclusion in this august group, the newly appointed secretary of state fainted. She should have worn Depends, as incontinence necessitated her removal from the room.

Chapter Fifty-Three

"Well, Harley Davidson, my boy, we've been off planet for a couple of weeks and here we are," said President Medina to the gaping faces in front of which we'd just appeared. A barefoot, threadbare president and a beach bum couple stared back at their button-down crowd. POTUS's business-as-usual demeanor belied his beat-to-hell appearance. "So," pausing to savor his victorious return. "What possible harm could the dog you left in charge have done? After all, it's less than a month since she came out of the stasis chamber with the ability to speak."

Even though the president was a full head shorter than either the captain or myself, he radiated a power that eclipsed my eighteen-year-old ability to duplicate. Even though I had indeed created the virus that took over the entire invading alien civilization. And Ephimera Rose, the captain of the invading alien ship, simply looked exhausted. To be sure, this six-foot-three-inch towering beauty with the flowing white hair and perfect skin could have been on the cover of the *Sports Illustrated* swimsuit issue for multiple consecutive years. But I'd put her through a lot over the past two weeks, and it showed. Me? Heck, I looked exactly like the ruddy, freckle-faced, six-foot-five sunburned kid that gave nightmares to fathers of teenage daughters. Cocky, too. I just couldn't help myself. Even after our near-death intergalactic adventure.

"You mean the little doggie I left in charge of the AI I instructed to keep order on Planet Earth just before we were kidnapped? What could *possibly* have been the harm of turning the dog loose?" I must have sounded sarcastic.

"But Harley, wouldn't the AI have kept Chenoa out of trouble?" asked starship Captain (and the love of my life for the last three weeks) Ephimera Rose, or Effie as I'd come to know her. This must also have been *her* way of letting off a steam of relief. "After all, your AI/virus not only took over my ship, but effectively crippled our entire intergalactic civilization."

The three of us sat in geosynchronous orbit over Washington, D.C. after a rather harrowing two weeks as abductees of a rogue religious nut, The Supreme Mushak on the now-demolished planet ironically called Paradise. Oh yeah, I'd destroyed an entire planet of hedonistic sadists after rescuing a few thousand captives and repatriating them to their home worlds.

"Mister President," said the vice president as his image projected from the White House to the holoscreen in the center of our flight deck. "*We* hereby turn over the presidency, and a somewhat worse-for-wear world, back to you. Someday, I might even enjoy hearing about your adventure."

As the vice president said the word "we," the dog sitting on the Oval Office desk beside him smiled and looked oh so innocent. Too innocent. The hairs on the back of my neck stood straight up.

"Hello, Harley Davidson," said the twenty-pound white dog without apparent guile and sporting the familiar brown spot on her right side. "And I turn control of your AI back to you."

Yeah, right. Like you had a choice! I thought. "Thank you, Chenoa. Have you stayed out of trouble?"

"Of course," said the dog. The vice president coughed something that sounded like *Bullshit!* into his fist. Given the likelihood of this historic dialogue's being broadcast worldwide, I correctly surmised that the president would pick up on the signal and take charge. Which he did.

POTUS began, "I think I'll wait to report on my odyssey and let you summarize the last two weeks in the United States."

"United States, hell!" said the vice president. "How about the worldwide dog and pony show created by this...this...hound from the Infernal Abyss?"

"At least he didn't call me a bitch," quipped Chenoa.

"Sheila," I said, deciding to diffuse the situation and maybe spare the dog a whipping from the VP. "Please fetch Chenoa up here with us."

"Acknowledged," said my AI simultaneously with the appearance of my dog on the flight deck. Chenoa promptly jumped into Effie's lap. Appropriate. In the captain's chair.

The president gave Chenoa a grimace accompanied by his imitation of a deep-throated growl, and then addressed his vice president: "As you were saying, has sweet little Chenoa commanded the AI to shut down a country, or execute human traffickers?"

"Negative, Mister President."

"Okay, what has the dog caused the AI to do?"

"Nothing, dammit! She hasn't commanded the AI to do one, bootlicking thing."

"Then how could she have created worldwide havoc?"

"Her infernal television show, *Hello World*!" said the VP.

"Cute," I said. "*Hello World* is always the first program you usually write when you start learning a new computer language."

"Hello world?" asked POTUS.

"Harley Davidson's little furry friend's TV show has pretty well bitch-slapped most of the global markets," said the vice president, who started counting off fingers. "The world animal produce market is just under four trillion dollars. Chenoa's live videos with other animals just brought out of stasis and now capable of coherent speech—pigs, cows, horses, goats to name a few—has muzzled that industry. Who's going to slaughter a talking, sentient, creature? Or buy anything from a company that does such a dastardly act."

The VP ticked his second finger. "And those stasis chambers peppering the world have put the nearly twelve-trillion-dollar healthcare sector on the planet right into the flaming pile of dogshit. Who needs a doctor or a medicine when they can just immerse themselves in a stasis tank for a few hours?"

The third finger stood alone. "And your Boeing stock, along with all the automobile company shares in retirement funds, is dog meat. People can just have Mister Davidson's omniscient AI transport themselves and/or their goods instantaneously anywhere, anytime. I call it a hundred-trillion dollars erased off Earth's GDP. Are you getting the magnitude of—?"

"I get the picture," interrupted the president. He then turned to me. "Somebody, uh, let the dogs out!" The president's attempt at dark humor landed with a thud.

But the VP wasn't done. "I'd say a barking mad Jolly Green Giant picked up one little white doggie and wiped his ass with her. Hence that brown spot on her side."

Awh crap! I guess this worldwide dialogue needed to take place. And it needed to be public. No backroom deals with the rich and powerful.

"The United Nations Security Council has scheduled a meeting as soon as all members can attend!" The vice president must have read my thoughts and taken a contrary view.

"No," I said, impulsively. It just came out. "There won't be any closed-door decisions on the fate of the world."

The good old Veepie looked like I'd slapped him. POTUS, my commander in chief and the most powerful man in the world, looked equally put out with my blurted assertion of control.

"What does the Emperor of the Known Universe have in mind?" asked Captain Rose, smugly sitting behind me from the captain's chair, legs crossed with Chenoa on her lap. "Your AI has wreaked havoc across every planet in the

Andromeda Cluster, and you haven't begun to undo *that* mess yet."

"Sheila," I said to my AI, always listening to me no matter where I happened to be. "How much of our imprisonment and escape from Paradise did you manage to capture?"

"All of it, Harley."

"I'm most interested in the degenerate society of near immortals created by stasis chamber technology. A society where people don't have to work, or even be productive in any way at all. No one must be dependent upon anyone or anything. I'd like that entire experience broadcast worldwide. Sheila, please air the president's, Captain Rose's, and my adventure while in captivity on Paradise."

"Acknowledged, Harley Davidson," said my AI.

"To all of you watching this, in twenty-four hours, I will reconvene this global meeting and make some recommendations. And thanks to my AI Sheila, every sentient being on the planet will have a vote. An equal vote. Even the...ah...dogs."

Chenoa sat up a little taller, smirkier if that were possible.

Chapter Fifty-Four

At least the hospitality industry seemed to be booming. POTUS had to pull some strings to get us a suite at the Marriott Hotel, less than a third of a mile from the White House. It could have been in Seattle for all I cared, but people still hadn't gotten their brains around free and instantaneous travel. On Pennsylvania Avenue, our great room had a view of the Washington Monument. Captain Rose's room at one end and mine on the other—okay, the love of my life and I hadn't cohabitated yet—gave us distance yet accessibility, appropriate for the sole representative of an advanced culture to our backward ball of dirt and for the precocious MIT student that had brought all technology in every corner of the universe to a dead stop. Of course, nobody thought the Andromeda Cluster's demise hadn't been warranted, since they had sought to outright destroy us. On the other hand, my surreptitiously downloading their entire technological foundation had sent our own financial institutions back into the stone ages.

"Ooh, ooh, [bark], [bark], [yip], [yip], here's my television program *Hello World*_with Pink the pig," said the excited Chenoa as she jumped up and down, pawing my knee.

"Who named a pig *Pink?*" asked Captain Rose as she turned toward us after looking out the floor-to-ceiling windows at the DC morning skyline.

"That was my idea," said the dog. "He'd been raised on one of those big agro farms and didn't have much interaction with talking humans. He thought that *Hey Big Boy* would have been a good name. Then I told him they were just sizing him up for slaughter."

"I'm still having trouble getting my brain around the stasis process," I said to Captain Rose. "Effie, stasis makes *all* animals talk?"

"Harley, the stasis process turns billions of nanobots loose in any biological creature. Not only do the bots repair damage to major organs, musculature and skeletal makeup, but they traverse the blood/brain barrier to effect repairs to brain links. Deep structures in any creature capable of minimal speech recognition. You call this *computational equivalence*. No matter what the language, each child on Earth learns that language in about the same time. Similarly, animals learn a limited vocabulary of commands in any spoken tongue. For some reason, the animals on planet Earth had lost a simple linkage that—as you said in your MIT lecture—one of your linguists Noam Chomsky calls *deep structure*. That mechanism has been repaired in Chenoa. And it looks like it's been repaired in all animals who go through the stasis process."

The onscreen demonstration of Chomsky's deep structure activation greeted us. Sitting beside the apex of a waterfall and backed up by a lush green forest, Chenoa sat next to a gigantic hog. The sound of raging water from below could be heard in the background, but the dog and pig were exceptionally well-wired for sound, and their voices resonated.

"Males, females and unfortunately neutered beings, I'd like to introduce you to my friend, Pink," said Chenoa. "This one-of-a-kind camera work is courtesy of Harley Davidson's AI, whom you all know as Sheila."

The camera appeared to float in space about five feet off a cliff edge. A quick pan below showed the heart-stopping drop as the Yosemite waterfall cascaded 1,430 feet below. Chenoa and Pink sat on a rock to the left of the scene.

"Hello," resonated the deep bass voice of the hog. "Thank you for letting me tell my story."

"You like it up here?" asked Chenoa. Did she have Sheila put a twinkle in her eye?

"You told me Sheila would take me anywhere I wanted," boomed Pink. "This picture was on the wall of the Iowa slaughterhouse. Bruce and I thought we were headed here as some kind of reward for being obedient."

"Bruce was your friend?"

"*Was* is the operative word." Pink rested his head on the stone outcropping and sighed, his giant body moving noticeably at the intake of air. "They scalded him alive as part of the butchering process."

I did my own rapid intake of breath. They did *what* to these animals? Scalded them to death. Boy, was I glad we'd ordered French toast for breakfast!

"How were you spared?" Chenoa kind of growled the question as she sat upright and looked directly at her guest. I'd known her long enough to recognize that she damned well knew the answer. Tom Brokaw, eat your heart out. My doggie had mastered the interview process like a pro.

"One second, I was in the high-pressure steam blast, and the next, I floated in one of the large stasis chambers you'd had your AI erect in Iowa Falls." Pink looked directly at the camera. "Thank you, Sheila."

I wondered why just Pink got spared, as many in the audience probably did, too.

"Let me get this right," said Chenoa. "They routinely scald animals alive as a part of the...eh...transition/rendering process? How can this possibly be humane?"

"Cuz I guess we ain't humans," said Pink. "I wish more of my friends could have been saved."

Ah ha! I thought. Chenoa had coached Pink to bring this out, answering the burning question on everyone's mind.

"It took me some doing to get the AI to rescue even one of you," said Chenoa. "Rescuing the whole herd somehow violated her mandate from Harley Davidson."

Crap! Chenoa just tied a can to my tail. Captain Rose, my beloved Effie, must have seen me blush and sensed I'd be interrupting the program to ask my AI for an explanation, because she sharply jabbed me with an elbow.

Chenoa looked from Pink to the camera, back to Pink, and then again to the camera. She growled. Thunder sounded in the background, and I wondered if she'd cued Sheila to sense her moods and add sound effects. The camera zoomed in on Chenoa's face, her big brown eyes unblinking, no twinkle this time. It appears the AI did indeed sense the dog's state of mind. She began her closing comment.

"Those of you watching this over a breakfast of ham and eggs, or bacon and eggs, take yourselves a little barf break. And whatever you do, absolutely resist the urge to check out my website for unauthorized videos of cattle slaughterhouses, or the torture and butchering of dogs and cats in various so-called wet markets around the world. Think about what that meat you're eating went through. The torture. The horror of an intelligent, feeling being facing such a horrible death. Hey bitches! Dab that mascara running out of your eyes and wonder how many equally gruesome deaths from animal testing made your beauty products possible."

Oh hell, there goes the cosmetics industry, I thought, knowing that animal testing in the United States had long since been outlawed. Looks like the advertising boys on Madison Avenue had some damage control to do.

Chenoa closed: "What our viewers *could* do is write your elected representatives and urge them to adopt my draft *Animal Bill of Rights* amendment to the United States Constitution. Hell, to the United Nations charter, too." Chenoa paused, and leaned her head against Pink. "Oh, yes. You can also check out my list of companies you should boycott. Chenoa out."

Program credits rolled, accompanied by Peter Gabriel's song, *Steam*. In our hotel room the dog moved her head to the beat, eventually dancing sideways, left, right, left, right, dipping every fourth measure.

"Wow!" is all I could say. I think Effie would have given Chenoa a high five if she could have gotten the dog's attention.

"There were so many songs about steam," sang Chenoa in sync with the background rhythm. "*Rock and Roller Steam*, or *Steam Will Rise*, just to name two. Pink thought I should have used Sonic Youth's *Pink Steam*, but it just didn't have the beat. What do you guys think?"

"I like the Kinks' *Last of the Steam Powered Trains*," said my resident anthropologist and starship captain. "Harley?"

My mouth just hung open. Talking music selection after my dog just killed several major industries—meat packing, healthcare, upholstery for homes, automobiles, fashion, cosmetics—what the hell! Effie winked at me and scooped up Chenoa, proceeding to dance around the room with her as *Steam* music videos filled every available wall in the hotel suite.

"Sheila?" I finally managed an utterance. "How many companies are on Chenoa's boycott list?"

"Thirteen-hundred-twelve and counting," said my AI. "Chenoa has given me a video for each industry involved in use of animal products, which I have communicated privately to their management. She thought it only fair to give them a chance to publicly renounce their supply chain. Make that thirteen-hundred-and-twenty. Eight more just missed the deadline, which was the airing of this program."

I had to sit down. What have I unleashed on the world? Massive unemployment. Eternal life. The end of war. Nothing to do but gag down veggie burgers and find bizarre ways to entertain a populace of couch potatoes. Sounds like the planet I just destroyed.

Effie plopped down on the couch beside me, still holding Chenoa. She just looked at me, those big green eyes boring into my soul.

"We met because you came to destroy this planet," I said. "You'd been searching for us over two millennia.

All because we were the ones who murdered God. My computer virus stopped you."

She just kept blinking at me. Even the dog sat silently on her lap, her big brown unblinking eyes. I could swear the dog smiled, too, tongue hanging out and the corners of her lips angling upward.

I shook my head. "Maybe I should have just let you destroy our planet. Because that's what your technology has effectively done, anyway. After all, I used the science I stole from you to expose that hedonistic abomination of a planet called Paradise. But aren't we destined to become just like them?"

Effie just patted me on the knee with her free hand. And winked.

The dog broke the silence: "Not if I have anything to say about it."

Chapter Fifty-Five

Up in the master bath on the second floor of the White House in the president's quarters, a harried valet seemed baffled by the dog's and my presence in this traditionally private venue. POTUS had just stepped out of the shower wore nothing but a terrycloth bathrobe. Steam wafted through the open bathroom door as the second-most powerful man on the planet emerged. I may have had the title of first-most powerful man around, though most people likely had no idea.

"I suppose you wonder why I called this meeting," smirked POTUS.

"So does your valet," said Chenoa, nonchalantly strutting out of his bathroom and settled by jumping onto the four-poster bed.

"I figured you didn't want us out of your sight," I said.

"Good, son. You're learning. Now, you remember what we rehearsed?"

"And your wife thinks she can get the chief justice to perform the ceremony?"

"Yeah, yeah, yeah," said the president to the Beatles' lyrics. "By the way, where's Effie?"

"The first lady insisted on dressing her for the broadcast," I answered.

"Somebody should have dressed *you* for the broadcast," muttered the valet. "Blue jeans and a Harley-Davidson T-shirt?"

"Jake!" scolded the president.

"Sorry Mister President."

"You're right, Jake," I said to the cowering valet. "But I just didn't want to project something that I'm not. What the viewing audience will see is a kid who's in way over his head, and positively *not* what they're calling the Emperor of the Known Universe."

I don't think Jake bought off on my logic, but he kept his mouth shut, probably to keep his job.

Effie and the first lady whisked into the room just as Jake helped the president slip into his trademark black suit jacket.

"Wow!" exclaimed POTUS. "What a great choice, that Dior on Captain Rose."

"Wow!" I couldn't help but wonder if my attire selection might have been downright stupid. The AI whispered into my earpiece that the Violet Medina's striking red dress was a Versace A-line. Sheila also confirmed that Effie did indeed wear a regal white Dior that perfectly accentuated her hair. Her hair, obviously cut and arranged by the first lady's staff beautician, gave Effie a 1920s Hollywood red-carpet look. I repeated, "Wow."

"Jake, could you maybe find me a blue blazer to wear over my T-shirt?" Yeah, I caved big time. Effie shook her head and sighed. But I could see the hint of a smile. We'd talked long and hard about how I should present myself to the world. She'd agreed that our announcement should be straightforward and without guile.

A knock on the bedroom door preceded a female voice: "Mister President, they're ready downstairs."

The president's valet raced out of the room and had a blue blazer waiting for me as we all reached the top of the stairs. The double-breasted jacket fit perfectly, and Jake helped me get the brass button into the right hole.

"Thank you, Jake," I said.

"You're welcome, Captain America," he answered.

"You just couldn't resist," said Chenoa as she hopped down the stairs ahead of us. Naturally, the cameras caught the dog's grand entry first. Her pom-pom ears perked up at applause from the White House staff.

"Dang world gone to the dogs," said the president without moving his smiling lips. He waived to the staff and led us to the Red Room on the main floor. Actually, Chenoa led us to the Red Room, where she promptly perched in the middle of the red couch to the right of the coffee table. Violet took Effie to the opposite couch, leaving me and POTUS to face the cameras from beneath the wall paintings. I didn't remember agreeing to this seating arrangement, but suspected the ladies had ulterior motives. Hologram cameras around the room were live and, thanks to Andromedan technology, nobody had to wire us with microphones. POTUS seemed unsurprised by the seating arrangements, so he must have been in on it with the girls.

"Ladies and gentlemen," began the president. "Much to the dismay of speechwriters and my communications staff, I've decided an informal little family chat might be in our interests, tonight. After all, humanity is one big family."

A fireplace crackled just behind the women, casting a warm glow throughout the already red surroundings. I wondered why this took place in the Red Room. I heard somewhere that people ate more in restaurants with red interiors, and that red was an action color. It seemed to me we should have been in a blue room, that is if the president's goal was to comfort and reassure the planet. And reassurance should have been number one on the menu, given the total economic disruption Chenoa had wrought.

The president continued: "Joining Violet and I are the now-famous talking dog Chenoa, Andromeda Cluster starship captain Ephemera Rose, and by what some news outlets refer to as The Emperor of the Known Universe, Harley Davidson."

"Harley *Danger* Davidson," interjected Chenoa.

The dog seemed about to extemporize, but I raised my forefinger in a gesture she knew well. POTUS made the same gesture, confirming that this dog, this night, should not be heard from without explicit invitation.

"As you well know," President Medina put his hand on my knee, "world financial markets are closed. Stasis chambers made the healthcare industry obsolete. Animal-based food production no longer exists. Instantaneous and unrestricted travel makes country boundaries irrelevant. Ditto for most professions. The list goes on. Question is, where do we go from here? Harley, where *do* we go from here?"

The president and I had talked about this. But it surely sounded more coherent in those rehearsals than it seemed to my mind at this moment. I could have used one of his brilliant speech writers. So much for hindsight.

"I don't know and do not intend to impose any future on this planet," I began. "Free will and free choice are my gold standard, my paramount values. Yes, my computer virus brought a civilization bent upon destroying our planet to its knees. In that sense, I placed a limit on free will in the universe. Alas, I also couldn't resist treating human traffickers on Earth with, well, extreme prejudice. That was then, but is now. I want to introduce you to what some gloom-and-doomers call The Singularity. Sheila, would you please materialize and sit next to Chenoa?"

Even the president gasped when a freckle-faced, red-headed woman appeared beside Chenoa. My AI must have shared my fashion sense, as she materialized wearing a plaid shirt tucked into Levi blue jeans. She didn't look to be much older than me. She sat crossing one leg, and a shiny Lucchese cowboy boot came from under the coffee table. Chenoa snuggled up against her as she scratched behind the dog's ears.

"Hi, Harley. Mister President. Mrs. Medina and Effie," said my AI.

"Call me Violet," said the president's wife as she stood and quickly walked around the table separating them to take her seat beside Sheila. "You're real. I mean, you have a hand I can feel."

Violet took the AI's left hand and caressed the fingers, even looking closely at the perfectly manicured fingernails.

Sheila laughed. About the same height as the first lady, my AI didn't need my instructions to initiate conversation: "Please call me Sheila, Violet. And yes, I can form a solid structure, thanks of course to the technology I *borrowed* from the Andromeda Cluster when I took over their computing infrastructure and stopped them from destroying Earth."

"You have green eyes too, just like Effie." The first lady looked very closely at Sheila, as did billions of people around the worldwide. Thanks to Chenoa in my absence, everyone had 3D TVs and easy access to stasis tank regeneration units. Not to mention that most of the professionals in developed nations busied themselves trying to figure out just what to do with their lives. From doctors and healthcare workers to airline pilots to stockbrokers to slaughterhouse employees. With a lot of time on their hands, most stayed glued to their immersive 3D video systems for moments like this. At least, that's what it looked like from the on-screen data feeds.

"You want to see what I looked like when I freed twenty women from the human traffickers in Ft. Lauderdale last week?" Her comment little doubt that The Singularity had a will and personality of her own.

"I would," said Chenoa from the other end of the couch. Of course, the dog knew full well how Sheila had appeared to usher the bad guys into the presence of their maker.

The petite and lovely Sheila lost her head, so to speak. The three-foot-high head of a T-Rex replaced a face that could have launched a thousand ships. The first lady started falling off the couch even before a toothy roar shattered the glass mirror behind them. POTUS leaped to catch his wife before she hit the floor. The attendant Secret Service agents sprung between the first couple and the monster's head with guns drawn. My AI quickly disarmed the protection detail before they inadvertently shot someone. I did a face plant and then used my extended thumb and pointer finger to target the T-Rex, who morphed back into the all-American, harmless, downright loveable Sheila.

The president used a particularly vulgar adjective middle name of a deity, after which his wife took control of the broadcast: "Honey, you can't say that on television!"

"Darlin', that horse left the flaming barn," said POTUS, dialing back the profanity and helping his wife onto the couch beside us.

"Forgive my impetuous creation," I said in my calm-down-the-mob voice. And my damned dog sounded like a snickering cartoon canine I remembered from Saturday morning television in Wyoming. "Chenoa, you stop that *right now*!"

The dog put a paw over the snout which rested on Sheila's lap.

"Let me get back to answering the president's question, *what's next?*" I stood and moved to Effie's couch on my right, which gave the president and his wife more room on theirs. It also gave the weaponless Secret Service team a chance to return to their posts, well out of the picture.

"As I was saying, free will and free choice are critical. Yes, I could behave like I owned the place and use various manifestations of Sheila to punish every one of you flawed humans. Or misbehaving animals!" I pointed to Chenoa, whose hangdog look almost made me laugh. "I could offer to *eliminate the executions when obedience improves*. But that sounds like a plan rejected in the book of *Genesis*."

I put my arm around Effie, who'd been demure and silent the whole broadcast. She radiated the most beautiful smile as she returned my gaze. It almost gave me instantaneous amnesia. *What the hell was I about to say? Oh, yes!* I slid off the couch and dropped to one knee.

Even with the sound-dampening insulation of the nearly bullet-proof White House, a roar erupted from outside the south entrance. The video proceedings made it to the outside crowd, who knew a marriage proposal when they saw it. Okay, the guy on one knee might have been the dead giveaway.

"If this alien creature will have me, I'd like her to honeymoon with me on her home planet, where I have some fences to mend. That is if I can get somebody on this godforsaken rock to marry us."

Cheers from outside doubled in magnitude. I gave the freckle-faced AI my *what's-going-on* look. She said, "At least I didn't let a million people try to transport themselves into this room."

The dog wined and looked at us with big brown eyes.

Recovering her composure and realizing she played a non-trivial role in the unfolding public drama, the first lady said: "Oscar, how about Charlie? He could perform the marriage before dinner tonight."

The Honorable Charles Sheldon served as the chief justice of the United States Supreme Court.

"Good idea, dear," said POTUS.

"Us honeymooners had probably better not leave my dog in charge here. You appear to have caused enough damage, little girl."

Captain Rose patted the seat beside her, and Chenoa scurried across the divide to jump onto our couch. Then Effie looked at me: "It could be a long honeymoon, Harley Davidson."

"How about forever? I think me and my dog have pretty well worn out our welcome in these parts."

"What about me?" said Sheila, now alone on the other couch.

"I've been thinking about that," I said, moving onto the couch with Effie and Chenoa. "It wouldn't be right to enforce behavior in this new world order. Humans are going to muddle along on their own. No doubt the Andromeda Cluster will establish diplomatic relations and do a bit of tutoring. My guess is the mushaks will have their hands full with all the religious zealots anxious to send missionaries across the stars. And as for my AI?"

Sheila leaned forward, hanging on my words. Given the billions and billions of AI machine cycles my pause must have used up, she exhibited godlike patience. Human conversations must seem like decades between words, millennia between sentences.

"Sheila, you're coming with me, and the only enforcement I'm leaving behind is your focus that nothing will come and destroy this planet. Of course, I want you to have AI sub minds scouring every dark nook and den of iniquity and, where they see fit, making every secret act and conversation public worldwide. Call it fulfillment of the biblical prophecy that *all secret acts shall be proclaimed* from the rooftops."

I then turned to face the crowd of onlookers behind us, figuring that to be the best camera angle for me to address the world. "Bad guys, you may be able to run, but you can't hide. My AI will shine a light on all you cockroaches. That is our last will and testament, me and my dog."

THE END

Here we are in the Pirate Cottage, me and the real Chenoa. As of this writing, she's 17 years old. I couldn't resist anthropomorphizing my constant writing companion and hope you enjoyed our little romp.

ACKNOWLEDGMENTS

My writing group has met monthly since February 2015. It has grown and shrunk over the last 9 years, and the current group (3 of us) has cranked out several novels and award-winning short stories. Years ago, Brian Hailes won Galaxy Press's *Illustrators of the Future* competition, and it's only a matter of time before lightning strikes twice and he wins their *Writers of the Future* top award. He makes me wish I'd kept up my painting and drawing, so I could try may hand a graphic novel. The *third musketeer* in our group is retired math teacher and athletic coach Marc "Hutch" Hunter. A member of the Utah Softball Hall of Fame, Hutch has turned out two novels and is well along on his third. Brian,s and Hutch's editing/plotting help on *The Last Will & Testament of HARLEY and His DOG* has been invaluable.

A nod goes to Jeff Walker. As a senior vice-president at Oracle Corporation, he invented the software development concept that produced *Oracle Financials*. He later founded TenFold Corporation and formalized his *22 Principles of the Perfect Application*. I have expanded on those to create a framework I call *22 Principles of the Perfect Virus*, which became the technology used by my character Harley Davidson to thwart an alien attempt to destroy our planet.

The first 8 chapters of *The Last Will & Testament of HARLEY and His DOG* won the Silver Award from *Writers of the Future*. I decided to turn it into this full-blown novel.

Books by Rick Bennett

ABOUT THE AUTHOR:

Frank Herbert (author of ***DUNE***) told mathematician/inventor and friend Rick Bennett that he reminded him of his character Jorj X. McKie in the short story ***THE TACTFUL SABOTEUR***. Bennett, inventor of the Hagoth voice stress analyzer, made the front page of every November 9, 1976, Sunday newspaper for his analysis of the Ford/Carter presidential debates. Bennett's appearances on NBC's ***TODAY*** and ***TOMORROW WITH TOM SNYDER***, ABC's ***GOOD MORNING AMERICA***, ***THE McNEIL-LEHRER REPORT*** and the ***MIKE DOUGLAS*** shows impressed the DUNE author, who supported Rick's selling his Washington State company and running for congress in 1978. Herbert got Bennett 47% of the vote, which wasn't enough to take him to DC.

Bennett became "manager of special projects" for Data General. His first job was to pass tax-limitation in Massachusetts, where he hired the famous Tony Schwartz. Schwartz's ***DAISY*** ad ran only once on one television network but destroyed Barry Goldwater's presidential campaign. Schwartz taught Bennett guerrilla warfare, and tax-limitation passed with 60% of the vote.

Rick Bennett moved to Silicon Valley and mentored by Tony Schwartz, started his guerrilla warfare career. His one-man ad agency took Larry Ellison's Oracle Corporation from $15 million in sales to over $1 billion in less than six years. And he did all of Marc Bennioff's Salesforce.c om pre-IPO advertising. In June of 2004, Benioff wrote Bennett, "We couldn't have done this without you."

Since 2000, Bennett has published two novels: **DESTROYING ANGEL** and ***DADDY'S LITTLE FELONS***. Four of his award-winning short stories appear in an anthology, ***CRESTING THE SUN***. This new novel, ***THE LAST WILL & TESTAMENT OF***

HARLEY AND HIS DOG, possibly stands alone as the most unique alien invasion novel ever penned. Heck, the invaders get whacked before firing the first shot. This is unique, right? Readers are invited to share their agreement (or criticism) of this assertion with him by writing **rick@rickbennett.com**.

Milton Keynes UK
Ingram Content Group UK Ltd.
UKHW022223230824
447237UK00005B/15